With every page equal parts eerie and enchanting, Hollowed is absolutely legendary.

CASEY L. BOND, AUTHOR OF
WHERE OCEANS BURN

This dark and atmospheric Sleepy Hollow reimagining had me turning pages late into the night! An eerie paranormal town and a chilling mystery make it a haunting gothic tale while the heart-healing romance and themes of self worth made it a moving one too. A great read for fall!

TESSONJA ODETTE, AUTHOR OF
CURSE OF THE WOLF KING

A little dark, a little spooky, and the perfect mix of Sleepy Hollow legend and Jessica's own lore made this book an intriguing read from start to finish.

MELISSA ROEHRICH, AUTHOR OF
LADY OF DARKNESS

Also by Jessica S. Taylor

The Seas of Caladhan Duology

The Syren's Mutiny

The Captain's Revenge

Standalones

Hollowed: A Sleepy Hollow Reimagining

A SLEEPY HOLLOW REIMAGINING

JESSICA S. TAYLOR

A SLEEPY HOLLOW REIMAGINING

HOLLOWED

JESSICA S. TAYLOR

To those who battle themselves every day.

Playlist

Afraid of the Dark - Unions
Crazy - Adona, Seibold
Dark Side - Bishop Briggs
Looking at the Devil - Siebold, Neutopia, Leslie Powell
I Feel Like I'm Drowning - Two Feet
Down - Simon, Trella
Get Free - Whissell
Dead of Night - Ruelle
What You Can't Kill - Merci Raines
Fight for Survival - Klergy
Legacy - FJØRA
Bloody City - Sam Tinnesz
Straight for the Kill - Unsecret, Anna Renee
How Villians Are Made - Magdalen Duke
World on Fire - Klergy
Play with Fire - Sam Tinnesz
Angel of Small Death and the Codeine Scene - Hozier
Wicked as They Come - CRMNL
Scars - Boy Epic

Pronunciation Guide

People:

- Katrina (kah-tree-nuh) – pure
- Alexander (ahl-uhk-zand-er) – defender of man
- Ichabod (ick-uh-bohd) – inglorious, without glory
- Ciara (kee-ruh) – dark one
- Loralai (lore-uh-lie) – bringer of death
- Dullahan (dull-uh-han) – mythical Irish folklore figure

Other Terms:

- Roghnaithe (row-nayth) – the chosen
- Ciallmhar (keel-var) – wise
- Sluagh (slouw) – hoard of restless spirits from Irish mythology
- Ellén Trechend (ell-in trekh-end) – mythological three-headed vulture

Before You Begin

This story contains dark elements that may be difficult for some readers. Some of the darker themes include:

- Recurring instances of parental neglect and emotional abuse
- Explicit depictions of depression, anxiety and panic attacks
- Moderate but brief depictions of suicidal ideation
- Explicit descriptions of death and murder

If you need a full list of content warnings, along with chapter locations, please go to the last page of the book, or visit my website.

If you need support or resources for suicidal thoughts or mental health concerns, please contact a local helpline.

You are valued, you are loved, and you are important.

There is a sacredness in tears. They are not the mark of weakness, but of power. They speak more eloquently than ten thousand tongues. They are the messengers of overwhelming grief, of deep contrition, and of unspeakable love.

WASHINGTON IRVING

"And he would have passed a pleasant life of it, in despite of the Devil and all his works, if his path had not been crossed by a being that causes more perplexity to mortal man than ghosts, goblins, and the whole race of witches put together, and that was —a woman."

-Washington Irving,
The Legend of Sleepy Hollow

One

My eyes tracked the spinning lump of clay atop the wheel, round and round and round. My stomach churning, I clenched my eyes shut and sucked in deep breaths until the nausea faded and I no longer felt like the floor would come up to meet me.

I had to stop watching the wheel as I daydreamed.

"Your clay is going to dry out, Katrina," a gruff voice called from nearby.

I glanced at the occupied stool next to me and sighed. It was the only response I could muster for my grizzled mentor. Henry, the earth mage who owned the pottery shop I'd come to think of as my home, leaned forward, resting his elbows on his knees as he held his chin in his palm. "What is it, dear girl?"

"I'm tired, Henry," I said, dipping my fingers in the bowl of water beside my foot before bringing the shapeless lump of clay in front of me back to life. I turned to sculpting as a form of escape, a way to channel my emotions into something productive. It was a far better method than my previous attempts to manage my feelings, which had only served to decorate my body in small scars, now silver with age. Here, my fire magic was welcomed, not something to be smothered and hidden.

The old man sighed, pushing back the sparse gray hairs that refused to stay in the tie at his nape. "You need out of that house. It's draining the life from your eyes day by day."

"I have nowhere else to go." My frustrations began and ended with my parents; their disappointment in me was a heavy cloak that shrouded my entire life. "They would never let me leave."

"Pah," he snorted, waving a hand dismissively as he leaned forward to watch me form the clay. "They cannot stop you. You passed your initiations; you are a full citizen of Sleepy Hollow now and can do as you please."

His words, however inspiring, were dangerous. Dangerous for him to speak aloud and for me to listen to. If my mother ever heard the sentiment... I shuddered at the thought of what she'd do.

"You know it's not that simple." My gaze fell to the floor.

His hand, a rich brown and worn from the sun, landed on my forearm, pausing my movements. "What do *you* want, Katrina?"

My foot stuttered, and the wheel slowly came to a halt as tears choked me, burning my throat and stinging my eyes. I could not want. Could not dream. My future was at the whims of my mother, and if she had her way, I would be locked away in that cursed manor and left to rot for the duration of my immortality. "It doesn't matter what I want, Henry. It never has."

"It always matters," he told me. Standing, he squeezed my shoulder before leaving me to my creations. From the corner of my eye, I watched him move to his patch of dirt, where we'd pulled up the floorboards to reveal the earth beneath. His eyes closed and his hands and lips moved as he manipulated the mound. One benefit of working for an earth mage, I supposed, was that we never ran out of clay.

When I spun the wheel back to life, I added more water to the clay, trying to resurrect the vase as I pondered Henry's words. What did I want? My childhood had never been joyous, and from the moment I could remember, I'd only ever had two aspirations: gain my citizenship in Sleepy Hollow and earn my own living working at the pottery shop.

With the recent initiations complete, I'd achieved both. My mother had wondered how I'd tricked the evaluators into believing my magic was stable, but we both knew I'd spent days in bed after, recovering from the mental and physical toll the tests had taken on me. I had barely passed.

Since meeting Henry when I was merely ten summers old, I'd achieved the latter goal. The old mage took me under his wing the second I'd walked into his shop in search of a way to fix the plate I'd broken before my mother discovered it. Shortly after, he'd brought me on as his apprentice and spent every spare minute tutoring me in both magic and the mundane world outside Sleepy Hollow. He worked to ensure I missed nothing, refusing to leave me ignorant about how the world worked.

His efforts were far more than that of my mother. One session with a magical tutor when I was seven had her quickly deeming me a magical failure. After that assessment, she saw no reason to further pursue my education.

Despite Henry's tutelage, I knew there were gaps in my knowledge, especially around the inner workings of Sleepy Hollow. But I knew the town was a haven for the magical. I knew the magical barrier that kept humans away was a natural occurrence and no feat of spell work. I also knew that the ominous Dullahan roamed the forests beyond the barrier.

My mother claimed Sleepy Hollow as her pride and joy. Her creation. Her legacy. And I wanted out. My mother demanded perfection, and those she found lacking often found themselves the recipient of her ire. Unfortunately, I was her most favored target to extoll her disappointment upon.

Now that Henry had put the words into my ear—the one that worked, at least—a life away from my mother was all I could think about, and moving out of that godsforsaken manor would be the first thing I needed to do. The sprawling house was far too big for our pitiful family of three and served as nothing more than a monument to my mother's ego. I had no happy memories from that house, and the sooner I could leave, the sooner I could move on.

But I could not begin to fathom a life beyond my mother's rule until I was out of the manor and in my own space.

I needed somewhere that was mine. Somewhere I could control.

"I want to move out," I muttered, more to myself than to Henry, though my eyes drifted to my mentor. He was like a father to me, more than my own had ever been, and I wanted—

No, I needed his approval.

As he lowered his arms, the swirls of earth moving from the pit into pitchers at his feet collapsed, and he raised his brow. "From the manor?"

I nodded.

The pride that shone in his eyes as he made to stand in front of me caused my heart to squeeze. No one had ever looked at me like that. He took my hands in his, neither of us minding the dirt and wet clay covering our palms.

"Katrina, I think that is probably the best idea you've ever had."

Tears stung my eyes again, but for the first time in a very long time, they weren't tears of sadness or frustration. "I want my own life, Henry. One of my own making and under my own power."

"Then you shall have it." His hands squeezed mine. "And I will do anything in my power to ensure that, my dear girl."

Sniffing back the tears, I couldn't stop the watery laugh that bubbled up from my chest. "I'm going to move out, Henry."

He laughed with me, his voice vibrating through my chest, where it curled into a warm glow. A fire that welcomed rather than raged. "Yes, you are, Katrina." He cracked his knuckles, nodding toward the table at the back of the room. "Now, let's see what we can find."

"How will I find somewhere without my mother knowing?" I asked, running my hand through my wild curls and gripping the back of my head. For nearly two hours now, every available residence we discovered was owned by a friend of my mother's. And while it wasn't surprising, it had me ready to upturn every piece of furniture in sight and set it all ablaze. Sighing, I leaned back from the papers strewn about the table in front of Henry and me and crossed my arms over my chest.

Henry's sigh echoed my own as he rifled through the papers again. "Surely, there must be something. Let me speak to a friend. She might have space available above her shop." He paused his movements, looking up at me with a frown. "You know I would take you in if I had the space, my dear. But we both know that a spot on the floor by my fireplace is not what you're looking for."

"I'll take anything at this point," I grumbled, desperation leaking into my voice. Was I doomed to fail before I'd even started? My dreams were already succumbing to the will of my mother.

I shook my head. No, I *would* move into a place of my own. I would have something to call my own, even if it did end up being a spot on Henry's floor.

"I'll talk to Ciara as well," I said. "Maybe she heard something from her customers."

At the mention of my only other friend, Henry's face brightened. "Brilliant." He craned his head back to look out the windows at the front of the shop. "It's getting late. Why don't you go on ahead before she closes for the day?"

I gaped at him. Despite his fatherly affection, Henry was a demanding boss. He'd never let me go early, and certainly never before we'd finished our orders for the day. "Are you sure? I told her I'd collect some flowers she needed before I stopped by next, so I'd need to go gather those first. I was planning to do that tonight, so I can see her in the morning."

He laughed loudly, shooing me away. "Go on, girl. Pick your flowers and go see Ciara before it gets dark. Getting you out of that manor is far more important than finishing those blasted vases."

Jumping from the table, I pressed a kiss to the old man's cheek, ducking as he swatted at me. "Thank you, Henry!"

He grumbled, but neither of us could deny the twin smiles across our faces as I pulled on my cloak, fastening the button at my throat over the gleaming ruby necklace he'd gifted me just the year prior. Stooping to pick up my spade and basket, I rushed out the door before he could change his mind.

I would move out of the Van Tassel manor. I would live my own life under my own control, and I would do it if it killed me. And given my mother's propensity toward violence when challenged, it very well might.

The smile slipped from my face at the thought.

"There is something at work in my soul, which I do not understand."

-Mary Shelley,
Frankenstein

Two

There were several reasons I volunteered to collect flowers for Ciara's apothecary. The first being that my friend—one of my only friends in Sleepy Hollow—had planted the grove with her brother.

And just two short years ago, her brother had been sacrificed to the Dullahan by my mother. A yearly sacrifice, intended to placate the horseman of death in exchange for his continued protection. I found it to be a barbaric practice that made my stomach revolt every time someone mentioned it. Ever since her brother's death, Ciara had been unable to return to the grove without breaking down. I'd gone with her several times, and each time the journey had ended the same. I'd held my friend as she sobbed, screaming to the skies and pounding the earth with her fists, her magic crackling around us in a need to be released. She just pulled into herself until her sobs turned into hiccups, and she slumped in my arms.

Since then, I'd volunteered to go to the grove as often as she needed me to. Anything to spare her from that pain. From those memories.

The other reason for collecting Ciara's flowers was far more selfish. I relished the solitude of the isolated grove, which was in a clearing of the forest on the edge of town. Despite being a burden in the home I was born in, I rarely found myself left alone. At least physically.

My time in the forest was *mine* and was one of the few things that truly belonged to me.

Pushing aside the last branches, I finally entered the clearing, stopping at the edge to take a deep breath. Closing my eyes, I tipped my head back and inhaled the blessed silence.

Opening my eyes and entering the clearing fully, I decided that wherever I ended up, I would have a garden. Somewhere to grow flowers and watch as their petals turned up to the sky.

As much as I wanted to sit and relish the quiet solace of the grove, I needed to gather Ciara's supplies and meet with her. Daydreaming about a garden would mean nothing if I couldn't escape the manor.

Sighing, I dropped to my knees beside bunches of evening primrose and began my work. The bright yellow flowers taunted me with their happiness, stark against the gloomy afternoon sky. At least I could be useful with this and help my friend.

With each bunch of flowers I placed in the basket, some of the tension bled from my shoulders and neck. The repetitive movement—the thoughtless motion—slowed my racing mind and calmed the burning in my blood. Tilting my head side to side, I stretched out the loosening muscles even more.

As I moved on to the dandelions, digging them up for their roots, movement at the edge of the clearing caught my attention. Rocking back to sit on my heels, my eyes scanned the tree line. Leaves shifted in the wind, but there was no sign of any other disturbances.

The back of my neck prickled, hairs standing on end at the weight of someone—or something—watching me. A gust of wind crossed the grove, lifting my hair from my shoulders and swirling it around my face as the cold cut through the thick wool of my cloak. Spitting hair from my mouth, I tamed the wild curls behind my ears, my eyes frantically searched for a sign of whatever was with me.

There.

By the edge of the forest, directly across from me, a thick fog gathered around the base of the trees, twining through the branches and consuming the forest floor beyond.

It was October, yes, but it was also the middle of the afternoon, and fog like that should only form in the mornings. I swallowed hard. It definitely wouldn't be moving as if it were crawling across the earth.

Katrina... The wind seemed to whisper like an eerie voice, whose talons slowly dragged down my spine.

I shot to my feet, whirling around as the wind continued whispering my name.

"Who's there?" I demanded, holding my spade out to use as a weapon. It would do nothing against anything magical, but it made me feel slightly better. Once again, I wished my flames would respond to my demands, rather than erupt whenever they chose. They typically appeared when my emotions raged, but now, the flames in my soul were dormant.

Katrina...

The feeling of being watched increased, and a branch snapped behind me. Turning again, I searched the tree line but again came up empty. Whoever was watching me and whispering my name did not want to be seen.

Warnings rang in my head, but my feet remained frozen

to the earth. I couldn't make my body move, despite my quickening breath and the sweat rolling down my forehead even in the cold air.

I needed to *move*. To *run*.

The air chilled as another gust of wind rolled through, and the fog across the clearing began creeping beyond the bounds of the tree roots, spreading like fingers over the grass. Five large strides would have set me inside the fog, and despite its languid movement, it was growing closer. Three strides away. Then two.

I didn't want to find out what would happen if it got too close.

The tendrils of fog reached the first bed of flowers, thick and undulating as it obscured the grass and leaves beneath. If I leaned forward and stretched, I could have touched the first wisps of the mass.

KATRINA.

The booming whisper of my name, clearer than the first two times, pulled me from my stupor. Dropping the spade on the ground, I picked up the basket of flowers and ran back the way I'd come through the forest and into town. I needed to get out of here.

Now.

The forest faded behind me as I ran, ducking beneath branches and dodging trees, moving as quickly as possible and panting with the exertion. My vision tunneled as the town grew clearer through the trees. I was so close to safety. Once I was out of the forest, someone would see me. Surely someone would help if the fog swallowed me or attacked with some invisible force.

At least, I hoped they would.

I'd almost made it and was about to clear the last few strides out of the forest when a hand wrapped around my arm, pulling me to a stop. I couldn't stop the scream that escaped my throat. Couldn't stop the flames that erupted from my hands as I dropped the basket of flowers.

Of course, now the flames would choose to make their presence known.

"Gods, Katrina!" The voice of the person who'd grabbed me was familiar, but I couldn't breathe. The grip eased, and I yanked my arms back, folding my hands to my chest as I whirled to face whoever had followed me.

The flames bled out as my eyes finally focused, taking in the man before me. My shoulders slumped, and I released a heavy breath. "Ichabod. What are you doing here?"

Without waiting for his answer, I bent and picked up the basket of flowers before continuing forward until I was fully out of the forest and back on the dirt path that led into town. The feeling of being watched faded with each step away from the trees.

"Katrina, stop," Ichabod said, jogging to catch up with my frantic steps. He pulled around in front of me, reaching his hands out as if to grab my shoulders. His eyes flicked down to my hands, stained with soot, and he pulled them back, searching my face as a frown formed. "Are you all right?"

"I..." I held up the basket of flowers, struggling to catch my breath. "I... was getting flowers... for Ciara. Something in the forest..."

His stormy blue eyes widened. "There was something in the forest? What was it?"

I shook my head, still unable to form the words.

His hand faltered, again hesitating as he reached out in the space between our bodies, but he eventually placed it on my shoulder. "Let's get you to Ciara's then. You can tell me when you're ready."

There was no force in this world that would ever make me share my secrets or emotions with Ichabod Crane. The tall and lanky schoolteacher and master alchemist could rarely keep anything he learned to himself. Without a doubt, anything I told the man would be common knowledge in Sleepy Hollow by sunset.

With each step we took away from the forest, my heart calmed. Taking deep breaths, I walked myself through one of the calming routines I had in my repertoire. Five things I could see: Ichabod's black leather boots, the gates of Sleepy Hollow Cemetery, the leaves rustling above us, the wicker basket in my hand, the townspeople ahead of us. Four things I could touch: the scratchy wool of Ichabod's coat, the metal of my necklace, the soft petals of the flowers, and the dirt beneath my nails. Three things I could hear: Ichabod's breathing, the whistling of the wind, and the creaking of the basket in my hands. Two things I could smell: the fragrant blooms of flowers and the stale sweat beading on my upper lip. One thing I could taste: the tangy metallic of blood from biting my cheek as I'd run through the forest.

Ichabod was quiet, keeping in step beside me and not saying anything as I moved through my routine. He'd seen me do it once before, and though I hadn't expected him to recognize that I needed silence, I appreciated it. Finally, I was able to speak. "There was someone—some*thing*—watching me in the forest."

I felt his curious gaze, but I didn't look over as we continued to walk. Heartbeats passed before he spoke again. "I'm certain it was nothing, Katrina. Just an animal."

I bit my lip to keep from snapping at him. An animal could not whisper my name on the wind or cause that unnatural fog. But as much as I wanted to correct him, it would do no good.

Forcing a nod, I clasped my fingers tightly around the basket handle; the knuckles turning stark white against the brown wicker. "Yes, you're likely right."

The doors of Ciara's apothecary came into view. I turned to Ichabod, my boots scuffing in the dirt. "Thank you for escorting me."

Without waiting for his answer, I quickly pushed into the apothecary and leaned against the door once it closed. My eyes slid shut as I steadied my breath once more. I heard Ichabod scuff his boots against the dirt as he turned and left the shop. I was safe here, if nothing else.

"Katrina, is that you?" Ciara's soft voice would have gone unnoticed if I hadn't already overloaded my senses with the calming exercise I'd done. My hearing was faulty, and I often had to ask Ciara to repeat herself.

"Yes," I called, wincing at the hoarseness and the twinge in the back of my throat. "I have your flowers."

Ciara's head of sleek auburn hair popped out from a curtain behind the counter. "Oh, good. Bring them back here, please?"

On shaky legs, I followed her instructions and stepped into her potion room. Ciara was truly gifted at mixing potions and making cures for any ailment. I was hopeless at potions; everything I attempted turned sour or bitter. I was more apt to poison someone than cure them. No, my magic was a blunt instrument, whereas Ciara's was precision. Setting the basket on the counter, I settled onto the stool by the door to watch her.

"So, why have you come by today?" Ciara said, pulling the flowers out of the basket and inspecting them. She paused, meeting my gaze with an arched eyebrow. "Surely it was not just to bring me flowers."

"I'm..." I weighed the words on my tongue. "I want to move out of the manor."

She froze, her lightly freckled hands poised over the dandelions. Her voice was sharp. "What?"

Heat burned my cheeks, and I ducked my head, letting

my curls fall forward to cover my face. "I want to move out of the manor, away from my parents. Do you know anyone who has space available, and who would not tell my mother I'm looking?"

Her head tipped to one side as her brown eyes studied me, and her voice slowed as she considered each word before speaking aloud. "I don't. But I can ask around if you'd like."

"Discreetly?" I asked, wincing at the request. I hated asking for help, especially help that could get one or both of us in trouble with my mother. "Yes, please. I would appreciate that."

Ciara nodded, humming as she went back to her flowers. I was grateful she hadn't asked about my reasons for wanting to leave the manor. Though she likely already knew, or at least suspected, not having to say them aloud was a grace I hadn't realized I needed. I didn't want to talk about it. Not until it was real.

The silence was comfortable as she harvested the roots from the dandelions before moving on to the evening primrose buds. It was something I appreciated about her. She and I could sit in each other's company, not uttering a word, and feel completely at ease.

I wanted to ask about the forest, but the idea of bringing up the grove had me wary and weighing my words. I tried to find a combination that would not send her into a spiral of tears. "Have you heard anything unusual coming from the forest?"

She froze again, sending me a quizzical look. "No, why?"

The curiosity on her face told me that any kind of hedged answer I gave would not be enough for her to believe me. "No reason." I leaned back to peek beyond the curtain separating her space from the shop. "It's getting late. I better go before my mother starts to wonder where I am. Thank you for keeping an ear out for a space."

Her expression was unreadable, but she nodded slowly. "Of course, Katrina. Be safe getting home, please."

Nodding, I stood and rushed out of the shop. Despite Ciara being one of my only two friends here, I was still... apprehensive about sharing my burdens with her. She'd already gone through so much with the death of her brother, and the grief-stricken state of her mother. The last thing I wanted was to force her to carry the weight of my feelings as well.

Dusk was falling, the sky turning a cool gray as I made my way down the path and toward the ornate Van Tassel manor. Dread bubbled low in my stomach as I thought about the isolated path that traced along the edges of the forest. My mother had set the manor apart from the town, and so the only way to get there was down a path no one else would ever take, unless they too were coming to the manor.

My fingertips heated slightly as the sound of the Hollow faded behind me. Despite being able to see the outline of the manor from here, I knew better than most just how long the path from town to the front door would take.

Long enough for trouble to find me.

And it didn't take long for my thoughts to become reality.

Along the edges of the path, that same unnatural fog gathered, wrapping up the tree trunks and spreading as I walked. I sped. So did it. The prickling feeling along my neck was back.

Someone was watching me again.

I kept my eyes forward and moved along, careful not to make sudden movements. Jumping at the sound of a cawing crow, I broke into a run.

Keep your eyes from the forest, I told myself. I knew it was a foolish superstition, but I couldn't help but hope it was true. *If you don't look at them, they won't notice you.*

Logically, I knew danger wouldn't care if I noticed, but I could still hope as I kept moving.

A branch creaked behind me, and a jolt flinched down my spine. Wings fluttered as a single crow landed on the path in front of me, drawing me to a sudden stop. It tilted its head, its glassy eyes studying my every move. A breeze caressed my back, like fingertips tracing my spine. With my eyes fixed firmly on the crow, I skirted around the edges of the path, hurrying past it. Turning to look over my shoulder, I saw the crow in the same spot, turning to watch my retreat.

My heart pounded as I started to run once more, barely stopping when I reached the covered porch of the manor. I pushed open the door and slammed it shut behind me in a single breath. Panting against the door, I gave myself one heartbeat, two heartbeats, to catch my breath.

I couldn't risk staying here. My mother would find me and question why I was out so long after my workday ended, and why I returned home out of breath, sweaty, and drenched in fear. I didn't have the energy to deal with it right now, so I forced my feet to move, climbing the stairs to my room.

Once inside my room, I locked the door and slid to the floor. I took a deep breath and thought about the day, combing through every detail in my mind and searching for answers, for anything I could have missed that might have explained this.

My magic was unique in that it didn't need a spoken spell or incantations to activate. It responded solely to my will, or at least it was supposed to. But today, it hadn't responded *at all* until Ichabod had grabbed me. Usually, my fear, anger, or sadness would set it off, but today I had been frozen in fear and not so much as an ember had escaped.

Moving to dress for bed, I stepped past the window and

froze at the touch of icy fingers wrapping around my throat. Fog surrounded the edges of the garden down below, forming around what looked like a person. The phantom fingers squeezed tighter, cutting off my air as the room spun slightly and the figure blurred. My feet froze against the floor. I couldn't quite make out the features, but I knew in my soul that the figure in the fog was looking right at me.

A breeze blew through the trees, shaking the branches as the figure vanished. The hand around my throat disappeared, and I slumped forward, rocking the breath back into me.

Dressing quickly, I climbed into bed, leaving the candle on my desk lit as I pulled the quilt tightly around me. Turning to roll on my hearing ear, so that only the wild thumping of my heart filled my head, I squeezed my eyes closed and tried to sleep.

If you don't look at them, they won't notice you. I repeated this, over and over and over, never daring to open my eyes until sleep claimed me.

"Love will have its sacrifices. No sacrifice without blood."

-J. Sheridan Le Fanu, Carmilla

Three

It was raining outside, the heavy drops hitting against the glass with a sharp tapping before sliding down the windowpane like tears. My eyes tracked over the trees through the dining room window, searching for the figure that had been watching me last night, searching for anything unusual.

"Katrina," my father said from his place across the breakfast table, rapping his knuckles on the wood. Reluctantly, I pulled my attention away from the rain outside, allowing my gaze to linger a second longer before turning to meet my father's. He sighed deeply, no doubt irritated by having to wait for my attention. "The town is in danger."

I froze. Did he know? Was he talking about what was in the forest? Studying his face, I tried to figure out what he meant, but without more information, I couldn't know. According to my parents, Sleepy Hollow was constantly in danger.

My father likely expected a reaction showing my immediate concern, but without knowing what danger he spoke of, I couldn't bring myself to give any reaction.

I couldn't fake a reaction this morning as the sleepless night lay heavily across my eyelids. Chewing on my lip, I knew I had to give him some response, though, or I'd regret it once my mother joined us.

"In danger from what?" I asked, feigning interest with a tilt of the head and a widening of my eyes. Dropping my hand from my necklace, I leaned forward slightly, resting an elbow on the table to move this conversation along. I needed to leave the Van Tassel manor and return to my kiln at Henry's. But pretending would only work for so long. Eventually, both my parents would see through my apathy, like always.

"Mundanes, of course," he replied, turning up his nose in the air as if the word smelled foul to him. I finally exhaled, the air pushing out of my lungs as the words settled over me. Perhaps I should have predicted his answer, given that my parents continually blamed all our hardships on the humans surrounding our town. He wasn't speaking of the forest, but rather of the usual argument they often made against humans. "The barrier seems to get weaker with each passing year, and if we do not act soon, we fear the town will be exposed to the human world. That will surely bring our ruin."

I tried not to roll my eyes at his words, though I admittedly didn't try very hard. My parents were dramatic about most things, though this was their favorite topic. The humans surrounding us had nothing to do with the supposed challenges the town faced, especially given Sleepy Hollow was far better off than the surrounding human towns. Yet, it was a continual discussion—a blame placed on those around us rather than taking responsibility for their own mistakes.

A small sigh escaped my lips. Now, there was an actual threat, something in the forest, but he only focused on the humans and the natural barrier of magic that had been here long before my mother founded Sleepy Hollow. "Father, you and mother say this every year. Nothing has ever happened. The barrier is safe. The town is safe. The Dullahan and the veil protect us."

A cup slammed down beside me on the wooden table. Flinching at the sudden vibration against my hands resting on the table, I jerked my hands back, but I was too slow to avoid the steaming liquid that sloshed over the side of the dainty teacup and sprayed onto my skin. The burn stung, but I didn't dare let it show.

I looked up at my mother's face. Despite her skin being as smooth as the porcelain of the cup by her hand, her expression twisted with rage, painted on like the twisting vines that decorated the teacup she'd nearly shattered. Her lip curled as she snarled at me, stooping to bring her mouth closer to my hearing ear. "Katrina Van Tassel, do *not* speak to your father like that."

My cheeks burned hotter than the tea could ever hope to, and I ducked my head, my shoulders hunching as I slid down into my chair to avoid my mother's wrath. Rolling my eyes had been a foolish move, but all I could do now was apologize and hope she moved on from my indiscretions as quickly as possible. I cleared my throat, my eyes still fixed on the table in front of me. "Yes, Mother. I apologize."

A beat of silence passed, and dread crawled up my spine with each passing tick of the clock in the corner. There was no way of telling if my words would appease my mother or anger her further. Given that I'd already angered her yesterday morning by asking her to repeat herself at breakfast, I wasn't hopeful I'd make it out of this encounter unscathed.

"This town is the only sanctuary our kind has left. If the barrier falls, humans will expose paranormals and hunt us down like they did to the witches in Salem a century ago," she snapped. She straightened and exhaled, adjusting her hair and smoothing her hands down over her pristine apron as if that would take away the violence that whirled around her like a cloak of death and anger. "Only those chosen as Roghnaithe can keep us safe and keep the barrier alive. The Dullahan requires a sacrifice to continue protecting the town. It is an *honor* to be given to him."

"Who will be chosen as Roghnaithe this year?" I asked before I could stop myself, my stomach churning in anticipation of who they would sacrifice to the Dullahan—the Headless Horseman—this year. Which unfortunate soul would my mother turn loose in the woods to wait for the Horseman to whisper their name and lead them to their death? Too often, it had been someone important to the town, and too often, it was someone I knew.

According to my parents, it was the only way to appease the gods who determined our fates, and the only way to protect Sleepy Hollow—and the supernaturals who lived here—from the mundane world. It was a heinous practice and one that should have never begun, but in the decades following the war of independence, staying protected had been the town leaders' only concern.

And so began the deplorable practice of condemning a random citizen to death at the hands of the Dullahan once a year, and it had remained unchanged for the last century.

Over one hundred people dead. Sacrificed in the name of protection.

I froze in my chair as a realization tingled down my spine. The stories said the Dullahan whispered the name of those he killed. Had the Dullahan been the one to whisper my name in the forest? How was I still alive? My breathing quickened, and I dug my nails into my palms to ground myself and keep my fire from erupting as it warmed my chest.

Mother snapped her fingers at me, but before I could react, she grabbed a fistful of my curls and pulled my gaze up to her once more. My stomach lurched when her long fingers curled into the strands and tugged sharply. I tried not to wince, for I knew showing her pain would only spur her on. The dread that coiled in my spine snaked up, wrapping around my throat as I realized the gravity of my situation. Only my father made an effort to ensure I was looking at him when he spoke. My mother much preferred to speak and then berate me for not hearing her.

That she'd ensured my focus was entirely on her now... the words that followed could not be good. She pushed my head away, releasing my hair as she wiped her hands on her dress. I sat up, fighting back the tears from the pain radiating through my scalp. I pulled my hands into my lap and took fistfuls of my dress, twisting the heavy fabric as I waited for her to speak.

"You will be." Her voice was calm, the anger that had been there before now replaced by the cold indifference I'd long since learned to emulate. "Your sacrifice is called for this year, and it will bring peace to Sleepy Hollow."

My mouth dropped open, and the room faded away with a whoosh in my ears. I must have misheard her or misread her lips somehow. My parents were two of the original founders of Sleepy Hollow, and surely, they could not mean to sacrifice their only child to this barbaric practice. The Ciallmhar council supposedly chose the Roghnaithe at random, not intentionally.

Despite my disbelief, I could see in her face that I had

not misheard her, and more so, that she did not care about my impending death.

"Beg your pardon?" My voice was raspy as my lungs contracted at the news of my forthcoming demise. I whipped around to look at my father, still hoping that my mother had misspoken.

"You are, Katrina," my father said, pushing his glasses up on his nose as he straightened in his chair. The softness of his words held a hint of regret, but it vanished quickly, replaced with the pious air of duty I had grown so familiar with in my almost twenty years of life. "The Ciallmhar has agreed to name you as the Roghnaithe this year. We need the Dullahan to strengthen the barrier before any humans can see past it, and the spirits have decided it is time for a... more *significant* sacrifice. You will go to the Dullahan at the Samhain celebration this year."

"But..." I protested, my words trailing off as the breath rushed out of my body. The room began to spin as the news settled deep into my stomach. My fingers, still twisted into my dress, began to heat up. I clasped my hands together, trying to avoid my magic burning my clothing.

The fire constantly bubbling beneath my skin could not erupt now, not when my mother was already furious with me. If it did, she would likely kill me before the Dullahan would ever have the chance.

I dug my nails into the flesh of my palms even harder, pulling my focus away from my growing panic and pushing it toward the stinging pain. The heat dulled, and the fire eased from my hands. The fiery tendrils slowly withdrew from my fingertips and slithered back into my chest, curling up and waiting for the next moment they might be unleashed.

I swallowed, pushing down the burning clog of tears

that threatened to spill out. I didn't want to die. And certainly not for these people and this town that only echoed my mother's disdain for me. My mother was two hundred years old, and I would not even live to see twenty.

My mother raised her hand up, her lips thinning like they always did when she was angry. They twisted into an incantation, and although I could not hear the words she uttered, the room chilled drastically. My right ear ached at the sudden change in pressure, but again I masked the discomfort and fought back the urge to rub at it, knowing it would only anger her further.

Despite the serene expression on her face, she was furious enough to control the air. The only way to avoid her ire was to be silent and still. Something I had perfected during my childhood.

"You will be *honored* to protect this town, Katrina," she hissed.

"Why would you choose me, though? It could be anyone," I said, my desperation clear.

I knew better than to have said anything, and I would pay for it, I was sure. My father seemed resigned to my fate while my mother seemed to embrace it, both entirely unconcerned that the Dullahan would kill their only child.

But of course, the town was always their favorite child and their highest priority. I should not have been surprised.

The Hollow will always come first.

It was impossible to count how many times I had heard that phrase throughout my childhood. Impossible to count how many times they'd told me how utterly unimportant I was. A single tear spilled from my eye and rolled down my cheek, dripping from my chin onto my hand. Quickly, I sniffed back the other tears, hoping that my mother hadn't seen it.

"Allowing you to be Roghnaithe shows our dedication to Sleepy Hollow," my mother said through gritted teeth, as if she were talking to a stupid child. And in her mind, I was sure that was what she was thinking. My mother had always valued the town above me, her defective daughter that could not hear and whose magic was unpredictable. "This town needs us."

"And do I not need you?" I wanted to scream at her. But I bit my tongue, the copper taste flooding my mouth as I remained silent. Anything I said now would only result in a strike to my face, or worse, a punishment from her magic. I wanted neither. I needed to get to Henry, and the only way to do that was to remain silent, remain complacent, and bend to the will of my mother.

Lifting my head slightly, I could almost see the anger radiating from her body, but she controlled herself, keeping her fists bunched at her sides. My gaze fell back to the ground. The disgust in her eyes was clear and more painful than any physical blow could have ever been.

She said something under her breath to my father, but I couldn't hear it. He shook his head in response, his eyes downturned as they swung back to me.

"You will be honored to protect this town," she repeated, her voice even colder than the surrounding air. She sniffed, raising her chin. "The decision is final."

With that edict, my mother turned and left the dining room, the ornate lace hem of her black skirt swishing over the floor behind her.

I turned to look at my father across the table, finally reaching up to rub at the ache in my ear. He was always softer than my mother, though never willing to protect me from her ire while she raged. "Am I truly the Roghnaithe?"

He reached across the table to grasp my hand, but stopped at the last minute, his fingers closing around nothing as he pulled them back. He still had sadness in his eyes, but I was not entirely convinced it was because of me. "Yes, Katrina. I know this is not ideal, and I am sorry. We love you dearly, but this is what the town needs."

"She has never loved me," I mumbled, looking down at my cold, empty hand.

They never touched me. Not out of love, at least. Perhaps I should not have voiced my musings aloud, but that did not change the truth behind them. My mother had only used me to increase her status in Sleepy Hollow and grow her power.

I brought my gaze back up to his. "I have only ever been a tool for her."

"That is not true," he blurted, as if by instinct. But I could see the truth in his eyes. He knew it as well as I did. My mother only loved the town—not my father, and certainly not me. I had been born only because a child would further solidify her legacy.

"When is the ceremony?" My mind worked, trying to figure out what day today was, and how close we were to Samhain, but my emotions were swirling too much to allow my thoughts to clear.

"The full moon, and the night of Samhain. In five days' time."

Such a short time. There was nothing else I could say, nothing else I could do. There was no escaping being named Roghnaithe, not without sentencing someone else to death in my place. And though I was certain Henry would offer, I could not bear knowing he had died in my stead.

Moving out of the manor now was meaningless. I would be dead in five days' time. And when it came to my mother, no one would stop her from getting what she wanted.

My appetite now gone, I pushed my breakfast plate away, the ceramic skidding across the wooden table in a pitiful imitation of my heartbeat. "I should go to the shop. I'm late, and Henry is likely waiting for me."

My father merely nodded, turning his attention back to his own breakfast and letting me leave the room without another word of apology or comfort. I didn't know why I even expected any.

"If ever I should wish for a retreat whither I might steal from the world and its distractions, and dream quietly away the remnant of a troubled life, I know of none more promising than this little valley."

-Washington Irving,
The Legend of Sleepy Hollow

Four

My mind was churning as I escaped from the manor, though I mostly felt numb. A normal person would be raging, screaming at the sky, and doing anything possible to plead with my parents to change their minds. But I knew none of that would work.

I kept every ounce of emotion bottled up, pushed down, and locked away until the front door of the mansion closed behind me, the dulled booming echoing in my ears.

Stepping out from beneath the porch's covering, I took a deep breath and embraced the icy rain that spilled from the low-hanging gray clouds. It had let up some but was still readily coming down, beating against my skin, and soaking into my hair and dress. Tilting my head back, I released a heavy breath from my lips, puffing into a white cloud in the cold of the morning. It was not quite time for frost to form, icing over the grass, but it would not be long now.

Too bad I wouldn't live to see it.

I straightened my head and flexed my jaw as the raindrops clung to my eyelashes. The path in front of me was muddy, but unlike my mother, I didn't care if my dress became dirty. I stepped down from the porch, my boots squelching in the mud. Each step away from the mansion left me feeling physically lighter as the weight crushing against my lungs eased slightly.

Likely, I should have still felt fear from what had followed me down the path the night before, but the anger and despair that filled my veins overpowered it. I was going to die, regardless. What difference did it make now if that death was from the Dullahan or a mysterious forest spirit?

Stopping at the bend in the path that would take me to town, I turned around to look back. The manor was a prison to me. It was a symbol of wealth and status to those who called on my mother and fawned over the opulent furnishings and carefully arranged décor, but all I could see was pain and anguish. It was in the very foundations of the structure.

Scoffing, I turned back to the path and put the manor behind me. Questions swirled in my mind as I walked, passing the trees—their leaves heavy with rain—as I made toward town. I kept my eyes on the path but felt no eyes on me and noticed no fog around the bases of the trees this morning.

It was a blessing and a curse. Without fear driving my steps, my mind wandered. Unbidden, my thoughts returned to my parents, to their decision, and to my childhood.

While they had never been what one would call loving parents, they prized the appearance of the perfect family more than anything.

My defective ear was hidden from everyone, and I had been forced to adapt to reading lips as soon as my parents realized I could not hear well. Although a language that would allow me to use my hands to communicate existed, my mother forbid me from learning it, saying it would have brought too much unnecessary attention upon me, and thus, upon her. The hearing loss was only in my right ear, and its ache often made me question if there was more to it than just a simple hearing loss. My mother would never take me to a physician to investigate it further, so I conceded to the pain.

We never spoke of my magic publicly, though those who knew me knew I had little control over the flames that lived in my heart. The only time I'd heard my mother speak of it, she'd told those asking that I was merely being stubborn, refusing to exercise my magic at that moment.

Anything to keep from telling the truth. That their only child was a failure. A disappointment.

Tears burned in my throat, blurring my vision.

"'*You are nothing, Katrina*,'" I muttered, exaggerating my lips as I mimicked my mother's voice.

Fire burst from my hands, the raindrops sizzling into steam as they met and dispersed into the dismal morning sky. This time, I didn't try to smother the flames. Instead, I stopped to gaze down at my hands and watch the flames flicker, licking up my wrists and dancing out from my fingertips. The flames would not last long... they never did. But even as they faded into steam, they pushed a warmth into my soul, blanketing it like a heavy quilt, soft but not smothering.

The flames, unable to survive any longer outside of my chest, extinguished and my cooling hands fell back to my sides as I refocused on the path in front of me. I took a deep breath, leveling my gaze at the mud ahead of me. "I am not nothing, Mother."

The tears that'd been building overflowed, warming my skin briefly before the cool of the morning clung to their wet tracks. Continuing my trek, I kicked my foot out to disperse the thick layer of mist gathered above the ground, wiping at the angry tears that spilled down my cheeks.

This mist was not like the fog from last night; this was natural, expected for such a fall morning. It did not creep like fingers, but instead spread like a thin layer over everything the sun touched. The rain clung to me like a smothering blanket, pressing against every inch of my body and soaking through my thick dress. It felt both oppressive and comforting.

Turning onto the final path that led into town, the trees gave way to buildings, rows of shops, and large looming homes. Their pointed rooflines reached into the morning sky, kissing the mist. Passing the small school that had taken over an older manor home, I made my way to the center of town.

The lanterns that hung around the corners of the town square still glowed, not having yet been extinguished in the early morning air. A large oak tree sat in the center of the square, its branches naked and gnarled, twisting up into the sky. As I passed it, the wood groaned with the morning wind. I spared it a glance, looking up at the noise. A large crow sat alone in its branches, staring at me with its eyes unblinking. I stopped short, turning fully to look at it.

Was it the same one from last night? Crows were common here, but they usually traveled in pairs. To see a lone one twice in a row made the hairs on the back of my neck stand up as fear clamped around my throat once more.

I cocked my head, studying the bird. It mimicked the movement, tilting its own head as its onyx eyes continued to hold my gaze. It stared at me as it opened its beak, cawing loudly and shattering the peace of the morning. I flinched, the noise startling me as it stabbed painfully into my ear, leaving behind a faint ringing I knew would echo for hours.

As I reached up to rub at the ache, an eerie feeling washed over me, like someone had stepped up behind me and was breathing on my neck. Goosebumps skittered down my spine and fear clung to the hair on my neck and arms. Clenching my fists, I whirled around, but there was no one there. Again.

Nothing was behind me except the empty town square and the soft noises of the town beginning to wake. My heart raced as I turned back to look at the crow, but it was gone, only a slightly wobbling branch a sign of its presence.

Pressing my hand to my chest to still the rapid thumping, my eyes scanned the entire square as I passed through, speeding up to get to the safety of my workplace.

Finally reaching the pottery shop, I opened the door and went inside. The familiar smell of wet clay and hot air filled my nose, and I took a deep breath, leaning against the door. Whatever omen had come with the lone crow, it could not harm me here. Or at least, that's what I would tell myself.

"Katrina, you are late!" Henry called from the back room. His voice was loud enough for me to easily hear it, an accommodation he had made when he hired me and had discovered my hearing was not quite what was to be expected. Before, he'd seldom raised his voice past a whisper. He popped out from the door frame to his office space, raising an eyebrow. "Where have you been?"

"I had breakfast with my parents," I said. With each step further into the shop, my heart lightened. The burden of this morning and my impending death slipped further away. As much as I wanted to fight, and rage, and march to the Ciallmhar, demanding they change their mind... it would do no good. In fact, the only thing I'd likely accomplish is getting Henry killed beside me as a punishment for my rebellion.

I would not risk his life. One of us was enough.

"Ahh," he hummed, coming out of the room and walking over to stand in front of me. Despite his old age, he moved spryly. He grabbed my chin and turned my head to one side and then the other, inspecting me with a grim expression. Letting go, his gnarled hand patted my cheek. "You have been crying, girl. Your face is swollen. And you are wet. Is it raining? Did you talk to Ciara yesterday?"

"I am the Roghnaithe this year," I breathed, ignoring his other questions and comments. He was simply trying to comfort me the only way he knew how—optimistic irreverence. There was no use in delaying the news. It would be announced to the town soon enough. My mother said the Ciallmhar had chosen me, so word would spread quickly.

"Oh, darling girl," he whispered, reaching down to take my hands in his wrinkled ones. His face fell, and he sighed heavily, patting my hands as silver lined his eyes. "I am so sorry."

"They did not even care, Henry," I said, the tears burning in the back of my throat. Even I could hear how pitiful I sounded.

I cleared my throat, pushing the tears back as my right ear popped at the pressure. I did not want Henry's pity, or anyone's, for that matter. And showing my pain would not change their minds. Nothing would. I had learned that much in my nearly twenty years of life.

Burying my emotions with a practiced ease, I sniffed my tears back and my throat again. "In any case, there's work to be done."

He looked at me, his old, clouded eyes full of sorrow. Staring for a moment, it was clear he wanted to argue with me; to protest that it was fine that I broke down sobbing in his arms over the thought of dying. But thankfully, he nodded, reaching up and patting my cheek once more. "Very well. Get to it. I shall be in the back."

Sighing heavily, I went to the counter and began going through the orders, working out what needed to be started today and what needed to be finished. I had broken down in

Henry's arms many times before, but this... there was nothing crying would do to fix it. Sobbing would not change my fate and would only make Henry sad. And I did not want that.

No, the more aloof I could appear to others, the less impact this would have on them. Henry was special to me, the father I never had, and I would do whatever it took to make this easier on him. He would be the one that had to live with my death, not me. I would do nothing to jeopardize his life after my mother took mine.

"Deep into that darkness peering, long I stood there, wondering, fearing, doubting, dreaming dreams no mortal ever dared to dream before."

-Edgar Allan Poe,
The Raven

Five

The morning sun had fully risen, though the thick gray clouds hiding it from view made it hard to tell. A cold blanket of dreariness smothered the town.

The lantern beside the door moved up and down, my cue that someone had entered the shop. Before I had joined Henry's employ, it had been a small tinkling bell, but we quickly realized I could not reliably hear it every time. One too many broken dishes after I was startled by a customer had quickly deigned the need for an alternative.

Removing my foot from the pedal of the pottery wheel, the vase I'd been working on slowly spun to a stop. Two familiar faces entered the shop, swirls of morning mist fading around their feet. Though calling them friends was certainly an overstatement, Ichabod Crane and Abraham Van Brunt were two of the only people who ever actively sought my company, whether I wanted them to or not.

I stood, leaving the wheel to approach them from behind the counter. My previous encounter with Ichabod still burned in my mind, and from the frown that set across his pale face, it still burned in his, too. Abraham—Brom, as he preferred—was all smiles as he strode inside the shop.

"Katrina!" Brom greeted, stepping around the counter and pulling me into an uncomfortably tight hug. I never had to ask Brom to repeat himself, as his voice boomed, bordering on the edge of being too loud. Flinching at his touch, I gritted my teeth to keep my body from reacting too noticeably. I did not enjoy being touched; the contact was foreign and uncomfortable given my childhood held little affection. But I knew resisting would only prolong the contact, so I squeezed Brom's arm briefly before stepping back, trying to hide my grimace. If he noticed it, he would only ask questions, pushing and pushing until one of us snapped, and I was far too tired to deal with him right now.

Thankfully, he finally stepped back around the counter, moving to inspect the shelf of drying pottery along the wall.

"Good morning, Katrina. Lovely morning, isn't it?" Ichabod greeted. A forced smile stretched across his face as he pulled the door shut behind them and walked up to the counter, leaning against it.

I raised an eyebrow. "Is it truly?"

Brom, a large man in both appearance and personality, turned from where he'd been inspecting the pieces I'd made yesterday, hands clasped behind him in a guise of dignity. "Well, it was for us, but it appears that's not the case for you."

It was not unusual for them to visit me, but the timing of their visit was something that had me watching a bit more closely than usual. One of them—or both—knew something.

Ichabod glared at Brom before softening his gaze as it moved to me. "What's happened, Katrina?"

"I'm this year's Roghnaithe." There was no point in dancing around the subject with either of them. The town knew what being the Roghnaithe meant. The public sacrifice was a yearly occurrence. A spectacle.

While I had never attended one out of silent protest, I knew what happened. After the Samhain party at my parents' house, the poor, unfortunate soul was taken to the cemetery after being stripped of their magic by the Ciallmhar and then stripped of their belongings by my mother. Then they were sent into the forest on the north side of the Hollow, into the Horseman's territory. No one had ever returned.

And from the lack of surprise on Brom's face, he'd known my news before he ever stepped foot inside the shop.

Both men froze, their voices echoing as one. "What?"

Ichabod's surprise appeared genuine, but Brom was as good an actor as he was a friend. Which was to say, not very. It should have irritated me that he had come here looking for some kind of reaction. He'd likely heard from his father, who sat on the Ciallmhar council with my parents, but that wasn't enough drama for Brom Bones. No, he had to come witness my assured despair and grief over being chosen.

Well, he wouldn't get it.

I knew they both heard me, but I repeated myself anyway, keeping my voice flat and disinterested despite the wild thumping of my heart. "The spirits have apparently chosen me this year. My parents informed me this morning."

"They surely cannot mean to sacrifice you," Ichabod said incredulously, his eyebrows shooting up his forehead. "You are their only child."

"Ichabod," I said dryly. He, of all people, knew how my parents truly viewed me, and for him to say those words to me was foolish and ill-advised. We'd been close once, as children. Ciara, Ichabod, and I had gone to school together—the quiet outcasts banding together in a pitiful attempt at a friendship that never truly took hold. But he knew. He knew exactly how my parents treated me when they thought no one was listening. He'd ruined any potential at that friendship last year, and I doubted he'd be able to repair it in the next five days. The truth of my situation was much less sentimental and far more practical than he was pretending, and to deny it under the guise of sentimentality was ignorant. "We both know my parents care more for this town than they *ever* could for me."

He sighed and fell silent, the pity clear on his face. He knew my words were true and there was nothing he could say that would ease the burden of my newfound situation; nor did I want him to try. I knew my situation, and I was dealing with it the best I could—by shoving down my emotions and not letting myself feel them. But soon, everyone would look at me with pity and remorse. I wouldn't be surprised if Ichabod's first stop after visiting me was to go tell everyone he could find. He was one of the town's biggest gossips, and everyone loved him for it.

I went back to sorting through my orders, trying—and failing—to avoid thinking about my impending death.

Ichabod rapped his knuckles against the counter, pulling my attention back up to him. He looked at me the same way he looked at his often-spooked horse, and I bit the insides of my cheek to keep from curling my lip up at him in response. "What are you going to do?"

Pausing, I sighed and set the stack of papers down. "There is not much I can do. We all know my parents will not change their mind, and I have no one to offer to take my place."

"I suppose Henry will want to sell the store?" Brom asked, moving over to the counter next to Ichabod and leaning to rest his chin on his fist. "It's well known he cannot run the shop without you."

"No, I was planning to continue making pottery in the afterlife," I replied dryly, rolling my eyes. While I needed to consider what would happen to the store and to Henry without my help, I was a bit more concerned with figuring out what would happen to my life. "Yes, I suppose I will need to talk with Henry and make a plan to find help for the store."

"I could buy it," he suggested, wiggling his eyebrows at me.

Brom would be the last person I would ever trust to take over this store. He was lucky Henry was still in the back, or he would likely have smacked Brom across the back of his head before literally *kicking* him out of the shop. He'd done it before, after all.

"Absolutely not." I shrugged. He drew back as if I had physically struck him. I would rather the store rot into ruins than give it to Brom. "Brom, you are not the type to run a pottery store. You'd likely die if you got a little clay on your hands."

"She has a point," Ichabod chimed in, smiling widely.

Brom grumbled something I could not make out and crossed his arms over his chest. He sniffed haughtily. "Then who is Henry planning to sell it to?"

"I suppose that will be up to him, considering it is his shop. *If* he even decides to sell it," I said, raising an eyebrow. "But we have time, considering it has not even been an entire day since I found out about my impending doom. We have four more days to figure it out."

"Of course, you have time, Katrina," Ichabod mumbled, but loud enough I could still hear. It helped that he was on my left side, too. "And we will assist however you'd like."

"Katrina, you know, if you truly did not want to marry me, there are much easier ways to get out of it," Brom teased, as a serene smile found its way back to his face, his previous embarrassment quickly forgotten.

I narrowed my eyes, trying to keep my temper from bubbling up at his words. Brom never failed to bring up his failed marriage proposal whenever he could. He and Ichabod had spent much of the prior summer trying to win my hand, despite me explicitly telling them I was not interested in marrying anyone... a fact Brom seemed to repeatedly forget. Ichabod had at least been interested in romancing me for my personality, while Brom had clearly only cared about the status he foolishly believed I could bring him. That, and he was constantly seeking to one-up Ichabod.

"Brom, I already rejected your proposal, remember? I won't marry anyone unless I decide to, and this will not change whether I am the Roghnaithe or not." My jaw ached from how hard I was clenching it, trying to keep a lid on my frustration with the two men. My mother had encouraged the engagement to Brom, and when I had publicly rejected it, I'd had to stay in my room for two weeks while the bruised eye she gave me healed.

But unlike my mother, who seemed able to douse all the fight from my body with a single glance, it wasn't the same with Brom and Ichabod. With them, I had to work to restrain my temper, trying to uphold the propriety and manners expected from me.

"Ichabod here will not mind," Brom pushed, clapping a hand on Ichabod's shoulder. Ichabod flinched under the rough blow.

Crossing my arms over my chest, I felt fire build in my palms. I clenched my fists to keep my power from erupting. Burning down the shop would not bode well for my last act here.

"Now, now, there is no need to get hysterical," he said,

sniffing as he looked down at my hands. "I was simply teasing you."

Teasing or not, I had grown tired of this conversation before it even started. Ever since I rejected Ichabod and Brom's marriage proposals, there had been constant "teasing" from them both. Mostly it was needling remarks here and there about how I was only getting older, and how I would find no one else willing to put up with me for the rest of our practically immortal lives. It truly showed how foolish they were for thinking that insulting a woman was the way to get her to agree to marriage. I pitied the woman who settled down with either of them.

Clearing my throat, I tried to keep my voice aloof and soft. "I think I would like to be alone, if you both would not mind."

"See what you have done, you fool?" Ichabod hissed, smacking Brom's arm.

"Me?" Brom hissed back, once again unable to keep his voice lower than a soft bellow. "She is the one being unreasonable."

"Oh?" I crossed my arms over my chest, my hackles rising instantly. The word—and the accompanying tone—had spilled from my lips before I could swallow it down, and now that it was out there, we'd all have to deal with the consequences.

"You are the heir to Sleepy Hollow," said Brom, his voice slow as if I were a stupid child and not a fully capable adult woman with enough power to burn him to ash where he stood. It reminded me all too much of how my mother had spoken to me this morning. "If you die before you are married, no one will inherit the town after your parents eventually pass."

As if my parents would not try for another child, a boy this time, before my body was even cold.

"Brom, this is hardly appropriate to discuss so soon after she got the news," Ichabod scolded. He frowned at me. "I apologize for his insensitivity, Katrina."

"You do not need to speak for me, schoolteacher. Katrina knows I am speaking the truth. We do not have the time to sit and dawdle."

"Please leave now," I said, my voice cold and harsh, echoing that of my mother's. When I pointed at the door, my fingers were smoking. I took a deep breath, trying to keep my fire under control, but the thread of willpower was quickly unraveling with every word Brom and Ichabod spoke. My powers bubbled beneath my skin, begging to be let out to destroy everything in sight.

"You are being unreasonable," Brom protested, taking a cautious step toward me, his palms out as if he were trying to calm a wild horse. "You must think of the town."

"Brom does make a valid point," Ichabod added, shrugging. "If not one of us, consider marrying someone before the ceremony."

"Though really, it should be me," Brom chimed in again, tugging at the lapels of his jacket and sniffing. If he sniffed once more, I might consider cutting his nose off.

"No, you have made her angry. It should be me."

"Ichabod, you are a fool."

"A fool? You are the one who continues to insult her!"

"STOP," I roared as flames erupted from my hands and shot down into the floor. As quickly as they ignited, I smothered them out, drawing the burning anger back into my chest and pushing it low into my belly. Only the smell of acrid smoke and singed hair remained.

Both men froze, their eyes wide and mouths open as they looked at me.

I raised a shaky finger, pointing to the door again while

the smoke still smoldered from my now blackened finger-nails. "Get out. Now."

"Fine, we will leave. But when you calm down, we should discuss this more," Brom said, collecting himself and straightening his clothes.

"You fool," Ichabod grumbled as he pulled Brom out of my shop and closed the door, giving me an apologetic look.

Finally alone again, I slumped to the floor, my back against the counter. Surprised that Henry had not come out at the commotion, I grabbed a rag off the floor and used it to scrub the soot from my hands. My fire never burned me, but it left its traces behind on my skin.

It was not even midday, and I was already beyond ready to crawl back into my bed and hide from the world beneath my covers. As upsetting as Brom and Ichabod's words had been, there was an element of truth. I needed to face this at some point. The itching desire to find a way to escape my fate sunk into my bones, but the fear of failure paralyzed me, wrapping around my lungs and squeezing tightly until I dismissed the idea.

Complacency and courage warred inside me, one side pushing me to give in and do what everyone expected, while the other whispered that I should burn my own path into the world... One of them sounded like my mother.

Sighing, I pulled myself away from the counter and crawled over to the scorched floor, rubbing at the soot and ash with the rag. Henry had enough to worry about without me burning down his shop.

"I am tired of myself tonight. I should like to be somebody else."

-Oscar Wilde,
The Picture of Dorian Gray

Hours passed, and I was still here, working on the same vase I'd started the previous day. My thoughts raged like a storming current, and I couldn't focus long enough to perfect the form.

For years I had simply turned a blind eye to the way my parents, as heads of the Ciallmhar, led Sleepy Hollow. It was foolish and privileged; I knew that, but it was all I had known. Now that I was facing certain death, I had questions. Concerns. I did not want to die. And I did not want anyone else to die, either.

Sighing, I slammed my hands down into the mound of wet clay on my wheel. The vase had once again not been going the way I intended, like everything else in my life right now. It was time to start over.

In all my life, I had never seen any sign of the danger my parents continually spouted about. No mortals had ever seen the bridge leading into Sleepy Hollow. The barrier did its job, concealing us and keeping them out, though some had wandered near it, oblivious to the magically shrouded structure just meters away from them.

The Horseman had never sought to punish us, and no one in the town had ever seen him. Had anyone stopped to question the practice? I doubted it. My parents' word was law in Sleepy Hollow, as it had been for longer than I'd been alive. And no one dared question them.

My hands wobbled over the clay as my mind wandered. My parents knew I disapproved of the practice, despite never saying it aloud, and I couldn't help but wonder if that was the reason I was named as Roghnaithe, along with my other perceived failures. I should have been married off by now, and yet I still lived with my parents, no doubt a product of both my own design and my parents' belief that I would never be good enough for anyone. Especially since I wasn't good enough for them. I pushed my hands into the clay, the wet earth squishing between my fingers as I squeezed. I closed my eyes and drew a shuddering breath.

My parents—my mother in particular—had never been shy about letting me know how disappointing I was. And given their prolonged mortality, I had no doubt my parents would try for another child after my death. Maybe one that would live up to their unattainable expectations; one that was not broken like me.

"What did that clay do to anger you, girl?" Henry asked as he walked up in front of my wheel. I opened my eyes, pulling my fingers from the mound of clay and wiping them on my apron. He smiled, but I could still see the sadness in his eyes.

My heart felt like it weighed a thousand pounds. I did not want to leave Henry or Sleepy Hollow. "Nothing," I sighed. "I am thinking too hard, I suppose."

"Well, pottery is good for calming your thoughts. But I am a good listener if you speak loudly enough." He patted my shoulder and lingered for a moment. "I will be here when you are ready to face it, Katrina."

My eyes blurred as I focused on the wet clay in front of me, channeling my frustration into the vase to distract myself from the tears building. If I ignored them, maybe they would not fall.

At the very least, I could make this vase. Smoothing my hands up and around the curve of the clay, I wondered what I could do to escape my fate. As quickly as the thoughts came, I shook my head to clear them. There was no escaping this. No escaping Sleepy Hollow. No escaping death and the whisper of the Horseman that would spell my demise.

As a witch, I had nowhere else to go.

Supposedly.

But... perhaps my mother had lied about that as well. Maybe there was another haven for me, another place where paranormals would be safe and not persecuted by the humans. It was a risk. Too big a risk for me to take without proof, and too big a risk to leave without knowing where to go. Even if I managed to suppress my erratic powers enough to blend in with the humans, a woman my age, who was not married and unable to hear from one ear, was not exactly a common societal norm. I would stand out immediately, and that would almost certainly end in my death.

Sleepy Hollow was my home, for better or worse, but I couldn't let it become my grave as well. I had two options: stay in Sleepy Hollow or try to escape... both ended in my demise.

Frustration bubbled up in my chest, marrying despair and clawing its way from my throat with a choked sob. Tears fell, streaking down my face and dripping onto the vase in front of me. A lump of misshapen clay stared back up, taunting me and whispering that I was a failure and could do nothing right.

Standing, I wiped my tears with the backs of my hands

and picked up the lump of clay, dropping it back into the container for tomorrow.

I washed my hands off slowly, the cold water grounding me. It would be wise to talk through my thoughts with Henry. He might not help me find a solution or a way to escape my fate, but I knew, if nothing else, he would hold me as I cried.

Before I could go find Henry, though, he came out from the back office and pulled his stool up beside the counter. "Come sit and talk with me, Katrina."

My heart squeezed at the sadness in his voice, but I listened and pulled up a second stool beside him. Despite my desire for him to tell me how to survive, the voice in my head escaped my lips before I could stop it. "I suppose you want to tell me I must accept my fate?"

He reeled back as if I'd physically struck him. "Heavens no, girl." He pulled my hands into his. "I want to tell you to do whatever it takes to stay alive. Perhaps you should stop by Ciara's for some tea. Seeing her might help clear your mind and help you explore your options."

I had already been planning to see Ciara once I'd finished my work. "Yes, I need to go see her."

One of Henry's hands reached up, meeting my cheek. "I know you are smarter than most, but you've lived a sheltered life. Have you considered leaving the Hollow?"

For a moment, the only sound I heard was the thump, thump, thumping of my heart in my ears. "What?"

"There is a world beyond Sleepy Hollow, you know."

"*Can* I leave?" In all my years, I'd never imagined leaving Sleepy Hollow. This was my home, and though I was often unhappy, I had considered nothing different. "Who would they have take my place?"

He shrugged. "That hardly matters, so long as you're safe."

"I can't do that to someone," I croaked. There was little doubt in my mind who they'd choose to take my place if I left, and I would not leave Henry or Ciara to suffer my fate while I ran away. If I was to die, I would die in Sleepy Hollow; not at the hands of fearful humans whose path I crossed attempting to escape.

"Katrina Van Tassel, there is little you couldn't do if you set your heart to it," he said, smiling as he patted my cheek again.

"Where would I even go?"

"Go talk to Ciara. Have some tea, and then if we still need to discuss it, we will." He stood, pulling me up with him. "Now, go clean that clay off your face and go before Ciara closes."

As I approached the apothecary shop, the sun's fading rays colored the town in flaming orange and yellow, and a crisp, sweeping breeze cooled the sweat on my brow.

I saw the bells on the door move as I entered the shop, though I could not hear them. The smell of pungent herbs and sharp medicines overpowered my senses, causing my nose to itch. Warmth from the fire along the wall rushed over me, folding me into its embrace as I closed the door behind me.

"Katrina," Ciara greeted, moving out from behind the counter to greet me. She hugged me tightly before resting her hands on my shoulders as her swirling hazel eyes roved over my face. "Something has happened since yesterday."

"You heard," I said, defeat hanging on each word.

Her eyes darkened slightly, and she let out a sigh that held the weight of the world as she squeezed my shoulders.

"Yes, I did. I am sorry. They should have abolished this barbaric practice long ago."

"Katrina, dear, come sit with me," a female voice called from further in the shop.

We both turned to look. Adelaide, one of the few female members of the Ciallmhar, was sitting alone with a cup of tea. My stomach flipped and my heart sped as I twisted my hands, sharing a look with Ciara. Perhaps this would be my chance to make my case to the Ciallmhar to put an end to the sacrifices. I had never entertained the notion before, knowing that my mother would have me turned away from the Ciallmhar house before I could even raise a hand to knock.

But Adelaide was here, alone. Since there were no other Elders in sight, maybe I could plead my case without anyone turning me away. Adelaide was an extremely powerful diviner able to see the future at her will. Surely, she would be the one to help me stop this practice.

"Go," Ciara mouthed, gently pushing me toward Adelaide.

Slowly, I walked over and took the seat opposite Adelaide. Her milky white eyes studied my face, scanning up and down.

"You wish to change your fate?" she asked, setting her teacup down on the saucer.

I fidgeted in my chair, tucking my hands beneath my thighs and locking my feet behind the legs. "Yes. I do not wish to die. And I am questioning—"

"You are questioning if the sacrifices are truly warranted," she finished, lacing her fingers together and resting her hands on the table in front of her.

"Surely, the Horseman cannot—"

"Call him by his appropriate title, child. The Horseman is the common name."

I ducked my head, my cheeks heating. "Yes, ma'am. I meant the Dullahan."

Ciara came over, setting down another saucer and teacup in front of me before disappearing into the back once more.

Adelaide nodded her approval, raising a grayed eyebrow as she sipped her tea. "And I assume you are now questioning our tradition because of your newfound fate as one of those sacrifices?"

The intensity of her gaze froze the words on my tongue, the retort dying on my lips. "Yes."

"And you think that is not a noble sacrifice to make?" She sipped her tea, her non-seeing eyes staring through me. "You think you are above being sent to the Dullahan for the good of our town?"

"I think it is an unnecessary sacrifice." The muscles along my spine quivered, forcing me to slouch and wrap my arms around myself. But I fought against it, keeping my chin high and my shoulders back as I met her eyes. If this was a test to see if I was worthy of the truth, cowering would certainly show my worthlessness.

"How would you know what is necessary and what isn't? You are barely older than a child. Your parents—your mother especially—have lived in this Hollow for nearly two hundred years, since before the War for Independence. I have lived here for nearly one hundred." She sipped her tea, setting the empty cup down roughly on the saucer. "What makes you think you know the truth behind how the veil works?"

I picked up the teacup in front of me and took a sip, considering my next words and contemplating the best way to make my case that I should be allowed to live or at least be allowed to leave.

"You cannot leave, child."

My eyes widened as she answered the thoughts I'd not spoken aloud. "How—"

She traced her finger around the handle of the teacup, watching me as I struggled to form words. Her eyes blazed a glowing white as she leaned toward me, her voice like shards of ice piercing my skin. "Sleepy Hollow will be destroyed if you leave."

The teacup in my hand slipped from my fingers, dropping to the floor and shattering into tiny shards of porcelain. My heart thundered against my ribs, which seemed to constrict around my body like a corset, tightening to the point I couldn't breathe. Each heartbeat felt like an eternity before I was finally able to peel my dry tongue from the roof of my mouth and wet my lips to speak. "Pardon me?"

She leveled a look at me. "Did you truly not hear me? Or are you simply hoping that if you ask again, my words will change?"

Blood rushed to my cheeks, and I fought to keep my head held high. I had heard her. The quiet of the apothecary shop and the ringing clarity of her voice made that certain.

"You underestimate yourself," she said, wagging a finger at me as she pointedly ignored my not answering her question. Her voice never wavered, and her chin never dipped as she continued. "Your mother is one of the most powerful witches to ever live. You were bred for power. You're one of the few witches in recent history to have control over pure flames."

I shook my head, sweat dampening the back of my dress. I couldn't be powerful; I'd been told my entire life I was *not* powerful. "I am not—"

"*Bred* for power," she repeated, holding that same finger up and pursing her lips. "Not trained for it. Your mother sees your potential, and she doesn't want you to usurp her." She picked up her teacup, sneering as she raised it to her lips.

"It's a waste of magic, if you ask me. But your mother never does ask for anyone's input."

"Usurp?" I asked, my surprise showing through my voice. My mother had never treated me as anything but an inconvenience. Could she really consider me a threat? She hadn't even been willing to train me when my magic set in. And while it was true that my fire magic was rare, it was hardly notable. Elemental magic was considered basic, and anyone with any magic worth mentioning had achieved their status through spell work and practice.

Adelaide returned her teacup to the saucer, clearing her throat. She reached over and patted my hand. Her skin was cool and dry against my own warm, damp skin, and I was uncertain whether the touch was supposed to be comforting or a warning. "Two months ago, the Ciallmhar discovered a prophecy. It says your mother must sacrifice her bloodline to save the Hollow, otherwise death will destroy us all."

My stomach dropped to my boots, my heart racing. Perspiration gathered on the back of my neck and my palms as my throat grew tight. I clasped my hands together to contain my flames. My voice was a hoarse whisper as the room spun slightly. "I cannot destroy Sleepy Hollow. I do not have the power to do such a thing."

My mother had founded Sleepy Hollow. Surely, she would never have had a child if she knew I would be destined to destroy it.

She waved a hand, scoffing. "Your mother may have coddled you, but your fire *is* the most powerful in Sleepy Hollow."

My panic subsided momentarily at her words, immediately giving way to the red that bled into my vision. Smoke drifted up from my clasped hands. "If there is one thing my mother has never done, it is coddle me."

She sniffed, nodding at my hands. "Your fire is itching to

escape and protect you, which proves otherwise. Your mother let you be complacent in thinking your flames were not powerful and never pushed you to be more. Others with fire magic in the Hollow are nowhere near your level, and they have trained for years."

"Why did she wait?" I asked. "If she knew my sacrifice would save the Hollow, surely she'd have done it long ago."

She cocked her head to the side, as if she were listening to something far off in the distance. For a moment, she was silent, and I almost repeated my question. But at last, she straightened her head and turned her unseeing eyes back to me. "The prophecy has just come to light. And even then, we know only a small portion of it. We're certain there's more."

"Then how do you know it's even about me?" I asked, keeping my hands clasped together to contain the flames. They would not burn me, but they would burn everything around me if they escaped. "It could be about anyone if you only have a small piece. How do you know? She would kill me based on supposition. What does it say? Show me the piece you have."

"Calm yourself, Katrina," she scolded. "The last thing we need is you burning Ciara's nice shop to the ground because you cannot control your emotions."

My hands burst into flames as I shoved back from the table and stood. "Control my emotions? I am being sentenced to *die* over words that may or may not be about me."

Before, when my mother had made it seem like this was nothing but a need for a more personal sacrifice, I had almost made peace with my fate. But now, knowing she made this decision based on an incomplete prophecy brought to Adelaide, my ire had pushed itself out of the cage I'd built in my mind.

My body was too hot, too tight, and the flames grew, crawling up my forearms and singeing away the fabric there.

Adelaide merely sat there, sipping her tea. "Are you finished? Or are you truly intending to burn this shop to ashes?"

No, I did not want to burn Ciara's shop down or harm anyone... except my mother. Closing my eyes, I inhaled slowly through my nose; the smoke stinging my nostrils and settling deep in my chest. I repeated the process, blowing the breath back out through my nose. Again, and again, and again. Finally, the warmth surrounding my hands receded, and I opened my eyes.

I could not talk about this any longer. I *would* leave the Hollow. I would *live.* Apart from Henry and Ciara, I was a no one here. Adelaide was wrong. I was not surprised my mother didn't investigate the prophecy more. My life—and my death—meant little to her. But that did not mean I would stay to accept her decision. I would ensure Henry and Ciara's safety however I could, and then I would leave. "Do you truly believe we need to make a sacrifice to the Horseman each year to maintain the barrier?"

Adelaide sighed, setting her teacup down and pursing her lips at me. "Go home, Katrina. Make your preparations for the afterlife. *Stop meddling*."

Before I could say anything else, she stood, leaving the apothecary with a tinkling of bells. Of course, I could hear those bells.

"*A drowsy, dreamy influence seems to hang over the land, and to pervade the very atmosphere. Some say that the place was bewitched...*"

-*Washington Irving,*
The Legend of Sleepy Hollow

Seven

A s soon as Adelaide left, Ciara hurried to the front door, locking it, and pulling the heavy fabric blinds down over the window. She turned and took the seat Adelaide had occupied, leaning forward on her forearms. "What are you planning, Katrina?"

"What makes you think I am planning something, Ciara?" I asked, crossing my arms over my chest.

She gave me a pointed look. "I have been your friend since we were schoolchildren. I know when you are planning something. You came here knowing she comes here every afternoon for tea. You had to know something like this was a possibility."

I slumped backward in my chair, slouching in such a manner I knew would have earned me a lashing from my mother had she seen it. Ciara was right, of course. And I had known she would ask for details as soon as Adelaide had left. "Yes, I am planning something."

She rolled her eyes with a scoff. "Of course you are. Tell me what you are planning."

"I cannot stay here, waiting to be slaughtered," I whispered, sitting up straighter in my chair, and tucking my hands into my lap beneath the table.

Suddenly, my lap was more interesting than Ciara's all-seeing gaze. While I knew she would support me, I also knew her feelings about Sleepy Hollow. The good ones and the bad ones. This was her home, the only one she'd ever known, and while it was also the place that sacrificed her brother, I knew she would never leave. None of the residents here would ever leave. My mother had ensured their loyalty to the town and their unending dedication to tradition and safety, above all.

Only silence followed.

I raised my head to see her staring at me, though I could not decipher the expression on her face. Defensiveness rose in response to her studious gaze. "What?"

"Do you think the prophecy is about you?" Her voice was quiet and carefully calm.

I shook my head, reeling back in horror at the implication. "No, of course not. Ciara, you know me. I could *never* harm this place, no matter what I feel about it."

I hated my mother. I hated the sacrifices. I hated Ichabod and Brom for pushing for marriage. I hated many things about this town, but I loved many things, too. Henry and the pottery shop had shown me true love and had given me purpose. Ciara had given me companionship, a respite against the meanness of other children.

I could not destroy Sleepy Hollow. Not even if I wanted to.

"I have seen what your powers do when your temper is out of control." She huffed a small laugh, though there was no amusement in the sound. "And your temper is not exactly what I would classify as stable."

I leveled a look at her. My temper, while notoriously volatile, was under my control, despite what many thought.

Ichabod and Brom merely had a way of bringing it out more than others. And I could not fathom my temper ever becoming so volatile that I would destroy my home. "I will not stay here to die."

"Your parents and the Ciallmhar know better than anyone what is best for the town, Katrina," Ciara said, worry creasing her forehead. Her eyes glazed over, as they often did when she was thinking about Torin, her brother who had been in my place just years ago. "It is not wise to question them."

"No one has ever questioned them. The Horseman has never tried to attack us." I wrung my hands together, desperate to get someone to see my side. Ciara, of all people, should have been supporting me. I'd been gentle with her, never questioning her own feelings on the sacrifices or the Dullahan, knowing what they'd be and that the conversation would only devolve into me holding her as she cried.

But she should have been on my side.

I thought she would have been.

I should have told Henry my plan before I left for tea. At least he would have supported me or told me outright I was being foolish. "This is a tradition that no one has stopped to question. Do we have any proof that it's even necessary?"

Ciara's gaze hardened. "Do not say that."

"But—"

"If that is true, why have you done nothing about it before now? I know you have not asked my opinions out of fear or respect, but you know how I feel about it. You know it's barbaric. You know how it has torn families apart and left them broken. We cannot question them, Katrina, but they are your parents. If anyone could have stopped this before now, it would have been you. And if you are right, how many people could we have spared?"

My cheeks burned. She was right. I should have pushed back long ago. Even though she knew about my home situation with my parents, I understood her anger and hurt, and it was justified. Her words burned in my chest, and I wanted to defend myself and remind her of what little influence I truly had over my parents. I had little freedom. But the pain in her eyes stopped me, pushing my retort back into my throat.

Ciara sighed, pushing a strand of shiny auburn hair back behind her ear. "It is too late, Katrina. The town has rules for a reason. To protect us. Your parents know that better than anyone. Although I detest the practice and the fact this cruelty separates families, I must acknowledge it. And so must you. Maybe it is best to not risk you causing even more death and pain."

I reeled back at her words as if she'd physically struck me. "How can you say that? You are my only friend here."

She didn't respond—not with words, at least. But the icy countenance rolling from her shoulders spoke plenty about what she thought of my statement.

I took a deep breath, pushing my own emotions down for the sake of hers. I had done it my entire life in my parents' presence and had done it for Ciara herself since Torin's death. Perhaps it should have disturbed me how easy it was to stuff my anger and hurt down until it was a dull ache instead of a sharp pain. I knew the words she wanted to hear. *Needed* to hear. "I am sorry, Ciara. You are right, of course. I should have questioned this practice sooner. We all should have. But to say that my parents are right... It is wrong. But I will not go quietly. I cannot."

She looked at me for a moment, her face unreadable. Would she turn me in to my parents? Would she stand with me? I had thought I knew that answer, but now, I was not so sure.

Tears of embarrassment and frustration stung my eyes. I reached up to wipe them away roughly. Crying would serve no purpose, yet I couldn't stop; the room blurring behind the tears.

"You are my friend. You know that, Katrina," she said, her voice barely audible now that I could not see her clearly.

"Say again?" My cheeks burned in shame over having to ask her to repeat herself.

She sighed. "You are my friend."

Shutting my emotions down until I bordered on complete numbness, I nodded. I twisted my fingers together in front of me, itching to get away from this conversation, to run and hide and be alone. No one could hurt me when I was alone.

"You are my friend," she repeated, reaching her palms out to me. When I didn't respond, she shook her hands slightly. Hesitating, I lifted my own to meet hers, our fingers twining as her icy hands contrasted with my hot skin. "You are my friend, but I cannot help you. Not the way you need me to."

My breath left my chest in a rush, causing my ears to ring slightly. I wanted to be upset, but felt nothing but a heavy weight in my stomach. I swallowed hard, pushing past the taste of ash to continue my request. I may not have her support, but perhaps she would be willing to give me information. "Your friendship is important to me, Ciara. *You* are important to me."

"And you are important to me," she said, squeezing my hands again.

"I need to leave the Hollow," I said, tenuously trying to keep the peace and not upset her. "Do you know how I can do that without being stopped by my parents or the Ciallmhar?"

After what felt like an agonizingly long time, she spoke

again, her voice quiet. "I have heard there is another haven in Saint Augustine, in the far south."

"How do you know?" I asked.

Ciara ran this apothecary, and while she had her fair share of Ciallmhar visits, I had not expected her to have this kind of information.

"Several moons ago, I heard some of them discussing a visitor that was coming from there. He never showed, but they spoke of the town as if it were like ours." She pulled her hands from mine and laced her fingers together. She shrugged slightly. "They never notice me. I am the help to them, so they are not careful with what they say when they are here alone."

"Another haven? Does it have sacrifices as well?"

I would not trade one death sentence for another.

She shook her head. "I don't know, Katrina. They didn't speak of it again." Her head tilted. "We can assume, though, can't we? If we need to sacrifice to ensure protection, wouldn't they need to as well?"

"Perhaps..."

If there was even a chance they did not require sacrifice, I needed to take it.

It did not surprise me they had ignored her presence and spoken so freely, but now my mind was spinning. How could I get there? The journey would be long and arduous, and I would need many supplies. Adelaide's words came back to me with a vengeance. Would my magic be stable enough for me to travel? Was it tied to the Hollow? Could I suppress it, as I had my whole life, long enough to get to safety?

"That is a very long journey."

"I can get you supplies," Ciara offered in a whisper.

I couldn't catch the words. "What?"

"Supplies," she said with the slight raise of her voice. "I

can help you. If you truly are planning to leave."

"You would do that?" It pained my heart that I would leave her behind to face whatever consequences awaited. I reached out to take her hand once more. "Would you come with me, Ciara?"

Tears welled up in her eyes. She squeezed my hand and smiled, but as someone who had faked smiles her entire life, I could see right through it. "You know I cannot, Katrina. My mother is not well enough to travel that far, and I will not leave her behind. Perhaps if Torin was still here, but not now. I am all she has left."

"I do not wish to leave you here," I said, my throat growing thick with unshed tears. "Are you certain you want to risk helping me?"

"I'm not certain about anything," she admitted. I opened my mouth to tell her I could find another way; a way to not involve her, but she held up a hand to stop me. "I will help you. I just need you to consider something, Katrina."

I nodded, still holding her other hand. She brought the hand she had raised down to hold mine between hers.

"If you leave—" She took a deep breath, and I saw the slight quiver of her bottom lip. "If you leave, who do you think your parents will choose in your place? You have no family to take your place, but you have me. You have Henry. What will stop them from simply choosing one of us? And what happens if Adelaide is right?"

My stomach curled. I knew the requirements; they had been my reason behind forcing myself to accept my fate. I wouldn't put Henry in that position. But if my mother found out that Ciara had helped me... I could certainly see my mother choosing Ciara as punishment. "I had not—"

"I know," she whispered. "And as much as I love you, I cannot die for you."

My stomach heaved, and bile rose, burning my throat. I

had to get out of here. I rose from the table, my vision blurry with tears. "Thank you, Ciara."

"Come by tomorrow and we will discuss the supplies you need."

I couldn't bring myself to return the smile, but I squeezed her hands before walking over to raise the blinds and unlock the door. Her eyes were heavy on my back as I left, but she said nothing else.

Opening the door, I stepped back out into the crisp air, inhaling deeply. The light was fading into the early evening, a purplish gray creeping in along the horizon. Needing to get home before darkness fully took hold, I turned down the path leading into the town square. The rows of small buildings rose into the night, greeting me as candles flickered in each of their windows. Passing through the main thoroughfare, I felt the stares on my back as the townspeople stopped to look at me; to gawk at the one marked for death. My steps quickened, wanting nothing more than to be out of the center of attention. Getting back to the manor was my only focus.

How ironic that the manor I had so desperately wanted to be free of would now be my solace.

"Am I to be thought the only criminal, when all human kind sinned against me?"

-Mary Shelley, Frankenstein

Eight

"You are late. Again," Henry said as I entered the shop the next morning. He was sitting at the counter, his fingers steepled beneath his chin as he struggled to keep a smile from his serious expression. "You know, a death sentence does not entitle you to slack off, girl."

I scoffed at him, grateful for the humor. He knew me better than I knew myself, and I appreciated his attempt to distract me. I shook my head. "You rarely come to work on time, old man."

He tried to keep the grave look on his face, but the smile broke through quickly as he chuckled and stood from his stool. "Yes, yes. I know."

"And tea was a terrible suggestion." I walked around the counter and pulled my apron on, tying it behind my back. The sharp pinching against my waist was a welcome distraction from the ache in my heart.

All I could hear was the echo of Ciara's final words, that either she or Henry would have to take my place.

He raised a bushy eyebrow. "Oh?"

"All it got me was a lecture, and then a strike across the face this morning when my mother discovered it."

"Your mother is a—"

"Do not say it," I muttered, reaching around him to pull out the stack of orders. "She has ears everywhere."

He sighed. "Fine, I will not say it. But I am thinking it. Loudly."

I smiled at him, grateful for his support. "Thank you, Henry."

"Do not thank me, girl. I simply do not wish to train a new apprentice again," he said as he stood from his stool. "Do we need to discuss getting you out of the Hollow?"

Rubbing my temples, I exhaled, and a hysterical laugh bubbled out. His question had broken through the dam I'd placed on my emotions to block out all that had happened yesterday afternoon.

Henry paused at my outburst. "What is it, girl?"

"My mother specifically chose me as the Roghnaithe this year," I told him, the words stabbing my heart and ripping into my soul. Acknowledging it aloud made it even more real. It had been my mother's choice, and not a random choice given to the Ciallmhar by the spirits. "And I... I can't..."

He shook his head and pulled me into his arms. The moment my face pressed into his chest, the tears began to flow. I balled my hands into fists, tucking them behind my back as I sobbed in the arms of my mentor. My mother truly did not love me, and though on some level I'd known that was my reality, seeing it result in my death was overwhelming.

"Tell me what happened, Katrina," he whispered, rubbing my back.

Sniffing, I clenched my throat and swallowed back the sobs, wiping at my eyes with my smoking hands. "There is a prophecy. It says unless my mother sacrifices me, I will bring death to Sleepy Hollow."

"That is utter nonsense." His answer was immediate and firm. "How convenient for that to come out now, just as you were getting the confidence to escape from under her thumb."

I shrugged, unable to voice any other words.

"You must leave, Katrina. I cannot bear to watch you stay and be killed." His voice cracked, and the sound made my tears begin anew. "Please, you must leave."

"I cannot," I whispered. "I cannot risk your life, Henry. You cannot ask that of me. I have no family to take my place, and everyone knows who you are to me. I cannot risk them choosing you instead."

He cupped my face in his hands. "And you cannot ask me to watch you die and know I could have prevented it."

We looked at each other for a long moment, both of us teary-eyed.

"What should I do?"

"Did Ciara have any insight?" he asked, reaching up to wipe away the tear that fell to his cheek.

I sniffed and leaned back, wiping my face with the sleeve of my dress. "Yes, she said she'd heard the Ciallmhar speak about another haven in the south, near Saint Augustine. She offered to get me supplies."

"Then that's what we shall do," he said, reaching over the counter and pulling a piece of parchment toward us. "We will make a list of what you need, and I will take it to her."

Nodding, I watched as he scrawled the list. Each line he wrote caused a new fissure to form in my heart at the thought of leaving him behind, of him possibly facing the Horseman. For me. Just like Ciara, I knew he'd never join me. But I had to ask.

"Henry," I whispered, my voice cracking. I cleared my throat as he lifted his head and paused his writing. "Would you come with me? When I leave?"

Tears welled in his eyes, and he shook his head. "No, darling girl. This is my home."

"Why?" I wiped the tears away again, my throat burning. "There is nothing for you here, and no one to help you. Why won't you come with me?"

He grasped my hand. "Katrina, I will be fine. If I went with you, I would only slow you down. I cannot move as well as I once could, and this is too important to risk. You will go without me. You will be fine, and I will be fine."

I couldn't form the words to reply. My body froze as the tingling traveled down my limbs and my head spun. I wanted to beg him, even if it meant getting on my knees, but if I learned one thing about the old mage, it was that no one could easily persuade him to do anything. He'd taught me to stand my ground, but I couldn't ignore his request. I forced myself to nod.

He nodded back, patting my hand. "All right then, it's all settled. You will go, and I will stay here."

"You will write to me?" I hated the meek sound of my voice, but I had to know. I couldn't lose him. He was my only connection to kindness and love.

"You could not stop me if you tried," he said with a smile. "Now, let me finish this list."

Silently, we finished the list, and I bit my tongue to keep from asking him to reconsider. As soon as the ink had dried on the last word, Henry stood. "I am off to Ciara's. When I return with the supplies, you will be on your way."

"So soon?" I asked, my stomach knotting at the thought of leaving everything I'd ever known behind, especially without knowing what lay ahead.

"We cannot risk anyone finding out about our plans,

girl. You yourself mentioned your mother having ears everywhere," he said, tapping at my cheek. "Now, I'm off. I shall return soon."

I blew out a breath once Henry had left. Was I truly doing this? Leaving the Hollow had never been an option I would have considered before, but now it seemed to be the only option I had in order to live. And I wanted to live.

"You are stronger than this, Katrina," I muttered to myself, wiping at the tears on my face as I stood from the stool.

Moving about the shop, I filled a bag with the belongings I'd left here for safekeeping: my journal, which certainly would not have been safe in the same residence as my mother, money I had tucked away for any emergencies, and the red crystal necklace Henry gave me... the only gift I'd ever received.

I packed my meager belongings in the satchel with room to spare for whatever Henry returned with. I pulled out a fresh piece of parchment and began penning a letter to the old earth witch, spilling my emotions and several tears onto the paper. Folding it neatly, I placed it on his desk in the back office, and then I sat, taking in the shop for the last time.

What had only felt like seconds passed before the lantern flashed and Henry returned with a small bag over his shoulder. "Are you ready, my dear girl?"

Taking a deep breath, I nodded and met him at the front door. Despite my earlier resolutions to not ask him again, the words came spilling from my lips. "Won't you please come with me, Henry? They cannot sacrifice you if you are not here."

He chuckled, placing the bag over my shoulder. "I have lived a long life, and I am too stubborn to leave it now, Katrina. But you, you have your entire future ahead."

Tears welled in my eyes again, blurring my vision and burning my throat. "Henry..."

He waved his hand and pulled the door open. "None of that now. I expect you to write once you have arrived somewhere safe. Keep those hands of yours out of trouble."

The watery laugh that escaped made me feel slightly better, though not much. I leaned in, pressing a kiss against his cheek while trying not to think about how it might be the last time I touched him. Tears slid from my eyes, wetting both our cheeks as I lingered. "Thank you for everything, Henry."

"You be careful, girl."

"I will," I said, smiling reassuringly at him as I adjusted the bag on my shoulder. "I promise."

Reluctantly, he let me go, holding the door open. "I pray I never see you again, Katrina Van Tassel."

His words may have been harsh, but the waver in his voice gave away everything he left unsaid.

Before I could change my mind, I turned and stepped out into the fading afternoon light and began my walk down the cobblestone streets leading through the Hollow. Staying to myself, I could only pray no one would notice that my path was leading toward the cemetery and the covered bridge that led out of town.

The bridge finally came into view just over the hill and my heart sped up, my palms slick with sweat as I adjusted my grip on the bags in my hands. The worn wood. My breathing sped up. The flaking, once-white paint. Sweat beaded on the back of my neck and rolled down my spine. The shadows cast across the planks of the floor. My throat grew dry, and my tongue felt heavy. The gaping entrance that led to freedom. My knees shook as I walked.

This was it. After twenty years in Sleepy Hollow, I was finally leaving.

It wasn't the relief I'd been expecting.

Instead, each step felt like a weight attached to my ankles. My heart shattered with each breath, thinking only of who I was leaving behind; of what pain Henry and Ciara might suffer on my behalf. Or those who would become a victim of my mother, never seeing a way out.

I closed my eyes and took a deep breath, pushing it all away.

For the first time in my life, I needed to be selfish. Or I was going to die.

I opened my eyes.

Staring at the bridge, all else fell away. Only the weathered wood and the sound of running water in the river beneath remained in my awareness. My feet pulled me in the direction of the bridge, the energy from the magical wards pulsing and drawing me in.

A hand wrapped around my arm, clamping tight like a vise, before pulling me from the trance the bridge had pulled me into. Turning to face my captor, fire built in my chest. "Brom? What are you doing?"

"Where are you going, Katrina?" he asked, his hand squeezing tighter. His brows furrowed as he took in my cloak and the bags I had with me. "Are you trying to leave?"

"You are hurting me." I tugged against his powerful grip. Fire erupted from my fingertips and twirled up my forearms, singeing away the sleeves of my dress and licking at my captor's hands. Yet Brom did not release me. The smell of burning flesh entered my nostrils, but his grip only tightened. "Brom, stop this!"

He did not answer and began pulling me toward the bridge. I dug my heels in, but it was no use. Brom was nearly a full head taller than me and moved me with ease.

"I must protect the Hollow, Katrina," he said, and then grimaced as he pulled me to the side of the bridge, just above the rocky embankment leading to the water below. If he threw me down there, it would be too steep to climb back out. "You must be the sacrifice. You cannot leave Sleepy Hollow."

My heart raced, and blood pounded in my ears. I whipped my head back, hoping to call to someone nearby for help. My eyes landed on Ichabod, his lanky figure peeking out from behind a tree as he stood there watching the scene unfold. He did not look surprised as he watched Brom drag me across the grass.

Before I could open my mouth to shout for his help, Brom pushed again, and I clung to his arms as one of my feet slipped over the embankment.

"Brom, no. Do not do this."

"There is no choice. I must sacrifice the life of one for the safety of the town." He pried my fingers from his arm. "You must be given to the Dullahan. You cannot leave."

And then I was falling.

I landed below on the bank with a rough thud, crying out at the impact of my shoulder slamming against the earth. Panic seized my lungs as the steep embankment tilted me toward the river, rolling side over side. I scrambled to find purchase on the grass and rocks, desperately trying to cling to anything that would keep me upright and keep me out of the river, but I only succeeded in pulling a rock down onto my head and coming away with clumps of earth in my fingers. The blow landed and a sharp pain radiated through my temple as the rock tumbled down beneath me. My vision blurred, and I lost what little grip I had.

All too quickly, I left the earth and fell into the river's icy water. A gasp escaped my lips as my body absorbed the shock of the cold. I pressed my fingers to my head, coming away sticky and dark with blood. Blindly reaching for the shore to pull myself out of the water, I could feel my consciousness fading as a thick haze of black moved in from the edges of my vision, consuming everything. I fought against it, pushing to keep my eyes open despite the stinging pain in my head and the heaviness of my body.

My fingers wrapped around a log, but it was too late. My vision blackened further, and I fell back, smothered by the icy hands of the water, pulling me beneath the surface of the current.

The Horseman would surely find me now. If the river did not claim me first.

"*The boundaries which divide Life from Death are at best shadowy and vague. Who shall say where one ends and where the other begins?*"

-Edgar Allan Poe

Nine

Fingertips pressed firmly against the skin of my neck. The sensation of cool fingers and pressure tugged me back from the brink of unconsciousness, and I jerked back from the startling touch of a stranger. I pried my eyes open, struggling with the exhaustion that plagued my body.

I blinked rapidly to clear my blurry vision, trying to focus on the dwindling evening light. Shaking my head slightly, the fogginess dissipated only some, but I was able to form a coherent thought. How long had I been unconscious? My hair was damp against my forehead, but it wasn't dripping, so I'd been out of the water, at least for a bit. I pressed my fingers against my forehead, shaking away the pain again as I looked up.

"May I assist you?" The tall man who'd had his fingers pressed against my neck now had his hand extended toward me, as if to help me to my feet. His voice was like smoke and silk. It washed over me with a calm my body fought to embrace.

"Who are you?" I asked, carefully sitting up and slowly edging back along the grass.

Still hovering near me, the fading sun glinted off the man's short hair, reflecting strands of gold woven through a darker brown. His brow shadowed his eyes when he bent toward me, but the sharp line of his jaw was unmistakable and covered in a light dusting of hair. He extended a hand toward me, and I stared at it, my eyes quickly scanning our surroundings before returning to him.

Despite my hair having dried some, the rest of me was still soaking wet, my dress heavy with the touch of the river. A crisp breeze flowed over me, rustling the grass that tickled against my wrists.

There was no one around to help me if this man was not intending to help me. Trees extended in every direction as far as I could see, and the only sound I heard was my panting breaths in the wind. We had to be deep in the forest. Even if we were closer to Sleepy Hollow than I suspected, no one from town would dare venture into these woods after dark.

I licked my lips as I studied him, waiting for him to answer me. Nerves coiled in my stomach and my hands shook at my sides. The breeze rustled a tree branch nearby, and I flinched at the noise, curling in on myself while keeping my eyes fixed on the figure in front of me. He peered down at me, his face void of any indications of his intent. Like a statue.

"I believe your people refer to me as the Headless Horseman." His voice was calm, but I still jerked as he spoke again. He tilted his head as he looked down at me, studying me with a careful stillness I knew had to be intentional. "I am the Dullahan."

The world around me froze for a moment as his words washed over me, clinging to the hairs on the back of my neck and gripping my heart as it skipped a beat. Brom had succeeded in delivering me to the hands of death, after all.

My eyes closed briefly, squeezing tightly, but I snapped them back open, remembering who was in front of me. My escape from death had failed. I was here, in front of the Dullahan, and though he'd pulled me from the river, my fate had been sealed.

"But you have a head." As soon as the words left my mouth, my eyes widened, realizing the offense I'd surely caused. That was likely not the best thing to say as my first impression, especially to an entity that was rumored to both protect and threaten my home. An entity that was supposedly waiting for my soul to venture into these very woods. There were so many questions that would have been better suited to ensure my survival.

One side of his mouth twitched upward slightly. His bare hand was still outstretched, the other covered in a thick black leather glove. "Yes, I do indeed have a head. It would prove quite difficult to speak to you if I did not."

I almost narrowed my eyes at his jab, but my mind was finally beginning to catch up with the reality in front of me. Despite the quivering in my gut, my voice was steady as I spoke again. "The stories say that you only speak to call someone's name for death."

"And do you believe every story you are told?" he asked. His raised eyebrow fell as he finally dropped his hand, and he squatted beside me as his eyes drank me in like he'd been thirsty for far too long.

Orbs of blue swirled as they moved over my face. They seemed to be searching. For what, I wasn't sure, but I could only hope that he would find whatever he was looking for in my face. His gaze traveled down my neck, skipping over my torso in a flitting movement before focusing in on my hands, which were resting on the grass at my sides.

Clenching those hands, I tried to keep from squirming under his gaze. No one had ever looked at me so intently before, so openly. It made my face hot, and I wanted to turn away from him to escape the intensity. It was as if he was looking through me, rather than looking at me. Goosebumps formed on my exposed forearms.

"I believe there is some truth to every story," I replied slowly, weighing the words before letting them escape. The last thing I wanted to do was offend the Dullahan. If he hadn't killed me outright, or left me to drown in the river, perhaps there was a chance I could convince *him* to let me live. "Else they wouldn't have been told to begin with."

He hummed, nodding once in tandem with an easy shrug. "I suppose you are right. In any case, I can speak, I have a head, and I have no plans to murder anyone tonight."

Tonight. His emphasis didn't go unnoticed.

"Were you the one to pull me from the water?"

The chill of the night cut like daggers through the sopping wet material of my dress. A shiver wracked my body as the wind picked up, and I gritted my teeth to keep them from chattering. Now that the shock was beginning to wear off, the cold had set in.

"Yes. You nearly drowned." His voice was blunt as he stood, straightening his heavy jacket before pulling a second glove onto his other hand. He reached out once more, looking down at me. "Would you allow me to take you somewhere to warm up? It would be a disappointment if you were to die from exposure after I went to such lengths to pull you from the river."

I chewed on my lips, my hands tangling into the damp grass at my sides. Warmth sounded nice, but I was not foolish enough to believe that going with a man I'd just met —no matter what mythical being he claimed to be—was an intelligent choice.

"If you do not wish to accept my help, that is your decision. Though I fear you will not last much longer in the cold. Your lips are already turning blue, and you've not stopped shivering since you woke. We would not want you to die."

My body was hesitant whether to scream or laugh at the statement. Eventually, my anger won out, heating my blood better than any shelter could. It was foolish, given that the Horseman was even larger than Brom, and had a menacing aura to him, despite his carefully neutral expression. I saw steam rising from the grass, where my fingers were digging into the dirt, but I didn't care.

"They sent me to die." I inhaled sharply through my nostrils, quelling the fire in my belly. "I hardly see how the manner of my death would matter."

"Something offered does not always need to be accepted." He cast a pointed look at my hands. "And that will do you no good here."

The irreverence in his voice only spurred my temper. Thankfully, years of practice enabled me to keep my tone steady and my voice soft. "What have you been doing with the people offered to you?"

"I am more than willing to have this conversation," he said, still extending his gloved hand to me. "However, I would prefer it indoors, once I am certain you will not become ill from the cold and the wet."

"Why should I go with you? How do I know you are being truthful?"

He held his hand out for a moment longer, his gaze heavy on my face. Finally, his hand dropped to his side, and he straightened up. "Fine, enjoy your night in the cold. I will collect your corpse in the morning."

The fire inside my veins moved from my hands to flush my neck and face. Likely, he was right. Being wet in this crisp autumn air overnight, with no shelter from the wind and no dry clothes—even if I could start and sustain a flame on my own, I likely would be dead by morning. Reluctantly, I swallowed my pride and cleared my throat. "Where will you take me?"

His eyebrow ticked up again. "To my home."

My breath hitched in my throat. His home? This ominous figure had *a home*. One he planned to take me to. He could not possibly live nearby. Sleepy Hollow was a small town, and we would have quickly noticed an outsider. My brows furrowed as I pictured my mental map of the Hollow, trying to decipher where he could hide a home that no one had seen. I licked my cracked lips. "Where?"

"Close by," he said mysteriously, once again contradicting everything I'd assumed. I shook my head to clear to fuzziness once more. Was everything I had been told about him a lie? My heart raced and my breath quickened, but I fought to control my emotions, forcing my breathing to slow. He held his gloved hand out to me again, shaking it slightly when I still only looked at it. "Take it. I will not hurt you."

I curled my fingers tighter in the grass, smoke still rising. My fear, as much as my anger, fueled my magic now. "I might hurt you, though."

Wouldn't that be ironic? Little Katrina, failure at everything, was the one to maim the Dullahan. My tongue felt like lead as I swallowed.

For a moment, I would have sworn his eyes softened toward me, glinting in the evening light. But as quickly as I thought I had seen it, it was gone, the uninterested expression back in place. He extended his hand further. "You will not hurt me."

Hesitantly, I reached out to him. I held my breath as my hand slipped into his, waiting for the cry of pain from the heat of my skin. My fire had hurt Henry once, when he'd tried to pull me out of a panic attack by hugging me, and while he had forgiven me, I doubted I would survive the slight if I burned the Dullahan. Maybe the gloves were thicker than they appeared, or perhaps he had some magical protection, as he didn't even flinch with discomfort. His fingers tightened around my hand, and he pulled me to my feet with ease.

"Are you able to walk?" he asked as I swayed slightly.

The ground spun in my vision, but I knew closing my eyes would only make it worse, so I focused on the Horseman's boots until the world stilled once more.

He moved to drop my hand, but I held on tightly, using his grounding touch to help stop the movement of the forest. My dizziness always passed faster with touch, but I had so few willing to touch me, to help ground me to the steadiness of reality. But the Dullahan had not even blinked when I'd kept hold of his hand, not dropping it until I finally felt steady on my feet. "Thank you."

He nodded his head and raised an eyebrow. "Can you walk, Katrina?"

"Yes, yes, I think so," I replied, touching the side of my head.

Brom and Ichabod had betrayed me, but I could not bring myself to think about that now. I would get my revenge on them, but first I had to face the Horseman and go to his home. I looked around the ground, finding nothing but damp grass as panic rose in my throat. "Did you find a bag with me? When you pulled me from the river?"

My journals. My necklace. Tears burned at the thought of losing the gift Henry had given me.

He shook his head slowly. His brow furrowed as he studied me again, searching my face for answers I could not give. "No, there was nothing with you when I pulled you from the water. Why? What is missing?"

My heart sank. All my writings and the only kindness I'd ever received were gone, washed away in the cold water. "I had a satchel of supplies and personal belongings."

There it was again. A flash of sympathy in his dull blue-gray eyes, gone as quickly as it came. "I apologize, but there was no bag near you. Perhaps it will wash up in the morning."

Nodding, I smoothed my hands over my sopping dress; the movement was born of pure habit, but this time only smeared mud and clumps of dirt and grass down my front. "No need to apologize, Horseman."

"Best be off." He turned away from with a sharp step and began deeper into the forest. He glanced over his shoulder. "We need to get you into dry clothes."

And so, I followed the not-so-Headless Horseman away from the river and into the dark of the woods, toward his home and whatever fate he'd decide for me.

"Certain it is, the place still continues under the sway of some witching power, that holds a spell over the minds of the good people, causing them to walk in a continual reverie."

-Washington Irving,
The Legend of Sleepy Hollow

Ten

I followed the Horseman along the riverbank for several tense moments, apprehension building in my chest, telling me to run as far as possible. The evening light filtered through the tree canopy, cutting swaths of silver across the grass as I stumbled after him. Still uncertain of what would await me at the home of a being so closely tied to death, my heart thundered in my chest, clawing up to stick in my throat.

I balled my hands to keep my powers under control, but my emotions were seeping through and caused smoke to trail from my blackening fingertips. I stumbled, trying to keep up with the Dullahan's long, smooth strides. The last time I'd been in this forest, the fog and the whispers had sent me running. My eyes scanned over what I could see, which wasn't much. The evening was quickly giving way to the darkness, and the fading light was all I could rely on.

As we rounded another bend in the river, a loud rustling sounded in the trees. Whatever had been following me had found us. I immediately stopped, my eyes darting around, trying to find the source of the noise. The Horseman looked back at me over his shoulder, his eyes tracking down to my hands, still smoldering though no flame had erupted. "You are fine. It is just Liath, my horse. She will not hurt you either."

The panic subsided slightly as I took a few more cautious steps forward and looked to my right to see a jet-black horse standing behind the trees, its dark eyes reflecting otherworldly flames as it watched me. A black leather saddle sat atop her back, and her muzzle strapped around with the same dark material. The only color visible was the bands of white above her hooves, glowing in the evening light.

A sigh of relief escaped as my shoulders slumped. "A horse."

"Yes," the Dullahan said, his voice sounding amused at my reaction. "You *have* seen a horse before, right?"

I scowled at him, my cheeks heating. "Yes, of course I have seen a horse before. I simply was not expecting one to be here. I thought it was the fog again."

The Dullahan whirled so fast I'd barely seen him move, and his gloved hands grabbed my shoulders. "Fog? What do you know of the fog? Tell me everything."

The utter command in his voice made me shrink away, my body falling into the patterns my mother had created as my mind shut down, protecting myself from the anger and pain that would surely follow.

"I—There... was a-a fog." I cursed myself as I tried to move my tongue, paralyzed by the fear that leaden my mouth.

His brow furrowed and his gaze tracked down to where his hands rested on my shoulders. In a smooth motion, he stepped away and tucked his hands behind his back, bowing his head. "I apologize for grabbing you, Katrina."

My head was spinning, though not from the change in spatial orientation this time. The Dullahan was apologizing to *me?* Licking my lips, I pushed out the words that had grown jumbled in my throat. He had no reason to apologize to me, not when I was the one who had failed to answer his question.

"I was picking flowers, and there was a strange fog. Perhaps it was two days ago? Or maybe yesterday? And I heard something whispering my name."

His jaw ticked, the shadows in the hollows of his cheek becoming more pronounced in the moonlight. He looked like a carving—a sculpture of marble in the image of a man.

"My home is a way away from here. This is the best way to get there." He walked over to the horse and patted her nose gently as he untied her leads from the nearby tree.

I watched as he adjusted the saddle. My breath rushed from my nose, fanning against my upper lip. "The fog? Do you know about it?"

"It's not safe to discuss it openly. I will tell you more once we're inside," he said. His hands fell from the saddle as he turned to face me fully. I could not decipher the look on his face. Pity, perhaps? Again, as quickly as I noticed it, it was gone, hidden behind carefully constructed irreverence. He held his hand out to me once more, a motion that was quickly becoming familiar. "Come now, I will not let you fall off, I promise."

Stepping up next to the horse, I took his hand gingerly. Despite my apprehension, the idea of showing any weakness to this man—to the Dullahan—was even less appealing. But I'd never mounted a horse before, and without his help, I had no doubt I would make a fool of myself.

I hesitated, and a warning fell from my lips before I could stop it—another thing that was quickly becoming familiar. "If I fall, you will find your moniker to become suddenly accurate."

I froze, almost able to see the words hanging between us,

101

but I couldn't snatch them back. They were something I would have said to Henry, a teasing promise to a friend. They should have stayed tucked behind my teeth. I braced myself for the retaliatory strike I was certain would follow.

But nothing came.

A smile broke out across his face, and he bowed his head, attempting to hide his amusement. Of all the things I could have said, it was clear he was not expecting that. "Noted. Now, put one foot in the stirrup and swing your other leg over. I will climb on behind once you are comfortable."

My stomach clenched. While logically, I knew we would have to be on the same horse, hearing it said aloud was unsettling. The Dullahan, the deadly protector of Sleepy Hollow, would sit, pressed against my back as he took me to his home. This was certainly not how I had planned to spend the evening.

Pushing it from my mind, I slipped my foot into the stirrup, gritting my teeth as I grabbed hold of the saddle and pulled. His hands wrapped around my waist to hoist me up, and I nearly lost my balance at the contact.

The Dullahan was *touching* me. And I was still *alive.*

Swinging my other leg over, mindful of the way my dress bunched around my thighs, I settled into the saddle, panting slightly at the exertion. My hair had come loose from its bun and the wild curls now fell into my face. I shoved them back, gripping the horn of the saddle in front of me. The breeze quickly cooled the sweat beading on my forehead. I was skeptical whether the heat came from the physical movement or the idea of having the Dullahan at my back.

I supposed it didn't matter.

"Move up slightly, please."

I barely had time to follow his instructions before he

rose himself onto the saddle behind me with a practiced ease that made me dizzy. He was not even out of breath. Scowling, I tried to focus on my jealousy of his physical prowess rather than the feeling of his thighs bracketing mine, or his front pressed against my back, seeping warmth into my stiff body.

Needless to say, it did not work.

While I was stuck in my head, his thighs flexed, and Liath began moving.

"Steady," he said, his voice low as my entire body tensed and I gripped tighter to the saddle. I'd felt his words more than I'd heard them, the rumble moving through my back. I bit my lip, not wanting to admit any more faults. He spoke into my right ear, and if we weren't pressed so closely together, I wouldn't have been able to hear him.

"If you need to speak, please talk into my left ear," I said, my chest tight with anxiety. Would he look at me with disdain, as my mother had? Would he be accepting, like Henry? Everything I'd suspected about the Dullahan had been wrong so far, but I couldn't bring myself to hope his reaction would be pleasant. "I have no hearing in my right."

"Of course," he quickly agreed, and I felt his breath puff against the left side of my neck. If my request surprised him, he took care not to show it. I appreciated it, the nerves bleeding out of me—at least the nerves about his response.

I would have squeezed my eyes shut had I not thought it could make things worse. Being this far off the ground, astride a large, powerful animal while sitting in front of another large, powerful being, was unsettling. Keeping my eyes open was the wisest decision, else my dizziness would likely return with a vengeance. Even the fabled Horseman could not keep me from falling as the world spun.

We traveled along the river for a while, before the horse took a path off the side, carrying us up a slight embankment to a well-worn trail between the trees. We had to be completely on the outskirts of the Hollow, deep in the forest. I doubted anyone had ever ventured this far out.

We moved down the path for several more minutes until the trees parted, revealing a sprawling solitary stone cottage. It looked like it had been here for years, well before the war with Britain had even begun. The stones were smooth with age, and moss crawled up the sides. It was remarkably well kept, the roof seemingly in good repair as we grew closer.

The Horseman pulled his mare to a gentle stop as we approached the large wooden stables off to the side of the house. In one breath, he had dismounted and was standing next to me with his hand extended again.

"Here, let me assist you."

Clambering to find my footing in the stirrup while I simultaneously tried to pull my other leg over the saddle, it was not a surprise when I lost my balance. Tipping to the side, my foot slid from the precarious grip, and I braced myself to hit the ground. But the impact never came. The Horseman caught me, righting me in one movement and setting me on my feet. His face remained as neutral as ever, while my cheeks blazed in embarrassment. This mythical being likely thought me a clumsy, foolish girl, and I had done nothing to prove him otherwise.

"The front door is not locked," he told me, taking Liath's reins once more. He nodded toward the house, and all I could do was follow his gaze. "Please let yourself in while I put her away. There is a fireplace in the sitting room. Once I get back, I will show you to your room and get you dry clothes."

Nodding wordlessly, I turned away from the stable, taking a few steps toward the house before I stopped. I was willingly about to enter the Horseman's home, and I had been about to do so without hesitation or even a second thought. What was I thinking?

The Horseman was a being of death, yet he was being kind to me, and sending me into his home without hesitation. What would be waiting for me inside? Was it a trap? My breathing quickened.

Standing in front of the house, I studied it with narrowed eyes. It seemed like a normal house, aside from the same ominous aura that radiated out from the Horseman himself. Cold. Solid. This house unapologetically occupied the earth it was built on, unyielding to the vines that tried to reclaim the space. But, as I was quickly learning, things were not always what they seemed. What lay waiting once I stepped over the threshold? Was that when I would finally meet my end?

A gust of wind washed over me, wracking a shiver from my body as it chilled my wet dress. My fingers flexed, stiff from the cold as the shivers continued down my spine. My muscles ached, and suddenly, thoughts of warmth and a blanket had been all I needed to enter this harbinger of death's stronghold.

"Are you well?" His deep voice made me jump as he approached from behind. Pressing a hand to my chest, I steadied my racing heart. He stepped up beside me, understanding dawning on his face. "Apologies. I didn't mean to approach you from that side."

"It's fine," I dismissed, dropping my hand from my chest. "What did you ask?"

He examined at me for a moment. "You are still apprehensive about me. I have told you, I will not harm you. I have no use for sacrifices, Katrina."

"What do you have a use for?"

He smiled wryly and nodded toward the house. "Go

inside and warm up. We will discuss this more once I join you."

I forced my body to go against every instinct to turn and run. Walking up the door, I counted my steps, intently setting each foot down on a stone. I would be fine. I could do this.

Reaching the front door, I paused with my hand on the handle, taking a deep breath to steady my nerves as I pushed it open and stepped inside. My eyes adjusted to the dim lighting, and I blinked at what lay before me.

The inside of the house was nothing like what I expected, and yet everything I expected all at once. A wall of bookshelves framed a stone fireplace that sat cold and dark. Potted plants sat on large windowsills across the back wall. The smell of warm parchment, leather, and moist dirt cocooned around me, lingering in the air, and settling into the dampness of my dress and hair.

I flinched as the fireplace crackled to life with a sharp pop, spitting light and heat even though no one touched it. My eyes drank in the flames, searching for any signs of illusions. Embers crumbled off the end of a log, sifting down into ash along the bottom.

Walking further into the house, the crackling fire called to me, pulling me in like a moth to the flame. Picking up the ends of my dress to avoid tripping, I hurried over to the wide cushioned lounge placed near the fireplace. I almost sat down, but at the last minute, removed the cushion and placed it on the floor so my wet clothes would not ruin it. The warmth was amazing, and as much as I wanted to explore the rest of this mysterious house, I held my hands up as close to the flames as I could without sticking them into the fire itself. A deep sigh escaped as I felt the heat seep into my skin.

Exploring could wait until I regained feeling in finger-tips once more.

Settling in deeper, I closed my eyes for a moment. The Dullahan could take as much time as he needed to put his horse away. This fire was all I needed right now.

"What has life given me? The beginning is fire; the end is a heap of ashes; and between the end and the beginning lies all the pain of the world. Let me sleep, since I cannot die."

-F. Marion Crawford, The Dead Smile

Eleven

I knew little about putting a horse back into a stall, but the Horseman was gone for quite a while. My dress was nearly dry, and I was comfortably warm now. I wanted to move from the bench and explore the house, but I doubted the Horseman would appreciate my snooping. He may have been kind to me thus far, but his motivations were clearly beyond simply saving me from drowning in the river. I wasn't foolish enough to believe he would let me explore his home without supervision or consequence.

Even so, my body ached to get up and wander, to discover what lurked in the shadowed corners of his home— to see what secrets the Horseman might be hiding. He had been far kinder than I'd expected, and either my entire life had been a lie—which, while entirely possible, wasn't something I wanted to consider right now—or the Horseman was hiding something from me. Or perhaps it was both.

Rocking back and forth on the bench, I shoved my hands under my legs. Idle hands and a damning curiosity never made for a good combination. Forcing my eyes away from the rest of the room, I focused back on the fire, watching the flames dance in the fireplace, twirling, spinning, and sputtering as if they were aware they now held my attention.

Jiggling my legs only eased my restlessness so much, and after what felt like an eternity, I gave into my impulsiveness and rose from the bench, walking over to the floor to ceiling bookshelf. Books of history, books in languages I did not recognize, books on magic I had never seen before—I ached to read them. I longed to learn everything I could about magic; everything my parents denied me as a child. Dragging my finger along the cracked leather spines, I perused his extensive collection.

An image of the Dullahan in all his ominous black riding gear, sitting on the bench by the fire while reading a book, popped into my mind. I smiled at the thought as my attention swung to a book at the end of the shelf. The shiny black leather and gold lettering on the spine caught my eye, as it seemed alive. It writhed in the firelight, embossing the text in flames rather than gold. Everything else in the room faded away as I heard the loud thumping of my heart and saw the liquid flame of the words on the book.

I was not in control of my body as my fingers reached out toward the book. I was merely a witness as my hands ghosted along the spine, not quite touching it. Black spots danced across my vision and my breathing quickened, tight in my chest.

Katrina, the book seemed to whisper, just like the wind had. *Come closer, Katrina. Discover our secrets. Listen to our stories.*

My fingers were a mere breath away from touching the book when the door swung open, thudding softly against the wall behind it. The noise broke whatever trance I was in, and my hand dropped to my side. I snapped back to reality as if I had been dropped into an icy river.

The Dullahan had returned just as I was snooping through his book collection.

"Have you found something interesting there?" he asked. His face was void of emotion, though his eyes remained locked on the book I'd been about to pick up.

I looked back at it, noticing the title was now still, just simple gold lettering embossed on the spine. Had I imagined it? I clasped my hands in front of me and ducked my head. "I apologize. That was invasive of me."

"Be careful what you touch, Katrina," he warned. "Some of my collection may not appreciate it."

"Where did you get them all from?" I asked, looking back over at the shelf as he stopped in front of me. He was uncomfortably close; I could feel his body heat radiating into me.

He tilted his head, his forehead wrinkling slightly. "Here and there."

I opened my mouth to question him more, to ask if the books ever whispered to him, but he held up a hand to stop me.

"Let me get you some dry clothes. After that, we will talk." He held his hand out, pointing toward a hall that snaked off from the opposite wall. "I told you I would answer your questions, and I will."

"My dress is mostly dry now," I said, holding up the fabric. The dismissal of his concern was more for the sake of getting answers than a desire to stay in my damp clothes. They would dry eventually, but I was uncertain I would get a second chance at answers. Especially from such a mysterious and deadly being. Deciding to push my luck, I dropped the fabric of my dress and asked, "Why are you so willing to answer my questions?"

"You are damp and covered in mud. Are you saying that is your preferred state?" He raised an eyebrow, pointedly ignoring my last question and replacing it with his own.

My cheeks burned. It was clear that my answers would be on his terms, or not at all. A draft blew through the house, sending a shiver down my spine.

With a heavy sigh, he nodded at the way I'd wrapped my arms around my body and then began leading me down the hall. We moved down the short stone hallway, stopping in front of a heavy wooden door across from another. He pushed open the door. "There is a trunk full of clothes just inside the doorway. Take whatever you please."

I nodded my head in thanks and followed his direction to the bedroom, pulling the door closed behind me. The curtain hanging over the windows was a heavy green fabric that reminded me of the moss that threatened to overcome the rocks along the riverbeds. Pulling it closed, the room darkened considerably, leaving the only light from a pair of candlesticks along the dresser. I turned to the trunk and opened the lid, and clothes of all sizes and types spilled out.

I dug through the clothes as I forced myself not to consider the source of the clothing. I found a simple wool dress that appeared to be about my size and pulled it out. Shucking off my dress was harder than I had expected, as the fabric was not entirely as dry as I had believed.

I quickly pulled on the thick green dress, trying to fight the chill washing over me. Now that I had stepped away from the fire in the main room, I was feeling every bit of the cold. The dress fit better than I had expected. Pulling my hair out of the collar, I twisted the damp curls off my neck, looking around for something to pin them back with. When I found nothing, I sighed and let the strands tumble down my back.

Easing the door open, I trailed my fingers along the stone of the hallway as I made my way back to the sitting room. The stones were cold and rough against my fingertips but then warmed under my touch, despite no flames unfurling from my body. It was as if they were welcoming me. Turning to look at the wall as I walked, I watched my fingers dip *into* the stone, disappearing to the first knuckle.

Air escaping my lungs in a gasp, I snatched my hand away from the wall.

Hurrying my steps and ensuring I touched nothing else, I returned to the sitting room once more, stopping short at the sight in front of me. The Horseman was sitting at the small table and chairs in front of the bookshelves, stirring a small spoon into the teacup in front of him. He appeared remarkably normal. The Dullahan had a fire that lit itself, books that whispered to people, walls that sucked in those who touched it, and yet here he was, drinking tea.

"Ah, you found something suitable," he said when he noticed me. He pushed a teacup and saucer to the other side of the table as he beckoned me to sit down. "Here, I made you cinnamon tea."

Accepting the invitation, I sat and pulled the saucer closer, wrapping my hands around the warm cup. "Thank you."

"I imagine you have questions, Katrina. Those chosen as Roghnaithe often do, though they have never come to join me quite as you have." He waved a hand. "Please, ask whatever you would like."

I had so many questions swirling in my mind, and I was unsure which of them I wanted an answer to first. "How did you know my name?"

He raised an eyebrow. "That is your first question?"

My cheeks burned, but I held my resolve despite wanting nothing more than to crumble under his careful stare and retreat to the safety of the room he'd shown me. "Yes. It is."

"I know the names of everyone who lives in Sleepy Hollow," he explained, taking a sip of his own tea. "I am tasked as its protector. How can I protect it without knowing those who live there?"

That made sense, but it also brought more questions. And now that I'd asked the first one, the rest were spewing out of my mouth. "Who tasked you with protecting the Hollow? How long have you been the Horseman? Why do they call you the Dullahan? The Headless Horseman? Why haven't you killed me yet?"

"The Dullahan are a type of people, like mages or shifters, not one singular person. While we do not have enough time to go into the origins of us and the specifics of our magic, it is quite simple. We are children of Death, sent forth to protect our assigned domain." He paused, tilting his head slightly. "And as for the reason they refer to me as the Headless Horseman, it would be better to show you. But I'll do that later."

"Children of Death?" I asked, quite impressed that my voice did not come out as a squeak. Part of me noticed he still had not answered why he hadn't killed me yet, but I had more pressing questions burning on my tongue. "What does that mean?"

He waved his hand dismissively. "That part is not important. I have magic that allows me to control the spirit realm. I can kill with the magic, or I can protect. My brothers kill to protect, but I have a different philosophy. Sleepy Hollow rests on a natural well of magic, and I am responsible for protecting that well."

I was left uncertain of what to say. There was so much new information, I was indecisive on where to start. His history, his house, his magic, and those were only the questions I had about *him*.

I weighed the two most important items I needed

answers on: the fog and those sacrificed. Ciara's pained sobs filled my ears, and I'd made my decision.

"The sacrifices. You said before that something offered did not always need to be accepted. Is that why you haven't killed me?"

"Do you want me to? I could have left you in the river, I suppose," he said with the raise of his eyebrow.

"Why do you continue to accept the sacrifices the town sends if you do not need them to protect the wards?" My jaw clenched at his irreverence, but I tamped down my temper to hear his response.

"The town continues to offer them. I take them and send them to safety, giving them a chance at a new life elsewhere."

"Elsewhere?"

"Yes." He took another sip of tea. "There are many other naturally occurring supernatural towns such as this one, and many more created ones. There are always places for those who are sent to me."

My stomach dropped, and the room spun slightly. There were other sanctuaries for supernaturals. Other places where we could be safe. Thoughts of Ciara's brother filtered through, along with memories of the sadness she continuously experienced over his loss. But he was alive.

White hot anger surged through my veins, and I let go of the leash I'd kept on my tongue. "Why don't you approach the council and tell them you do not need sacrifices? This has torn families apart."

He sighed. "Drink your tea, Katrina. It will warm you."

"I do not want your tea, Dullahan. I want your answers."

"Fine," he said, leaning forward and steepling his fingers together. "I have told your town's leaders before. When I first came into my powers, I approached them, informed them it was unnecessary. They cared not for my words. I am convinced they did not believe me. Tradition is difficult to break, and the Dullahan in the old world did take sacrifices, quite enthusiastically."

"Instead, you continued accepting people offered to you?" My mind was spinning with questions, shifting too fast for me to latch on to any singular line of thinking. Did they still take sacrifices elsewhere? Would the other haven in Saint Augustine truly have been safe for me? Did he know the other Dullahan? Were they close? Did he write to them? How did they kill if it wasn't by whispering our names?

So many things spun wildly in my mind, but they all kept coming back to one thing: that these sacrifices were unnecessary. My vision tunneled as my veins throbbed against the skin of my neck, pulsing in time with my rage.

"Yes," he said bluntly, staring at me unblinkingly. "Your town has chosen these people to die, and if they are not willing to listen to reason, I will save those people. They are all happy in their new lives."

"And those who left families behind?"

"Of course, there is some sadness, but they are alive."

"But their families do not know that," I snapped, thinking of the pain and agony Ciara and her mother had to endure after Torin's death. The weeks Ciara spent in bed, crying until her eyes were red and had left the skin around them dry and flaky. I took a harsh breath, reigning in my temper and locking it back down. Softening my tone, I continued, "I have seen those left behind, mourning friends and family they believe to be dead."

"What would you have me do?" His words had no bite. Instead, it seemed as if he were genuinely interested in how I would address the situation. It threw me that someone other than Henry would value my opinions. His fingers tapped against each other as he inclined his head.

"Do not give them a choice. Return those given to you and make it known you do not accept sacrifices." Anything would have been better than leaving those to believe their loved ones were dead. I sucked in a harsh breath, trying to quell the heat in my blood. "Why could you not at least tell the families of those you rescued? Give them some form of closure; some way of knowing."

He shook his head, settling back in his chair. "It is not that simple, Katrina. There are things at work that you know nothing of. Not everyone is as honorable as you appear to be, and not everyone would think my acts are out of kindness."

My cheeks flushed at the admonishment, embarrassed tears burning in my throat. Those had been words I'd heard my entire life. *You are too stupid to understand, Katrina, and I do not have the patience to explain it.* That was what those words truly meant. "Then explain it to me."

"Sleepy Hollow's Elders believe giving me sacrifices will protect them for a reason." He paused. "In the old world, when Death came calling, she delivered the news on the screams of a banshee, and then a Dullahan would carry the person away and deliver them to Death. They believed Death had marked their chosen. If they discovered I was not shepherding the chosen to their fates, what do you think they would do then?"

I wrapped my arms around my middle. They would simply kill the chosen themselves. If my mother knew the Horseman was not killing the sacrifices, she wouldn't even hesitate to make the sacrifices herself. Anything for the good of the town.

He picked up his story. "People of old believed that giving someone willingly to their Dullahan would satiate them and keep them from carrying off those called for Death. And for some, it worked. That practice evolved, and the Dullahans became the protectors of their towns, accepting sacrifices to keep the townspeople alive and to protect them from anything threatening. More and more, that threat is becoming the humans around us. They are growing scared of what they do not understand. But in any world, with any people, there are those that wish to harm others, and those that wish to take what is not theirs."

"But—"

"This will take longer if you keep interrupting me."

My mother would have hissed the words, her lips snarling to frame her teeth, but the Dullahan said it softly, like the interruption was amusing to him.

At this point, I would not have been surprised if flames were coming out of my skin through my cheeks.

"I have been here for a long time. I stopped aging at twenty-one years, but I've been alive for nearly one hundred years. Death sent me here as a child, and I grew up in this house, watching the town from the shadows. The town has always clung to the ways of the old world, more so than other havens. They fear humans, and in some ways, even though they do not know it, humans fear them. It's clear in their stories and the tales they tell around fires at night to scare each other. If they knew we truly existed, they would destroy us for no other reason than they do not understand us. And this town... this town is not ready for that."

I sat silently, waiting for him to continue. But he didn't. I chewed on the inside of my cheek, trying to find the words I wanted to say.

He huffed a small laugh. "You may speak now, Katrina. I am finished."

There were many things I wanted to ask, to say, but nothing would come out. His notion was correct, and I could not argue about it. "Do you protect us? Has there ever been a threat to Sleepy Hollow?"

"Yes," he replied. He hesitated for a moment, opening and closing his mouth.

"Now, or in the past?"

"Both."

"What is threatening us now?" I asked, my heart speeding up. "The fog?"

"There are many threats. Humans wandering too close, exploring the lands. Things slipping out from the Otherworld that shouldn't be here. Other supernaturals who do not have good intentions when crossing the bridge." He shrugged, exuding a careful irreverence. "Lately, there have been more and more things slipping out from the Otherworld."

"Is that what the fog is?"

"The fog." He sighed heavily. "The creatures and spirits that escaped the Otherworld started as harmless and irritating. They weren't dangerous, but lately—lately they're becoming something more."

"What is the fog?" I pressed harder, trying to pull the answers from him. Henry flashed through my mind. He was far too old to protect himself from something the Dullahan considered dangerous. "You know what it is, don't you?"

He leaned forward, the intensity of his stare burning hotter than any fire I could ever conjure. "Tell me what you think you've seen, Katrina. And perhaps I will be able to tell you what you actually saw."

"Several days ago," I started, twisting my fingers in my lap. Would he believe me? Or would he dismiss me just as Ichabod had? I had to take the risk and hope that he would take my word, or at least be able to explain what truly had chased me through the trees. "I was in a grove in the forest, and there was a fog. It crept along the base of the trees, staying out of the grove at first. It was so thick; you couldn't see the ground below it. And then something whispered my name, and the fog started creeping toward me, like fingers reaching out."

He was quiet, and I noticed an unnatural stillness about him as he looked at me. "Did it touch you?"

I shook my head. "No, I ran before it could, but I also felt it chasing me. It stopped when I left the forest."

"Was there anything else?"

"A crow," I answered, the image of its glassy black eyes staring back at me filled my head. "I've seen a crow twice, and it acted oddly both times. The first time, it stopped on the path directly in front of me and just stared, never moving even as I ran around it. Then I saw it again on a branch in the town square."

Shivers went down my spine, and despite the fire raging in the fireplace, the air around the Dullahan seemed to darken and crackle with energy, like lightning about to strike.

"Have you told the council about the threat?" My voice was barely above a whisper as fear kept me from speaking louder. "Do they know about the fog?"

He sighed, reaching up to rub at his temple. The darkness surrounding him faded and the hairs on my arms no longer stood on end. "No, I have not told them. I have not approached the Ciallmhar in decades."

"Why?" Though I'd tried to keep my voice carefully neutral, the cutting disapproval was far too clear.

"I don't answer to them, Katrina. No matter what they may think." His eyes narrowed slightly. "And why should I? They've made it clear they would not listen to my words. They only want me to protect the town, take my sacrifices, and stay in the shadows." His jaw flexed, and he reached up to run a hand through his hair. "And as for the fog, why would I tell them when I believe it is one of them summoning these creatures? There have been too many to simply just slip through the cracks. This is intentional."

"What creature is causing the fog?" My voice was steadier, but the understanding in his eyes told me he knew I was hanging on by a thread—a sparse, fraying thread that anchored me to reality. A whisper could have snapped it, but I still clung to it, desperate to repair it with my curiosity and quest for knowledge.

Silence filled the room as I waited for the answer to my question. I could not bring myself to break it. I wished I could say I didn't believe him, but I couldn't. I'd seen the Ciallmhar and how power hungry some of them were.

"I may be Sleepy Hollow's protector"—He interlaced his fingers, leaning onto his forearms as he stared into my eyes, holding my gaze as if he could see into the very recesses of my soul—"but after meeting you and seeing your magic, I believe you are its savior, Katrina."

"Pardon me?" I felt myself sit back in the chair with a thump, as if I were outside my own body. Keeping up with his changing topics was making me dizzy, and I couldn't gain my balance, not before he'd already moved on to his next earth-shattering revelation designed to upturn my world.

I leaned back, blinking at him.

The Horseman could not have just said what I thought he said. Over the past three days, I had been told I would destroy Sleepy Hollow, and now I was being told I would save it. My head was swimming, waves of confusion crashing down and threatening to drown me where I sat.

My voice was almost a squeak as I shook my head. "I am no savior. I barely have magic."

"You have more magic than you suspect," he told me, raising his eyebrow back toward the singed spots on his table where I'd been holding onto it. "I can see the vast well of power you hold."

"How? Is that part of your magic?"

I clung to anything that would keep me from spiraling down into panic. Facts, questions, answers. I was collecting as much information as I could hold, cataloging it for later.

"My magic allows me to enter the spirit realm, among other things."

I swallowed hard, my next question sticking against the back of my tongue. "You said I have more magic. How? My mother always told me I had low levels of magic because my control is unreliable."

He tilted his head as he studied me. Something akin to pity flashed in his eyes briefly. "You have never been properly trained, have you? Were you ever taught how to access your magic, to hone it, or has it only ever erupted with your emotions?"

Adelaide's words came back, and realization washed over me. "With my emotions, I suppose. I was not even taught spell words until I was thirteen."

"Useless," he spat, disdain in his eyes.

My heart dropped, a hollow ache filling the cavity where it sat. I'd heard the words before, mostly from my mother, but hearing them from the Dullahan was different. It cracked against my soul like a whip, flaying it raw.

I couldn't bring myself to reply.

The Dullahan ran a rough hand over his hair. "Those fools had no idea what they held. They just tossed you aside because you did not conform to their ideas of how magic should manifest. They are the ones who failed you, Katrina, not the other way around."

I blinked. He was calling them useless, not me? "But I... I just *make pottery*."

His look could have wilted even the strongest of flowers.

"You are capable of making far more than just pottery, Katrina."

Sighing, I shifted in my chair, clasping my fingers together to keep from crossing my arms impetuously. I needed to remember that despite how kind he had been so far, despite how willing he was to answer my questions, this was still the Dullahan, a self-professed child of Death. And even if he was telling the truth about my magic, his magic likely far outweighed anything I could ever achieve, and to show him disrespect would certainly result in a death sentence.

"Why do you think I have this power? Why do you think I can save the town? Is that not what you are here for?"

"What is threatening the Hollow now is beyond what I can stop on my own."

That was far from encouraging to hear. "Do you know what the threat is? What the fog is?"

"I believe I do." Again, he spoke so casually. "It's a horde of spirits who feast on the souls of the living."

"Why is it following me, then? How do you think I can help you stop it?"

He hesitated, tipping his head to the side as he stroked his chin, studying me.

"Tell me," I demanded, leaning forward.

"If I tell you, you would be agreeing to help. It would mean you have to stay in Sleepy Hollow."

"Forever? Or just until we have dealt with the fog?" I narrowed my eyes.

Staying in Sleepy Hollow was not an option, but if I could at least know what the threat was, I could get word to Henry and Ciara and, at the very least, get them to safety. Perhaps this would push them to leave with me. We could all leave the Hollow behind.

The Dullahan continued to look at me.

"Tell me."

He leaned back in his chair, crossing his arms over his chest. "I will not waste my breath on explanations to someone who will not stay to help. I have answered all your questions and then some. I have told you about the reality behind your Hollow. Now, will you save it and the people who live here, or will you leave and save only yourself? That is the question you must answer now."

I blinked at him. "That is..."

"Quite a bit to digest, I know."

"You make me sound selfish for wanting to leave this place," I said, my heart splintering. "I have known only pain here."

"Only pain?" he asked, a frown pulling at his lips.

"Mostly pain," I murmured.

The Dullahan stood from the table and picked up his gloves, tucking them into the pocket of his coat. "You can stay and fight for the town and all of its residents, or I can send you on your way to another haven where you will be free from Sleepy Hollow like you wished." He paused. "Just know that there will likely be no Sleepy Hollow for you to return to."

My stomach clenched. There was too much to think about, too many conflicting emotions warring in my chest. The thought of Henry and Ciara alone would make me stay and fight until my last breath. But my mother, my father, Ichabod, Brom, the Ciallmhar—did they deserve to live? Why should I have the right to choose?

Oily shame curled in the pit in my stomach and my cheeks flushed. I couldn't stomach the thought of being the cause of Sleepy Hollow's destruction, but at the same time, I couldn't help but hear Henry's voice telling me they didn't deserve my empathy.

"May I have some time to consider my options?" I asked, carefully controlling my voice despite the raging tempest in my soul.

He nodded, motioning toward the room where I'd changed clothes. "Of course. Take what remains of the night to rest and consider it. I shall need your answer in the morning, though. We are running out of time."

With nothing left to say, the silence moved in, covering us like a thick blanket.

He looked at me for another moment before turning to walk toward the door along the far hall across from my own. Pausing at the door with his hand on the knob, he turned back to me. "If you stay out here much longer, please remember what I said earlier about not touching things."

The click of the latch as he closed the door behind him echoed through my chest. I slumped into the chair, suddenly exhausted. This was all too much for one day, and my mind was spinning faster than the potter's wheel I used at the shop. Rubbing at my temples, I debated what I should do.

This town was the only home I had ever known, but both my parents and the Ciallmhar were so quick to condemn people to death in a needless sacrifice that apparently did nothing. Why should I try to save them?

The more I thought about it, the more my blood boiled. Other than Ciara and Henry, no one else in Sleepy Hollow had done anything to help me after being named Roghnaithe. My only other almost-friends, Ichabod and Brom, had knowingly pushed me over that embankment, sending me plummeting to my death. Even thinking about them made my fists clench, itching to strike the smug smile from Brom's face and see blood pouring from Ichabod's nose.

They deserved none of my kindness and none of whatever refuge my powers could supposedly provide. They deserved whatever was coming to the Hollow. Just as my mother did.

My mind turned back to Ciara and Henry, who did deserve my kindness. Even Ciara, whose words had stung deeply. The practice of the Roghnaithe had upended her life, but I knew that despite it all, she cared for me in her own way, with what remained of her heart. And the children and other townspeople in Sleepy Hollow were too innocent to know better. They deserved my kindness as well.

I sighed heavily and stood, walking into the room the Horseman had directed me to. Maybe I should sleep on the decision. Perhaps rest would make the decision easier. Against the far wall was a small bed with a ragged quilt across it. Pulling the quilt back, I climbed into the bed.

The silence was overwhelming, and I felt lonely once more. Tears burned at my throat as I turned to lie on my left side, my hearing ear pressed against the pillow to block out the world with the thumping of my heartbeat. I squeezed my eyes shut, ignoring the tear that streaked down my temple and into my hairline. There was no place for weakness in the Horseman's home. I would not give him any reason to think I'd be better off dead.

"*I have lost the faculty of enjoying their destruction, and I am too idle to destroy for nothing.*"

-*Emily Brontë,*
Wuthering Heights

Twelve

The next morning, I sat across the small table from the Dullahan, sipping my tea while my stomach was a ball of knots. I waited—impatiently—for him to speak as he prepared his tea and breakfast.

"Did you sleep well?" the Horseman asked, spreading jam across his bread.

"I did," I replied quickly, although I was not foolish enough to tell him I'd cried most of the night. Despite his words the night before, I still didn't trust him, and certainly not enough to share my emotions. "Thank you."

"Have you decided?" he asked, putting down his knife and turning his entire attention to me. His eyes were brighter than fire, and far more intense, as they looked deep into my soul. It was as if he knew my answer before I did.

"I will help you." I swallowed hard, my words sticking in my throat. His gaze was so intense I looked away, focusing on my fingernails as I picked at the edges of the skin. "Sleepy Hollow may be hell for me, but two of the most important people in my life live there. If there is anything I can do to protect them and the other innocent people, I will do it."

For a moment, his silence was deafening, and I thought I had answered incorrectly. But as I lifted my head to meet his gaze and opened my mouth to take it back, he nodded. "Very well."

I sucked in a breath, rolling my shoulders back. "Now, tell me what I need to know."

"Eat," he told me, waving his hand at the platter of food in front of him. He picked up his bread and took a bite. "We will talk over breakfast."

My gaze drifted to his throat as he swallowed. My cheeks burned even hotter, and I felt my hands heat from where I had shoved them beneath my thighs. Quickly, I pulled them from beneath my legs and clasped them in my lap to keep from burning another piece of the Horseman's furniture. "Tell me what the threat is."

"I am not completely certain, but I believe they are summoning the sluagh." He hesitated over the last word, as if it was not what he had been planning to say.

Icy fingers trailed down my spine. I only knew a little about the sluagh, but what I did know was not good. Sluagh were malevolent spirits, ghosts of those who had died horrible deaths, roaming where they died and seeking to cause havoc and pain everywhere they could. The idea that someone was attempting to summon them was far from reassuring.

I cleared my throat, pushing back my fear of facing down a horde of evil spirits. Instead, I latched onto the deception and hesitation in his voice. "You know more than that."

He raised an eyebrow. "I have suspicions that more is at play, but all the evidence I have at the current moment points toward the sluagh."

"What evidence?" I pressed. "And who do you suspect is summoning them?"

"The fog that has been circling the Hollow is not natural. Even peaceful spirits have been more restless than they typically are, and animals are behaving strangely at night." He paused and looked up at me. "You've seen that yourself. All those things point toward someone summoning something to Sleepy Hollow. And from what I have found, the disturbance of the existing spirits is pointing to sluagh."

"I thought that was impossible." A passage from a children's book of legends came to mind, one Henry had read to me when I was far too old to listen to such stories, yet still young enough to cherish them all the same. "Once sluagh are in the Otherworld, we cannot bring them back to earth. They're supposed to be locked away for good."

"Nothing is impossible, Katrina," he said, his voice dropping an octave as he leaned in. "Not when it comes to magic."

Another chill rolled down my spine, along with a bead of sweat. "What threat would the sluagh pose to Sleepy Hollow specifically?"

"Beyond attempting to pick off souls? It is unknown." He released a heavy sigh. "One or two sluagh would not be much of a threat, but based on the intensity of the omens I've seen, I believe it will be a great many sluagh. And that would be very dangerous to any living creature that winds up in their path. At the very least, we can be grateful they don't seem to be powerful enough to cause any real harm. Yet."

"What omens?" Goosebumps broke out across my arms. Had I missed them? Or were they only for his eyes and his magic to be aware of? "The fog? Or something else?"

"There have been..." He tilted his head from side to side, as if he couldn't decide what to say. "There have been rumblings in the spirit world. Disturbances in the magic.

Yes, the fog is an omen, but the animals are acting oddly as well. We can feel most of it in the magic of the veil around the town." He pressed his fingers together, resting them under his chin. "What do you know about the sluagh?"

I had learned most of what I knew from a tale of a heroic mage fiercely battling them and sentencing them to the Otherworld, escaping with nothing but a scratch across his chin. Pushing past the burning in my neck and chest, I gave my answer. "They scavenge souls and try to lead people to their death to get the souls, right?"

"Yes," he confirmed, his eyebrows rising as though he wasn't expecting me to know that. "And until we can discover more about how many sluagh are coming, and figure out who is summoning them and why, we are at a disadvantage."

My stomach twisted and my mind flashed to Ciara and Henry. They had no way of protecting themselves from the sluagh. Gods, no one did, really. The sluagh would destroy the entire town and serve up souls on a silver platter, ready for the taking. "How can we find out more? And what difference will my magic make?"

"You are very powerful, Katrina." He spoke slowly, as if he expected me to bolt like a frightened animal. "There is little you could not destroy if you put your mind to it."

I breathed a shaky sigh. I was not powerful, no matter what this mythical being before me said. No matter what prophecy my mother believed was about me. My powers had been a threat to my safety my entire life. At first, they induced the rage of my mother, and now, they had caused my death sentence. But I was not the solace, or the *savior*, the Horseman made me out to be. I was nothing.

"I am not," I whispered.

"Certainly not with that approach to things," he said, taking a sip of his tea. "Tell me, has anyone ever truly pushed your powers to its limits? Or have they simply let you fall into complacency when you assert you cannot do something?"

My cheeks burned at his insinuation, and I had to fight to hold my head high. "I had some training as a child, but my mother determined I had low-level powers and stated it was not worth continuing the lessons."

His face darkened, obviously displeased by my words. "You should still have been trained. Powers like yours need to be honed, not left to fester and evolve on their own."

"How do you even know what my powers are?" I asked, feeling panic build in my chest. I closed my eyes for a moment and took several deep breaths, digging my nails into the flesh of my palms and pushing my fire back down to burn low in my stomach. "How do you know all of this?"

I saw the hesitation on his face as he leaned back in his chair. "It's the same answer as how I knew your name. It is part of my magic. I am a protector, and to do my job, I must know what I am dealing with. I can tell that you have a great well of power, but it is repressed and untrained."

"You can sense the powers of everyone in the town?"

"Yes. Once I lay eyes upon them, I can see their magic pooling around them, like an aura of sorts." He stood from the chair. "Now, if you are serious about helping me find out more information about the sluagh, the first thing we must do is teach you how to access and utilize your powers. All your power."

Unease simmered in my stomach, and I looked up at him, channeling the simmering into false confidence. "And where do you propose we use my powers? I'm positive you have noticed we are in the forest, and my magic is fire."

"Do not worry yourself, Katrina. You will not burn down the forest." He held out his hand, looking at me more patiently than I would have expected from the dreaded Horseman.

"What is your name?" I asked, my cheeks flushing once more at my careless statement. Perhaps he did not even have a name. "I apologize. You don't have to answer."

He paused for a moment, tilting his head to the side as he continued to hold his hand out. Quickly, before I could tell myself how bad of an idea it was, I took his hand, standing from the table with him.

"Alexander," he said, so quietly I almost did not hear him.

If he had been on my other side, I certainly would not have heard him.

I paused, looking up to take in his strong features. Alexander. It fit him better than the Dullahan or the Headless Horseman did. I wondered if someone gave him the name Alexander, or if he had chosen it for himself. I wouldn't be foolish enough to ask that question aloud, though.

Nodding, I forced a smile onto my face. "Thank you, Alexander."

He squeezed my hand once before dropping it. My fingers twitched, missing the contact more than I expected. "Now, will you train? Will you let me show you how to use your magic?"

I hesitated, but the utter ease with which he looked at me—so confident that I would do the right thing—was addicting. I wanted him to keep looking at me like that, to keep believing in me, until I could do it for myself. But I had to remind myself he was still the Dullahan. Still a child of Death. Did I truly have a choice here? I doubted it.

"Y-yes, I'll train. But only if you're certain I won't hurt anyone."

The room stood still as his hand reached for my face.

Smiling wryly, he tucked a loose curl behind my ear, moving it from my forehead. "I promise, Katrina."

My heart squeezed, like a fist wrapping around it and crushing it slowly. Until he had taken my hand—until he'd briefly grazed his fingers against my face, I had not realized how little others touched me. This kindness was foreign, but I enjoyed the feeling. I wanted it again, even if it was just holding his hand once more. I curled my toes in my boots, focusing on the sensation.

"If I burn down your house, you will feel very foolish, Dullahan."

The only response I got was a half-smile as he turned and led me out into the yard. The sun was battling against the clouds, the oppressive gray wisps winning the war against the bright light. Stepping into the large clearing on the side of the cottage, I took several deep breaths. I was about to use my power, after I was told that I could very well destroy the world if I tried hard enough. Despite the icy morning breeze, sweat trickled down my spine, dampening the back of my wool dress.

The Dullahan—Alexander—took a few more steps before turning back around to face me. He lifted a hand, waving it in a half circle motion above his head, and the world shimmered. His head disappeared, and he stood, a truly headless being. Where his head had been was now a swirl of purple magic, dark and curling around his neck, flicking lazily like a cat's tail. My eyes widened, entranced by the unfurling power spreading from his body and extending around us.

Everything dulled in color, taking on a grayish-purple haze, as if we had stepped into a room of violet smoke. Even the sound of the birds and wind was muffled.

"What is this?" I asked, wincing as my ears popped, distracting me from the unnerving bubble we'd found ourselves in. "Is this why they call you the Headless Horseman?"

"I surrounded us... spirit..." he began, his voice too muffled to hear him clearly. Honestly, I was surprised he was speaking at all.

I took a step closer to him and tapped at my right ear, frowning at my deficiencies and how much of a burden they again posed. "Please, speak up."

He cleared his throat, a sound I had not been expecting, given that he had no head, and moved even closer, raising his voice as his arm brushed against mine. "A veil of spirit magic surrounds us. Anything you do here will not harm the environment outside of it. You can use your magic freely."

"What do I do now?" I asked, glancing at the field surrounding us. My fists clenched tightly, and my breathing grew uneven, alternating between shallow breaths and panting gasps as my chest tightened.

I didn't know what he expected, and that never led to anything pleasant in my experiences. I needed instructions, explicit guidelines, and measurable goals. I needed to study and explore every detail of what was to happen, so I could do things perfectly the first time. Anything other than perfection was deemed a failure and met with punishment. But there was no instruction here. No books I could pore over to find these answers. I'd tried.

"Try conjuring your flames," he instructed. "How do you normally conjure them?"

"I never conjure them intentionally. Not since I was a child. They come out when they want to," I said, ducking my head. Admitting that out loud, especially to a man who obviously had a plethora of magic beyond what I had ever considered possible, was embarrassing to say the least. He thought I had more magic than him, which was impossible.

I could hear the irritation in his voice, even if I could not see it on his face. "Then how does your magic feel when it manifests? Your flames have come out several times since we met. What caused it? What did it feel like?"

"It feels hot, like it's burning up from my chest and trying to escape my body." I swallowed hard. Sharing what provoked my powers was not high on my list, considering that all reasons were because of my failings. "I have a temper. And anxiety. My magic spikes when I have strong emotions, and between my anger and anxiety, it happens quite a bit. I have worked most of my life to smother my flames, not release them."

He crossed his arms over his chest and walked closer to me. "Why?"

"Why, what?" I clenched my hands into fists at my sides. For my entire life, scrutiny only led to being told how much of a disappointment I was. I did not enjoy anyone, let alone someone like this man, looking at me too closely. He would be just like the others, disappointed by what he saw.

"Why do you hide from your emotions?" He circled around behind me, and I closed my eyes, tilting my head toward the sky and rolling my neck. I felt him move to stand in front of me, and I lowered my chin to gaze at his chest. Reaching out a gloved hand, he poked a finger at my chest, tapping lightly. "It sounds to me like the key to unlocking your powers is to give in to your emotions, not to suppress them."

"My emotions are a messy thing and not suitable for the public," I said, my voice hollow as I repeated the words I had heard my mother repeat my entire life. She had ingrained those words in me. My emotions were not for public consumption; *I* was not for public consumption. The disappointing, broken, unwanted child. Tears burned in my throat.

"Let it out."

My eyes snapped to him again; my vision was blurry with unshed tears. I found myself wanting to see his face, not wanting to focus on his chest instead.

"Let it out, Katrina. Do not bury what you are feeling. Embrace it, and let it out," he murmured, stepping closer until we were nearly touching. His coat brushed against me. "Your fire will not harm me. So, let. It. Out."

Doing as he asked was harder than I expected, but I forced myself to focus on the emotions I was feeling, on the feeling of disgust at being cast aside by the very people who were supposed to love me unconditionally. Rage and sadness washed through my body and tore across my mind. I released the tears that were burning in the back of my throat, their wetness spilling down my cheeks in rivers. My chest ached, but I stayed focused.

Fire flickered at my fingertips, and my first instinct was to draw them back inside to smother them. Alexander's voice sounded, but I could not make out the words as the blood rushing to my ears was deafening. I continued to focus on the hurt, the pain, and the sadness. It crested and erupted, flames shooting from my hands and traveling up my arms.

Tears poured down my face and I could no longer see anything in front of me except for flames. I squeezed my eyes closed, but I could still feel the fire erupting from my body, burning away my dress.

"Open your eyes, Katrina." His voice was so, so close to me.

No! I wanted to scream. *Get back!*

Hands wrapped around my arms, and the leather of his gloves on my bare skin startled me into opening my eyes. Flames fully engulfed my body and horror filled me. I must be hurting him. I could not control this.

My eyes widened, taking in the scene as I tried to

scramble away from him. I could not risk hurting him. I tripped over my own feet and fell to the ground. Even though my body was in contact with the earth and should have been incinerating the grass beneath me, it remained intact and only flattened beneath my weight.

Alexander bent down next to me, his gloved hand now resting on my back. "Breathe, Katrina. You are safe here. You are safe."

I nodded, sucking in breaths as I curled in on myself. This had been a foolish endeavor. Adelaide had been right. My mother had been right. Giving in to my emotions was more than just frowned upon to uphold a polite society. It was *dangerous*.

As I continued sucking down breaths, like my life depended on it, I focused on the grass in front of me. Alexander had told me to focus on my emotions, but I could not. I could not focus on that right now. The surrounding flames faded until I was no longer a walking ball of fire. I was now just a naked girl kneeling in the grass with tears streaming down her face.

It was pathetic.

I was pathetic.

"In the dark shadow of the grove, on the margin of the brook, he beheld something huge, misshapen, black, and towering. It stirred not, but seemed gathered up in the gloom, like some gigantic monster ready to spring upon the traveller."

- Washington Irving,
The Legend of Sleepy Hollow

"Here," Alexander murmured, holding out a blanket he had brought from somewhere. Kneeling beside me in the grass, he placed a hand on my back and lingered for a moment, concern radiating off him.

I felt even more worthless, my head hanging low and shoulders slumping in. This powerful being—this protector—was worried about me. And he should not have been. I didn't accept the blanket, flinching away from it, and instead wrapped my arms tighter around myself. I didn't deserve the kindness or the warmth it would bring.

He hesitated, then lowered the blanket, kneeling on the ground next to me. "What happened, Katrina?"

"It was too much," I whispered, shifting to hide my nakedness. Another dress I had ruined. Another failure.

Rage bubbled within me faster than I could stop it. A roiling cauldron building and building before finally spilling over. I tipped my head back and screamed at the sky. I screamed until my throat burned, cursing the gods that made me this way.

Why? Why? WHY?

Why did I have to be a constant failure? A worthless pit of nothingness.

My screams turned to sobs. I hated Alexander for suggesting this. My emotions were dangerous and had no place being acknowledged. Waves and waves of emotion after emotion washed through me, and I failed to recognize the sounds coming from my mouth. Slowly, the sobs subsided, but I could still hear myself panting for breath, shaky and brittle. The flames slowly eased, finally extinguishing, as I sat shivering in the cold.

I heard Alexander talking to me, his voice soft, but I could not make out the words. Fabric touched my body and a soft blanket draped over my shoulders. I shoved it off, wiping at my eyes. I did not need his sympathy or his concern. Wrapping my arms around myself, I tried to take deep breaths to slow my racing heart. Around me, the world popped, the veil of purple spirit magic fading as the sounds of the forest returned.

"Katrina, you are all right. I have you. Nothing will hurt you here." He wrapped the blanket back around my body once more, moving around to kneel in front of me. He took my hands in his with no hesitation, no regard for the fact they were still smoldering. "Katrina, look at me."

Reluctant to see the pity, or even worse, the disappointment, in his face, I kept my gaze on my lap, toying with the edges of the blanket he had wrapped around me as I continued working to slow my breathing.

An ungloved finger tucked under my chin, lifting my face. I squeezed my eyes shut as a stray tear escaped, carving its path down my cheek. His finger moved from my chin to wipe the tear away in a careful touch. It was gentle and unexpected, and something I did not deserve.

I couldn't do it. I couldn't control my magic, couldn't summon the flames needed.

I let out a sigh and opened my eyes. Alexander smiled wryly, his head visible once again. "Thank you, Katrina."

"For what?" I asked, my voice hoarse.

He squeezed my hand gently, pulling me back into the moment. "For trying. I could see that was a lot for you to endure. Thank you for trying."

I laughed, but it was not a humorous sound. Instead, it bit like a harsh wind, choked with words I could not say. "Trying. Unsuccessfully, though."

"It was your first time giving into your emotions, and to see even a glimpse of your full power is more than I expected."

I was uncertain what to say to that. It might have been more than he had expected, but I doubted it was far from the power he was hoping for to save Sleepy Hollow. Would it be enough to destroy Sleepy Hollow, though? Enough to make that damned prophecy come true?

I swallowed, tasting the ash in the thick air. "How long do we have?"

"Days. A week at the most," he said so quietly that I would not have heard him had I not been looking directly at him to see the words upon his lips. "The disturbances in the magic are becoming heavier and more frequent. The sluagh are close."

"Impossible," I whispered, my voice cracking. I cleared my throat and sighed. I could not possibly save Sleepy Hollow from a group of sluagh in a week, not when I failed to even summon my fire without an emotional breakdown.

He rubbed his hand on my shoulder, squeezing briefly. "Nothing is impossible. Let us go get you a new dress, and we can discuss what happens next."

"No, I want to try again," I said, sitting up straighter. I

would *not* be a failure, not anymore. My self-loathing was over. I needed to prove myself, and more importantly, I needed to prove my mother wrong. I rolled my shoulders back, lifting my chin. "I can do this."

He looked at me, furrowing his brows and frowning. "I know you can. That was never the question. But you have not used your magic like this before. It will tire you out, and that is normal."

"I cannot fail," I whispered, more to myself than to Alexander. The Horseman of Death knew nothing about my visceral fear of failure. He would not understand it, had never felt it himself. "I must do this. I cannot fail."

"You have not, and you will not, fail." His voice was strong and certain as he stood and held his hand out to me. "If you want to try again, you can. But only if you are sure."

Looking up, I saw only determination in his eyes now. No pity, no disappointment. My heart soared, and taking his hand, I stood, struggling to keep the blanket wrapped around my body. I was painfully aware I was completely naked in front of this man. My cheeks burned.

He didn't seem to notice, though, which left me uncertain whether I appreciated it. While I was grateful he was not ogling me, some small, foolish part of me wanted him to at least look. But he kept his eyes on my face, nodding once as I stood. "Now, this time, focus on the physical feeling of the fire consuming you. The more familiar you are with how your body feels when you are using your magic, the easier it will come to you."

I nodded, hesitating for a moment before dropping the blanket from my body and kicking it away. I had already destroyed enough of Alexander's belongings. The least I could do was spare the blanket. My stomach churned at the idea of sinking back into such harsh and bleak emotions again, but I took a deep breath to steady myself. I could do this.

I let the words of my mother fill my head. *You call that a flame, Katrina? You will never be worthy of our family name. You are a disgrace to this family and to Sleepy Hollow.*

The negativity fueled my anger and, quicker than before, my body erupted into flames.

While I wanted to smile, I gritted my teeth and focused on the sensations. The crackling in my ears resembled branches snapping. The faint tickle of the flames over my skin was like a warm caress. Flickering orange filled my vision, spreading out from my body in a cocoon of power and destruction. For the first time in my life, I felt powerful. I felt worthy. My mother was wrong.

As soon as it was there, though, the fire sputtered out, leaving me standing naked in the smoldering grass once more. The spirit veil had dropped, the purple haze no longer surrounding us and protecting the world from my magic, and I hadn't realized.

"I am so sorry," I sputtered, looking around at the destructive circle of scorched earth.

"No need to apologize." Alexander stepped forward and rested his gloved hands on my shoulders. "That was very well done. Now, what did you feel?"

"Fire." My cheeks burned at the stupidity of my response.

He laughed, a loud and deep sound that sent goose-bumps over my entire body. "Yes, I would imagine so. What made it stop at the end?"

"I felt proud of myself," I admitted, the meekness of my voice drowning out the pride I had just felt. Saying it aloud felt foolish. What did I have to be proud of? Holding a flame for a few seconds?

His face turned serious as he studied me. "You should feel proud of yourself, Katrina."

My cheeks burned at the compliment, and I ducked my head down, avoiding his intense gaze.

Once more, his finger found its way under my chin to lift my eyes back to his. His gaze flitted down to my mouth and his tongue darted out to wet his lips. For a moment, I thought he might kiss me, and I found myself leaning toward him. But as quickly as I had the thought, he took a small step back, clasping his hands in front of his waist and clearing his throat.

"Do it once more," he encouraged, inclining his head toward me, his bright eyes fixed firmly on my own. He waved his hand, and the world shimmered and turned purple once more as his head disappeared and the spirit veil surrounded us again. His voice became disembodied but firm. "This time, focus on trying to push the flames out from yourself. Target something. A tree, a blade of grass—try to power your flames toward it."

"But—"

"You will destroy nothing here, remember?" he said, waving one of his hands to the purple haze surrounding us. "So, pick something and try to burn it. The goal is to make your flames leave your body."

I nodded, silently admonishing myself for ever thinking he would want to kiss me as I squared my shoulders and recalled the feeling of the flames across my body. This time, I used my embarrassment to fuel the flames, and even quicker than before, I became the fire. Focusing on a small divot in the ground a few yards away, I raised my hand and concentrated on pushing the flame away from my body as Alexander had instructed.

Surprisingly, the fire obeyed on the first try. Flickering out from my palm in a dancing movement, the flames twirled and moved centimeters away from my body, stretching and twining as I focused on the clump of earth. They extended a few more centimeters before collapsing and rushing back into my hand.

Gritting my teeth, I turned my thoughts back to my mother, and the flames came back to life. They moved from my hand once more, reaching nearly halfway to the divot this time before rushing back.

I dropped my hand, clenching my jaw as I inhaled a deep breath. If I could not do more than simply stand here and burn, I was no good to anyone. I let my gaze flick briefly to Alexander, who was watching with his arms crossed over his chest as he shifted his stance. My body curled in on itself at the thought of disappointing him.

With renewed vigor, I squeezed my other hand into a fist, grinding my teeth as I focused once more. I could do this. I would not disappoint another person.

The flames shot from my hand in a tight ball of fire, digging into the ground where I had aimed. This was no trickle of magic, or tendril of flame. This was a sphere of fire and despite what Alexander had said, the ground smoldered, the grass catching alight.

My eyes widened, and in an instant, my flames disappeared. I could not burn down more of this land.

"Oh, my gods," I whispered.

Alexander rushed into action, grabbing the blanket to smother the flames quickly before they could spread.

"I thought I could not burn anything in here," I said, my heart launching into my throat. What if I had aimed at something else? What if I had accidentally focused my fire on him? If I could burn the grass inside this spirit veil, was it safe to be practicing here?

He waved a hand and the purple haze dropped, revealing the bright day once more. He looked up, kneeling beside the scorched patch of earth. "You should not have been able to."

I swallowed hard, fighting to keep upright and not collapse to my knees. "What do I do now?"

"For now, let's go back inside. I need to look at some books," he said, standing with the blanket. He held it out to me, but then immediately pulled it back with a grimace. "Let's find you something to wear first."

I blushed as his eyes roamed over my body for the first time. I could have sworn I saw a hint of appreciation. He cleared his throat and held his arm out toward the house. "After you."

Walking back to the house, I knew I had not imagined the feeling of his eyes on my back.

"Even broken in spirit as he is, no one can feel more deeply than he does the beauties of nature."

-Mary Shelley,
Frankenstein

Fourteen

Dressed once again, I sat down at the kitchen table, looking up at Alexander, who stood by the bookshelf, his fingers trailing across the spines. I tracked every movement, entranced by how the books seemed to rush toward him on the shelf, welcoming his touch. My leg was bouncing uncontrollably beneath the table, and I wiped my sweaty palms on my new black cotton dress as I forced my attention away from his hand. "What are you looking for?"

"Books on elemental magic or even journals from other magic users that might contain anything we can use." He tapped the spines of several books and they floated from the shelves, stacking themselves neatly on the table beside me. He paused, his hand outstretched for another book as he looked over at me. "Are you all right?"

"I could have hurt you," I said, somehow managing to keep his gaze despite the flush creeping up my chest and the tears burning in the back of my throat.

The last book he'd been looking at left the shelf, joining the others on the table with a thud. He turned his back to the books still waiting on the shelf and sat down. He met my gaze and raised both eyebrows. "You could not have hurt me, Katrina."

"You also said I could not harm anything within the veil you cast," I pointed out, twisting my fingers.

"You should not have been able to." Despite his kindness, the look on his face reminded me I was still dealing with the Dullahan, the legendary protector of Sleepy Hollow.

"Why did I?"

"I am not sure. That is why I need to search through these," he said, nodding down at the stack of books. "But first, I want to ask you more about the town."

"You truly think I can stop the sluagh from being summoned? That I can protect the town from being destroyed?" I asked, tilting my head to read the titles on the spines of the books. Most were in languages I vaguely recognized but couldn't understand. I looked back up at him, searching his face for any indication of lies in his words. "Truly?"

"With continued training, yes, I do," he said, then raised an eyebrow. "Do you not think you can?"

"My emotions are all over the place," I said, shaking my head. The sluagh were supposedly deadly, and I was far from confident in being able to even face them, let alone defeat them. "Even if I do manage to figure out which emotion triggers my powers the most, I doubt I can channel that emotion consistently."

"Which emotion did you use on the last try?" His gaze was heavy on my skin, but not uncomfortable, like my mother's. Her attention was ice and blades, but the Dullahan's was warm, like a tepid bath, lapping at my skin.

I did not answer. Did not want to answer. How could I tell him I was trying to focus on not disappointing him without seeming like a foolish child? There was no way to tell him that my intense, abject fear of failure had burned that patch of earth in an instant without sounding pathetic.

He raised an eyebrow at my silence. "Katrina?"

Shifting under his gaze, I cleared my throat. From the little time I had been around him, it was clear he would not move on until I answered. "Fear."

At my words, both of his eyebrows shot up. "Fear? Surely fear of your own powers would not cause them to explode in such a manner."

"No." I shook my head, chuckling at myself. Perhaps it was better to just admit it. To get the obvious out in the open. I was a failure, and now, Alexander would see it, too. "Fear of failing."

His face softened. The look was not quite that of pity, but more of understanding, and I was uncertain which I hated more. "You did not fail, Katrina. Not even remotely."

I scoffed, my frustration rising. I did not need coddling, nor did I want it. I'd survived this long in my life without it and would continue to do so.

"Well, Horseman, I certainly did not succeed."

He studied me, his eyes intensely gazing into mine. His fingers twitched and his hand moved forward, but he pulled it back quickly, picking up a book from his stack and sliding it across the table instead. "Here, read through this and see if you can find anything useful that might explain this."

"I thought you wanted to ask me about the town," I said as I pulled the book in closer.

I ran my fingers over the embossed leather. *A History of Elemental Magic*, it read. It was clearly old, given the age of the leather and the soft crinkling of the spine, as I opened its dusty pages.

"I do," he admitted, opening his own book, which looked to be a small journal based on the neat swirls of handwritten lines inside. "I can ask you questions while we read, if that's all right."

I nodded, turning to the first page of the book in front of me. This was good. Reading and answering his questions would be enough to hold my focus and keep my mind from wandering to dangerous avenues. "Yes, ask anything you would like."

"Is there anyone you think would try to raise the sluagh? For any purpose." His question was blunt, his eyes focused on the journal in front of him. I wanted him to look up at me, to feel the weight of his gaze. But he kept his eyes down as he turned to the next page.

I watched him for a moment, his eyes flicking through the pages in front of him, tracking the letters and words. My cheeks burned as I realized just how long I'd been staring at him without answering his question. I dropped my head and forced my eyes back to my book. "I suppose there would be several. Any of the Ciallmhar would have that power."

"Can you think of anyone in particular?" he asked. He paused and leaned back in his chair, its legs creaking under his shifting weight. "Is there anyone who is not an Elder that you might suspect?"

I opened my mouth but closed it when I realized the name I had been about to say. No, it couldn't possibly be him.

He raised an eyebrow. "You do. Who is it?"

The name was heavy on my tongue, and as much as I didn't want to believe he was capable of such evil, he'd already proven that he was.

"Brom Bones," I finally offered, sighing. At his quizzical look, I elaborated. "His name is Abraham Van Brunt. He is a rather... ambitious man. I could see him trying to raise the sluagh if he thought it would benefit him and cut down the competition."

"I know he has learned to manipulate the lightning around him," Alexander said, leaning forward on his forearms. "But is he powerful?"

"Not overly so," I explained, thinking back to all the times I had seen Brom use his powers. "I've never seen him do more than create balls of flickering light, and that's only when there's a strong storm overhead, but I suppose he could be hiding his true abilities."

"Are his parents powerful?"

"His mother can manipulate weather, and his father is a diviner." I flushed, remembering that he had told me he knew the names and powers of everyone in the Hollow. I cleared my throat and turned to the next page in the book in front of me. "I've been told his father has low-level magic, so I had always assumed most of his powers came from his mother."

"He was born in Sleepy Hollow?"

"As far as I know, yes. I believe his parents came from the north several years before he was born. He has been trying to marry into more power since we turned of age."

The Horseman's face darkened, reminding me that despite his kindness, he was still a bringer of Death and had likely earned that title. "Marry you, I assume?"

I raised an eyebrow at his reaction. Was the Dullahan upset Brom wanted to marry me? Surely not, yet the sharp crease between his brows and the set of his jaw told a different story. "Yes. And I have turned him down every time."

He hummed, tapping his chin. "He might be worth looking into. If he is as self-serving as you say. Who else?"

"My parents," I mumbled. "My mother, more specifically."

"Why your mother?"

For someone who said that he knew everyone in the

Hollow, he seemed genuinely interested in my views of the town and the people who lived there. It had been a long time since someone other than Henry or Ciara was genuinely interested in anything I had to say.

I shook my head, both in answer and to clear the emotions swirling in my head. "I would prefer to not discuss my mother right now. Can we look through the books, please?"

He looked at me for a long time, his expression unreadable. I was certain he was going to press me for more information, for more insight about my mother, but he simply nodded and returned to his own book, pulling it closer to him and running a finger down the page to find the spot he'd left off. The tension bled out of my shoulders as I realized he would not make me discuss her further. I didn't think I could do it. Not right now.

"Speak up if you find something interesting about spirit veils or fire magic. If we are going to work together, we must learn how our magic will interact."

"Of course," I murmured, turning my attention back to my book.

I felt his gaze on me again, heavy and intense. I itched to look up to see his expression, but I kept my eyes on the pages in front of me, trying to focus on the words instead.

Given how often I felt his attention on me, it would take me weeks just to get through the first page.

"*You will always be fond of me. I represent to you all the sins you never had the courage to commit.*"

-Oscar Wilde,
The Picture of Dorian Gray

Fifteen

"Here," Alexander said sometime later, tapping his finger on the page of the book in front of him.

I straightened, wincing at the soreness in my back. We had been at it for several hours now, the sun setting and the stack of books to be read dwindling. He had made it through several books, while I was still on the first one he'd given to me.

"This is another journal, from an old…" He tilted his head, as if he couldn't quite figure out the word he wanted to use. He turned the book to face me and tapped the middle of a page. "We'll call him a collector, I suppose. He talks about types of magic that can penetrate spirit wards."

I wanted to ask more about what he meant by a collector, but it wasn't the time. Curiosity itched beneath my skin, and I forced it down, turning to the words in front of me. My eyes flitted over the pages, scanning in the ancient language and the few words I recognized as fast I could. "It does not give specifics. What types of magic?"

He sighed, irritation accompanying the huff of breath that washed over the side of my face. "In an earlier entry, it said that spirit magic was sensitive—I think the word translated to—to certain aspects of fire magic. It has been a long time since I have read this language, and this mage liked to use multiple languages in his entries as a sort of code."

Dread settled low in my stomach. Fire magic. *My* magic. I was the certain type of magic that could penetrate Alexander's veils. As I spoke, it was as if I was floating out of my body, observing us from above. My voice echoed in my ears, sounding like I was underwater, muffled and fuzzy. "What does that mean? Am I a danger to you?"

Shaking his head, he reached across the table for my hand. As much as I wanted his comfort, I did not reach out to him, and he pulled his hand back after a moment, sighing again. "No, Katrina. You are not a danger to me. I touched you while you were on fire that first night and felt nothing but warmth."

Tears burned in my throat. I swallowed them down as I clenched my fists, settling back into my body, and the fuzzy thickness around my head subsided. "What does it mean by certain aspects of fire magic?"

"I believe it means levels of magic, or perhaps subtypes within a magic class." He stroked his chin, his lips pursing as he looked between me and the book. "The fire that comes out when you do not want it to is one level, and the fire that takes over your entire body is another, and the ball of flames you push out is yet another. Just like the spirit magic I use to see people's magical signature is one level of mine, and the active use of it to create the veil you saw earlier is another."

I nodded, though all I really wanted to do was cry. I felt foolish, though I knew in my heart that even if I had pushed for training, my mother would have refused. But Alexander seemed willing to train me, and though I very much doubted his faith in me to learn quickly, at least it would be more than I'd ever had before. But would it be enough?

I swallowed down the acid that rose in my throat, coughing to clear the sting. "So, higher levels of fire magic? How can I have different types of fire?"

"I told you before, you are more powerful than you know. The magic is simply stuck behind a wall in your mind, waiting to come out." He took the book back, flipping through a few pages before turning it back around to me. "This passage here documents a meeting with a man in Sleepy Hollow who had knowledge of the more powerful kinds of magic. It does not say what the meeting discussed, but I assume fire would be one of those kinds of magic."

"Did it say who he met with?" I asked. Surely if there was someone in the Hollow with knowledge of fire magic, my mother would have sought them out when I was a child, hoping to explain why I had little magic.

"Cyrus. He is still on the Ciallmhar, yes?" he asked.

"Yes. He is, but he rarely takes visitors now."

Cyrus was old. Not just in appearance, but in age. He had come to Sleepy Hollow well after my parents, but had clearly been alive for much longer. Why hadn't my mother gone to him? If he knew about these types of magic, I should have been training with him my entire childhood. And yet, I'd only ever seen him in passing.

"We need to speak with him." He stood from the table, pacing around the small kitchen. "Do you know where he lives?"

Cyrus had never been cruel to me, preferring to stick to the shadows during the Ciallmhar meetings. Unlike the others who enjoyed my mother's cruelty, Cyrus had always seemed ambivalent. Bored. I wasn't certain he would help us, but I wasn't going to set my hopes on a man who had yawned when they announced the Roghnaithe's name last year.

"I thought you knew everyone in the Hollow," I questioned, clinging to anything I could to keep myself from spiraling. I watched him pace back and forth and studied the muscles in his thighs as they bunched beneath his pants when he moved. The power was unmistakable, yet subdued. Just like the rest of him. Realizing I'd been staring at his legs, I cleared my throat and pulled my attention back to his face. "Why are you asking me?"

"I know the powers of those in the Hollow, and I know the names of most. But I am not all-knowing, Katrina. Things happen in private that I'm not always privy to. No one is all-knowing."

I fought against the uncomfortable feeling tingling through my body. It had been a valid question, and I would not cower at it. But despite my words, my shoulders slumped in and my chest curled around my breastbone in an ill-fated effort to protect my heart from whatever stinging admonishment would come next. "Adelaide claims she is all-knowing. She is a powerful diviner."

"Adelaide's powers come more from idle gossip than from anything she has seen with her magic," he said dryly. He waved a hand, and the fire crackled loudly in response. "Take little that woman says at face value."

"She told me I would destroy the world. That I was bred for power and would burn Sleepy Hollow to ashes if I left before they could sacrifice me." My voice was steadier than I had expected it to be, even as my heart thundered against my ribcage.

I would not shake. I would not slump in my chair. I would be strong. Perhaps if I told myself that enough times, it would be true.

He stopped pacing abruptly, his boots scuffing against the floor as he turned to face me. The blue in his eyes blazed like icy fire, churning around the irises in a way that looked purely inhuman. "She said that?"

I nodded slowly, grimacing at the anger radiating from him. Surely, he couldn't be angry on my behalf, but I could think of nothing else that would warrant his anger. "Yes, she did. Why?"

"She must have been trying to frighten you into staying. What else did she tell you when you spoke?"

I tried to remember what else she had said, but my mind was racing. It didn't surprise me that Adelaide had lied, as the lies still buzzed in my ears like a swarm of bees in the summer. Were none of the Ciallmhar honorable? I'd long grown accustomed to my own parents' faults, but sitting here, talking to the Dullahan... The more I learned, the more I wondered why he was working so hard to convince me I would save Sleepy Hollow. What was there to save?

"She said she believed I was part of some prophecy, but she would not explain. She said I should accept my fate and stop trying to fight my destiny as Roghnaithe. But, if you do not take sacrifices offered, what do they think it is accomplishing?"

He shook his head. "I do not know. But we need to find out who is summoning the sluagh, and quickly. If someone unleashes them fully, no one will be safe."

"Have you heard of the prophecy she mentioned?"

"I know many prophecies, Katrina," he replied. "Any of them could be the one she mentioned."

Sighing, I wrung my hands in my lap but nodded. Certainly, a being like the Dullahan would know of many prophecies, and without specifics, I could not ask him more.

Unease gnawed at my stomach, its teeth sharp, but I ignored it, turning my focus back to the task at hand. I would prove Adelaide wrong; I would save the Hollow, not destroy it. If only to spite them all. When I was the hero of Sleepy Hollow, they would finally see. My actions would show them my value. They would see that I deserved respect and kindness instead of disdain and dismissal. They would have no choice but to acknowledge me.

"We would need to question the townspeople. Knowing more about their motivations could help us determine why the sluagh is being summoned and perhaps give us a clue as to how many." My parents kept me isolated, but I knew starting with their closest confidants and the townspeople who sought the Ciallmhar's respect would give us an abundance of knowledge, even if they didn't know it.

"That is precisely what we will do. No one in the Hollow has seen my face. The Ciallmhar only knew my father's face. I've only ever appeared in my spirit form, and I've remained hidden when I've ventured near town."

"They know me, though," I pointed out. "Quite well, in fact."

He smiled, the genuine expression of joy showing his teeth and crinkling the corners of his eyes. It was the biggest smile I'd seen from him, and even so, it wasn't a friendly one. It was one of confidence and boasting. "Yes, but my magic can disguise you."

I was certain my face conveyed my shock. "Spirit magic can do that?"

"There are very few limitations to spirit magic," he explained, patient with me and my unending questions. In a way, it reminded me of Henry teaching me how to use the pottery wheel for the first time. "Which is why it is so rare. But yes, I can alter your appearance so no one will recognize your face or your voice."

"My parents and some of the other members of the Ciallmhar always greet new members of the town," I said, thinking through the best way to get the information we would need. "We could simply approach from the bridge and request residence."

"Who do you suppose would be the best person to speak with first?"

"Ichabod Crane," I answered immediately. At Alexander's raised brows, I elaborated. "He is the school-teacher in the Hollow, but also the town's most notorious gossip. If there is any news about members of the town, he would be one to know it. Or at least could point us in the direction of someone who would know more."

His eyes darkened slightly, but the shift was so brief, I couldn't be definitive it wasn't a trick of the shadows as the flames flickered over the walls. "A friend of yours, I presume?"

"Not anymore," I replied, my voice hard. My fingers began smoking, and I started to push my anger back as I thought of Brom's betrayal and Ichabod's complacence. We'd never been friends, but I'd never thought they would have tried to kill me.

"Let it out," Alexander said, his voice firm. He nodded at my hands. "Do not fight your emotions, Katrina."

"If I let it out, I will burn your house to cinders."

The corner of his lip twitched up. "I wouldn't be so quick to assume the house cannot protect itself."

At his words, the fireplace flared, crackling and spitting embers into the room.

Emboldened by the fire, I moved my fingers away from anything flammable instead of shoving my anger down. I stared at them; the fire twirling over my fingers and pushing out into the air. My flames twitched, mirroring the flames in the fireplace. "He was with me when Brom pushed me over the riverbank. He stood there and did nothing."

"They are the ones who tried to send you to me?" Now his voice was hard and filled with a darkness that would have me afraid if he had directed it at me. "And you believed them to be your friends?"

I squirmed under his intense gaze, my flames sputtering out as embarrassment cut through the anger, extinguishing it with a gust of shame. "More like acquaintances, but yes, they were the ones who pushed me over the bank."

"We will start with him then," he said, standing from the table. "Now, let us prepare to go into the Hollow. There is a small bag in the trunk that you can put clothing into. I will get Liath ready to travel and then we will be off."

"So soon?" I croaked.

I wanted to save Sleepy Hollow to spite the notions of the Ciallmhar, to save the innocent people, and to prove to my mother I was not the worthless waste of life she believed me to be, but the idea of going back so soon to face those who had sentenced me to death—I was not eager to revisit it.

He paused on his path to the door, his large hand wrapped around the frame, flexing as his fingers tightened around the wood. I swallowed heavily and tore my eyes away from the strength.

They are just hands, Katrina, I told myself, blinking rapidly as I tried to listen to his words.

"Yes. We do not have much time, Katrina. We must find out who is summoning this evil and stop them before they succeed."

"Of course." I jumped up and moved down the hall. My cheeks flushed, as I felt thoroughly reprimanded. Glancing back over my shoulder, I paused, feeling as though I needed to say something else to him. I wanted to thank him for believing in me, for taking me in and not killing me. But the words that came out were weak and pitiful in comparison. "Thank you for the clothing."

He hesitated for a moment, and I could feel his eyes on my back. I hoped he would say something. I wasn't certain what, but in the end, the door opened and closed, and I was alone once more.

Sighing, I opened the trunk and began piling dresses into the small bag inside. I would have to face my town, whether I was prepared to or not.

"There is no such word as indifference in my apathetic nature."

-J. Sheridan Le Fanu,
Carmilla

Sixteen

The sun was high in the sky as Alexander climbed onto Liath behind me. I didn't want to admit his presence comforted me, but it did. The heat from his body warmed my back as his thighs bracketed my own. A shiver coursed through me and my cheeks instantly blazed. This man—this being—was on an entirely different level than me, and my naïve attraction, stemming from my prolonged lack of affection, would not be welcome, I was sure.

"Pass me your bag," he said gruffly, not even noticing my turmoil.

Flustered, I tried to lift the strap over my head, but managed to get it tangled in my curls, wincing as I pulled my own hair.

"Here," he muttered, wrapping his arms around me to reach up and untangle the strap from my hair. Lifting the mass of wild curls, he freed the strap and leaned in to grab the bag, securing it behind him.

"Thank you," I said, glancing over my shoulder to offer

a smile. It was the least I could do after making an utter fool of myself.

His eyes flicked down to my lips before his face shuddered and his gaze moved out to the field beyond. His thighs flexed, and he dug his heels into Liath's side. "We should be off."

Alexander's body only amplified the swaying of my body as he pressed up against my back. I turned around, focusing intently on Liath's mane in front of me. I needed to get myself under control. Alexander—no, *the Dullahan* —did not find me attractive. This was no time or place for attraction; we were facing a threat to our town. Perhaps acknowledging that I was touch starved would be enough to remind myself that my feelings were not real, and even if they were, the Dullahan did not reciprocate them.

This was just a professional arrangement, built on the desire to save Sleepy Hollow. And though our reasonings for wanting to save Sleepy Hollow might differ, the goal was ultimately the same. And as its protector, that was the Horseman's only concern. Not me.

Perhaps after this was over, if we succeeded in this impossible task, I could continue my journey to Saint Augustine and begin a new life. One where I could entertain these feelings for someone else.

Liath jerked as she began to trot, and I pulled my mind back to the present. There was time to dream later, now was time to investigate.

Riding into town was extremely nerve-racking; my body was achy and tense by the time the bridge came into view. The journey had felt like an eternity. Approaching the bridge, he pulled Liath to a halt, his thighs flexing around mine.

"How many will be there to greet us once we cross the

bridge?" His voice was soft, and the puff of breath against the left side of my neck sent shivers down my spine.

I briefly closed my eyes as we approached the entrance to the bridge. "There will be a fairly sizeable crowd waiting for us by the time we make it into town."

"I need to apply the glamor to your appearance," he said into my left ear. He had remembered what I had said about speaking when behind me and was the first person other than Henry who had adapted to my needs. It warmed some part of me that I kept covered in ice for far too long.

"What will I look like?"

"The magic required to change your entire body would be too taxing to hold for long, but I can change your face shape, hair color, and your voice," he said as a wave of magic washed over me. It tingled across the bridge of my nose, tickling down my neck and over my chest, moving through the rest of my body.

"How long will it last?" I asked, reaching up to tug on my hair. It still felt like my dark, coarse, and curly hair, but when I lifted a strand, it was silky smooth and blonde in my fingers.

"For however long you are in my presence," he answered. "Which means you need to stay near me at all times, lest the magic wane."

While I had been prepared to be around him for this investigation, something about hearing the requirement was jarring. "What if we get separated?"

"Get away from people and make your way back to wherever we are staying without being seen. If you can't do that, meet me beneath the bridge by the water." He hummed, a low sound that vibrated against my back. "It will be all right, Katrina. I swear, no one will harm you."

Without another word, he urged Liath over the bridge. A crow cawed loudly as we passed, making me jump and look at the sky. Alexander pulled on Liath's reins to slow her as my head whipped around, searching for the source. There, perched in the tree just next to the bridge, sat another lone crow, staring at us.

An uneasy feeling nagged at my mind, like claws scraping down the back of my neck. I felt a whisper of a threat not yet said aloud, and without a doubt, I knew it was the same crow that had been in the town square.

"That is the third time I've seen that crow," I whispered, keeping my eyes locked on the creature.

Alexander hummed again and flexed his thighs around Liath to speed her up, not hesitating for a moment as we began down the path that would lead us into the town's center.

True to my word, there was a small crowd gathered as we neared. My anxiety flared and my heart pounded against my ribs, my legs vibrating with unspent energy. I clenched my hands into fists. I had to control my flames, or I would give myself away before we even began. Gloved hands slowly wrapped around mine.

"Stay calm, Katrina," Alexander said, his lips pressed against the shell of my ear, effectively distracting me from the growing feelings of panic. Now, all I could think about was his lips against my ear and his breath puffing against my skin. One of his hands moved from my own and wrapped around my stomach, pulling me back tightly against his chest. "They will not recognize you, but I need you to trust me."

I nodded, breathing through my nose as we approached the crowd. Recognizing my parents, my heart raced, trying to escape my chest and flee back to the Horseman's cottage. They looked the same as they had the last time I saw them. Regal and apathetic like the morning they told me the news.

Alexander squeezed my waist, and the touch eased my

racing heart. I felt calmer knowing he was with me as we faced my parents and several of the other Elders waiting for us. Adelaide was with them, as were Brom and his parents. It nearly made me smile to see Brom's bandaged hand; the same one he'd grabbed me with the night he threw me over the embankment. It pleased me to know I had burned him after all. Ichabod was not present, but given the time of day, I assumed he was at the schoolhouse.

My mother approached us first, a serene smile on her unnaturally smooth face. "Hello, welcome to Sleepy Hollow."

I felt Alexander's head bow. "Greetings. We were told this place was a sanctuary for those with magical abilities. Is that true?"

"Certainly," she said, her hands clasped in front of her waist, as if they had not struck me across the face little more than a week ago. My blood bubbled beneath my skin, but I pushed it back, focusing on the feel of Alexander's hands around my waist. "Where are you traveling from?"

"Near Virginia," he replied smoothly. "The town we were living in discovered our true natures and forced us to leave. My wife and I are looking for a safer place to live and potentially raise our future family, and we were told this town was a refuge."

"Well, we are pleased you have joined us. What are your names?"

I froze. We had not discussed what my name would be. He squeezed my side briefly before smoothly replying. "This is Katherine Elizabeth. And I am Alexander."

"We welcome you both." My mother turned to Brom. "Abraham, dear, can you please escort Alexander and his wife to the stables, and then to the inn? We will house them there while we look for other lodging."

"We can pay for our own lodging," Alexander spoke

quickly, playing the offended husband, who did not appreciate charity. It was almost convincing. It impressed me.

"Of course," my father interjected, stepping up beside my mother. "Let us at least pay for your first night. As a welcoming gift."

"How gracious of you." Alexander bowed his head again and cast his warmth against my back. "That's very generous."

"Abraham, please," my mother said, waving Brom forward.

He stepped up, and I could see the grimace he was poorly hiding. His gaze flicked over me, and his eyes lit up in a way I did not care for. Alexander must have noticed it too because his grip tightened around my waist. In an instant, he slid from behind me, and the cold rushed in, sending a shiver down my exposed spine.

Alexander extended his gloved hand to Brom. "Hello. Abraham, was it?"

Brom tugged on his coat, clicking his heels together and bowing slightly. He did not take Alexander's hand. "Yes, but please, call me Brom."

I did not miss how Alexander kept his hand extended, staying quiet until Brom finally reached for it with his unbandaged hand. It was an unspoken game of dominance, and Brom had lost.

I bit the insides of my cheeks to hide a smile.

Alexander exchanged polite words with the others and then took Liath's reins in his hand as we followed Brom to the stables. "Have you lived here long, Bram?"

"Brom," my former friend corrected through gritted teeth. "I have lived here all my life."

I knew Alexander hadn't mistakenly used the wrong name, and it made my insides warm. Alexander fell silent as we continued the short walk to the stables. Pulling Liath to a stop, he held his hand out to me and assisted me with dismounting. Thankfully, it was much smoother than the first time I had attempted it. I smiled at him, ignoring Brom entirely. It would only irritate him further, and if I could not burn the man to a crisp, irritation would suffice. For now.

Alexander led Liath toward a stall, and I trailed behind him. Brom quickly sidled up beside me. "Hello, Katherine, was it?"

"Katherine Elizabeth," I said with a tight smile. My voice sounded unfamiliar to my ears, silky and high pitched in a non-threatening and innocent way mine had never been. It was odd to not recognize my own voice.

"How long have you and your husband been together?" he asked, slipping his hand in the crook of my elbow and pulling me to a stop. He turned me around to face him.

I did not want him touching me, but I knew if I gave in to my flames, it would destroy both my dress and our cover. "Remove your hand."

"I simply would like to get to know you better," he said, still holding my arm. "I am trying to be welcoming to my new neighbors."

"I advise you to remove your hand from my wife," Alexander's voice was so cold, I expected frost to form in the stables. It sent chills down my spine and goosebumps along my flesh, though they were not all from fear.

At Brom's lack of response, Alexander's voice grew even colder, like thick layers of ice over a pond in the middle of winter. "Before I remove it for you."

Brom quickly snatched his hand away. "My apologies."

"I believe we can find the inn on our own." Alexander's gaze did not waver from Brom. "You may leave us now."

Brom began to protest. "No, I was told—"

"That is all, Bron." Alexander waved his hand in

dismissal before pulling our bags from the saddle. He then took my hand in his. "You may go."

"My name is Brom." Brom's face turned bright red. He crossed his arms and I could see his lips moving as he muttered something else, but could not hear the words. Thankfully, he listened to Alexander and left the stables.

"What did he say?" I asked, turning to Alexander after Brom had fully departed. While I should have removed my hand from his, it felt comforting.

Alexander smiled, his lips thin. "I do not think it would be appropriate to repeat."

A genuine smile crossed my face. "I have never admired someone more. Thank you for putting him in his place."

"No one touches you without your permission," he said, pointedly looking down at our hands. "Not even me."

"I do not mind you touching me." My cheeks burned, realizing what I had said. "I mean... I do not mind you holding my hand."

He smiled, but his expression was unreadable. "Let's get to the inn. I have little patience for prying townspeople."

"You realize we will have to interact with them quite a bit to get what we are searching for," I muttered, careful of listening ears.

He sighed. "Yes, I know. How unfortunate."

"*Gigantic in height, and muffled in a cloak, Ichabod was horror-struck on perceiving that he was headless! But his horror was still more increased on observing that the head, which should have rested on his shoulders, was carried before him on the pommel of his saddle!*"

-*Washington Irving,*
The Legend of Sleepy Hollow

Seventeen

As we arrived at the small inn, I was far from surprised to see Adelaide waiting for us with her apprentice at her side. Her white, unseeing eyes seemed to track my every move, and sweat rolled down my spine. Could her magic see through my disguise?

"I did not get to speak with you when you first arrived," Adelaide said, still staring at me even though her body faced Alexander.

"This is Adelaide, one of the Ciallmhar of Sleepy Hollow and a seer," Edmund, her young apprentice, said as his chest puffed with pride. He had shown promise as a young diviner, and Adelaide had quickly swooped him up to study under her. Not all the Ciallmhar took apprentices, but Adelaide had been one to take them frequently.

"A pleasure to meet you," Alexander said, bowing slightly before extending his hand out for her to shake.

"Mistress Adelaide is blind, sir," Edmund said, his voice sharp. Adelaide was mostly blind, and everyone in the Hollow knew that, but I could see why they would want to keep that information from strangers.

Alexander pulled his hand back, blinking slowly at the young boy. "My apologies."

"And you are Katherine?" Adelaide asked, her voice sugared as she folded her hands in front of her stomach. "A beautiful name."

"Katherine Elizabeth, yes. And thank you, that is very kind," I replied, keeping my voice carefully slow. Of all the Ciallmhar, Adelaide would have the best chance to see through Alexander's disguise. I could only hope that he was as powerful as he believed.

"We are having a town meeting before sunset," Adelaide said, still gazing at me. "We would be honored if you would attend."

"Certainly," Alexander answered. "Where is the gathering?"

"The town square. I will send Edmund here to fetch you after supper, if that is amenable? We would love for our newest town members to join us." She smiled slightly. "I know you must be tired after your long journey, but it will be good to have you involved in the town."

"That would be wonderful," I replied, forcing a smile of my own. "That is very kind of you."

"We will let you settle in now," Adelaide said. She reached one of her hands out to Edmund, who offered his arm. "We shall see you at sunset."

Our guests walked away, and I let out the breath I'd been holding. Going to a town meeting led undoubtedly by my parents on my first expedition back in the Hollow had not been what I was expecting.

Tears burned in my throat as I clenched my hands. I did not want to see my parents again. Not after they had sentenced me to death. Seeing them at the bridge greeting us was hard enough, but having to interact with them, speak to them... I could not do it.

"Hold it together until we get to the room." Alexander's voice was a rough whisper as he stepped up to my left and placed his hand on my lower back, pressing gently to guide me through the inn's front doors. "You will be safe, I promise."

Alexander procured us a room, though I was so caught up in trying to breathe that I did not hear a word he said to the man running the inn. He guided me away from the front desk and up a set of creaking wooden stairs, my gaze so unfocused it was a miracle I did not fall.

"We are here," he said, pushing the door open for me. I followed him inside, and as soon as the door was closed behind us, Alexander moved in front of me. "Katrina. You are safe."

I looked up at him, his eyes shining with concern brighter than I'd ever seen them before. All I could do was nod, over and over. I knew in my head I was safe, but my body was telling me a far different story.

"What are you worried about?" he asked, guiding me to sit on the bed. He sat next to me, reaching for my hands, but paused. "Can I touch you? Just your hands."

I nodded, and he took my hands in his. The leather of his gloves felt soft against my skin. Clenching my jaw, I bit down hard on the inside of my cheek, thankful for the sharp sting of pain that brought me back to focus. I sucked in a deep breath through my nose and let it out slowly, centering myself on the touch and comfort of the Headless Horseman.

"I thought I was ready to face them again, but I was not ready to see my mother. And I do not think I will be ready to see them again tonight."

He looked at me for a long time, rubbing his thumbs over the tops of my hands. "I think you are stronger than you give yourself credit for. What are you afraid of?"

I wanted to fidget under his gaze, but I clenched my leg muscles and forced myself to meet his eyes. He had saved my life. I could tell him what I was afraid of. "I have been a disappointment my entire life. To my parents in particular. Facing them again... I do not think I can handle them treating me nicely, simply because they believe I am a stranger."

"Why do you believe you disappointed them?" he asked. He stood from the bed and knelt at my feet, looking at my boots. "May I take these off for you while you tell me?"

Grateful to have him focus on something else while I spoke, I nodded quickly. "Yes, thank you. And I know they were because they told me. Often. I was a disappointment from the moment of my birth because I was not a boy. Then, I was a disappointment because of my defective hearing. Then, it became all about my magic, and how it was disappointing I was not more powerful."

Alexander scoffed as he pulled off his gloves and started to unlace my boots. "You are extremely powerful. The only disappointment they should feel is with themselves for failing to train you."

"I doubt they would have been pleased with me even if they did believe I was powerful," I said, shrugging indelicately. "All they wanted was to marry me off, so they could try for another child—a boy to inherit the town."

"You were to inherit the town?" He pulled my boots from my feet and moved to work on his own. "And the Elders still chose you to be sacrificed?"

"If they don't have a boy before they pass, I would inherit the town. But I imagine that's partially why my mother chose me as the Roghnaithe. If the choice was between me and the survival of Sleepy Hollow, there was never an actual choice," I said, watching him as his thick fingers worked at the laces of his own boots. His hands flexed, rippling the muscles of his forearms. I shook my head, pulling myself from the distraction. "They'll likely try for another child after my death."

He moved to sit back on the bed next to me, taking my hands in his again and turning to face me. "I am deeply sorry, Katrina. No child should grow up feeling unloved."

"Thank you," I said, my eyes flitting down to his lips. Idly, I wondered what it would be like to kiss him. I blushed at the thought. He would never want to kiss me. "Would you mind if I lay down for a quick rest before the town meeting?"

"Of course," he said, standing abruptly. "I will close the curtains."

As he walked over to the small window, I stood from the bed, pulling back the blankets and settling in on the mattress. In my panic, I had not noticed there was only one bed in the room, and the only other furniture was a small chest of drawers in the corner. But now it was all I could focus on.

I opened my mouth to speak. What I had been planning to say, I was not sure, but it did not matter. The thick curtains closed, and the room plunged into darkness. Footsteps sounded as Alexander padded back over to the bed.

"I can sit on the floor or go downstairs." His voice startled me, closer than I had expected based on his footsteps.

I shook my head, though I wasn't convinced he could even see me. "No, please stay. You can lie in the bed with me. You should rest as well."

"Only if you are sure, Katrina," he said, his voice carefully neutral.

In that instant, I was grateful for the darkness. My cheeks burned. Of course, he would not want to share a bed with me. Only Henry and Ciara could bear to be in the same room as me for anything longer than a moment. How could I expect anyone to want to be so close, so intimate? I cleared my throat. "I am sure. But if you are not comfortable with it, I understand. We can figure out a sleeping arrangement."

He did not reply, but I felt the other side of the bed sink down, and suddenly, his warmth was against me as he slid under the blankets. "Get some rest, Katrina. I will watch over you."

"You need to rest as well."

"I will," he said, shifting in the bed.

I turned on my side to face him. "Thank you."

He shifted again, and his breath washed over my face, inches from my lips. "And what have I done to earn your gratitude, Katrina Van Tassel?"

"You have treated me like someone worthy of friendship. Someone worthy of existing." My voice was so quiet, I could barely hear myself.

He was silent, breathing slowly and evenly in front of me. "You are worthy of far more than simply existing."

Boldness flowed through me, and I reached a hand up to rest gently on his cheek. In the darkness, it felt even more intimate than it really was. The stubble on his jaw felt prickly against my palm. His breath remained steady against my face. My thumb ran over the skin, and a part of me that had never surfaced surged upward, longing for me to lean in and kiss him.

But as much as that part of me wanted to, the familiar part of me that knew I could never be enough for someone. Slowly, I let my hand drop. Before it made it more than a few inches away, he reached up and pushed it back to his face, trapping my hand against his.

His breath washed over my face again, closer this time.

Unable to handle the pressure of knowing he was

watching me in the darkness, I let my eyes slide shut. Anticipation fluttered through me, like butterflies swarming in my veins.

"I have to go," he whispered into the darkness as the accompanying puffs of breath moved my hair.

And then Alexander pulled away from me and the coldness rushed in. I kept my eyes shut, listening to the bed squeak as he moved, the thump as he pulled on his boots, the soft footsteps as he left the room, and the door closing with a click behind him.

Shame heated my cheeks now instead of attraction, and I slumped against the bed, silently hoping it would swallow me whole and end this misery. At least he had left, rather than try to discuss it. Rejection and disappointment were both best handled in silence. I had misread the signs, the glances, and his kind comments. They were not what I had thought or what I hoped I might have.

Pulling the blankets up to my chin, I rolled away from the door and closed my eyes tightly, balling my hands into fists. Now, I would sleep, and when I woke, I would shove my emotions down and face my family once more.

It would be easy. After all, it'd once been my daily routine.

"I want you to believe...to believe in things that you cannot."

-Bram Stoker, Dracula

Eighteen

My rest was fitful, but I must have drifted off, because the door closing woke me with a start. Alexander turned from the door and grimaced. "I did not mean to wake you."

"Is it time to go to the town meeting?" I asked, sitting up in bed. The room was still dark from the heavy curtains, but a sliver of light traced a line down the window and across the floor to the door.

"Nearly." His footsteps sounded as he walked over and leaned on the wall across from the bed. Even in the darkness, I could feel his eyes on me, heavy and watching my every move.

"Then it was time for me to wake up."

"About earlier..." he trailed off, the discomfort rolling off him in thick waves.

I held a hand up, not wanting to have this conversation. Heat burned in my cheeks, knotting my stomach and pushing the sour taste of embarrassment to the back of my tongue. "No. There is nothing for you to say. I apologize for making you uncomfortable. It won't happen again."

He was silent, the unsaid words of rejection hanging in the darkness.

"Please, we don't need to talk about it." I was nearly begging at this point, but I couldn't bear to hear the rejection said aloud. "I made a mistake."

"As you wish," he said, bowing slightly. He moved to the window and pulled open the curtains, bathing the room in dying light. "Edmund will be here shortly. We need to discuss our plan for the meeting with the townspeople."

"What is there to do?" I asked, rubbing my hand over my face to clear the sleep. "Except listen, that is."

"After we listen to what they have to say, I want to speak with some of the other Elders. Since you so strongly suspect Brom and his family or your parents, I want to make time to speak with them as well." He crossed his arms over his chest. "I want to get a feeling for them myself, to see if we can determine who would have the most to gain by summoning the sluagh."

I raised an eyebrow. "I sincerely doubt Brom will want to speak with you after your encounter earlier in the stables."

"He should not have touched you," he said, his voice hard again. "And I will speak to his family then. I have no patience for a man who believes he may touch a woman just because he pleases."

"What about my parents?" I asked, playing with my hands in my lap.

"I will speak to them as well. Unless you would prefer to?"

"We should speak with them together. I will be able to tell if they are hiding something," I said with a sigh. As much as I did not want to face my parents, I knew it would be a wise decision to have us present a united front.

"Is there anything you can tell me that will help? Have

you been to these kinds of meetings before?" He crossed his arms over his chest. The look on his face was stern, but there was something beneath it that was indecipherable. Something under the surface that was darker than the shadows trailing across the floor.

"We have only had a few new members join the town. Usually, it was to share important news or some announcement from the Ciallmhar," I said, thinking back through my childhood. "However, this meeting isn't just to welcome us to the town. They've never done that before. The Ciallmhar alone make nearly all the decisions, so I can't imagine what they'd be meeting about."

He looked at me, waiting.

Realization dawned. "They are meeting about me."

"You said that Brom is the one who pushed you down the bank?" His jaw worked, clenching visibly. "Would that have been enough in the eyes of the town for their... sacrifice? Or is the larger ceremony on Samhain also necessary?"

I shook my head. "I don't know. He certainly would have told them, but I do not know if it would be considered enough without the ceremony. We have never had anyone try to escape their death."

His eyes widened. "For nearly a century, people just accepted that they might die for this town? No one questioned or fought back?"

"They couldn't," I said, ducking my head at the implied admonishment. "We were told that if we refused the sacrifice, a family member would have to take our place. That discouraged any dissent rather well." My body stiffened. "I need to check on my mentor. He would be the one they use as my replacement if they considered my sacrifice incomplete."

Shifting, his arms flexed, and his jaw feathered again. He

remained silent, looking at me. Finally, he nodded. "Tomorrow, we will find your friend."

My cheeks flushed at his expression. Ciara had been right. Questioning these practices had come far too late. Perhaps I could sneak away from Alexander and see her. Tell her that her brother was alive and safe, that the Dullahan had not killed him.

"Once we learn who is summoning the sluagh and stop them, we will address that practice. It will not continue."

"What about those you sent away?" I asked, my mind going back to Ciara and Torin. "Could they return? To their families?"

I could only describe the expression that crossed his face as surprise, and I was hesitant to grasp why that irked me. Was he surprised I cared for those who had been sacrificed? Or was he surprised I had asked if they could return? Either way, I did not appreciate the look he gave me.

"If they remained in the place I brought them, I can send word. But if they have moved on, there will be no easy way to find them," he said, inclining his head. "But yes, we can try."

I nodded, biting the insides of my cheeks to keep from asking why he was surprised.

Thankfully, a knock sounded on the door. Alexander looked at me for a moment before standing up off the wall. With a graceful strength, he pulled the door open in one fluid movement.

Edmund waited on the other side, bowing to Alexander. "Good evening. Are you both ready to depart?"

Alexander looked back at me, raising an eyebrow. Quickly, I pulled my boots on, lacing them with fumbling fingers. Standing, I smoothed down my dress. "Yes, thank you. We are ready."

"Wonderful. If you will follow me," he said, bowing shallowly before turning and leading us from the room.

THE TOWN MEETING was not quite what I had been expecting. Instead of the entire town, a population of around one hundred, a much smaller crowd of about twenty congregated in the town square. I studied those in attendance as Alexander and I approached. My parents, Brom and his parents, the rest of the Ciallmhar, Ichabod, and many of the more prominent members of the town all gathered in the center, cast in glowing light from the lanterns that lined the square.

Henry was not present, not that I had expected him to be after I saw who was in attendance. Ciara was not either, which was surprising, given how important her apothecary shop was to the town. Henry's absence, though expected, only furthered my anxiety around the man's safety. He would have fought back, but he would be no match against my mother.

"Welcome, Alexander and Katherine Elizabeth, to Sleepy Hollow," my mother's voice boomed.

Alexander slipped his gloved hand into mine, squeezing slightly. The move was likely to keep up the pretense of our marriage, but it offered me comfort all the same, and I clung to it, especially after how terribly I had fumbled our previous interaction. His voice was smooth as he spoke. "Thank you. We are very pleased to be here."

My mother stepped forward, her chin lifted high as her eyes scanned over the audience in front of her. "As you know, Sleepy Hollow is in a precarious situation. We must all make sacrifices for the good of the town and our people."

Murmurs of agreement shuddered through the crowd, and Alexander's hand tightened around mine. Looking up at him, he kept his gaze firmly on my mother, but squeezed my hand once more before dropping it. I took a deep breath in through my nose, pushing back my disgust. She spoke of sacrifice, yet did not know what it truly meant. Sacrifice meant giving up something you loved and valued. And that had certainly never been me.

"Despite the..." She hesitated on her words, lacing her fingers together in front of her, "...unfortunate situation involving this year's sacrifice, we want to reassure everyone that the town will continue to be protected, no matter the cost. And we want to thank those who have sacrificed for Sleepy Hollow. It takes honorable and selfless people to ensure the continued success of a haven such as ours. The Dullahan will protect us, and we will continue to live in peace, safely away from humans. This year will be no different."

My body went rigid at her words, fighting to keep from looking up at Alexander. Were they talking about Henry? The full moon was in two days, and whatever it took, I wouldn't let them sentence anyone else—let alone my old friend—to death. I would burn this entire town to ashes before I let that happen. It was too risky to assume my mother would be content with sending the sacrifice into the forest. I couldn't risk that she wouldn't take matters into her own hands to ensure the death she believed the Dullahan needed.

"It's all right," he murmured, almost too quiet for me to hear, even on my hearing side. He never looked in my direction, holding his focus on my parents with a feigned interest that would have fooled me had I not known his true feelings. "Breathe."

Doing as he bade, I focused on the feeling of the crisp air in my nostrils. The world faded from the rest of my senses.

When my mother's speech was finally over, she stepped back into the shadows beneath the oak tree next to my father. I could see her lips moving, but I was too far away to hear her now that she'd lowered her voice. I watched closely, trying to make out the words, searching for anything that might indicate what she was planning.

A tap on my shoulder made me jump, whirling to face whoever had touched me. My breath rushed out at the sight of Alexander looking down at me, a half-smile on his lips.

"I apologize for scaring you. I was speaking to you." He reached for my hand, pausing halfway. "May I?"

My cheeks heated as I offered him my hand. "I'm sorry. What did you say?"

"I am going to speak to Brom's parents. Do you want to come with me, or will you be fine alone for a moment?"

"I'll be fine here," I said, still a little breathless. Despite my earlier desire to present a united front with Alexander, I had no desire—and no energy—to be around Brom or his parents, and though I also wasn't keen on being alone in this sea of people who'd been ready to sacrifice me, it would be easier for me to fade into the background and study those around us. Belatedly, I forced a smile on my lips. "Really, I will be fine by myself."

He looked at me for a moment, tilting his head slightly. Finally, he returned a single nod and released my hand, moving to tuck a loose strand of hair behind my ear. "Very well. I'll come find you when I'm finished."

I stood, watching his retreating figure, my cheek tingling where his hand had brushed against it, the ghost of his touch buzzing against my skin. He paused in front of Brom and his family, and I watched as he introduced himself, my gaze focused on the broadness of his shoulders.

"Excuse me," a voice said, eliciting a startled jump from me as I turned to my guest.

Ichabod Crane stood there, his eyes hopeful and bright.

He bowed low before straightening and extending his hand. "Hello. I wanted to introduce myself. I'm Ichabod Crane. I teach at the schoolhouse here and heard you and your husband will be joining our town."

I forced a smile and took his hand politely. "Hello. I am Katherine Elizabeth. My husband just stepped away, but it's nice to meet you. Have you lived here long?"

"All my life," he said with a smile, tugging proudly on the lapels of his coat. His face turned somber, and he nodded toward my mother. "I suppose you heard Loralai's speech? What did you think of it?"

My heart took off at a sprint. *Be careful with your words, Katrina*. I cleared my throat to disguise my hesitation. "It was interesting. I've never heard of a sanctuary needing to sacrifice members of the community to ensure their safety. Do people truly think it's an honor?"

He bristled, clearly offended by my words. "Yes, of course. Our sanctuary differs from most, I suppose, but yes. The chosen, the Roghnaithe, feel honored to play their part in protecting our town and our people."

"Really?" I managed to force out, hopefully feigning interest instead of letting my disgust bleed through.

"Quite," he said. His eyes shifted, and he adjusted his coat again. "In fact, the Elders chose one of my best friends this year. And despite her initial fear, she was happy to fulfill her duty to the town."

Bile rose in my throat at the story he wove. "Is that the unfortunate situation that was mentioned? What happened?"

He rubbed at the back of his neck. "Well, it's not my place to say, truly. My friend allowed her fear in at first, but she quickly realized the town needed her sacrifice and honored it."

My stomach churned, acid coating my tongue as my vision blurred. "Excuse me, I need to go."

I didn't hear what he said as I turned away, my eyes fixed on Alexander as I moved closer to him. Thankfully, he was walking toward me and was alone. Nearly running into him as I approached, one of his hands caught my waist to steady me.

"What's wrong?" he asked, his eyes scanning the town square above my head.

"I need to get out of here," I whispered, reaching down to tug on Alexander's other hand. My emotions were running rampant, swirling higher and higher inside my chest, and I feared if I didn't escape soon, they would explode. I looked up at him. "Please."

He hesitated for a moment, looking around at the crowd in front of us, his eyes flitting back and forth between the faces of all those in attendance. Finally, he turned his gaze to me.

"All right," he said, his face annoyingly passive as he studied me. Nodding politely at my parents, he put his hand on my back and guided me away from the crowd and back to the inn.

Only once we'd reached our room did my body relax, no longer wound tight with anxiety. The door shut behind us and Alexander stood in the middle of the room for a moment, his back to me. He turned and his eyes roved over my body, assessing, as if he were looking for a physical reason for my pain. "Are you all right, Katrina? What happened?"

I took a deep breath, the movement shuddering through my body. My palms were damp, and my cheeks burned as I admitted my reason for leaving. "I got overwhelmed.

Ichabod started talking about me and saying things about my sacrifice, and it was just too much."

His brow furrowed and his mouth turned down, looking grim as he stared at me. "The survival of this town is on the line. We needed to get more information tonight."

"You do not need to tell me that, Dullahan. You could have stayed." The disappointment was clearly visible in his face, and that only made me feel worse. But I shouldn't feel bad, coming face to face with my past. How could he expect me to suddenly be fine while interacting with them? Quickly, anger took the place of embarrassment, and I felt my fire flickering to life beneath my skin, begging to be unleashed and scorch whatever was in its path. My words were venom as they came out. "And if the town's survival was truly your concern, you would have stopped the sacrifices centuries ago."

"I do not accept them. The townspeople sacrificed to me are all still alive," he said, raising his eyebrow; his voice was sharp to counteract my own stinging words.

I scoffed, clenching my fists as I crossed my arms over my chest. "We are devolving to semantics now? How charming, Horseman. We both know that if you had wanted to stop the sacrifices, you would have."

With a growl, his presence seemed to grow larger. A smoky darkness pulsing out around him in thrumming waves as he glared down at me. For a moment, his eyes flashed, changing from their normal blue to a burning red. But as quickly as it had appeared, it was gone, leaving behind a darker blue and flickering tendrils of violet shadows that snaked toward me. My pulse quickened and fear clawed at my throat as I continued moving backward until his magic pinned me against the wall.

Trapped between an angry mythical being of death and the wall, fire erupted from my fingertips, sending the shadows skittering to Alexander. They coiled around his arms and neck as the darkness of his eyes faded, and the bright blue returned.

His eyes widened, and he took several steps back, holding his hands up. "Stay calm, Katrina. I will not hurt you."

"What was that?" I asked, thankful my voice was not shaking, though my knees were. I sucked in a breath through my teeth, not lowering my hands or pulling my flames back into myself yet. "What were you going to do to me?"

He took a step closer to me and my body flinched against the wall involuntarily. The hurt that spread across his face almost made me feel bad, but not bad enough to lower my hands. I knew that if he wanted, the Dullahan *could* kill me with his magic, but I had no desire to find out if he *would*.

He crossed the room to sit down on the bed. "I apologize, Katrina. I lost my temper for a moment, and my magic responded. I would never hurt you. I can promise you that."

I stayed silent, the pounding of my heart steadily slowing until it faded entirely, along with the flames at my fingertips. Only then did I meet his gaze. "Do not do that again."

Our eyes locked for a second before he nodded. "Of course."

"What did you learn from the meeting tonight?" I asked, still pressed against the wall. I flexed my fingers, slowly continuing to work up my arms and then down my torso and legs as I unlocked my muscles. My shoulders slumped as the terror finally dissipated, taking my energy with it.

"I don't believe Brom is summoning the sluagh," he

said, still watching me from the bed. "No matter how annoying he might be."

"I don't think it is Ichabod either," I agreed, crossing my arms behind me and leaning back against the wall, rocking on my heels. "But we should not be so quick to dismiss Brom's family."

"Why?" He remained stoic, the only movement coming from his eyes and the rise and fall of his chest.

"Brom is too concerned about finding someone fool enough to marry him, though that may very well have led him to turn to magic as a solution. It is unlikely to meet anyone who is dense enough to willingly tie themselves to the man. Ichabod is too concerned with his school and his gossip, but beyond that he is too... gentle. But Brom's parents are very concerned with staying in the good graces of my parents and the other Elders," I explained, my surety of each word slowly replacing my anxiety. I knew this town and these people. "I would not put it past them to summon a sluagh and get rid of anyone in their path."

He nodded. "That was the impression I got as well. Ichabod is likely not the summoner."

"Now we are down to my parents or the other Ciallmhar," I said with a sigh, reaching up to rub at my forehead. "They will be far more difficult to question."

"Then I suppose we will have to be creative at the party tomorrow." He grimaced. "But we must not be too quick to dismiss anyone. With the right spell, anyone can summon anything, no matter their reasoning."

"I suppose we will," I said, pushing off the wall and bending to unlace my boots, ending the conversation. I had wanted to get away from my parents, and now I was running right back into their stronghold.

What could possibly go wrong?

"Quiet minds cannot be perplexed or frightened but go on in fortune or misfortune at their own private pace, like a clock during a thunderstorm."

-Robert Louis Stevenson, Dr. Jekyll and Mr. Hyde

Nineteen

J ust as I had fallen asleep, I woke up alone. I was not
certain where, or even if, the Dullahan slept, but he
had not joined me in the small bed. I was not
convinced he would have fit if he wanted to.

Rising from the bed with a sigh, I wondered if my life
would always be like this: alone.

"Did you sleep well?" Alexander's voice startled me
from a darkened corner of the room.

Squinting in the direction of the voice that had made
me flinch, I exhaled. Alexander sat in a chair, one ankle
crossed and resting on the opposite knee, watching me. Had
he been watching me sleep? My cheeks flushed at the
thought. I cleared the grogginess from my throat, pressing
my hand there to feel as my pulse returned to normal. "Yes,
thank you."

He hummed, and the sound rumbled through my chest
as his body remained still, like a gravestone in the cemetery.
His head tilted slightly to the side, studying me more
intently than I had expected this early in the morning.

"Did you?" I asked, disliking the silence and the attention. Belatedly, I wondered if an old childhood habit of talking in my sleep had recurred. My cheeks further reddened at the thought and what I could have possibly said to result in this much attention.

"I rarely sleep," he said. His boot thumped against the floors as he straightened and stood before I could ask what kept him awake at night. "We need to go somewhere before we go to your parents' house this evening."

"Where?" I asked, still standing awkwardly beside the bed. Without waiting for an answer, I bent down to pick up my bag at the foot of the bed. I set it down on the blanket, careful not to make eye contact with Alexander as I pulled out a clean dress.

"There is a bookstore here," he said. "I need to speak with the owner."

There was only one bookstore in the Hollow, and I could not imagine the Headless Horseman ever speaking with the owner. Even most of the townspeople avoided speaking with the owner beyond placing orders for the books they needed. The owner, Priscilla, was a powerful water witch who many people found abrasive as she always spoke her mind, a trait not well-received in the Hollow. I thought Priscilla was a pleasant woman, and she was very close with Henry. I had spoken with her on several occasions, picking up books for Henry, Ciara, or for myself. We'd never spoken at length, at least not on anything important. Nevertheless, I couldn't fathom what she would have that would interest the Horseman.

My brows furrowed. "Why do you need to speak with Priscilla?"

He arched one of his brows, surprise clear. "You know Priscilla?"

"I am a resident of Sleepy Hollow, and I do read," I said dryly. Sleepy Hollow was a small town, and although I may have been sheltered, I was not a complete recluse. "I have been to the bookstore before. What do you need to speak to her about?"

"Get dressed and you can see for yourself." He nodded down at the mossy green dress in my hands. As he headed to the door to give me some privacy, he paused and glanced over his shoulder. "That color looks nice on you, Katrina."

My eyes widened at the compliment, but before I could respond, he slipped out of the room and pulled the door closed softly behind him. Scrambling, I pulled the gray dress I had slept in over my head and tugged on the green one, letting it settle over my body. It was a good color on me, though I had not been expecting Alexander to tell me that, especially not after the obvious regret he felt for losing control over his magic around me.

I was both proud of and sad at how easy it was to shove down my embarrassment over the rejection, but now was certainly not the time to moon over the Horseman—no matter how distractingly attractive he was, or how closely he watched me.

Rolling my shoulders and taking a deep breath, I smoothed my hands over the fabric, calming my nerves as much as I was calming the wrinkles. My feet remained rooted to the floor as I stared at the door, knowing I should leave the room but unable to take a step forward all the same.

A soft knock pulled my focus back into the room, and the door pushed open. The Horseman's broad shoulders filled the doorway, and his brows raised as he looked at me. "Are you ready to leave?"

I felt heat rise in my cheeks as I nodded. "Yes, I apologize for taking so long."

He frowned. "You did not take long. There is no need to apologize."

"Let's go," I said, smoothing my hands over my stomach again before wringing them together.

The room was stifling and felt ever smaller by Alexander's presence.

He held his arm out, inviting me to leave the room first. "I take it you know where we are going?"

I nodded, reviewing the path in my head. He ran into the back of me as I stopped short. The touch made me jump slightly, but his gloved hands reached down, grabbing my waist to steady me. "My apologies. I was just thinking, should we ask for directions to keep up our appearances?"

His hands flexed on my hips, lingering for a moment before they dropped. "You do not have to keep apologizing. You have done nothing that warrants it."

My mouth opened to apologize once more, but I closed it, biting my lip as I nodded.

"And yes, I think asking for directions is a good idea."

Somehow, I held myself together enough until we had asked the innkeeper for directions. Stepping up to the book-shop entrance, I clenched my fists at my side. I could do this. I could prove I was more than a naïve child, ruled by her trauma and afraid of everything. I would help save my town.

Entering the shop, the small bell to the side of the door-frame swung back and forth, no doubt signaling an alert I couldn't hear. Shelves lined the walls in every direction, and a pair of plush velvet chairs sat on either side of a round wooden table near the front bay window. Smaller shelves jutted out of the middle of the room, creating a labyrinth of books. Candles and soft glowing lanterns filled the space with a welcoming light and the comforting scent of warm parchment and vanilla. Taking a deep breath, my shoulders relaxed as the tension slowly seeped out from my neck and arms.

Stepping out from behind one of the shorter shelves, Priscilla appeared with a stack of books cradled in her arms.

She smiled widely at Alexander. "Ah, welcome back."

He inclined his head in greeting. "Thank you, Priscilla."

I bit my tongue to keep my mouth from falling open at the realization that Priscilla recognized Alexander. Clearly, he'd been here more often than he'd let on. How many other people had seen him and not realized who they were looking at?

Turning away from us, she began shelving the books in her arms. "What can I help you with today, dear boy?"

"We are looking for information on the sluagh," he told her, his voice more casual than I could have ever managed. "Specifically, how one would summon and control them."

She paused, raising an eyebrow. "You never cease to surprise me. I think I have just the thing."

Hefting the remaining books in her arms to deposit them on the top of the shelf, she crooked a finger, motioning for Alexander to follow as she made for a shelf on the far back wall.

I hesitated, rocking on my feet for a moment. Alexander looked back over his shoulder, jerking his head slightly and holding his hand out for me to take.

Despite my feelings about his rejection of my advances, I was quick to take his hand, the leather of his gloves soft against my skin. I followed as we walked to the back of the store, to a shelf filled with aging books. I itched to run my fingers over their tattered spines, to read each title, giving them the attention they craved.

The witch said something as she confidently pulled book after book from the shelf. She stood with her back to me, and the pages absorbed her voice so that I could not make out the words she said.

"Yes," he replied, squeezing my hand lightly before

letting it drop. Taking the books from Priscilla's arms, he glanced at me and then answered the secret murmurings I was straining to hear. "She is."

Priscilla turned, placing a final book onto the stack Alexander was holding. She looked me over, her eyes running from my face down to my boots. The warm pools of brown landed back on my face, and she stared long enough that my body itched to move, to turn around and escape the intensity.

But I clenched my muscles and held my ground, letting her study my glamoured appearance. Her lip curled slightly, a movement so small I likely would have missed it had I not been staring at her mouth. Her chest moved with the soft grunt she let out. "Well, those books will get you started."

"Thank you, Priscilla," Alexander said, bowing at the waist as best he could while holding the seven thick books she gave him. "Do you mind if we read them here?"

"I insist upon it," she said, waving at the chairs at the front of the store. "Those books must not leave my shop."

"Of course." He set the stack on the table between the chairs. "I will return them when we are finished."

Priscilla gave me another lingering look before she turned and made her way back to the shelf she had been working on when we entered.

Taking a deep breath in through my nose, I sat down on the chair on the right, putting my hearing ear toward Alexander. I desperately wanted to speak. I needed to ask about Priscilla's reaction to me, what she said, and what books these were. But until I could learn more about Priscilla and why she looked at me with such intensity, I would hold my words back. Biting my tongue to keep the questions from spilling from my lips, I slid the top book from the stack and opened it in my lap.

"You have been quiet," Alexander murmured, picking

up his own book from the stack. He did not look at me as he pulled his gloves off and began thumbing through the pages.

The prominent veins on the backs of his hands and the strength evident beneath the skin caught my attention. His bare hands were comforting to me, and yet looking at them now, I knew without a doubt they could cause death in an instant. A shiver ran down my spine.

I cleared my throat, discreetly pinching my thigh to bring myself back to reality. "I have much experience knowing when my words would not add value to a situation."

Before I realized what was happening, his bare hand was holding my chin, tipping it up to make my eyes meet his. My heart fluttered at the sudden touch. His eyes darkened as he intensely held my gaze, studying me again. "Never say that your words do not add value."

My cheeks heated yet again, and I tried to turn my head away from his attention.

He pulled at my chin, his fingers firm and warm against my skin. "No. Look at me and listen. Your words, your thoughts, your actions—*you* have value. Never let anyone convince you otherwise. They are either ignorant or jealous."

"Thank you," I whispered, afraid that raising my voice any higher would allow an emotion to escape. Apart from Henry, no one had ever said anything this kind to me. And no one, not even Henry, had ever said it so emphatically. I almost believed his words. Almost.

Gripping the book in my lap, I tried to look back down at it to begin our research. Alexander was not having it though, and pulled my chin back up, leaning in so close I could feel his breath wash over my face, warmer than his touch. "I mean it, Katrina. You are valuable simply by existing. You burn with a fire brighter than the sun. Do not let anyone dim you."

Fighting the urge to look down, I kept his gaze, nodding once. My confidence, typically fueled by my anger, was nowhere to be found in the face of this man.

"Thank you," I said again, my voice louder this time.

He held my gaze a moment longer before nodding and releasing my chin, turning back to the book in his lap. "Good. Now, let me know if you find anything worth sharing. We have a lot of reading to do before this evening's party."

"I am all in a sea of
wonders. I doubt; I fear; I
think strange things,
which I dare not confess to
my own soul."

-Bram Stoker, Dracula

Twenty

The sun was setting, and we were on our last books, leafing through the pages with a palpable franticness. We had learned nothing valuable from our readings, much to both of our frustrations.

"I know all of this already," he muttered, mussing the carefully kept dark blond strands on his head. He turned through more pages, muttering to himself.

While I had been learning interesting information about the sluagh, including how they were formed and how they occasionally manifested as a flock of large gray birds, anything I shared with Alexander, he claimed to already know. Still, he had asked me to share anything I thought would be helpful. Though I was doubtful we would find anything before we had to leave.

Turning the page in my book, my eyes landed on something interesting. "Did you know that some think the sluagh can only roam during the night?"

His head popped up with almost comical speed. "What? No. Show me that."

Wordlessly, I passed the book over to him, tapping at the

passage in the middle of the page. "It says that direct sunlight is deadly to them, and if they are manifesting when the sun rises, they will die? Disappear? Can they truly die if they're already dead? Perhaps if the sunlight is harmful to them, my fire is as well." I rubbed my chin and pushed my fingers through my hair. "But then, why did the fog show up in the afternoon? It was overcast, certainly, but the sun was out."

"Perhaps it was overcast enough to risk. Did you see anything about whether the summoner could control or unleash them?" he asked, flipping through the pages ahead and behind the one I showed him. "Or are they at the sluagh's mercy with the rest of us?"

I shook my head. "No, nothing of that sort. Though I would imagine no one would summon something they have no control over."

He sighed, reading over the page again and again, as if it would have new information. "This is more information than we had before, I suppose."

"Perhaps we can discover something else at the party tonight," I offered, my habitual nature of placating those around me shining through. It made my jaw clench, but it was a safety mechanism that had kept me out of my mother's attention in the past.

Alexander looked at me, setting the book on the table softly. "Yes, I think we will."

Priscilla approached, having made herself scarce as we pored over the books. "Are you both finished, then?"

We stood as Alexander collected and passed the entire stack of books back to Priscilla with an easy strength. "Yes, thank you very much for allowing us to borrow these."

Her gaze passed over me, growing so cold I was surprised icicles weren't forming along her eyelashes. "You seem familiar, girl. Have you been here before?"

I opened my mouth to say yes, I had, but thankfully remembered that Alexander's magic had transformed my appearance. I cleared my throat to cover the pause. "No, I'm afraid I haven't."

I looked to Alexander for guidance, pleading to know if I should say more. His head shook minutely. I turned my eyes back to Priscilla.

She hummed, studying me for a moment longer. "I suppose not, then."

"Thank you for your hospitality, Priscilla," Alexander said again, his voice harder this time. "But we must be on our way now."

"Ah, yes," she said, an uneasy smile crossing her face. "The big party at the Van Tassels."

"Are you attending?" I asked before I could stop. I did not truly want to know, but my practiced politeness had necessitated the question leaving my lips.

She scoffed. "Certainly not. Even if I wanted to attend that ridiculous excuse to show off obscene wealth, I doubt I would be welcomed. No, better for me to just stay here with my books."

"Enjoy your evening then, Priscilla," Alexander said, placing his hand on my lower back and ushering me to the front door.

I let myself be guided out of the bookstore, focusing on the reassuring weight of his hand on my back. Tension pulsed from him in waves. For whatever reason, he wanted to leave, and he wanted to leave now. Looking back over my shoulder, Priscilla closed the door behind us, peeking out through the curtain unabashedly.

"Keep going," Alexander murmured, pressing more firmly on my back. "Before she realizes I took a book with us."

Biting the insides of my cheeks to hide my smile, I

remained quiet as we walked farther from the store. The only sound was the soft rustle of leaves in the crisp wind and the faint clopping of hooves in the distance. The sun was dipping lower in the sky, casting a soft glow between the buildings. A fog built along the grass, hovering low and kissing the damp blades. Passing an alley that smelt of burnt bread and ale, Alexander pulled us to a stop.

"You must be more careful. You almost gave it away," he snapped despite his whispered tone. "If they discover you are alive before we discover who is summoning this demon, all will be lost."

Indignation prickled through me, heating my skin as my fire licked beneath my skin, begging to be set free. "*Me?* You are the one who didn't tell me you knew her well enough for her to recognize you! We've been telling the town we just moved here, and she clearly already knows you. If she hears them talking about the new couple in town, surely, she will know. How can we trust her?"

He sighed heavily, his jaw working as if he were chewing on his words. After a moment, he inclined his head. "You are right, Katr—Katherine. I have not been holding up my end of the farse, and I apologize for being cross with you. We can trust Priscilla, though. We'll talk more back in our room, and I'll explain better."

Even though I had wanted it, the apology made me uncomfortable. Farse. That's what it was, though. Any affection I had imagined had been just that, my imagination. His earlier rejection had made that clear, and I needed to do better at remembering it.

My fire extinguished as quickly as it had come. "Thank you. Now, what do you propose we do tonight? Who should we speak with?"

"I am not as positive as you that it is your parents. Some of the Ciallmhar can be quite conniving. I would like to speak with as many of them as possible without being suspicious," he said, reaching up to rub his chin. "Have you ever been to one of these parties? What do they consist of?"

Shrugging, I tugged my sleeves over my hands, guarding them from the cool air washing through the alleyway. "I suppose it is like a normal Samhain festival. There will be a feast, a fire, and an altar for everyone to honor their ancestors. After the party is when they usually send the Roghnaithe off to... Well, off to you."

He hummed, his eyes darkening. "The party may be our best chance to speak with the Elders then. Perhaps we could even get inside the manor."

"I doubt that. My mother rarely allows anyone inside the manor during events. Too much trouble." The sky had turned a dusty purple, casting a gray haze around the Horseman's face. I sighed. If we were going to be facing down my parents, I would need time to wrap my head around it and prepare. "We should be going. The manor is a ways away and if we are late, my—Mistress Van Tassel will likely disapprove."

The Dullahan simply nodded, turning toward the mouth of the alley. He stepped away and hesitated, turning back to me and extending his gloved hand. "Would you do me the honor of allowing me to escort you... wife?"

I forced myself to ignore how my stomach flipped at the word, which was easy given it sounded as if Alexander would have rather swallowed glass than uttered the sentiment.

Reaching out, I slipped my hand into his, proud that it only shook slightly. "I would be delighted, husband."

And together, we walked to the Van Tassel manor, despite the growing pit in my stomach warning me that nothing good could come of this.

"I profess not to know how women's hearts are wooed and won. To me they have always been matters of riddle and admiration."

- *Washington Irving, The Legend of Sleepy Hollow*

Twenty-One

As we approached the Van Tassel manor, the noise of the gathering crowd began to filter out into the night air. Smoke rose over the roof from behind the mansion, casting dark tendrils into the graying sky. Evening mist was gathering, cool and damp against my skin. The front of the manor itself was as daunting as the idea of facing my mother in mere moments. Large windows gaped like a monster with its maw opened, and candles flickered on the banisters inside, adding to the menacing effect.

"Do you know where we're going?" Alexander asked, jarring me from my silent agony as I studied the home I had grown up in. The home that was my prison. My tomb.

I stared at the house a moment longer before tearing my gaze from it and turning to Alexander. "Yes, I apologize. There is a path to take us to the back. That's where they'll gather."

He moved closer to the path I had pointed at, pausing, and holding his hand out to me. "Are you ready?"

I was far from ready, and yet, something about seeing that gloved hand outstretched made me feel like I could make it through this event. Taking a deep breath, I nodded and set my hand in his. Alexander's fingers closed around mine, squeezing gently before letting our joined hands fall between us. We turned down the path lined with perfectly manicured steppingstones and made our way around the side of the house.

The party echoed around the manor, voices bouncing off the stone walls and filtering in from the falling night. The night grew brighter as we approached, the bonfire well stoked and breathing its flames up into the darkening sky. Soon, it would be the only light.

"Ah, welcome!" my mother greeted, her arms opening wide. Those who knew her well knew the smile plastered on her face was fake. "Alexander and Katherine Elizabeth, welcome to my home."

"It is a beautiful estate," Alexander said by way of greeting, inclining his head. I plastered a polite smile on my face, nodding in agreement.

"Yes, it truly is." She smiled at her home. "Now, you must tell me more about yourselves. You came from Virginia, you said?"

"Yes, near Williamsburg," he replied. I was grateful he at least knew our cover story, though I was irritated he decided not to share it with me. I hoped no one would ask me anything directly if we got separated.

"And you were run off? How did they discover you were supernaturals?" She appeared genuinely concerned, but I knew better. My mother was incapable of concern for anyone, save herself and Sleepy Hollow. She was really asking if we had been pursued.

I saw Alexander's hesitation, but he covered it flawlessly as he nodded and began to speak. "There were some shifters who had caught the attention of the town several months ago, so it was already a restless time. One of our neighbors, I believe, suspected us, and we found out he had been spying on our house and witnessed us using our magic through the curtains."

"Mundanes truly have no shame," she said, her lip curling in disgust.

"It's only fear." Alexander shrugged. "There is no reason to blame them for a natural human response to something they do not understand."

"They are beneath us," my mother sniffed. "They *should* fear us. They should also leave us alone."

"No being is beneath another," he said without a trace of disagreement in his tone. I was too familiar with the fake smile he had pasted on his face, but his emotional control still impressed me. I was barely holding onto mine at my mother's answering sneer. Alexander tracked it, his hand tightening around mine, but the smile on his face only widened. "But I do understand the reason for these sanctuaries existing, and my wife and I are endlessly grateful for them."

"Well, we are pleased to have you join us." Irritation flashed in her eyes, but she covered it quickly. Disagreeing with her was the quickest way to provoke her ire.

I couldn't take any more of this, these forced pleasantries while Alexander worked up to asking questions.

"Excuse me," I mumbled, interjecting in a pause in their conversation. "I am going to go pay my respects at the altar."

They both nodded, but Alexander's eyes lingered on mine for a moment before turning back to my mother and resuming his conversation.

"So, Loralai," Alexander started as I walked over to the altar. It was far enough away from my mother that I could finally breathe again, but still close enough that I could hear their conversation if I was focusing on them. I took a deep breath and focused on Alexander's voice, running my hands over my stomach and smoothing my dress. "Tell me about the town's history, if you wouldn't mind."

My mother was likely preening under his attention, but I didn't dare turn my head to look, instead focusing on the figurines and offerings people had left for their ancestors. Her voice faded out as she talked about the town. While Alexander had her focus, perhaps I could sneak inside the house. My mother was smart, but she would keep anything she had in her study—a room that was always forbidden to me.

"Katherine Elizabeth, was it?" The voice came from my left, startling me out of my thoughts. Adelaide. Looking around, Edmund was nowhere to be found. The seer and I were alone. Wonderful.

"Yes, and you are Adelaide, correct?" I said, feigning a smile.

"You and your husband seem like nice people," she started, tilting her head as she studied me. "I suggest you go back to where you came from."

The hairs on the back of my neck rose. "Pardon me?"

"Sleepy Hollow will not be safe for much longer," she muttered, her eyes staring off into the distance above the altar. "You should make plans to travel."

"We were told this was a haven," I said, keeping up my pretense despite the thundering of my heart at the implications her words held. "Is that not true?"

"It was true. But it will not be true very soon." She reached out and patted my hand as if she could clearly see where it was resting on the altar. "Trust me, dear. You seem like too nice of a girl to stay here for what is brewing. Take your husband and leave. Quickly."

"What is brewing, exactly?" I asked, narrowing my eyes at her. One thing I despised most about the members of the

Ciallmhar was their collective propensity to speak in riddles. "Speak plainly, please."

She smiled. "Something that has been coming for a long time."

And with that, she patted my hand once more and turned, disappearing into the crowd. I needed to get inside the manor. Now. Whatever Adelaide was alluding to was clearly frightening her enough to warn complete strangers to leave the town she'd dedicated her life to.

Chewing on my lip, I studied the party, thinking through the best way to get inside. Asking for something to drink or eat wouldn't work, given the platters of food and pitchers spread across the tables. For a moment, I considered if Alexander's glamor would hold if I was in the house, but since he'd not told me the distance it would work in, I had to take that risk. If it faded, I had to trust that I could get back outside without being seen.

Taking a deep breath, I leaned into my anxiety and every emotion I had ever pushed down, recalling how they felt coursing through my body. I focused on the speed of my breathing and wrung my hands together, darting my eyes back and forth as I pretended to be looking for an escape. Small steps, shifting to move to the house, and then back, turning toward the forest, and then back to the party.

Dragging my hands through my hair, I focused on the physical sensations, trying to keep my pretend emotions from turning into real ones. I was safe here, with Alexander, despite the proximity to my mother.

A hand on my shoulder pulled a genuine yelp from my lips as I whirled.

"Oh, I am so sorry, miss," Niamh, one of the maids, said, pressing her hand to her chest. "You looked like you were in distress. Can I help you with something?"

This was my chance. "Uh, um, I think I just need a

moment. Is there somewhere I can just take a moment to myself?" I darted my eyes back to the forest. "I was going to step aside, but..." I bit my lip and wrenched my hands together, lowering my voice and my eyes. "I'm afraid of the dark and don't want to go away from the house."

Niamh hummed sympathetically, reaching out to pat my arm. "Oh, of course, miss. Here, come with me. You can take a moment in the bathing room to gather your thoughts."

I widened my eyes, forcing myself to grasp her hands. "Oh, thank you so much. I—I don't know what happened, I just got... I got..."

She smiled at me, tugging me into the house through the servant's entrance. "It's all right, miss. It happens to the best of us. Sometimes we just need a moment to collect ourselves. It's nothing to fear."

I returned the smile, following her through the familiar halls to the bathing room on the ground floor next door to my mother's study. "Thank you, truly."

"Let me get you some water while you take a moment." She squeezed my arm once more before turning and heading off.

Opening the bathing room door, I lingered in the doorway until Niamh disappeared around the corner and quickly changed my path, slipping into the study and closing the door behind me. Pausing at her desk, I looked over the layout of the papers, ensuring I could put everything back the way it was before picking up the first stack of papers.

Letters.

I recognized my mother's neat handwriting as I scanned through the pages. She hadn't listed a name in the salutation, but the more of the letter I read, the colder I got.

I fear Katrina has evaded her fate, though she remains

shrouded from my scrying. My magic is searching for her, and I am certain it will find her soon. Rest assured, she will be dealt with before Samhain, as promised. She does not know her true potential, nor the realities of her status as Roghnaithe, though I suspect...

The letter stopped there.

I read over the partially finished words, committing it to memory before setting everything back down and rushing back out to the bathing room just as Niamh's shoes clicked down the hall.

Leaning against the other side of the door, I slowed my breathing and pinched at my cheeks to bring color back to them. With one more deep breath, I pulled the door open, coming face to face with Niamh.

"Oh, good," she said, pressing the water into my hands. "You look much better now."

"Thank you," I said, honesty shining through my words as I tried to suppress the shaking of my hands and the pounding of my heart. She had helped me more than she knew. But now we both needed to get out of the manor before my mother returned. I needed to get back to Alexander and tell him what I'd found.

"Niamh!"

My thoughts had summoned her. Niamh's face went pale. I sympathized.

"Yes, my lady?" she responded.

"What are you doing in here? We need more food outside, now!"

I squeezed Niamh's hand. "Go," I whispered. "I can get back outside without her seeing. Thank you."

She smiled and mouthed, *thank you,* as she turned and bustled off to intercept my mother. I watched until she disappeared before making my way back outside.

A hand wrapped around my arm as soon as I returned to

the party, pulling me into the shadows. I bit my tongue as I faced Alexander.

"Where did you go?" he hissed.

"We need to go," I said, keeping my voice soft.

He opened his mouth, likely to argue with me, but something caught his attention over my head. Before I could turn to see what it was, his hands left my arms and one wound around my waist while the other tipped my chin up. And then his lips crashed to mine.

Sparks shot down my spine, branding my skin where he touched me. His lips moved against mine as his thumb caressed my chin until I was pulled from my shock and kissed him back. The rest of the party—the rest of the world faded around me. All I could focus on was his lips against mine, his hand on my face, and his touch on my hip.

Alexander's hands tightened, and the kiss deepened. My hands moved to his hair, gripping softly and tilting my head back to press us closer together. A groan rumbled through his chest, vibrating through me.

A soft cough behind us pulled us back to reality. His hands left my body as if I had burned him, and it took all my willpower not to look down and ensure I wasn't on fire. The kiss clouded my mind, and all I could do was stand there and stare at him. He lifted his hand to his mouth, wiping at his lips with the back of his sleeve. My stomach twisted at the sight. He was wiping *me* away.

"Apologies." Alexander's voice was like warm honey, but his words cut like icy rain. "We got carried away."

"Quite all right," my mother said from behind me, on my left side thankfully.

I fought to keep my body from stiffening as I turned and stepped next to Alexander, keeping a good distance between us as I found my boots the most interesting thing I'd ever seen. Alexander said something else to her, and though I heard it, my brain didn't quite register what the words were.

I followed them as we all moved back to the party. The kiss was still burning at my skin, etched into my lips. It was all I could think about. I needed to get it together. It had been a distraction to keep my mother from questioning why we were away from the party. I knew that, and yet... something in me had hoped. For one brief second, I had hoped that he was kissing me just because he had wanted to.

Shaking my head, I tuned back into the conversation between Alexander and my mother. Now was no time for fantasies. Especially not when he was clearly unaffected by our kiss.

"Well, the way Sleepy Hollow is protected is unique. Different from other havens," she said. I fought back a grimace at the unadulterated pride in her voice. "Sleepy Hollow was founded around a natural magical ward that only allows those with magic to enter." Her voice dropped to a conspiratorial whisper I had to strain to hear. "Spirits protect our haven, and they demand payment for the protection."

"Payment?" Alexander asked. I was impressed with how well he faked the curiosity in his voice, as if he were hearing this for the first time. "Do you mean a tithe?"

Oh, how I wished to turn and see my mother's expression at that moment as she explained to a stranger that they sent innocent people to their death each year in a vain attempt to appease spirits who did not want their sacrifices.

"Not exactly," she said slowly, her voice back to its normal volume. "Each year, a person is offered to the spirits in exchange for their continued protection."

"A sacrifice, then." Alexander's voice was blunt as he spoke.

"Yes, quite right. It is an honor in the town to be chosen as the sacrifice each year."

I could not take anymore, and turning away from the altar, I made my way back to Alexander's side. "Your altar is lovely, Mistress Loralai."

"Why thank you, Katherine," she said, sniffing lightly. She turned her attention back to Alexander as if I had not interrupted. "As I was saying, it truly is an honor amongst the town people to be chosen. Why, even this year, my husband and I chose our own daughter to go to the spirits."

The hand Alexander had placed on my lower back twitched. "You chose your own daughter? Willingly?"

"To keep the town safe, yes," my mother said, her face hardening at his obvious disgust. I couldn't breathe, couldn't move. Knowing it was my mother's choice was one thing, but hearing her admit it and be prideful about it was another thing entirely. "As I said, it is an honor to be chosen to help protect Sleepy Hollow."

Alexander's disapproval was palpable. "Well, I suppose we will leave you to attend to your other guests. Thank you for your hospitality."

"You are leaving?" My mother's eyes narrowed, an unnaturally cold breeze washing over us. For a moment, I feared she would attempt to stop us from leaving. "The ceremony has not yet begun."

"Yes, I believe we are," he said, his voice smooth and polite in the face of my mother's barely contained rage. "Please, enjoy the rest of your evening."

Without another word, he turned and guided us away with a confidence I desperately wished I had. He bunched his shoulders around his ears and his grip tightened on my elbow slightly. Purple haze smoked out from his gloves, a clear sign of his dwindling control.

Approaching the front of the manor, I pulled us to a

stop. "What are you doing? We have not spoken to everyone here yet."

"You wanted to leave earlier." His expression was unreadable as he extricated himself from my grip and continuing his path away from my home, his steps quick but determined. "We are leaving, Katrina. Now."

Huffing, I picked up the ends of my dress and hurried after him. So much for working together to discover who was summoning the sluagh. Once again, I was dismissed by the Dullahan.

"I knew nothing but
shadows and I thought
them to be real."

-Oscar Wilde,
The Picture of Dorian Gray

Twenty-Two

He continued into the woods, stopping only once we were surrounded by trees. Whirling around, his eyes so dark they were nearly black. "You did not say that your mother was the one to choose you as my sacrifice."

"What importance does that hold?" I asked, immediately growing defensive and crossing my arms across my chest. I had hidden nothing from him and resented the implication hidden in his words. "It was never a choice if it was between my life or the town. I told you that. Why is this a shock to you?"

"It makes quite a difference for your own mother to condemn you to death, Katrina." He spoke as if I were a child who had failed to understand some complex topic. It brought me back to conversations with my mother. "It would have helped me understand what we were truly getting into here. Before, I thought you were merely..."

"Merely what?" I demanded, my icy voice a stark contrast to the fire building in my veins. "Merely being dramatic? That I truly hated my parents for no reason and thought they would summon the sluagh for my own amusement?"

His silence was answer enough.

I scoffed. "You truly believe I am that much of a child that I could attempt to convince you my parents were summoning a horde of murderous spirits for no other reason than I was *angry with them?* Do you truly think so little of me?"

He did not reply.

"Let me tell you about my childhood, Alexander. From the moment I was born, I was a disappointment to my parents, and my status in their eyes only went down from there. From the moment I could speak, and my hearing defect was discovered, I was a shame to my parents. From the moment of my first magic lesson where I could not do as my mother instructed, I was a burden to my parents."

He opened his mouth to speak, but I kept going.

"My mother has *never* held me. Not once in my entire life. The only touch I ever got from her was in anger. My father is a spineless man who bends to her every whim. I was never loved. The only affection I have ever received as a child was from my governess, who my mother fired and banished from Sleepy Hollow when she thought I was growing too reliant on her. The only love I have ever known comes from an old man named Henry, who took me in and taught me how to make pottery. The only gift I was ever given came from him. The only comfort I was ever shown came from him."

My chest was heaving, and my hands were engulfed in flames, illuminating the surrounding darkness. Taking a deep breath, I willed the fire back inside me, plunging us back into the night while my eyes adjusted to the nearly full moon's light. The only sound around us was my panting and the rustling of crisp leaves.

"I apologize, Katrina," Alexander said, his voice careful and quiet.

"What are you sorry for, Horseman? For your words? Your assumptions? Or for kissing me?" I asked, my anger still simmering, though I had successfully put the lid back on it. I had never let my anger out so freely, had never let my words go with such abandon. It felt like a weight had been lifted from my chest, like I could breathe freely, even though a part of me still feared reprisal. "Simply saying you are sorry is not adequate. You must mean it, and to mean it, you must admit what you have done."

"Of course," he agreed, nodding. He reached a hand out to me. I hesitated for a moment, but gave mine to him. I was woman enough to admit that despite my anger, his touch was welcomed, even through his thick gloves. He smiled slightly. "Thank you. I apologize for assuming you were intentionally hiding that your parents chose you for the sacrifice. And I apologize for implying that you were being childish in your suspicions of them. It was wrong of me."

"Yes, it was," I agreed. As angry as I was over his assumptions, I did not enjoy the feeling. I knew I was sheltered and naïve in some aspects of life, but I was far beyond what was considered an adult here, and I did know what I was talking about. Part of me noticed he hadn't apologized for kissing me, but I'd had enough disappointment tonight to bring that up. "I need you to take me seriously, Alexander."

"I do take you seriously, Katrina," he said, squeezing my hand. "I am sorry. It was wrong of me to say those things."

"Why did you?" I could not help but ask, my shoulders slumping. Since he had rescued me, the Dullahan had been kind. This was out of character. Perhaps I did not truly know him, but I felt compelled to ask. He studiously had not mentioned the kiss, and so I wouldn't either. The lack of acknowledgement was clear enough of a message. "And did you truly mean them?"

"Of course I didn't mean them." He hesitated, studying me. "I suppose it struck a personal chord, hearing that your own parents were honored by killing their only daughter."

Now it was my turn to fall silent. Alexander had been private about himself, only divulging information to provide context to our research. Despite my curiosity, I could not bring myself to ask the questions lingering on my tongue.

Alexander stepped closer to me, folding our joined hands in the narrowing space between our bodies. In the cool of the night, his body radiated heat.

"No child deserves to feel unloved by their parents." His thumb traced over my cheek. The touch extinguished the rest of my anger like a bucket of water poured over a smoldering fire.

"You've said that before. I am sensing there is a story," I said, my voice as quiet as his touch, afraid that if I spoke too loudly, I would fracture the tenuous peace between us. My curiosity had never been easily sated, and this tender moment between us made me want to know more about the man behind the Headless Horseman legend. This insight into his childhood was intriguing.

He sighed, pulling his hand away from my face, though he did not step away. "We should get back to the inn. The night is cold, and there is no need for us to continue conversing in the woods. I will tell you my story once we are inside."

It was clear he was looking for an excuse to put off my questions, perhaps to build his nerve. I understood that. "Let us get back then."

Though we had both said we would leave, neither of us moved.

Alexander's eyes flicked down to my mouth, and I tracked every single twitch of his eyes. While I desperately wanted to kiss him again, the rejection of the first time I had initiated the contact and the dismissal after our kiss at the manor still burned in the back of my mind. I would not be so foolish to open myself up for that hurt again. Gathering strength I had not known I had, I dropped my hand from his and stepped back.

I would not be rejected again, and Alexander had made himself clear before. The only thing between us was the mutual desire to save Sleepy Hollow from being devoured by the sluagh.

"We should be off." My throat felt thick, and I could only hope it did not sound obvious.

After another moment of neither of us moving, he nodded and stepped back, clasping his hands behind himself. "Yes, we should."

Silently, we left the forest and made our way back into town and to our shared room at the inn. The silence was agonizing as we walked, and I wanted nothing more than to ask a dozen questions.

Finally, the door to our room closed behind us, and I sighed in relief.

"Are you all right, Katrina?" Alexander asked, pausing to lock the door behind us.

My face flushed. "Yes, simply grateful to be back here, away from the manor."

He nodded and finished securing our room. Leaning back against the door, he unlaced his boots, pulling them off and setting them beside the door. Still watching me, he removed his coat and hung it from the hook on the wall. "Sit, Katrina. Take off your shoes and get comfortable. This story is not a happy one, as I am certain you have guessed."

Following his lead, I sat on the bed, removing my boots

and setting them beneath the bed. My dress was comfortable enough, having not donned a corset beneath it. Reaching up, I pulled the pins holding my hair back and shook it loose as the relief on my scalp thrummed through me. Moving further up the bed, I patted the space beside me. "You can sit down, Alexander."

He hesitated, but sat down next to me, his eyes fixed firmly on the wooden planks of our floor. "I told you before that the Dullahan are the children of Death."

I nodded, unsure if he wanted a response, but giving him one anyway. "Yes, I remember."

The sigh he let out moved through his whole body, and his shoulders fell. "Death created us, but Death did not raise us. All Dullahan are given to human parents to raise—servants, humans, and sometimes even other paranormals that were in debt to Death in some way. I was sent here, to a family of paranormals that lived in the area before the War for Independence. My adoptive mother left when I was an infant. According to my adoptive father, she decided she did not actually want to be a mother any longer. He raised me and taught me how to be a good man. It was hard, being a soldier and a father to an infant at the same time. He tried to balance caring for a child with his duties, but it was hard, and I was often alone, much like you."

"Your father fought in the war?" I kept my voice as soft as possible.

"Yes, he did." He nodded with a heavy sigh, pulling his gloves off and tossing them onto the bed. "As I grew older, he took me with him when he could, teaching me how to be a good soldier, talking about how to control my magic when it came in. This was before Death came for me, but we had to do something to keep from attracting attention. He taught me discipline, control, and I was able to keep my magic reigned in until I received formal training. But the distraction of worrying about a child at home took its toll. My father went out one night to patrol the land, and he was killed. I only found out when he was not there the next morning."

"How did he die?" I wanted to reach out and take his hand to comfort the obvious hurt on his face as he recalled his loneliness.

"He died during the war, but not in battle." I didn't push—didn't breathe as I waited for him to continue. "I was only a boy then, and though it was early in the war, it was still hard to continue without him. My magic settled in shortly after his death."

"How were you expected to learn your magic, then?" I asked. "If you were alone, who taught you?"

"Death knows when our magic settles in and takes us for training. I trained with Death for several years. But time passes differently in the Otherworld—"

"You've been to the Otherworld?" I asked. My cheeks burned as I realized what I'd done. "Apologies. Please, continue."

"Anyway, he didn't die during a battle. Sleepy Hollow sent people hunting down a rogue mage. When they ran across my father, walking our land to ensure its safety, they overreacted and killed him." His voice was hollow, as if he'd recited the words enough so they no longer elicited emotion in him. They were just facts he was repeating now.

I had no words. Nothing I could say would comfort him. My teeth dug into my lower lip, trying to keep it from trembling or falling open in horror. This was about Alexander, not me. I didn't want him to try to comfort me, or to stop sharing his story.

He sighed again, the movement slumping his shoulders, a far cry from the careful posture he'd always carried himself with. "I do not know all the details of that night. I still haven't discovered who from the town took his life. All I know is that he is dead, and I became an orphan at fourteen years old and went back to Death to learn my magic, without a parent."

He ran a hand over his face roughly. "So, I apologize for my anger earlier, but hearing that your parents—your mother—willingly sent you to die brought back some of those feelings."

"I understand," I murmured. My fingers itched to reach out and soothe him, but I forced myself back. The moment he knew he was upsetting me—never mind that I was upset for him—he would stop. The look of sorrow on his face, even in the candlelight, was heartbreaking. "I apologize for my anger, too."

"Thank you." He inclined his head and offered a small smile. Politeness, I recognized. "Tomorrow, we should venture to talk to Cyrus. I would like to go back to the bookstore, too."

"Of course," I agreed, still observing his face.

He shifted to turn and face me, bending one of his legs up onto the bed. "You are a strong woman, Katrina. And your value is not held in the thoughts of others. I want you to know that."

This time, I did not hold myself back. I reached across the bed and took hold of his hand, squeezing gently. "And your value is not held in the town's view of you."

"Thank you, Katrina." He smiled, albeit a bit sadly, but returned the squeeze to my hand. The smile fell from his face, and his eyes dropped to my lips once more. His tongue darted out to lick his lips and his eyes returned to mine, smoldering with a darkness that should have made me nervous, but instead made my skin vibrate with anticipation. "Can I kiss you, Katrina? Please?"

Unable to speak, unable to breathe, I nodded.

Desperately. In that moment, I did not care that I might get my heart broken. All I wanted was to feel his lips against mine again. There was no one here, nothing to interrupt us or to use as an excuse. He was kissing me because he wanted to. And I wanted it as well.

Alexander's hand came to the side of my face. The touch was soft, though the kiss that followed was anything but. Our lips met, and I was lost, spinning in the sensation. My eyes slid shut, and it only intensified the experience.

A groan vibrated through him, moving from his chest and into mine from the bridge of our lips. His hand flexed on my face, moving to tangle into my hair. The tug he gave had me responding with a groan of my own, and the kiss only escalated. The hand in my hair tipped my head back, deepening the kiss as he shifted closer to me on the bed.

"Katrina," he sighed, his breath fanning against my lips as he pulled back to rest his forehead against mine.

"What?" I asked, my voice hoarse. I desperately wanted to lean back in and initiate our kiss again. So I did.

He responded by pulling at my hair to tip my head back, beginning a path down my cheek and over my jaw line before descending to my neck. A breath puffed against my neck, and suddenly both of my hands were being pulled away into one of his. "We should stop, Katrina."

"Why?" I asked, leaning back to get a better look at his face. His hair was mussed, and his lips swollen, and he looked more beautiful than any creature I had ever seen. I could kiss him for an eternity and drown in his eyes happily. "I don't want to stop."

"I don't either, which is why we should." He sighed again, and with the same easy strength, moved away from me on the bed. "We have more important things that need our attention."

"Surely there is nothing we can accomplish tonight," I

said, desire still pulsing through my blood, unfamiliar yet intoxicating.

He leaned over and kissed me again, gently this time, a mere press of lips against each other. "Let us get through this alive, then we shall revisit this conversation, yes?"

I held his gaze for a moment. The only reason I could stop the snarky reply was the desire swirling in his smoke-blue eyes. A desire I was certain mirrored in my own eyes.

"I shall hold you to that, Dullahan."

He smiled. "I would expect nothing less."

No more words passed between us as we prepared for bed, changing our clothes separately. I climbed into the bed, facing the window as Alexander extinguished the lamp. The bed dipped as he climbed in behind me.

"Blessed Samhain, Alexander," I whispered into the darkness.

His arms tightened around me, and he pressed a kiss to the top of my head. "Blessed Samhain, Katrina."

For a moment, I let myself be lulled into thinking that I could find peace and happiness, here in the arms of the rider of death. I let myself find comfort in his warmth and drifted off to sleep. Tomorrow, we would continue our search for the summoner.

"There are chords in the hearts of the most reckless which cannot be touched without emotion."

-Edgar Allan Poe,
Masque of the Red Death

My heart was thundering in my chest as I stood in front of Priscilla's bookstore. When I woke, Alexander was already up and dressed, leaning against the wall, and waiting for me, his eyes watching my every move with an indifference that opposed the intensity churning in them the night before. He had quietly informed me he would drop me off at Priscilla's and then go to see Cyrus alone.

He didn't say why, and though I didn't ask, I did not need him to say the words. The pinch of his brow and the strained muscles in his neck as he ran his hand over his chin had told me all I needed to know. He didn't think it was safe. He either didn't think I was strong enough to take care of myself or didn't think I would be able to control my magic in light of whatever information Cyrus shared. I didn't need him to tell me which one it was. Both were equally enraging.

I had dressed in silence, nodding my agreement, and followed him to Priscilla's.

Pushing the door open, we entered. The wave of old parchment was comforting.

"You have returned," Priscilla called, stepping out from between shelves. "Good. What can I do for you today?"

"You know I trust you, don't you, Priscilla?" Alexander asked, his tone grave and his brow low.

"Of course, Alexander," Priscilla said, pressing a hand to her chest, clearly both offended and confused by the question. "You know that you can trust me with anything. I would never tell a soul anything you share with me."

"I am going to leave my friend here with you for the day," he said, his hand moving to my lower back to urge me toward the suspicious woman. "I have had her glamoured, and when I remove that magic, you will recognize her. I need your word that you will protect her while I am gone."

My heart sped up, sweat beading, and rolling down my spine. I had forgotten that the glamor would only exist if the Dullahan was near me. While Alexander seemed content to take Priscilla's word for her trustworthiness, I was more skeptical. Would she turn me in to my parents? My breath quickened in time with my heart.

Priscilla eyed me, her sharp gaze traveling from my head down to my boots before she let it fall back to Alexander. "You have my word. Who are you, girl?"

The Horseman waved his hand and my skin tingled as the magic fell, my ears popping uncomfortably. Reaching up to rub at my right ear to ease the ache, I watched Priscilla's eyes widen. Slowly, I let my hand fall back to my side. Blood thundered in my ears.

"Katrina," she breathed. Her eyes softened from the suspicious narrowed gaze she'd had since Alexander spoke. "Does Henry know you're alive?"

"Who is Henry?" Alexander asked, his voice sharp as he looked between Priscilla and me.

Now, the hard gaze of the bookkeeper landed on him. "Henry is an earth mage who owns a pottery shop. He's Katrina's employer."

"How is he?" I murmured, unsure if I truly wanted to hear the answer.

Her eyes flicked back to me, offering me a small smile. "He is sad, as you would expect, but he is a resilient old man. How are you alive, child? They said you were sent to the Dullahan."

Now it was my turn to hesitate. Did she know that Alexander was the Dullahan?

I looked up at him questioningly.

He sighed, reaching up to run a hand through his hair as he hesitated. Finally, he sighed again, rolling his shoulders back and straightening his jacket. "Priscilla, I am the Dullahan."

"I beg your pardon?" Her voice could have cut glass. "Alexander Brannon, you had better be pulling my leg, boy."

"I am not." His spine was rigid and the discomfort coming off him made my skin itch. "And as much as I would enjoy explaining this to you, I have somewhere else I need to be."

Her eyes narrowed once more. "Do not dismiss me. I expect you to return and answer every single one of my questions."

He bowed his head. "Of course. Now, will you please protect Katrina while I am gone? No one can know she is alive."

"I would protect her even if it was not you asking me. I owe that much to Henry," she said, waving a hand at Alexander. "Go on and do what you need to do. We will be fine here."

"Alexander." I needed to speak before I lost my nerve.

"Can I come with you?"

His face hardened, and he stepped up in front of me, wrapping a hand around my elbow as he guided me away from Priscilla and toward the corner of the room. "No. I need you to stay here. Where it's safe."

"I can protect myself."

"That's not what I'm concerned about."

My eyebrows furrowed. "Then what? What is it? Last night, we agreed we would both go to Cyrus. What's changed?"

He sighed, running a hand through his hair. Stepping closer to me, his breath washed over my face. "The risk is if someone sees us on our way to his home. I can disguise myself in the spirit realm until I get there, and I plan to speak with him in my spirit form, so he cannot see my face. I cannot do that to you, Katrina. You will always have either your true face or the one from my glamor. And if anyone sees us going to Cyrus's together, and reports that back to your mother... our plans will be over before they even begin. We cannot have them be suspicious of us both."

My mouth opened and closed as I searched for an argument, but I couldn't find any. He was right, and I hated it. My cheeks burned, but I had to try once more. I needed the answers that Cyrus could provide to learn about my magic. "I can be stealthy, Alexander."

A small smile turned up his lips. "I have no doubt of that. For now, please ease my mind and stay here with Priscilla. We need to keep searching the books as well. Despite my suspicions, we need more information before we can say with certainty it is the sluagh. I want to be sure, with no doubt, what is being summoned here before we confront anyone. Find us that, Katrina. Help me discover that."

Pursing my lips, I raised my chin to meet his eyes.

"Please?"

The furrow of his brow, set over wide eyes that fixed on me so intently I might drown in the sea of gray-blue.

Exhaling, the fight left my body. I slumped down, crossing my arms and brushing against his stomach. "Fine. But I want to know everything he says when you return. Everything, Alexander. No matter how small."

"Of course." He bowed his head. Then he reached up and tucked a strand of hair behind my ear. Turning to Priscilla, who was watching us with an amused grin from her spot by the bookshelves, he raised his voice. "I'll be back later. Both of you stay safe."

Priscilla bowed her head but didn't say anything else.

The hesitation in his steps was clear, but after a moment of looking back and forth between us, he nodded and left the bookshop without another word. Priscilla followed him to the door, locking it behind him. He didn't turn back once as he moved down the road into town.

Turning back to me, she draped an arm around my shoulders, guiding me to sit on the chairs at the front of the shop. "Now, Katrina. You must tell me everything."

I hesitated, unsure of how much to tell her. I sank down into the plush fabric, anxiety gnawing at my stomach. Priscilla may have known Henry, but she did not know me. But if Henry trusted Priscilla enough for her to know I was supposed to have left before my death sentence, and if Alexander trusted Priscilla, I supposed I could, too. "What do you want to know?"

"You were supposed to be leaving." Her voice was much softer now that she recognized me as Henry's friend. She reached out and gently took one of my hands in between hers, patting the top of my hand soothingly. "How did you end up back here?"

"Brom saw me heading to the bridge. He grabbed me and..." I took a deep breath. "Brom pushed me over the embankment. I hit my head and fell into the water. Alexander pulled me out."

"I always knew Brom was an unsavory character," she said, tutting as she shook her head. "Anyone who does not appreciate good books is no one to be friends with, my dear."

Her words made me smile. Henry had said something similar regarding art. I could see how they got along. It made my heart squeeze, and I longed to slip into the pottery shop and hug my mentor tightly. "Yes, I agree."

She tipped her head to the side, studying me. "So why are you back, Katrina?"

My shoulders felt like they carried the weight of all the books in the shop. "Alexander said Sleepy Hollow was in danger and that I could help save it."

She pursed her lips. "This town did not care about you, and yet you care enough about it to sacrifice your own freedom. Perhaps you are more like Alexander than I thought."

"You truly did not know he was the Dullahan?" The words left my mouth before I could stop them.

She sighed, patting my hand. "I knew Alexander's father. I was friends with his mother, and when she left, I looked in on them when I could. Alexander was a sheltered boy; his father never let him come into town. For his own safety, he had said. I suppose it makes sense now. But I would visit him, bring him books, and read him stories while his father was away. He grew up, and I stopped visiting. He comes by now and then, always looking for something specific, and never staying in town long enough to be seen by anyone but me. But no, I did not know."

"Does knowing change your opinion of the Ciallmhar?"

She let out a loud and brutal scoff. "Girl, surely that is not a serious question."

I flushed under her admonishment, attempting to pull my hand back to my lap, but she held firm.

Her eyes softened. "I know you were just as sheltered as Alexander was. Differently, sure, but sheltered, nonetheless. Not everyone in this town believes the Ciallmhar is the ultimate authority. And not everyone in this town believes your mother should be in power."

"I will agree there," I muttered. "But, if there are those who disagree with the Ciallmhar, why has the Roghnaithe continued for so long?"

She raised an eyebrow. "You are more sheltered than Henry led me to believe."

My cheeks burned, but I did not try to pull away this time. My ignorance was embarrassing, but though she may chide me, there was no venom in Priscilla's words, only observation.

"Those named Roghnaithe were not randomly chosen, Katrina," she said, as though she were wary of my reaction. "They were those who spoke out against your parents and against the Ciallmhar."

All at once, I felt the overwhelming urge to vomit. My head spun, and I grasped Priscilla's hands with all I had. Her touch was grounding, but her words echoed in my head. Though I knew the Roghnaithe were not dead, it did little to ease the blow Priscilla had just delivered.

"You did not know." Her voice was a whisper, and I had to strain to hear her through the blood rushing in my ears.

I shook my head. "No, I did not. I would have—I *should* have done something."

"There was nothing you could have done, Katrina. I suspect your ignorance was intentional. You are not to blame for the deeds of your parents and the Ciallmhar." The pity in her eyes was softer than the chairs we were sitting on, but her voice was hard and brokered no arguments.

Taking a shuddering breath, I focused on Priscilla's worried eyes. I had to tell her they were not dead, that the Dullahan did not kill those who spoke out against my parents. The words stuck in my throat, but I managed to get them out all the same. "Alexander said that he does not take the Roghnaithe. He sends them somewhere safe. They are all still alive."

She smiled, the expression bursting with pride. Once, I would have killed for someone to look at me like that. "Good boy."

I nodded, unable to find any other words to say. There was nothing I could say. Nothing would ease the pain of knowing I was the product of people who sentenced their opposers to death at the hands of a mythical being. Nothing would ease the pain of knowing they were intent on sending me to that same death.

"That is quite enough of that, now," Priscilla said, patting my hand and standing in one fluid motion. "What did Alexander want us to research today?"

I took a deep breath, thankful for the change in subject. I could focus all my energy on this. "He thinks someone is trying to summon the sluagh to Sleepy Hollow. Or something else from the Otherworld."

"Someone?" She raised an eyebrow. "Does he know who?"

"I think it is my parents, but he is less sure." I stood with her, eyes roving over the massive shelves lining the walls. So many books, and I itched to go through them all to distract myself from the churning thoughts in my head. Blinking, I brought my focus back to Priscilla. "He wants to find out if it is the sluagh, or if it is something else."

"And why has he involved you?" She spoke her question cautiously, but I could see the suspicion beneath her gaze.

She wanted to know what I could do, especially after the entire town had been led to believe I had nothing to offer.

I sighed. "Alexander is under the impression that my powers will be the only thing to save Sleepy Hollow. Adelaide believes I am part of a prophecy that means I will destroy Sleepy Hollow."

She hummed, pursing her lips. "And what do you believe, child?"

I hesitated for a moment. The words I wanted to say were stuck beneath my breastbone. Clearing my throat, I freed them from my chest. "I believe that, for better or worse, Sleepy Hollow is where I belong. And I will protect those who live here."

She looked at me with the proud expression she had earlier when speaking of Alexander. "Then I believe we have some research to do, yes?"

"I believe we do."

She held out her hand to me, and together, we headed into the shelves. And for the first time in a long time, I had hope. Hope that I would succeed at *something*.

"Life, although it may only be an accumulation of anguish, is dear to me, and I will defend it."

-Mary Shelley,
Frankenstein

Priscilla and I began on opposite sides of the longest bookshelf in her shop, working our way toward each other and pulling out book after book that might help us. Books on magic, on the sluagh, on the Otherworld—anything that seemed even tangentially related to our search. The stack on the small chair between us was growing.

"I believe this is a good starting place," Priscilla said, setting two more books onto the towering stack. "Let's get through these before we search anymore."

Nodding, I dropped my hand from the books I was perusing, moving around the stack. Priscilla pressed a stack into my arms. She patted my cheek and smiled, her eyes flitting across my face before she dropped her hand. I walked back to the chairs by the windows and sat down, pulling them onto my lap. "I hope this has at least *something* we can use."

She laughed, mirroring my movements with her own stack. "We can only hope."

Both of us settled into the plush chairs and began leafing through the pages in front of us.

The endless tomes were interesting, but nothing helpful had come up. I had learned more than I had ever wanted to know about creatures of the Otherworld, enough to give me nightmares for years. Nearly an hour passed before either Priscilla, or I spoke again.

"Have you found anything useful?" she asked, looking up from the thick book in her lap. Her eyes were wide as she leaned into me, waiting for my response.

"No," I sighed, closing my book over my finger to keep my place. "Though if it is only sluagh being summoned, I think I will be immensely grateful. There are much more terrifying creatures in the Otherworld that could have been summoned."

She peered up at me, raising a brow. "Alexander only suspects the sluagh. Do not speak something worse into existence, dear girl."

My cheeks burned. "Of course. Have you found anything?"

She hummed. "Perhaps. There seems to be something about that prophecy you mentioned, but nothing certain yet."

"You know the prophecy Adelaide was speaking of?" I sat up straighter, desperate for any new information about that prophecy. "Alexander said there were too many prophecies to know which one she was referring to."

"This one seems to be the only one I've come across that could be relevant," she said, looking back down at the pages. "It mentions flames and death. I am still searching for a full translation of it, but this book only has vague references to it."

"Please let me know if you find it," I said, dread settling like a lead weight in my stomach. Flames could refer to me, but death was never something good to be associated with. Chewing on my lower lip, I turned my attention back to the book in my lap.

My mind struggled to pay attention as my thoughts slipped to what Alexander could be doing or discovering, if anything. Priscilla's earlier words about my parents also wormed their way back to the forefront of my mind. I had been blind for so long, and though Priscilla did not seem to fault me for it, I knew my ignorance was complacency. I should have pushed back sooner.

Shaking my head to clear those thoughts, I turned back to the book. I could not change the past, but I could change the future. Sleepy Hollow would not burn to ash, I would make certain of that.

After another long period of nothingness, a poem caught my attention. The words jumped out as I turned the page, dragging my eyes back to them and holding them there.

The poem detailed a dance between death and a bird of flames, chasing each other through time, only for the bird of flames to be consumed by a sentient mist and pulled beneath the earth to the Otherworld by a swarm of large black birds the size of men. The similarities to the sluagh were enough to give me pause.

"Have you heard of birds of fire?" I asked, not looking up at Priscilla as I continued reading over the poem again and again. She did not reply, and I lifted my gaze to see her looking at me contemplatively. "Priscilla? Are they actual birds or are they figurative?"

Her eyes refocused on me, and she sighed, closing her book. "I suppose that depends on who you ask. There were real birds of flames long ago—phoenixes—who served the sun goddess Brig, though one hasn't been known to exist for a long time."

"Could—" I swallowed, the words heavy on my tongue like ash. The question I wanted to ask refused to leave my lips for fear of the answer, so I settled for a different one. "This poem talks about death coming with a swarm of large black birds. Could that be the sluagh?"

Priscilla reached over and pulled the book from my hands. Her finger traced down the poem, her lips moving as she read. Once she was finished, she tapped at her chin. "It's quite possible. There are some similarities to the small pieces of the prophecy. The descriptors." She waved her hand, her words trailing off. "Let me keep looking at this. You find out more about the sluagh and what someone could hope to achieve by summoning them here."

I wanted to protest and pull that book back to comb through it myself, to be the one that found the information to save Sleepy Hollow. Instead, I nodded and opened another book, content to hide from whatever truth I might discover.

Unease gnawed at my stomach, but I ignored it, flipping through the pages of *A Comprehensive History of Creatures of the Otherworld*. It was organized as an encyclopedia, with entries on a vast array of monsters that existed in the Otherworld and their characteristics.

Turning to the S's, I began my search anew, putting the thoughts of the phoenix out of my mind. Priscilla would be more than adequate to research the prophecy, and I was uncertain I wanted to find out more.

Willful ignorance was apparently my calling.

Finding the entry on the sluagh, I settled back into the chair.

Sluagh (sla-ow): The sluagh are a host of the dead, an army of unforgiven souls who fly through the air as a host of gray birds or a thick mist. The sluagh are said to approach and pick up a person from anywhere, transporting them to their hiding place and draining the soul of its power. In instances where the humans have magical abilities, those abilities can also be taken. When summoned, the sluagh can be directed to target specific people and transfer the power drained from the target to the summoner.

While the sluagh would occasionally rescue humans from danger in old times, they are generally dangerous and deadly. If you see a large crescent swarm of gray birds, or an unnaturally thick mist, the sluagh are approaching. If possible, go inside immediately and close all windows, lining all possible entryways to your home with salt. The sluagh are only active during the night and more active as the autumn harvest begins, ushering in longer nights, though they can be summoned at any time. While the sluagh can still appear with the rising sun, they prefer the darkness of the night, which is often all that is needed to accomplish their tasks of destruction.

"Priscilla," I said, my voice trembling. "The sluagh can drain magic and transfer it to the summoner."

Her finger froze over the passage she'd been reading. After a moment, she closed the book in her lap and looked up.

"Do you really think my mother could be behind all of this?" I asked, though I feared I already knew the answer. "Could she really be this desperate for power? To risk her own magic like that?"

Standing, Priscilla approached me and rested a hand on my shoulder. "Katrina, I fear there is quite a bit you do not know about your mother."

"We have to stop her," I said. My grip on the book was the only thing keeping me grounded—the only thing keeping me from spiraling into a pit of darkness. I could not bring myself to look up at Priscilla and see the pity etched on her face. "She cannot be allowed to do this."

The hand on my shoulder squeezed lightly. "We will, Katrina. Between you and Alexander, I doubt there is little you could not accomplish once you set your minds to it."

"Is this my fault?" My voice was so quiet, even I could barely hear it. But I had to know. I had been so ignorant of my mother's influence, and I had to know if I could have prevented it.

Priscilla tugged the book from my hands, stooping down in front of me. "Katrina, no. None of this is your fault, and no one blames you. You could not have known the kind of person your mother is."

"But I did," I croaked out. My vision blurred with tears as I looked up at the older woman. "I did know. She is not a pleasant woman, and she has never loved me. I should have known there was more to it. I should have questioned. I should—"

"Shh, Katrina, shh." She shook her head, lifting her finger to my lips. "The only thing you should have done is what you did. Survive."

I opened my mouth to protest that there was still more I could have done to put a stop to her, but a scream sounded from outside the shop. The high-pitched noise filled me with horror, and my stomach dropped to my boots. "What was that?"

She stood, eyes searching the windows. "It can be nothing good."

"Should we go out there?" I asked, standing from the chair, and searching the window as well.

"You should not be going anywhere." Her voice was grave as she pointed a finger at me. "If anyone sees you, Alexander will have my head."

"We need to go see what has happened," I protested, the noise and chaos outside growing louder. Panic surged, twisting my stomach with the thought that we had stopped my mother too late from summoning the sluagh again. "We—"

"I will go," she said, her voice placating but firm. "I will see what has happened. You stay here."

Only the pointed look she gave me kept me in my spot as she pulled on her coat from the hook by the door. She unlocked and opened the noise, allowing the noise from outside in.

She pointed at the doorknob her hand was resting on. "Lock this behind me."

Following her instructions, I locked the door and immediately moved back to the window, parting the curtains carefully to peer out. Chaos was the best way to describe the scene framed by the ornate wood around the window.

People frantically moved about the square at the end of the street, their gloved hands pressed to their mouths and their eyes open wide in horror as they both hurried away from the scene and moved closer to peer at it. My eyes followed the throngs of people, and I wished they had stayed on the books.

In the square, feet rising above the low cover of mist gathered near the ground, Adelaide hung from the trees, body swaying from a rope tied across her chest and beneath her arms to loop her around the thick branches. And her eyes were missing, gaping bloody holes in their place.

Turning to the wastebasket beside the door, I vomited.

"The immediate cause, however, of the prevalence of supernatural stories in these parts, was doubtless owing to the vicinity of Sleepy Hollow. There was a contagion in the very air that blew from that haunted region ; it breathed forth an atmosphere of dreams and fancies infecting all the land..."

-Washington Irving,
The Legend of Sleepy Hollow

Twenty-Five

I couldn't be certain how long Priscilla was gone for, but my mind was spinning as I stared at the body of the Elder woman.

How could this have happened? The Ciallmhar House was protected by insanely strong wards; it did not make sense that someone could get past their protections and past Adelaide's assistant, to be able to harm her. And more, she should have seen it and been able to avoid it.

After a while, Priscilla emerged in front of the window, motioning toward the door with Alexander following closely behind her. Letting the curtains fall closed, I rushed to unlock the door, wiping at my mouth with my sleeve. I kept my eyes focused on their faces, and not the scene of pure horror that lingered behind them.

"Priscilla, was that..." I could not bring myself to finish the question as I stared beyond them out onto the bustling street. The screams subsided, but the feeling of panic permeated the town, creeping into the shop and clawing up my body, attempting to retake its hold of me.

"Yes, it was," she said, gripping my shoulders. She

turned me around and pushed at my me back inside. "Let's go now, child. Away from the doors and windows."

Alexander moved in behind her, closing and locking the door before securing the curtains over the windowpane. He filled my vision, stepping up close to me and cupping my face in his gloved hands. "Are you all right, Katrina?"

"Not even slightly," I said, my voice hoarse from vomiting. I cleared my throat, swallowing down the acidic bile still coating my tongue. "What was that?"

He blew out a harsh breath, rubbing his hand over his face. "I do not know, Katrina."

"What hap—"

I should have been with Alexander. I should have gone with him to Cyrus, to see what the man knew. His house was close enough to the Ciallmhar House, perhaps we could have intervened. Or at least we could have seen what had killed Adelaide and tried to stop it.

He shook his head, sighing again. "Not now, please. We can discuss it later."

My cheeks burned, the admonishment stinging as he walked away and talked with Priscilla in hushed tones. They kept looking up at me, but I could not hear them. I was tired of being excluded from conversations that clearly surrounded me, but I did not know how to interject myself or advocate for being included. So instead, I did what I had done my entire life, and sat down in the chair with a book.

Forcing myself to focus on the words in front of me was a futile task, though I tried desperately to continue reading, blocking out the whispers. It did not work, and Priscilla's harsher tone made me question what exactly it was they were saying about me.

Squeezing my eyes shut from burning tears, my hands balled into fists and I took a deep breath through my nose. I had gone my entire life without validation and acknowledgement; I did not need it from two strangers, though I desperately craved it.

"Katrina." Priscilla's soft voice made me open my eyes, sniffing back my tears. She moved closer to me, leaving a stiff Alexander standing at the shelves, an irritated look on his face. She bent down in front of me, taking my hands in hers. "Alexander is going to put the glamor back on you and take you back to the inn. You can come back and we will continue our research once we see what impact this is going to have on the town."

"Will you be safe here alone?" I asked. Her touch bringing my wits back about me. "You should come with us, Priscilla. Or at least go stay with Henry."

She smiled and reached up to pat my cheek. "I will be fine. I will go to Henry and ensure we are both safe. We will meet again tomorrow, after this has all settled down."

"Do not tell him I am alive, please," I whispered, though the plea tugged at every fiber of my being. "I do not want him in any danger for knowing."

"Of course." She stood, pulling me up with her. Her eyes searched my face, and she tutted softly, reaching up to wipe beneath my eyes. "There you go."

Alexander held out a hand to me. "Are you ready?"

I eyed his hand for a moment, debating whether I should take it or not. Deciding that if he truly did not want to offer it, he would not have, I placed my hand in his.

All at once, the wash of magic crashed over me, tingling against my skin. As it subsided, Alexander dropped our hands, tugging his glove back on and adjusting his coat. If I wasn't watching my hands, couldn't see for myself that my hands were not aflame, I'd have guessed I'd burned him with how quickly he dropped the touch. He cleared his throat. "Priscilla, thank you for allowing Katrina to stay here today."

She scoffed, waving her hand. "You do not need to thank me for that, Alexander. Get her back to the inn, and both of you stay safe."

With a nod, he motioned toward the door, and we left the safety of the bookstore. The stench of death and despair greeted and overwhelmed me, pressing down like heavy hands trying to hold me in place. The fog that rolled into town still lingered, curling up the trunks of the trees. I squeezed my eyes shut for a moment, trying to ignore it. Opening my eyes again, I kept them firmly above the level of the fog. I didn't know if it was normal fog, brought in by the damp afternoon, or if it was like the fog in the forest that signaled the sluagh were getting closer. I wasn't inclined to find out which.

I halted, my eyes stuck on the sight of the trees Adelaide had been hanging from. Someone had cut down the rope holding her body, and the crowd surrounding the square kept me from being able to see anything else, but I knew what was there.

I did not see my mother or father, but given the bustling of people trying to get closer to investigate, I was not surprised. They were either not here at all, or right in the middle of it.

A hand on my back pressed gently, guiding me away from the square and toward an alley behind the bookstore. "This way."

I felt like I was floating, watching my body from above as we made our way to the inn and up to our room. Only when the door clicked shut behind Alexander did I truly register that we had made it back inside. Shaking my head to clear my mind, I dug my fingernails into my palm, the sharp sting of pain bringing me back to reality.

Taking a deep breath, I centered myself, ready to face whatever was happening. Despite my day of overwhelming news, I needed to focus and hear what Alexander had to say.

"Are you all right, Katrina?" Alexander asked, sitting on the edge of the bed. He patted the space beside him.

I took his invitation, settling onto the mattress with a sigh. "I don't know what I am."

"I know that must have been a shock to see," he said slowly. "I apologize that you had to witness that."

"It's not that," I said, sighing again. I waved a hand, trying to clear the haze from my mind and find the right words. "Well, it is not entirely that. Priscilla shared some other news that was... enlightening. I don't think I have truly processed what happened to Adelaide yet, to be quite honest."

"I am certain you will have ample time to process it later," he said, bending to unlace his boots. He toed them off with a thump, straightening up and turning his body on the bed to face me. "What did Priscilla tell you?"

I chewed my lip. "My mother has always been choosing the Roghnaithe herself. The entire time. They are people who speak out against her or the Ciallmhar."

His expression was inscrutable. "And this surprises you?"

I glowered at him, the insinuation clear in his tone that I was naïve for being surprised by this news. "Yes. I was raised to believe the Roghnaithe was chosen by spirits and simply communicated to the Ciallmhar. And though I know my mother was not a good person, I had no reason to believe she was the one targeting people for death."

His face softened. "I apologize, Katrina. I did not mean to imply that you should have known that. I am sorry that you had to discover this truth as well."

A sigh escaped my lips, as heavy as the fog descending into Sleepy Hollow. "I—"

The fog. The memory hit me out of nowhere, but once it settled, I could think of nothing else.

"The sluagh are coming soon."

He straightened, looking around the room as if I had meant they were coming right to this moment, in this room. "What?"

"The fog. It means they are coming," I said, my voice frantic. I took a deep breath, trying to calm my racing heart. My hands flitted about as I spoke. "At Priscilla's, I found a book. It said that a sign of the sluagh being summoned was thick and unnatural fog. We get fog and mist in the fall, and in the spring, but it is never this thick. And it does not hover near the ground like this. Fog lifts as the sun comes out. This fog has stayed when it's been overcast enough. I cannot believe I did not notice this before."

He took hold of my frantically moving hands and held them steady in his own. "Breathe, Katrina. Start from the beginning. What did you learn?"

Despite the panic gripping my throat, I followed his instructions and took several deep breaths, organizing my thoughts in my head as I did so. I could do this; I could handle this.

"There was a book about creatures of the Otherworld. It said that when sluagh are summoned, they would manifest in a thick, unnatural fog or in a large swarm of gray birds. If the sluagh are summoned by someone, they can take the soul of those that fall in their path, and if those people have magic, the sluagh can transfer the power from those people to the one controlling them. And then they die."

He was silent, taking in my words, but his hands tightened around mine. The anger was palpable, and despite knowing logically that Alexander would never hurt me, my body responded as it had been trained to, to make myself as small as possible.

"The summoner is my mother," I whispered, fighting the urge to cower beneath the waves of anger washing from him. "Isn't it?"

"What else did you find out?" he asked, glossing over my question. It was probably for the better. I needed to pull myself together. I knew my mother was evil, and I did not understand why this was affecting me so much.

"Priscilla was doing some research on the prophecy and a poem we found about death and a phoenix," I said, shrugging. "She was still trying to find the entire prophecy when we were interrupted. So far, she had only found a few lines."

His hands tightened around mine again. "What did the poem say?"

My eyes flitted as I tried to recall the words I had read. "It described a dance between death and a phoenix, chasing each other through time. It said that death would always chase the phoenix, but that death could never catch it, could never succeed at destroying it, and so instead would burn the phoenix's home to ashes each time it caught up to it. I thought it might be useful in understanding the prophecy, but Priscilla did not find anything more."

The sudden darkness of his expression reminded me of what truly sat in front of me: the Dullahan, the rider of Death.

"I was too afraid to ask Priscilla," I said tentatively. "But do you think I could be a phoenix?"

Immediately, he shook his head. "No, Katrina, you are not. Phoenixes have been gone from this world for over a century. Do not worry."

"Then what are you worried about?" I asked. I wanted to lift my hand to rub out the lines between his eyebrows, but I kept my hands still.

"A phoenix is not the only creature that Death tends to follow." He rubbed his hands over his face once more, sighing heavily as he stood. Turning back to face me, he dropped to his knees in front of me, taking my hands in his once more. "Perhaps you should leave after all. This is much bigger than I suspected."

My eyes narrowed. "You know more than you are saying, Alexander. What is coming? Is it not just the sluagh?"

"Something Cyrus told me makes me believe that yes, it is not just the sluagh. Death is coming to Sleepy Hollow, and I do not want you anywhere near her."

"Her?" I asked, my eyebrows shooting up. "Death is a woman?"

He sighed. "Yes, Death is currently taking the form of a woman, though Death is whatever Death chooses to be."

"What did Cyrus say, Alexander?" I pressed, not wanting him to shut me out, but needing answers.

His eyes searched mine, pleading in a way I had never seen before. "It is not safe for you here anymore, Katrina. Please let me send you somewhere else. Somewhere safer."

"What did he say?" I asked again, my voice firmer this time.

"The sluagh always turn on their master once summoned," he muttered. "And then they tear apart that master and deliver them to Death. Death will follow them when they are summoned, to wait for the offering. I do not want you to see that, and I do not want you anywhere near here."

"Why?"

"Because the sluagh may not stop at just your mother," he said gravely. "They may very well turn on her entire family."

Ice ran through my veins. "I beg your pardon?"

He sighed, still holding my hands as they rested on my

knees. "You see? This is not safe for you anymore. You need to be as far from Sleepy Hollow as you can be."

"I thought me leaving would spell Sleepy Hollow's doom," I said.

Though hearing my mother had targeted members of her own town had set me into a panic, hearing this news was utterly indifferent to me. I did not understand it, but I would not question it. My anxiety didn't need any additional reasons to take charge of my mind.

"I do not care if it does." His words were so matter-of-fact, they startled me. As much as hearing the words made me want to hope that they meant he cared about me, I was not so foolish to let myself fall into that trap. Alexander was the Dullahan, and I was nobody.

"I will not run away like a coward. Not again. This is my town, Alexander," I said, tense and restless at the same time. "And I will save it, even if it does not want to be saved."

"I would rather you be safe than Sleepy Hollow survive, Katrina," he said, his eyes pleading with me. "This town can burn to ashes for all I care."

Not stopping myself this time, I reached for his face. His words were pretty, and they sent a pang through my chest, but I knew they were false. Maybe he wanted to believe them, but I couldn't. "We both know that is not true, Alexander. Something must be done. We must stop my mother."

"We cannot stop Death," he warned, his hand coming up to sandwich mine between the warm skin of his face and the slightly cooler skin of his hand.

I smiled. "Perhaps not. But we can certainly try."

"I suppose a cry does us all good at times-clears the air as other rain does."

-Bram Stoker, Dracula

Twenty-Six

Darkness was falling outside our room. My confidence in our ability to come up with a way to stop my mother waned as we discussed our options. Hours passed, and we were no closer to discovering a solution than we had been this morning when Alexander had dropped me off at Priscilla's. Now, we sat on opposite sides of the bed, our discussions going in circles every time the other posed a question.

Optimistically, Alexander believed we had less than two days to stop the summoning of the sluagh, and with them, Death. More realistically, though, we had until tomorrow evening at sundown. The moon would be full, and the sluagh would be at their most powerful once the sun set and plunged the town into darkness.

"Approaching them directly is our only option at this point," I said with a sigh, rubbing at my temples. "If whoever is summoning the sluagh know we know about the summoning, they wouldn't try to complete the spell, would they?

"They can do whatever they wish if they have enough

power," he grumbled. "No, our best solution is to keep researching when we return to the bookstore and find a way to thwart their evil plans from here. We cannot risk them knowing you are alive yet."

"Why?" My brows furrowed. It did not make sense to keep my survival a secret, not if it meant we could stop my parents.

"It is the only advantage we have, and we cannot give it up in a naïve attempt to appease to the nonexistent good in their black souls."

I bristled at the implication that rang in his words. "I do not think my parents have an ounce of good left in them. But I still think confronting them so they cannot deny their plans would save us valuable time we do not have. If we can stop them before the sluagh get here, before Death follows, it could make a difference."

"Or it could speed their plans up," he said with the raise of an eyebrow. The pulsing vein running from his hairline to his brow told me everything I needed to know about what he thought of my input. I smelt the smoke trickling from my fingers. "We cannot stop Death, Katrina. And though I know more about her than others, we can do little to even slow her down once she's made up her mind."

Just days ago, he had told me my words had value and now he was sitting in front of me, dismissing them.

"We need to confront them directly, not skulk about in the shadows trying to 'thwart their evil plans,'" I said, lowering my voice on the last bit to mimic him and show how ridiculous his words sounded. I took a deep breath to quell my building frustration. "At the very least, we can get this over with sooner instead of waiting until after they act to be able to rectify the damage."

"And if we confront them, then what? If they truly are the ones summoning the sluagh, they likely have more power than you know. They could kill you outright, or worse, summon the sluagh and Death sooner," he said, the muscle in his jaw twitched as he ground his teeth. "It is foolish to think that would be a good plan of action. We must be smart about this."

"Foolish?" I asked, my brow rising along with my quickly untethered anger. More smoke escaped my hands, drifting up into the air. "I am far from foolish, Horseman."

"You are a petulant, naïve child who does not understand how the world around you truly works." He took a step closer, looking up at the smoke before shaking his head. "Are you truly so stubborn to refuse to listen to my centuries of passed down knowledge on the subject? I know more than you about this town, about this threat, and about Death."

"Then do something about it rather than sitting here with me reading books." Flames erupted at my fingertips. His words had struck right through my heart, echoing the sentiments of my own parents' words that he had condemned just days ago. Heavy pressure grasped around my ribs as my vision danced with black spots. Beneath the fabric of my dress, I clenched my hands into fists, digging my nails into my palms. "You are as alone as I am, hiding in the forest, too afraid to confront the town that killed your father. Too afraid to tell them the truth. I may be stubborn, but at least I am not a coward."

He laughed, a harsh sound. "You? Not a coward? You forget, Katrina, how we met. You were running away from your fate, from your home. And for what purpose? To go run and hide somewhere else? No, I am not a coward. You are."

Red flooded my vision, and my flames moved up my arms, caressing my skin from fingertip to elbow.

"You say you need me to save this town. You say you

want to keep me safe and that you care about me. Yet you condescend me at every turn and continue to dismiss me as if I were a child. I know my parents, and I know the best way to approach this is to put it in their faces and stop it at the source."

Eyeing my hands, he waved his hand lazily, a thick blanket of purple haze coming down around us. He raised an eyebrow. "I would not treat you like a child if you did not act like one. A toddler could have better control over their magic than you. You would burn this inn down before you'd admit you're wrong."

Every fiber of my being wanted to blast my fire at him, to prove him wrong. My fingers twitched at my side, itching to blast a ball of fire at his chest. It would be a weak attempt at conveying my hurt and anger, though, so I clenched my jaw, tensing my neck and taking a deep breath in a pitiful attempt to calm myself. "I do not have to sit here and take this from you, Horseman."

He opened his arm, gesturing to the front door with a scoff. "Then by all means, please go attempt to pull this off alone. Your magic is uncontrollable. You do not know if it is your parents summoning the sluagh, and you have no clue how to stop them. Yes, I would be delighted to watch your failure. And right after, I will sit back and watch Sleepy Hollow destroyed at the hands of the sluagh. At least then, Death would not have a reason to be here."

My jaw clenched so tightly I was almost certain I would crack a tooth. For a moment, I considered staying to continue arguing with this cowardly death omen, but I knew it was an exercise in futility. Nothing we said to each other would get through. Closing my eyes, I willed my flame to extinguish back into the depths of my soul. And then I did exactly as he said I should and left the room, slamming the door behind me.

My feet thudded on the stairs as I descended them, leaving the inn with a trail of black smoke following me.

I would stop my parents, with or without his help. And I would prove everyone who ever doubted me wrong. He wanted me to save Sleepy Hollow, and that was exactly what I intended to do.

"I wondered why it was that places are so much lovelier when one is alone."

-Daphne du Maurier, Rebecca

Twenty-Seven

Without the Horseman's magical disguise, I was all too recognizable. Despite my anger, I was at least thinking logically enough to realize that. Pausing in the hallway, I weighed my options. Surely there was some way for me to get out of this inn without anyone seeing me.

I turned away from the main stairwell and moved down the back hall to the servant's staircase. Pushing the door open, I descended to the back door of the inn. A grin broke out on my face when my luck had turned, revealing a thick hooded cloak hanging on a hook beside the door. The hood would certainly be deep enough to hide my face if I kept to back alleys and avoided crowds.

Pulling it on, I pushed open the door, tensing against the cool night air. As I stepped out of the inn, I felt Alexander's glamor on me fall away, my skin tingling as I was once again myself. I tucked my curls back into the deep hood, pulling it up to rest over my forehead before buttoning it at my throat.

My heart was in my stomach as I walked, my palms

sweating despite the crispness of the autumn air. While I had initially planned to go to Henry for advice on how I should accomplish this, I could not risk him. And since Priscilla was likely still with him, given my request, she was no longer an option either. Turning my feet down the path that would take me to the apothecary shop, I could only hope Ciara was still there. I could only hope she would listen to me and would help me work through a plan to stop my parents on my own.

A breath of relief passed through my lips, causing a puff of cold air to form in front of my face. The candles in Ciara's shop windows were still lit. Looking both ways to ensure no one was looking, I stepped out of the alley and hurried across to her shop, pushing open the door quickly and stepping inside.

"I am closing for the evening," Ciara said politely, her back turned to the door as she cleaned the tables.

I took a deep breath to steady my nerves. "Even for me?"

The teacups she had in her hand clattered to the floor, shattering on impact. She turned around slowly, as if she were afraid of what awaited her. Her eyes were wide as they landed on me, but immediately narrowed with suspicion. "I thought you had gone, Katrina."

"Can you talk for a moment?" I asked, turning to lock the door behind me. "I need your advice."

A frown graced her face as she stooped to pick up the shards of porcelain from the wooden floor. "Why are you back?"

"Brom betrayed me." I paused to take a breath, debating how much to tell her. While I wanted to spill all my secrets and tell her everything I had discovered, I also knew she could not leave and needed to be protected from the wrath of my mother. And only ignorance could do that.

"I am shocked, truly." Her voice revealed that she was anything but shocked.

"He attempted to sacrifice me to the Horseman."

"Then why are you alive?" Her voice was hard and accusatory, as if I had done something wrong.

I reeled back from the vitriol in her voice. Of all the people I thought would be angry about my survival, Ciara had not been one of them. Despite her harsh words before I'd tried to leave Sleepy Hollow, I still considered her a friend. One of my only friends. "Are you not happy to see I am alive?"

"I am simply surprised," she said, her voice cool as she straightened from the floor, discarding the broken cups into the bin with a soft tinkling noise. "No one has ever survived the Dullahan before."

"He is not who we thought. Which is the main reason I am here. I need your help," I said, broaching the subject carefully. While I knew Alexander—even despite his outburst just now—was a good person, Ciara did not. And after believing for most of her life that he had killed her brother, I doubted she would be open to listening to me. "My mother is summoning beings from the Otherworld to steal the magic of those in Sleepy Hollow."

"And what do you want me to do about that?" She wiped the table down aggressively, focusing on the rag in her hands instead of looking at me. "We both know your mother is a dreadful person."

I nodded, my mind rushing between all the things I needed to tell her, trying to decide what to say first. "I need your help to stop her. I must confront her."

Pausing from wiping down the table, she stood and ran her hands over her apron. "Katrina, we have been. And those who do are sent to the Dullahan and never seen or heard from again. I will not risk leaving my mother alone just because you have finally seen what was right in front of you."

"That is not fair," I said, my voice wavering as the hurt washed through me. This was not the Ciara I knew, not the woman I had grown up with who had nurtured me and given me solace. This was not the friend I had held while she cried, and who had done the same for me after whatever venom my mother had spewed had sent me running for comfort. I had given everything I could to comfort Ciara after Torin's apparent death, had stopped asking for my own comfort in exchange for helping her. I had done it gladly to ease her sadness, but now I could see the sentiment would not be reciprocated. "Why are you saying these things, Ciara?"

"How did you escape the Dullahan, Katrina?" she asked, crossing her arms over her chest. The flare of irritation in her eyes spoke the answers to my questions far more than her words ever could have.

My heart broke in my chest, the shards sharper than the porcelain she'd just cleaned. It stabbed into my lungs and took my breath. But I could not cry in front of her, not now. Biting down hard on the inside of my cheek, my mouth flooded with copper. The taste was bitter, but the sting of the pain brought my emotions back under control.

"He saved me. And he asked for my help in saving Sleepy Hollow. He is not the destroyer, not the murderer we all think him to be. He is a good person."

"He is not a *person* at all, Katrina."

She fell silent and still, an eerie calm settling over the shop. Chills went down my spine. Opening my mouth, I went to continue, but she raised her hand to stop me, closing her eyes tightly.

"Anyone who is friends of the Dullahan is no friend of

mine." Her voice was ice as she pointed at the door, her hand trembling in anger. "Get out, Katrina. Now."

"But—" I wanted to tell her he had not killed her brother as she believed. That her brother was safe, living somewhere away from this wretched town.

"No. Nothing you say will fix this." She walked to the door and opening it, stepping to the side as she jerked her head toward the cold night. "Now. Get out before I say something I will regret. You should not be in Sleepy Hollow. You do not belong here. You are not welcome here."

My fire flooded from the sharp sting of hurt in my chest, flames licking down my arms and dancing from my fingertips. Taking a deep breath, I clenched my hands into fists, keeping my flames to myself as I stepped out into the night. "Ciara, I—"

She shut the door in my face, the lock clicking louder than any noise I had heard in my entire life.

Standing there, in the lantern's glow beside her doorway, I felt empty and hopeless. Alexander's words flooded back into my mind and all I could hear was his voice telling me I was naïve and foolish. His voice turned into my mother's, telling me I was a failure. Second by second, my mind threw every insecurity into my face. My breathing quickened and the edges of my vision blackened slightly.

I needed to get out of here.

As I escaped down the alley between the shops, I had to run my hand along the wall to keep myself from falling. My legs wobbled as I tried to control my breathing, but the words that had been hurled at me my entire life kept coming, louder and louder and louder.

Finally, I slunk into the darkness of the alley, turning my back against the stone and sliding to the ground. I did not realize I was crying until the tears trickled into the corner of my mouth. Licking my lips, I closed my eyes and tipped my head back against the wall. My heart felt like it was about to burst from my chest. I could not breathe.

I felt the heat begin to emanate from my hands, but I did not open my eyes to see the flames I knew were there. They only fueled my self-loathing and proved that the Horseman's words were right.

An unnaturally cold breeze washed over me. It pulled me from my spiral of emotion. I opened my eyes, looking around. A thick mist hovered above the ground, creeping from the mouth of the alley, closer and closer to where I was sitting.

The sluagh.

Scrambling, I stood from the ground and backed up several steps. Seeing the mist pulled me back into reality. I needed to do something, or this mist would take over the town and turn into something far more harmful than an unusual fog.

Taking a deep breath to center myself, I lifted my hands, palms out to the mist.

It was time to see if my fire would damage this.

Focusing all my energy on pulling at that ball of fire in my chest, I envisioned the flames traveling from my heart and down my arms. I would prove to myself, to Alexander, that I did have control over my magic.

Tendrils of flame emerged from my fingertips, lighting up the alley. My lips pulled back from my teeth in what was undoubtably not a friendly smile. Remembering how it felt when I lit the grass on fire in the clearing with Alexander, I pushed the fire from my body, willing it toward the mist.

Erupting from my hands, a ball of flame left my palm, striking at the center of the mass of thick fog. An otherworldly sound—like a pained shriek—sounded, echoing in the alley. I winced at the high-pitched whine but kept my hands directed there, sending another wave of flame at the mist.

With another shriek that faded into the night, the fog disappeared, leaving me alone in the alley. I panted as I looked at where the mist had been.

Slowly, as my heart and breathing returned to normal, a smile broke across my face, a genuine one this time. I had done it. And my fire could harm this mist, which would hopefully translate to the sluagh.

"You can do this, Katrina," I said to myself, rolling my shoulders back and lifting my chin. The words of those insecurities, thrown back in my face by the Dullahan and then again by my mind... they would not stop me. I would prove to myself that I could save Sleepy Hollow.

And I would say it until I believed it.

I will save Sleepy Hollow. I will save Sleepy Hollow. I will save Sleepy Hollow.

Chanting my new mantra in my head, I pulled the hood of my cloak up and set my feet in the direction of the Van Tassel manor.

I would confront my parents myself.

"Even with the utterly lost,
to whom life and death are
equally jests, there are
matters of which no jest
can be made."

-Edgar Allan Poe,
Masque of the Red Death

Twenty-Eight

P assing through the town, it was noticeably empty. The thick mist still hovered over the ground, but as I walked, it parted, almost skittering away from me. Part of me was proud that this mist was frightened of me, and the other part of me was horrified that this mist was intelligent enough to realize I could harm it.

Unease churned in my stomach as I passed by the closed shops. No lanterns were lit inside any of them, and those that had curtains had them drawn tightly over the windows and doors. It should not have been this empty, even though night had firmly settled in.

And I feared what it meant that I had not seen another soul since leaving the alley.

Continuing my journey through the town square, I swallowed down the bile that rose into my throat at the sight of the trees Adelaide had been hanging from. For the rest of my days, the image of her lifeless body and gaping eye sockets staring out at the town she had sworn to protect would be burned into my mind.

Shivers crawled down my spine, tickling like icy fingers. I

took a deep breath and continued my path, my eyes flicking up to the trees as I passed it.

Whispers filled the eerily silent night as I exited the other side of the square. The words were so soft that I should have not been able to hear them at all. I spun around, searching for the source, but again, there was no one. The mist was undisturbed, having already consumed the square in a thick blanket of gray.

With a pit in my stomach, my steps quickened, my eyes frantically scanning my surroundings as I practically ran toward my former home.

Whatever was lurking in the darkness of Sleepy Hollow tonight would not be friendly. And though I doubted what was waiting for me at home would be friendly either, it was at least a familiar evil.

By some grace, I reached the Van Tassel manor without any further whispers or encounters with the strangely sentient mist. Though the sight of my home laid before me did little to calm my racing heart, I kept moving forward. Stepping into the pool of light cast by the lanterns hanging on either side of the entryway, I took a deep breath to calm my nerves. The only way this would be successful was if I kept my wits about me. Panic would only benefit my mother.

Once my heartbeat steadied out, I stepped up onto the porch and raised my hand to push open the door. The creaking of the hinges echoed into the silent night beyond.

Keeping my steps light, I followed the hallway to my mother's study. My feet hesitated outside of the room, but after taking a deep breath, I pushed the door open, revealing my mother. Her eyes widened, taking me in from head to toe, before narrowing as she stood and crossed her arms over her chest.

"What are *you* doing here?" she asked, lip snarling up

slightly. "You are supposed to be with the Dullahan and long dead."

The venom in her voice roused nothing in my heart. There were so many things I wanted to say, but I settled on the quickest explanation possible that would get me in the door. "I was with the Dullahan. He let me live."

She scoffed, moving her hands to rest on her hips. "You could not even die properly, could you?"

My fire itched beneath my skin, but by some miracle, I held it back. Not even smoke escaped from my fingers as I clasped my hands in front of me and dug my nails into my forearms. "I know what you are doing, mother."

Her eyes narrowed further until I could barely make out the color of her irises. "And what is that?"

"You are summoning the sluagh here. You choose the Roghnaithe to silence any dissent." I was impressed with my ability to keep my voice steady. I channeled the apathetic tone I had heard from her throughout my childhood and continued, the confidence in my chest unfamiliar yet welcomed. "And I will not let you destroy Sleepy Hollow."

In an instant, her face changed from the twisted anger to a serene blankness, though the rage I knew simmered beneath the surface shone in her eyes. "Come in, Katrina. Let us discuss these ridiculous notions you seem to have about me."

Logically, I knew I should not have come to the manor alone, but I also knew I had no other choice. To get my mother to admit what she was doing, to convince her that the town would not abide this once they knew the truth, that the Dullahan would never allow her to accomplish her task... This was what I had to do.

My body was vibrating with nerves as I stepped inside the study and followed her to the sitting area by the far window.

I stopped just shy of sitting down. "Why are you doing this?"

"Doing what?" she asked, sitting down once again, her movements graceful and proper in a way mine could never have been. She lifted the teapot from the center of the table and poured two cups, setting the dainty porcelain onto saucers, and sliding one over in front of the other chair. "I am simply having a conversation with my daughter."

I bit out a laugh. "I have never been your daughter."

"I gave birth to you, Katrina. Surely that makes you my daughter as much as anything." She motioned to the other chair. "Sit and have some tea with me."

"You may have given birth, but that does not make you a mother." I sat in the chair roughly, not bothering to force the manners I knew she wanted me to display. The propriety she clung to, that she lorded over me. Here, in society, she was better than me, and she had no hesitations in reminding me. My lip curled up of its own accord before I schooled it back into a flat line. "You sent me to my death, and when I was so close to escaping, I am certain you are the one who told Brom to stop me."

She only hummed once more, lifting her teacup to her lips to take a small sip. When she set it back down, the porcelain chimed daintily as she re-crossed her ankles, settling her hands in her lap.

"Admit it." I was not sure what it was I was asking her to admit—if it was the sluagh, the Roghnaithe, or that she instructed Brom to push me over that embankment. Perhaps it was all three.

"This is your legacy, Katrina."

"It is my legacy to die?" I clenched my hands clenched once more, fighting back the sparking fire. I knew she had only given birth to me to have power, but hearing that she had truly only given birth to me to sacrifice me later was enough to bring the flames out. Smoke drifted up from my fists.

"Yes. It is." She raised an eyebrow at the smoke tendrils filling the surrounding air, but did not comment on them.

"I refuse to accept that. And I refuse to let you harm anyone else ever again."

"Have some tea, Katrina," my mother said, inclining her head to the teacups she had set out for both of us. "At least pretend you have manners."

"I am not here for tea with you, mother. You are trying to destroy Sleepy Hollow, and I will not allow it." I stood, my fists erupting into flames.

She laughed, a loud sound I had never heard from her before in my entire life. As quickly as the sound began, it ended. Her eyes were like ice as she stared at me, all amusement gone from her face. A long finger pointed at me. "Sit and drink your tea. I'll not converse with someone who has no manners."

A gust of wind came from nowhere and pushed me into the seat, holding me there. The abrupt movement quelled my fire for a moment, and I was able to pull the flames back into my chest. I scowled at her, and at the teacup in front of me. "This is not a time for tea. Why are you doing this? This town was the only thing that ever mattered to you, and—"

"Drink. Your. Tea."

Gods above. Huffing in frustration, I picked up the teacup and brought it to my lips. Anything to get her to move on and answer my questions. I drank the contents in one unladylike gulp before slamming the porcelain onto the table, wincing at the bitter taste of the tea as I wiped the excess from my lips with the back of my hand. "There, I drank the tea. Now, tell me why you are summoning the sluagh to Sleepy Hollow."

The answering smile on her face sent chills down my

spine. "I am not summoning anything, you petulant child. You never could see past your own imagination. Stubborn and wrong is a dreadful combination."

"Then who is summoning them?" I demanded. My vision blurred, and I blinked rapidly to clear it. My tongue felt like it weighed a thousand pounds. "Surely you have noticed the unnatural mist blanketing the town. That is a sign the sluagh are coming, and you are the only one who stands to gain from it. You have destroyed those you deemed to be against you by sending them to the Dullahan, and this—"

My breathing grew labored, and my vision blackened around the edges. Sweat beaded on my forehead and back, rolling down my spine. Phantom hands gripped my throat, cutting off my airflow. All the while, my mother sat, smiling at me.

"What—what are you doing to me?" I panted out. The room spun around me, and I tried to raise my hands to steady myself on the arms of the chair, but they would not move. I tried again, but none of my limbs obeyed me.

"It is henbane, Katrina," my mother said, smiling wider still. "And once again, your impetuousness will be your downfall."

The room faded as I slipped from the chair; the ceiling filled my remaining vision. My mother leaned over me, her features blurred and spinning, but I could still make out her grin. My mind betrayed me, and I could not focus on anything.

A shadow crossed the window behind my mother. Then everything went dark.

"All these, however, were mere terrors of the night, phantoms of the mind that walk in darkness; and though he had seen many spectres in his time, and been more than once beset by Satan in divers shapes, in his lonely preambulations, yet daylight put an end to all these evils."

-Washington Irving,
The Legend of Sleepy Hollow

My muscles screamed in protest, tingling uncomfortably as awareness spread down my body. My head hung heavily against my chest, and when I tried to open my eyes, the effort to lift my lids was far more than I had been expecting. Instead, I let my consciousness move through my body slowly, taking in what I could while I took stock of my body.

I could not yet open my eyes, but it was clear we were outside. The wind rustling through the trees was soft but clear, and the ground beneath me was damp in the cool night air. Awareness continued down to my arms and torso, which came with the realization that I was bound to something hard. Scratchy ropes dug into my stomach and wrists, and hard, cool stone sat at my back.

A soft clink of glass from something being set down upon a hard surface followed the sound of something being poured into another container. It was not far away, but I could not tell how close whoever was making the noise was to me.

Finally, I could lift my head and open my eyes. And

immediately I wished I had not. My vision was blurry, making everything muddied and wavy. Two figures stood in front of a small fire, and while I could tell they were moving, I could tell nothing else about them. Blinking repeatedly, my eyes cleared, the scene before me finally coming into focus.

I was in Sleepy Hollow cemetery, and based on my position amongst the graves, I was tied to a headstone. Testing my hands against the rope that bound me, there was no give and the material only bit into my skin, tightening further. The rope was wound around my wrists, and then another length of rope stretched across the front of my chest and shoulders, and another around my stomach, holding my lower back to the stone.

The light from the small fire made it easy for my eyes to adjust to the darkness, and I was able to finally make out both of my parents standing before me.

"She is awake, Loralai," my father said, pausing from his work in front of a large brass bowl sitting on a stone pedestal in front of them.

My mother looked up from her own work. "Good."

Tipping my head back, I let the gravestone take the weight of my skull. The henbane was still in my system, given how much effort it took to move my body. Anything I could do to conserve my energy would benefit me. In the same vein, I did not waste any of that energy on speaking. It would do no good.

"I am sorry it had to come to this, Katrina," my father said, walking from behind the stone pedestal and squatting down in front of me. He reached out and tucked a strand of my curls behind my ear. For a moment, I almost thought there was remorse in his eyes. "I do wish there was another way."

"Why?" I asked, my voice hoarse as I spoke. My tongue reached out to lick at my dry and cracked lips.

He sighed and stood, stepping around the crackling fire and back to my mother's side.

"The veil is crumbling. This unnatural fog and Adelaide's unfortunate death are proof of that, and if the Dullahan will not protect us, we will do it ourselves," my mother said, motioning toward the forest.

My eyes followed her movements, and I blinked to clear the remaining haze, revealing the thick undulating fog circling the bases of the trees once more. It didn't whisper. It didn't move any closer. It was as if it were watching us instead. Waiting.

Picking up bottles of liquids and herbs, she added them to the brass bowl. "Unfortunately, that requires a bit more power than we currently have."

"So you will summon creatures from the Otherworld to take the souls and power of the people who live here?" I asked, straining against the ropes, and wincing when they again tightened. "Then who will be left to benefit from the veil?"

"New people always come to town, Katrina," she said. "And people always leave."

"What will you do to me?" The ropes around my chest and stomach tightened uncomfortably, making my breath difficult. I winced, straining to catch a deep breath without pushing against the ropes more.

"We told you the truth before, Katrina," my father said. "Repairing the barrier requires a more significant sacrifice this year. And that is you."

"You could not even die properly, and that is the only reason we have not already repaired it," my mother bit out, scowling at me. "The Dullahan may have rejected you once, but we will ensure he takes you this time."

I wanted to roll my eyes, to scoff at her delusions, but the first motions of the expression sent a throbbing through my skull. Gritting my teeth against the pain as the henbane worked its way out of my system, I raised my eyes to my mother's. "The Dullahan does not take any of your sacrifices. He never has. He sends them elsewhere to safety. There was never a need to offer people to him."

They both paused for a moment at my words, looking at each other. My mother shrugged. "It is no matter. We will fix this town ourselves. It will simply require an adjustment to the spell. Your death will still power the veil; once we channel your life force into it, it will be whole once more. You see, we have no need to summon the sluagh you keep accusing us of. We are trying to fix the town."

With a wave of her hand, the ropes began tightening. Stars filled the edges of my vision. "Stop. Please."

They ignored me as they continued with their preparations at the pedestal, mixing the spell ingredients in the brass bowl. My mother stepped up to the fire with the bowl in her hands. The sound of hoofbeats and rustling leaves filled the air, stopping her in her tracks.

At once, all three of us turned toward the noise.

Out of the thick line of trees, the Dullahan emerged.

Even with my fading breath and blurring vision, I knew that much. Alexander rode in atop Liath, whose eyes were now alight with actual flames, the purple aura of his spirit magic around him, violet shadows pulsating. There was no head atop his shoulders, and in his hand was a long whip. As he slowed to a stop in front of my parents, Liath let out a snort, embers shooting from her nose into the night.

My heart leapt into my throat, but it wasn't from fear. Perhaps if I were seeing him for the first time, I would be, but now I could only exhale and slump back against the stone. He was here. A smile crossed my lips as I let my head fall back against the headstone for a moment, taking in everything.

He was here. For me.

He flicked the handle of his whip; the length shooting out to snap at the bowl my mother held, knocking it from her hands to hit the ground near the fire with a metallic thud. She curled her lip back in a snarl, but didn't make any moves to thwart him. "I believe you have something of mine."

Shivers raced down my spine that had nothing to do with the cool breeze. The fog skittered back, retreating to the second and third rows of trees along the edges of the cemetery. They, too, knew what was in front of them.

Raising his hands, a ball of swirling purple energy formed, and using a motion similar to the one I had learned with my fire, Alexander sent it hurtling toward my parents.

The magic blasted them in their chests, sending them off flying into the depths of the cemetery. Alexander slid from Liath, the purple aura around him dropping as his head returned. He ran over to me, his hands immediately going to the ropes at my back and freeing me.

The rush of breath back into my lungs was so rewarding I could not hold back the sob of relief. Alexander's attention came back to my face, reaching down to hold my cheeks in his hands, searching my face. "Are you hurt?"

I shook my head, still sucking down as many deep breaths as I could. He stroked his thumb over the fullness of my cheek, staring at me for a moment before pulling me into his arms. Freeing my aching arms, I burrowed my face into his coat, breathing in the smell of petrichor and warmth. Closing my eyes, I relished the warmth and comfort.

I was safe.

Pulling back slightly, his hands returned to my face. "I am so sorry, Katrina. For my words, for almost being late, for all of it. You are braver than I could ever imagine, and I hope you can find it in yourself to forgive me for words spoken in fear."

"Fear of what?" I croaked out, still trying to suck air into my lungs.

"Fear of this," he said, pushing a curl behind my ear and nodding to where my parents had been blasted off to. "I did not want you hurt any more than you already had been."

"This is quite touching," my mother said, her voice flat and apathetic. With no sign of hesitation, she sent a gush of air at us. "But we have a veil to fix, and you are both slowing the process."

Alexander moved in front of me, transforming to his spirit form in the next breath, taking the blunt of the strike. He staggered back half a step, and I surged to my feet, sending a ball of fire at my mother, fueled on instinct alone.

Alexander recovered easily, the whip returning to his hand. I spared it a quick glance. It seemed as though the whipcord was made from a human spine.

Tingles traveled down my own spine as he adjusted his grip on the handle, also appearing to be made from bone.

It should have been disgusting, should have made my stomach recoil in fear, but it didn't. It looked like it belonged in his hand, merely adding to the deadly aura of the Dullahan.

"You think to fight me, Dullahan?" my mother demanded, her voice shrill. "I am the leader of Sleepy Hollow. You exist to protect me."

"I exist to protect the town. To protect the magic that was here long before you," he snarled.

"I am better," she replied. Her gaze landed on me, and she scoffed. "I'm certainly better than my useless child you seem so fond of."

Alexander snarled, but before either of us could respond, her hand extended to me, and she closed her fingers in a fist. My breath caught in my throat, and as I tried to suck in a breath.

But I couldn't.

Eyes widening, panic seized my lungs, expelling the little oxygen I'd had left. I clawed at my throat as I fell to the ground, pulling at the invisible binds constricting my airway. My vision blackened around the edges, my chest heaved as I failed to breathe at the hands of my mother.

Alexander's whip cracked in her direction her, but my father raised his hand, roots shooting up from the earth to wrap around the whip, pulling it down with a sharp crack. The Dullahan growled, a menacing sound, and even without his head, I knew the expression on his face would be deadly.

"Harm her, and I will take great pleasure in removing your head from your shoulders."

My mother merely laughed.

Blood thundered in my ears, my heart pounding as my heart tried to keep up. Clawing at the earth, I tried to get away from my mother, to get out of the range of her magic.

Alexander stepped up to my father, shrugging off the roots my father tried to use to subdue him. With an effortless movement, Alexander pulled the root closest to him, yanking it from the ground and wrapping it around my father's neck, pulling him to his body as he cut off my father's airway. My vision had blurred, fading as I struggled to keep myself upright, but I saw my father's body slump before Alexander pushed it to the ground. From the ground, his unseeing eyes stared back at me.

I couldn't breathe—couldn't focus on his body as black spots dotted my vision.

My father was dead.

Instantly, my mother's magic relinquished its hold on me. My head spun as I sucked in a deep, gasped breath, then panted as my body tried to replenish its oxygen. Holding my throat, I studied my father's body, waiting for guilt, regret, sadness—anything to take hold of me. But the only thing I felt was my breath shuddering against my hand. It was as if it were a stranger lying on the ground. I felt nothing for him.

Just as he'd felt nothing for me.

My mother turned her focus to Alexander, face contorted and lips snarling, and she sent her magic toward him as he advanced on her. "You killed my husband?"

"You would kill your own child," Alexander shot back, brushing off her attempts at cutting off his oxygen as he approached her. Her wind did nothing to slow him, nothing to stop his heavy steps. "What is the difference?"

"My child is a waste of life who should never have been born," she snarled, blasting him with a wave of air that sent him stumbling back.

Her words echoed in my head, rattling off every corner of my mind and fracturing what little peace I'd created. Red tinged my vision now, my face heating with both anger and embarrassment. From the ground, fire engulfed my hands, burning at the grass. Raising one shaky hand, I launched a fireball at my mother, striking her in the side.

She cried out in pain, clutching her wound as she whirled on me. "You insolent child! How dare you?"

Another ball of flames left my hand, one after the other, fueled by my unending rage. Each was meant to hurt the woman who'd only ever made me feel less than. I was no longer shaking. I wasn't thinking. There was nothing on my mind except her words, the sneer on her face, the strike of her palm against my skin. Every instance of her abuse, of her disappointment in me, every barbed word and sharp slap flooded my mind. I let all of it fuel my magic, channeling it at her in unending volleys of flames.

My fire struck true, over and over and over, pummeling at my mother until she lay motionless on the grass.

My vision cleared, realizing what I was looking at: her body charred and blackened beyond recognition.

The breath rushed from my lungs and my knees gave out, no longer able to hold my weight. All I could do was stare at her body.

She was dead. Finally dead. I was finally free from her.

Unlike seeing my father's body, every emotion I'd ever felt before rushed through me, slicing through my mind in a whirlwind.

Relief. Fury. Regret. Pride. All of it and then some. There was too much—too many feelings to decipher.

But I knew, without a doubt, without an inkling of a question, that I was glad she was dead.

And I was glad I had been the one to kill her.

With one last look at my mother, I turned to Alexander, searching him out. He was standing, once again headless and shrouded in an undulating purple haze, over the bodies of the two people most responsible for my pain. The two people who should have protected me, who should have loved me more than anyone else. The two people who had been ready to murder me to protect themselves.

"It's over," I whispered, focusing on Alexander's chest, on the buckles of his jacket, on anything to keep my eyes from wandering back to their bodies. I didn't want to see them anymore, didn't care that they were dead. I wanted to feel remorse, and maybe I would, later. But only the unending wash of relief moved through me as I slumped against a headstone, tired beyond words as I stretched my legs out in front of me.

Alexander stooped in front of me, transforming back into his human form. His hands cupped my face as he turned my head to one side and then the other, inspecting me with narrowed blue eyes, the pupils blown wide as they roamed over my face and then down the rest of my body. "Are you hurt?"

Before I could answer, the sound of cracking branches emerged from the forest behind us. Turning, I held my breath as we both watched the tree line.

Alexander pulled me to my feet as the wave of purple magic took over him, turning him into the Dullahan once more. The sound grew closer, each step over the earthen debris making me flinch, the snapping too similar to the noise of bones snapping.

My breath froze in my lungs. The trees rustled along the edge of the cemetery and my body tensed, waiting.

"What fire does not destroy, it hardens."

-Oscar Wilde,
The Picture of Dorian Gray

Thirty

" I suppose their sacrifice will do instead." The voice was familiar, but as I searched the darkness of the tree line, no one appeared. "Even if they did not intend it."

A figure stepped out from behind a large tree trunk, covered in a blood-red cloak with a deep hood. The voice was female, but the hood shadowed her face. She moved closer to us, stepping over my parents' bodies and approaching the dying fire in front of me.

"I told you to leave, Katrina," the woman said, reaching up to push her hood back. "You never listen."

"Ciara?" I breathed. My knees buckled, and only Alexander's grip on my waist kept me upright. "What are you doing?"

She sneered down at me, the pure hatred on her face contorting her into someone completely unrecognizable. "You never could see what was right in front of you, Katrina."

Before I reacted, she pulled a bronze dagger from her cloak and sliced her forearm, letting the blood drop into the fire as she muttered a spell. Lightning cracked across the sky as her blood dripped into the flames.

The electricity struck my parents' corpses, illuminating them before retreating into the sky. A rumble of thunder crashed. Alexander grabbed my arms, pulling me into his chest to hold me back from surging at her.

"It is too late," he murmured. Pulling us another small step back from Ciara, the purple magic around him fell, revealing his face. His eyes were trained solely on Ciara. "We have failed."

"You always were smarter than they said you were, Dullahan," Ciara cooed, smiling at us. "But you are too late."

"So you will summon the sluagh to destroy this town out of revenge?" I asked, the heat of the now roaring fire washing over my face. Alexander tensed beside me. "Why? He is not the villain."

"This town took everything from me. *He* took everything from me and left me with a dead brother and a mother so destroyed by guilt she must be constantly supervised to keep from killing herself." Snarling, she pointed her finger at Alexander. Her face morphed into one of serene calm as she watched the flames surge. "And I am not summoning the sluagh."

"What have you summoned?" My voice shook, afraid of her answer.

As if the world were waiting for my question, unnatural tendrils of flame shot up out of the center of the firepit and sunk back down into the ground. It reminded me of veins.

Along those veins of flame, the ground split, the earth separating and shaking more.

"You summoned her," Alexander breathed. He grabbed

my hand and pulled me back, away from the flames until we were both pressed against the side of a mausoleum.

Ciara continued to stand, watching the fire. Her eyes flicked over to us. "I did."

"This never would have brought him back," Alexander said, anger in his voice as he grasped me tightly. "But now you have condemned everyone here to death. You truly think she will obey you?"

"The spell will ensure she does," Ciara said, eyes going back to the fractured earth.

Alexander laughed, a humorless sound, and tightened his arms around me even more. His touch was my only anchor, my only solace to keep from swimming in my head. If she had only listened to me earlier, when I'd tried to tell her, none of this would be happening.

Nausea swirled in my stomach, climbing up my throat as Alexander continued speaking. "Nothing can control her. Certainly no spell. She tricked you, as she does everyone. You will die with us, foolish witch."

The seams of the ground split wider, thick black smoke escaping out of the crevices and swirling to form a column behind Ciara, who closed her eyes but refused to turn to face it. What started as translucent smoke quickly grew opaque as tendrils of smoke escaped the earth and joined the group.

Alexander's grip tightened on me, but it barely registered in my mind. Finally, no more smoke came from the ground and the smoke that was already here collapsed, dispersing into the night.

In its place was a woman, tall and slender. Her skin gleamed unnaturally white, like freshly crafted porcelain. The night breeze picked up the long silky strands of her moonlight-colored hair, pushing it off her bare shoulders.

Her eyes... her eyes were pools of inky black—a soulless gaze, staring at Ciara.

"You are the one who summoned me?" she asked, circling around to stand in front of Ciara. She reached a blood-red nail out, tracing it down Ciara's cheek. "What do you ask of me?"

"Yes," Ciara said, holding her head high and looking straight ahead. "You can bring my brother back? The one he took."

She tutted, once again behind Ciara. Her voice was a sickly sweet coo as she spoke. "I cannot bring back your brother, little one."

Ciara's face contorted, whirling to face Death. "What do you mean? Why won't you bring him back?"

"I said I cannot. Not that I would not." A slow smile spread across the woman's face as she nodded to us, where Alexander was still holding me to him. "Because your brother is not dead."

Ciara's eyes snapped to us. "What?" she asked, her words merely a breath.

"Tell her, *Horseman*," the woman said, mocking Alexander's moniker with a snarl. "Tell her the truth you have hidden from the town."

"Your brother is alive," Alexander said, his voice flat. "I do not take sacrifices. I send them somewhere safe, where they can live happily."

The hatred in Ciara's gaze faltered, eyes softening as they shone in the moonlight. Quickly, she recovered and glowered at him, her attention flicking between Alexander and me. "You lie. You murdered him."

"I did not." Alexander remained remarkably calm. "Torin lives. He was sent to a haven in Kentucky. Whether he is still there or not, I do not know, but he was given money and supplies and left alive. They were always left alive."

A sob escaped Ciara's lips, her hand flying up to cover her mouth as tears shone in her eyes. "No."

"And now you've summoned Death to Sleepy Hollow, and she is not beholden to you. She can do whatever she wishes. *Take* whoever she wishes," Alexander snarled.

The woman stepped up behind Ciara, pressing her front against Ciara's back and resting her chin on her shoulder. Her teeth gleamed in the moonlight as she smiled, leaning her mouth to brush against Ciara's ear. The blood-red of her lips made it easy to read the words she spoke. "He is right."

Ciara's eyes snapped up, locking with mine just in time for the woman to raise her hands and snap Ciara's neck.

Her body fell to the ground with a sickening thud.

The woman stepped back, wiping her hands on her thighs. Black shadows spun around her fingertips, merging and writhing to encompass her hands before traveling up her forearms.

I squeezed my eyes shut and fought back the bile that surged.

Ciara was dead. My parents were dead. Adelaide was dead.

And we were next.

"We need to go," Alexander whispered, standing slowly, and pulling me with him as we backed away.

"Now, now," the woman said, stepping over Ciara's body to move closer to us, the same serene smile still on her face. "Where are you off to so quickly?"

Alexander remained quiet, his hand clasping mine as he observed the inhuman woman. He obviously knew who she was, yet his only reaction was to keep us still.

"Who are you?" My voice shook along with every

muscle in my body. I feared I already knew the answer, but something in me needed it to be said aloud.

Alexander cursed under his breath.

The woman smiled wider. "Well, hello, little phoenix. I am Death."

With a flick of her finger, Alexander was wrenched away from me and thrown across the cemetery, crashing into a stone mausoleum with a sickening crack. His body slumped to the ground, unmoving.

"Quiet minds cannot be perplexed or frightened but go on in fortune or misfortune at their own private pace, like a clock during a thunderstorm."

-Robert Louis Stevenson, Dr. Jekyll and Mr. Hyde

Thirty-One

The stomach-turning sound of Alexander hitting the stone echoed in my ears. Before I fully realized what I was doing, my hands burst into flames, and a fireball formed at my chest. All I could see was Alexander's bent and broken body, contorted where he'd fallen.

My heart clenched as I launched my ball of flames at the woman who'd called herself Death. All logic had left my body. The only thing remaining was pure rage. The fire hit Death square in the chest, sending her stumbling back several steps. Despite the blackened circle on her dress and the tightness of her shoulders, she smiled widely.

"Is that all you are capable of?"

Her words needled at me, sounding like my mother. But I knew I needed to get Alexander and myself out of here and somewhere safe. Pooling my rage and fear together, I hurled another blast of fire at her, this one larger than the last.

It hit her in the same spot on the chest, throwing her into a large headstone. She fell to the ground and her blackened hand went to her middle, holding her ribs.

Not wasting another moment, I ran over to Alexander.

He was moving some, groaning, but he still hadn't opened his eyes.

"Alexander, get up," I pleaded, pulling on his arm to get him upright. "We need to run, now."

He groaned again, his hand reaching up to hold the side of his head. "Katrina?"

"Yes, it's me," I said, looking back at Death, who was still leaning against the headstone she'd struck. "We need to go before she gets back up."

My words seemed to provide some clarity to him because he nodded, taking in a deep breath as I helped him up to standing.

"Where is Liath?" I asked, my voice strained from the exertion of bearing most of his weight.

"Trees," he replied, his eyes trained on the woman who'd created him. "Get to the trees. She will find us."

"Can you run?" I asked, urging my fire into my left hand and forming another sphere of flames.

He nodded, closing his eyes briefly. "I'll manage."

"Be ready to run, then."

Another ball of flames left my hand, crackling against Death once more and pushing her back into the headstone. The flames dissipated, leaving soot and ash along her neck and face.

"Now," I breathed out, tugging on Alexander as we ran into the tree line.

The sound of laughter followed us into the night. Turning over my shoulder, Death sat at the headstone, wiping at her smeared lipstick with her thumb. She smiled widely. "Run, little phoenix, as fast as you can."

Her words sent chills down my spine, like fingernails scraping against my skin. Keeping my eyes on her form, we finally made it to the trees, disappearing into the forest. Only when I could no longer see the light of the fire in the cemetery and the glow of Death's hair in the moonlight did I turn around, pulling Alexander with me as we ran.

Branches tangled in my hair and caught at my dress as we moved through the brush.

"Where is Liath?" I asked, panting for breath as I continued to lead us in what I could only hope was the right direction.

As if she'd heard us, hooves sounded nearby, and we both turned to see Liath, her flaming eyes alight as she stopped beside us.

"Alexander, can you get on the horse?" I asked. He swayed slightly, his eyes drooping. Reaching up my free hand, I patted his cheek roughly, causing his eyes to open once more. "Alexander, you need to get on Liath. Now."

By some miracle, I was able to get him astride Liath. Gritting my teeth, I slid my foot in the stirrup and pulled myself up, settling in front of Alexander and wrapping his arms around my waist as he slumped forward, his weight heavy and warm on my back.

"Liath," I whispered, taking hold of her reins. "I hope you know the way home."

She whinnied, and then we were off, her eyes lighting the way as she sped into a gallop, winding us through the trees and branches. My hands tightened around the leather of the reins, but I was careful not to put any tension to make her think I was trying to direct her.

I had a vague idea of where we were, but my heart thundering in my ears and the oily fear swirling in my stomach made it impossible for me to think straight.

With the moon high overhead, we burst out of the trees, Liath slowing to a trot and then a careful walk as we entered the clearing around Alexander's house. My breath left in a rush, the overwhelming urge to cry as safety greeted us.

But we weren't safe.

Not yet.

My luck with Liath had apparently run out, as I attempted to dismount. My foot tangled in my dress, and I fell to the ground, landing on my shoulder with a sharp pop. Gritting my teeth, I stood, reaching for the reins. Sudden pain flooded through my shoulder and neck, turning my stomach and pulling a shuddering gasp from me. I bit down on my lower lip to fight the noise escaping, and gingerly, I cradled that arm to my chest.

"Alexander," I called out, patting my good hand against his thigh. He'd somehow stayed upright during my less than graceful departure, but his eyes had slid shut again and the sway to his body was concerning.

His eyes fluttered, and his jaw tightened as he opened them fully. "Where're we?"

"Home," I replied, taking Liath's reins in my good hand and leading her to the stables.

"'S not safe here," he said, somehow dismounting from Liath while she was still moving and landing on his feet gracefully. "Need to cast wards."

"Wards?" I asked, dropping Liath's leads. She took off on her own into the stables, going into an open stall, where she began happily munching on whatever was in her feed bag. Letting out a breath, I turned back to Alexander, just in time to catch him before he fell, tucking my good arm beneath his armpit to keep his face from meeting the earth. "You're too weak to use any more magic. Tell me how to do the wards and I'll try to cast them."

The movement jostled my injured left arm, and I bit down on the inside of my cheek to keep from screaming, a burst of copper flooding my tongue. Panting as the pain dulled, I spat out the glob of blood onto the ground.

"Has to be me. Or she'll find us," he muttered. He raised his hand, and waves of purple smoke left his palm, spreading out and surrounding the clearing on all sides in a hazy dome. His lips moved as he mouthed words, but they were so quiet and slurred that I could not hear him with my deaf ear.

The dome shimmered before disappearing, the air the same as it had been.

"Done," he said proudly, smiling at me. And then his eyes rolled back and despite me holding him, he fell to the grass. I winced as he landed with a thud. Bending down quickly, I placed my knees beneath his head, barely making it before it lolled against the ground.

Despite how he got there, Alexander looked calm before me. The usual intensity that burned through his face was now smooth with unconsciousness.

A crow cawed in the distance, pulling a flinch from my body that turned into a wince as my arm jolted. After looking around for signs of Death, I turned my gaze to Alexander while I kept my injured arm tucked against my chest. Sighing, I slipped his head from my lap and stood.

I knew it would be a challenge to get him into the house, but we needed to get inside. The door was yards away, but it felt like miles with how heavy Alexander felt when leaning against me. There was no way I could get him inside by myself, but I also could not leave him here.

I knew I would need to use both arms to pull him inside. With my right hand, I sucked in a breath as I poked at the injured joint, probing the skin and muscle. The joint was certainly not in the right place; the abnormal lump at the front of my shoulder proved that. I had read about this injury before, in a book of medicine that Henry had left out on his desk one day.

Taking hold of the wrist of the injured arm, I focused on inhaling deep breaths, one, and then another, and another. Closing my eyes, I took one more breath and held it, blowing it out harshly as I pulled on my wrist and yanked the arm out and up.

Fire burned through my entire arm, and I cried out, loudly panting until the pain faded. Gingerly, I tested the arm, moving it slightly. I nearly cried out again, this time in relief, as the pain was only a dull ache instead of the stabbing white-hot pain it had been.

I could do this.

Bending, I looped my hands beneath Alexander's armpits. Flexing my core and bending my legs, I pushed my feet into the earth, pulling him up and dragging him toward the house. Pain radiated out from my arm, but I continued my path.

Finally, after what felt like hours, I deposited Alexander onto the bed in what I assumed was his room. Dropping his torso first and then bending to pull his legs to follow.

"Katr... na," Alexander mumbled, his eyes staying closed.

Sweat poured down my back and face, trickling in rivulets down my forehead and neck. Wiping it away with the back of my good hand, I bent down beside him, cradling my left arm to my chest. "What is it, Alexander?"

"Alone... blazing bright," he said. "Pure flame."

"What?" I questioned, leaning closer to his face with my left ear. "Horseman, are you with me?"

He didn't reply, his head slumping to the side once more.

Patting his cheek until his eyes opened again, I found the blue darker than before. "Horseman. What are you saying? Can you hear me?"

"Katrina," he said, smiling slightly. "You saved me. You're beautiful. My bright fire."

My cheeks heated at his words. I rested my hand on his forehead, finding it clammy with sweat. "Rest, Alexander."

"Spirit magic." His voice was weak, trailing off before he could finish. "Such a price."

As his eyes closed once more, I stood, taking a deep breath. Of course, his magic had taken a toll on him. He'd been using it constantly to disguise me and then to find me. Even my body was fading, eyelids heavy.

I stopped at the foot of the bed, debating on taking off his boots so he would be more comfortable. The twinge in my shoulder declared he could sleep in discomfort.

Moving to the room I'd slept in previously, I toed off my own boots and lay down on the bed. The tension bled from my body as my eyes slid shut and my breathing evened.

Maybe I would just rest for a moment.

"I have an empty sort of feeling; nothing in the world seems of sufficient importance to be worth doing."

-Bram Stoker, Dracula

Thirty-Two

Visions of flame and blood startled me awake, the images seared into my eyelids as my chest heaved. Sitting up in the small bed, I pressed my palms into my eyes, pushing until bursting stars filled the darkness behind my eyes instead of rivers of blood and fire.

My breath finally slowing, I stood, moving to the window to pull open the curtains. I'd slept longer than I'd intended, the gray of the coming dawn lightening the sky above the trees surrounding the cottage. From here, I watched the wind rustle the trees, picking up the autumn leaves and swirling them like a ribbon of flame around the ground.

Focused on the leaves dancing around the tree trunks, the sudden blur of darkness that filled the windowpane sent me stumbling backward. There in front of me, lighting on the small windowsill, was a crow. The inky black pools of its eyes focused intently on me, its head tilting back and forth as it studied me.

Unbidden, my feet carried me closer to the window, despite every instinct screaming at me to draw the curtains and run from the strange stare of the creature. But something held me there, pulling me closer as if entranced by its unblinking eyes.

It sat there, watching me as I placed my palm on the window. The cold of the glass was sharp against my skin.

Click. Click. Click.

The bird tapped its beak against the glass where my palm rested. It pecked once more and pulled back, its jerky head tilting one way and then the other. It blinked once, twice, three times. And then, as if it were an entirely different bird, it tipped its head back and opened its maw, screeching.

Stumbling from the window, I fell to the floor, my hands reaching out behind me to catch my body. The impact jarred my shoulder, wrenching a cry from my lips. Biting back the tears, I rolled to my knees and crawled to the window, using the frame to pull myself up.

My breath caught in my throat, waiting for the bird to stare back at me, but once again, it was gone. Without a sign it had ever been here.

Cradling my injured arm to my chest, I yanked the curtains closed, plunging the room into darkness. Tears pricked my eyes as both the pain of my injury and the events of the previous night cut through the adrenaline of my encounter.

My parents were dead. Ciara was dead. Death was in Sleepy Hollow, and was coming for me...

The breath left my lungs in a rush, the room spinning in the darkness as Death's words came back to me. She'd called me "little phoenix."

My vision swam as I stumbled toward the bed, my foot catching something in the room and sending me careening to the floor once again. My knees caught my impact this time, and I let myself slump to the side as I stared into nothingness.

I could not be a phoenix.

The poem I'd discovered at Priscilla's. The firebirds and their dance with Death. Had she known?

A noise outside the bedroom pulled my head around. Had Alexander known?

Squeezing my eyes shut, I let my head fall forward, curls dropping to cover my face. Tightening the fist of my good hand, I beat it against my leg, hard to feel the pain. A punishment for my naïveté. I was smart. I was the one who found the poem. I was the one who discovered the passages about the sluagh, though in the end, that hadn't mattered. Maybe they hadn't known.

With a shuddering breath, I raised my head, shifting my weight back on my heels and standing as I pushed my hair back from my face. My chin jutted out, and I kept my shoulders back as much as I could. A deep breath expanded my ribs. Another.

Alexander was injured, and though my anxiety pleaded with me to leave him and hide from the potential knowledge he had known things and not shared them with me, I knew I could not stop Death without him.

This was no time for me to break down, though all I wanted to do was hide in the darkness and slip, forgotten, away from everything and everyone.

But Sleepy Hollow needed a savior.

An inky thought slithered from the recesses of my mind, dark and twisted like the shadows Death had emerged from. Perhaps, if I died saving Sleepy Hollow, I would finally be enough.

The thought took hold of my heart, acid burning in my throat. I did not want to die, and yet, perhaps I did.

A rattling groan from Alexander's room yanked me

from the darkness, my eyes focusing on the floor before me. Taking a deep breath to settle myself, I pulled the door open, leaving my room and entering Alexander's.

His eyes were closed, but from how his hands balled at his sides and feet clambering on the blankets, his rest was fitful. Sweat beaded on his forehead, dripping into his hair.

Looking around the room, I grabbed a damp rag from the bowl of water the house must have left on the chest of drawers nearby and sat on the bed beside him.

"Shh," I whispered. The shame that had been burning through my soul deflated at the sight of his pain, my shoulders slumping in as I curled over him while wiping his brow.

His eyes fluttered, but his legs relaxed, feet stretching back out again. His lips moved, but no sound escaped, caught behind the weight of whatever price the spirit magic had exacted from him.

"Alexander." I raised my voice, so he'd hopefully hear me wherever his mind had taken him. I set the rag down on my knee, moving to shake him.

Stirring, he opened his eyes, his tongue darting out to lick at his cracked lips. "Katrina, are you all right?"

"Shh," I said again. I would not be answering his question, not when I couldn't trust my face to not give away the lie when I told him I was fine. "How are you feeling?"

"Tired," he replied, his voice hoarse. He licked his lips again, looking around the room. "How did we get back here?"

"Liath," I muttered, taking up the rag once more. "And then I brought you inside."

He looked at me, eyes tracking over every inch of me from my head down to my waist, before focusing back on my injured arm I held tightly against my stomach. "You're injured."

"I am fine."

"And now you lie," he said. He shifted, trying to sit up and hissed in pain, his hand going to cradle his midsection.

"Stay lying down," I scolded, standing from the bed. "You were thrown against that mausoleum."

"I should have healed by now," he said through gritted teeth. "Even with all the magic I'd used, it should not have affected me so."

I froze at his words. "Was it her magic?"

He licked his lips again, his blue eyes darkening as he studied my face for a long moment. "Likely, yes."

"You need to rest then," I said, placing the rag down at his side. "I will get you some water and then brew you some tea to help you sleep."

Without waiting for his response, I turned to leave the room. Before I could step out, though, a cup clattered from the dresser, sending me jerking back into the doorframe with a hiss as I held my shoulder.

There, sitting on the dresser, was a steaming cup of tea beside the rag and bowl.

"It's the house," Alexander said, trying to smile through his grimace. "I'm sorry it startled you."

"It's fine," I said, rubbing my collarbone as my heart slowed. "I'll let you drink your tea and rest, then."

"Katrina," he called. "Wait."

I paused in the doorframe, turning over my shoulder.

"Thank you," he said. The softness of his voice and his eyes were like daggers plunging and twisting into my heart. I wanted to lean over and question him, to ask if he had known all along what I was, but when he looked at me like that—like I was the breath in his lungs—all I could do was melt.

My throat burned, all the unsaid words scratching and clawing to get out. Unable to let any of them free, I simply nodded before turning away, leaving the room and drawing the door closed behind me.

My vision blurred with tears as I stumbled to the kitchen. Bracing one hand against the countertop, I took deep breaths, focusing on the wood grain beneath my hand.

A tear escaped from the corner of my eye. I wanted him. Gods, I wanted. Perhaps, in another life, perhaps we could have been together. But in this one, plagued by shadows of death and fire, we had no hope.

Something fractured in my chest at the admission.

Wiping away the tear from my cheek, I let my curtain of hair fall around my face. Just for a moment, I could mourn what I had lost, but never truly had. Just for a moment, before I needed to shove it all back and focus on the reality at hand.

It would be awhile before he woke, hopefully, so I turned to the rest of the cottage. The bookshelf caught my eye, sparking something in my mind. If Alexander had known the truth of his mother's words, perhaps he would have more information on phoenixes.

Tipping my head to the side, I scanned the titles, searching for anything that would stand out. Halfway down the third shelf, a faint tugging sensation in my chest guided me toward a thick leather-bound tome. The gilded title blazed like molten metal.

The book that had called to me the first time I'd seen it.

Without giving myself a moment to second guess myself, I pulled it from the shelf. My breath caught in my chest, and I froze, waiting for whatever Alexander had been warning me about to happen. Nothing did.

The book felt warm in my hands, like holding a warm mug, rather than a burning inferno. I took it back to the kitchen table.

Though I itched to dive right in, I stopped, filling the

kettle with water, and putting it on the stove to make tea for myself, since the house had only made enough for Alexander. Once that was done and my fire ignited, I slid into the chair at the table and opened the book; the leather cracked as the smell of worn parchment tickled my nose.

I flipped through the pages as the water heated. My eyes devoured every word. Turning to the next page, my hand wavered. An illustration of a great bird of fire looked back at me, its head held proudly, and wings of flame outstretched. My fingers traced over the lines, following the curve of its beak and the sharp points of its wings. Reluctantly, I pulled my eyes over to the accompanying text.

A flame grows in the darkness,
Alone and blazing bright.
Screams grow coldly in the wind,
On wings as black as night.

Death demands an offering,
Only those with sight can see.
Ashes and dust surround the world,
No one to hear your plea.

Veils of smoke and shadow hide
The truest hearts of stone.
And with the dead to help her,
Death will build a throne of bones.

Run, little phoenix,
Run far, run fast.
For Death will always find you,
Your peace
It will not last.

Blood and embers fill the streets,
The world ready to become
An endless maze of bodies.
Oh, how quickly you'll succumb.

THE SCREAMING of the kettle made my heart jump into my throat as I slammed the book shut once again, pressing my hand to my chest.

Numb, I stood and stared at the book on the table. I couldn't bring myself to touch it. Not even to return it to the shelf.

I'd brought Death to Sleepy Hollow. And now she was going to destroy it.

"His appetite for the
marvelous, and his powers
of digesting it, were
equally extraordinary."

-Washington Irving,
The Legend of Sleepy Hollow

My world spiraled as muted colors mixed with the smell of lavender. Ciara might have been the one to summon her, but Death was going to destroy Sleepy Hollow because of me. Acid burned in the back of my throat, and an oily sensation churned in my stomach.

Standing at the table in the kitchen, I lost all track of time. Visions of empty eye sockets, crackling fires, and the blood-red lips of the woman who'd sprung from the shadows ran through my mind over and over and over. I could hear nothing, save the pounding in my heart that echoed through my chest and into my head.

A hand came down on my injured shoulder and yanked me back into focus as a cry escaped my lips, layered equally in both pain and fear.

"Katrina, it's me," Alexander said, cutting through the frantic cacophony of my heartbeat.

Squeezing my eyes shut to fight the prick of tears, I turned to face him, sucking a breath through my teeth. "I didn't hear you."

"Did I hurt you?" he asked. As I slowly opened my eyes, Alexander's face filled my field of vision, pinched tight with worry. Or perhaps it was exhaustion. His hand reached out for my shoulder, stopping before he touched it again. "What happened?"

"I'm fine," I managed, through clenched teeth. The pain had dulled some, and as long as I didn't move my arm much, I could almost forget it was injured. "How are you feeling?"

"I am stable for now and will get better as more time passes," he replied, bending to catch my eyes. I attempted to turn away, unready—and unwilling—to face him, not with all the secrets he'd apparently been keeping, but he caught the hand of my uninjured arm and kept me still. "Please. You're obviously in pain. Tell me what happened."

Heat kissed my cheeks, but I knew if I did not tell him, he would only drag this out longer. "I fell from Liath getting you back here. I dislocated my shoulder when I landed on it."

"Is it still dislocated?" he asked, gingerly touching the neckline of my dress and peering closely.

"No," I replied, stepping away from him. He frowned at our separation.

"But how..." His eyes widened. "You put it back in place yourself?"

"I had to carry you to the house, and I couldn't do that with one arm," I said with a careful neutrality. The concern in Alexander's voice and eyes made my heart tighten despite the anger that still simmered. I desperately wanted to hug him, to reassure myself that he was safe, that I was safe, that we were both alive. But I would not. Not until I had my answers.

"You could have injured it further," he said. "Have you taken anything for the pain?"

"I've had other things on my mind," I said, letting some

of the fire in my soul seep into my words. "I was going to put herbs in my tea to help with the pain once you were back on your feet. We cannot both be impaired at the same time."

He didn't reply, but instead looked at me like he'd never quite seen anything like me before.

In the heavy silence, words clawed at my throat, begging to be spoken. Before I could stop them, they slipped from my lips. "She called me phoenix."

He froze, an animal caught in the face of a feared predator. And it answered all the questions I had left unsaid.

"You knew," I continued. "You knew what I was, and that she was coming."

"Katrina," he began, shaking his head. The guilt shining in his eyes told me everything.

"No, Dullahan. I want the truth."

He sighed, reaching up to run his hand through his hair as he turned and paced the room for a moment. He came to a stop in front of me, closer than before. "I didn't know for certain, but yes, I suspected. On both accounts."

"You lied to me." No anger or disappointment laced my words, just apathetic facts. Rage bubbled beneath the surface, dangerously close to boiling over and erupting in a white-hot plume of destruction. "You could have told me what you suspected. We could have prepared for this. Instead, you told me I couldn't be a phoenix."

He shook his head. "You cannot prepare for Death. And if I was wrong—I did not want to put any more of a burden on your shoulders."

"That was not your decision to make." My voice cracked as hot tears blurred my vision and spilled down my cheeks. Reaching up, I roughly wiped them away, irritated at myself for once again crying in front of the Horseman. I was not sad. I was not hurt. I was furious. "This is my life. Those were my parents, and this is my home. I had a right to know all the facts, theories, dreams, or guesses you had access to."

"I apolo—"

"Did Priscilla know?" I demanded, cutting him off as the fiery flames began cracking through the lid I'd put on them.

He shook his head again, his eyes pleading with me. "No. And if she suspected, she did not share her theories with me."

Closing my eyes, I took a deep breath, attempting to re-form the lid on the bubbling rage. With my arm injured and tucked closely into my stomach, I could not risk my hands erupting into flames. If I ruined this dress, I wasn't certain I'd be able to get into a new one on my own, and I absolutely would not be asking the Horseman for help. I didn't look at him as I spoke. "Why didn't you tell me?"

"Katrina, please. I understand I've hurt you, and I do apologize," he said, reaching down to take my hand in his. His other hand raised to cup my cheek, tilting my head up to meet his gaze. "I am sorry for keeping it from you. I'd hoped you not knowing would be enough to keep her away. But when Ciara summoned her, she sent her fog, and she sent her pets to watch the town. When she saw you, she knew anyway. I saw the crow at the party; she was there. I was still in denial, and now we will all pay the price for my stubbornness. I am so very sorry."

I built a wall around my heart, which strengthened again with those words, even though it had already crumbled a bit with the touch of his thumb on my skin. My parents deserved to die, but Ciara had not. "We'll never know if it would have changed things. Just like we will never know if we could have avoided this entirely by sending back those sent to you. Ciara summoned Death because of you. Not because of me."

He flinched, dropping both of his hands back to his sides, his eyes closing for a moment. I fought to keep myself from leaning in after the warmth of his touch. "You are hurting. You need to take time to grieve those you lost."

"No, Dullahan, I do not, and I cannot. Death is here, in the Hollow. And despite the many, many failings of my parents, they always believed they were working for the good of the Hollow. I will not mourn their deaths, but I cannot let your mother destroy my town. So, what shall we do?"

Taking a deep breath, I pushed back the voice that told me I was not enough to save Sleepy Hollow, that I would not succeed.

For a moment, there was nothing in the room between us. Not a breath or a whisper of a draft; not even the calling of a bird from outside the window. Finally, he nodded. "Fine."

Once again, ignoring the twinge of alarm, I nodded. "Should we go back to town first and ensure she's not already destroyed Sleepy Hollow?"

He shook his head immediately. "No, absolutely not. Unless I dreamed it, I cast powerful wards around the property. She won't be able to get to us here, but as soon as we step outside of them, she will. And without your powers focused and ready, she will kill you."

I searched his face for any hint that he was holding something back, but found nothing. Sighing, I nodded once more. "Fine. Do you have any other books about the phoenix? I found the one with the poem." I nodded my head at the book spread out on the table still. "Are there others that may help?"

"The first line of it—in its original language—could easily give the impression that your mother would have to sacrifice her fire since she was the first of Sleepy Hollow. I suspect Adelaide mentioned it," he said slowly, as if weighing the words on his tongue as he spoke.

I jerked back. Of all the things I'd anticipated, that had not been it. The admission, so freely given, was surprising yet welcome. I had many questions, but settled on the one I needed answered most urgently. Finding more answers about how much she did not love me could wait. "Is that the entirety of it?"

He shook his head. "I sincerely doubt it. Many poems in that book are only portions; whatever the author deemed important enough to include. If we want to find it in its entirety, we must search elsewhere."

I chewed on my lip. That poem had been exceedingly accurate in the events that transpired thus far. If there was more to it, it could prove invaluable in our efforts to stop Death. "Do you think Priscilla would know where to find the rest?"

"Perhaps." His voice was careful as he nodded at my shoulder. "But first, we need to get your pain managed and wrap your shoulder tightly before we go to work on your powers."

I fought to keep from scoffing. "I am fine. We should start with my powers now. I can only imagine the havoc Death will wreak on the Hollow once she discovers she cannot get to us here."

"I'm not compromising on this, Katrina," he said, crossing his arms over his chest. Though his stance was rough, his eyes were soft and full of worry. "Please, let me help you."

Chewing on my lip, I debated it for a heartbeat before finally accepting I would not win this battle. "Fine. But then, we train. And we don't stop until I'm able to conjure the full extent of my magic."

"It's a deal."

"It is true, we shall be monsters, cut off from all the world; but on that account we shall be more attached to one another."

-Mary Shelley, Frankenstein

"You're certain it's set properly?" Alexander asked, his hands hovering around my shoulder. His forehead pinched as he pulled his gaze away long enough to meet my eyes. "Would you mind if I made sure?"

"Go ahead, Dullahan," I told him as I clenched my other hand into a fist to stave off the pain I knew was coming.

"That is the third time you have used my title instead of my name since I woke," he murmured, his breath fanning against my neck as his fingers caressed along my skin. He paused, looking at me again with an unfamiliar swirl in the blue of his eyes. "Why?"

"Have I? I didn't realize." Despite knowing that I was well within my rights to be angry with him for what he'd done—or rather, not done—part of me was still tense, fearing retaliation for my words and tone of voice. I truly hadn't realized I put that distance back between us again. Taking a deep breath, I slowly blew it out, watching my breath flutter against the fabric of his shirt. "I'm sorry, Alexander."

His breath hitched slightly, but his fingers never faltered

in their gentle probing. I squeezed my eyes shut to keep from looking at him, though I could feel the weight of his gaze on my face. Thankfully, he said nothing and continued his examination. He trailed his fingers down my arm to wrap around my wrist, sending shivers through my spine. One hand moved my arm as the other pressed against my shoulder, prodding as the joint moved. I bit down on my lip, wincing at the dull twinge of pain while swallowing back any noises of discomfort.

Finally, he moved away, and I opened my eyes, only to find him staring at me. "Katrina, I—"

"You said you would bind my shoulder?" I asked, not wanting to hear what he had to say. Perhaps it was childish, but I wanted to stew in my anger and make him suffer for lying to me. And if I let him say whatever he'd been about to, I knew I would not be able to cling to that.

It was already dissipating each time I caught him looking at me, and I knew it would soon crumble entirely.

"I'm sorry, Katrina." He reached up to run his thumb over my cheek. And with that motion, all the anger I'd clung to bled out of me. I sighed, closing my eyes as I leaned into his touch. "I'm so sorry, Katrina."

"I forgive you, Alexander." My voice was a mere whisper. I opened my eyes to meet his intense gaze.

He pursed his lips, his eyes darting to my mouth and then to my shoulder. At the sight of my shoulder, his lips pressed into a firm line, as if he'd just remembered what we were doing here. "You'll need to remove your dress. I cannot bind it properly over your clothing."

Fantastic.

Fighting the sudden tempest brewing in my belly, I stepped around him and walked into the room. In some way, I was almost grateful for the situation. I needed to see his reaction to my body and see if this tension that had been burning within me since our almost-kiss was real, or if I was imagining it. But I knew better than to get my hopes up. I pushed those feelings down as far as they would go, praying to whoever was listening that they'd stay there.

Alexander stepped into the room behind me and pulled the door closed, making the room feel overwhelmingly small as his presence dominated the space. He moved to the chest by his bed, stooping to rifle through it before returning with linen bandages.

He stopped in front of me, holding the bundle of fabric up. "I can turn around while you undress, if it would make you feel better."

As much as I wanted to say yes, I knew I could not remove the dress by myself. My cheeks burned with embarrassment. "I'll need your help, if you wouldn't mind."

He answered quickly. "Of course not."

Gingerly, I tugged at the sleeve of my dress, pulling the neckline down until I could stretch it over my shoulder. Alexander's hands took over, easing mine aside as he raised my injured arm and nodded at me to raise the other. His hands landed on my waist, startling me.

"I'm sorry." He'd said the words too quietly for me to hear, but I'd read his lips. I nodded for him to continue, and he hesitated for a moment before pulling the dress up and over my head.

Respectable women wore a slip under their dresses, sometimes more than one. But I was not a respectable woman. Also, since I'd met the Horseman, I'd scorched all the clothing he'd lent me. Every decision I'd made since taking his hand that night after he'd pulled me from the water came back to laugh in my face as I now stood naked in front of the Dullahan. No, even worse... I now stood naked in front of *Alexander*.

If he was breathing, I could no longer hear it, and I

didn't see his chest rising and falling, either. He was staring at me, but not at my body like I'd feared. He was staring at my face, and the centers of his eyes were wide, with only a sliver of blue was visible around the edges.

Fire pulsed through my veins, crawling through my body and pooling low in my stomach. Reaching out my good arm, I pulled the discarded dress from his hands and held the fabric against my torso, covering my bare breasts. It did little to make me feel less exposed, but the exposure I felt had nothing to do with my nakedness; especially considering he'd yet to drop his gaze below my mouth.

He blinked once, twice, before clearing his throat. Holding up the bandage again, he took a small step closer. "May I?"

"Yes," I murmured, finding a knot in the wood of the floorboards to focus on as he began unraveling the bandage. He pressed the end to my collarbone, his fingers sending sparks down my spine from where they touched my bare skin. I surpassed a shiver, my fingers itching to reach up and pull him close to me.

"Hold this end." He pressed his fingers firmly into the skin above the dip in my collarbone.

Adjusting my grip on the dress covering me, I held the bandage in place with my forearm as my fingers brushed against his. His fingers lingered a moment longer than necessary, and he let out a soft sigh that moved my hair as he continued. Pulling the bandage taut, he lifted my injured arm and began winding the bandage beneath my armpit and back around the front of my shoulder.

"You can let go now," he said, bringing the bandage back around my arm once more. Letting go, I resumed my grip on the dress. He lowered my arm, bending it for a moment as he continued wrapping around and around. Stepping behind me, he gathered my heft of curls in his hand, easily holding the mass in one palm as he lifted it and draped them over my wrapped shoulder. The touch sent another shiver through me, and this one I could not suppress.

His fingers rested on the bare skin at the back of my neck, his voice a hoarse whisper. "Are you cold, Katrina?"

I *was* cold, but that wasn't why I had shivered. "No."

"You shivered."

"I did, but it wasn't because I was cold, Dullahan."

The heat of his body radiated into my bare back as he stepped closer to me, nearly touching my back to his front. My eyes squeezed shut in anticipation, hoping he would touch me again. His breath fanned against the back of my neck. "My name is Alexander."

"I know."

A heartbeat passed, and I waited for his response, my body buzzing. Would he touch me? Would he step up behind me and press his body into mine? My breathing quickened as I imagined what his hands would feel like on my skin when they weren't tending to my wounds, but exploring simply for the sake of it. But he did none of that. He simply hummed and continued wrapping my arm, anchoring my injured shoulder in place.

Rejection curled in my throat like the smoky taste of ash against my tongue. A taste that was getting far too familiar for my liking.

He tucked in the end of the wrap, wedging it beneath the fabric at my back. Despite his job being complete, he stayed—the fabric of his clothing brushing against my back, the soft puff of his breath against my skin.

"Thank you for bringing me back here, Katrina." His voice was like warm honey dripping over my skin.

I kept my eyes firmly on the floor in front of me. "I could not very well let her kill you, could I?"

"You could have," he said, reaching up to adjust the

bandage across my back, trailing his fingers over the skin. Goosebumps erupted, and I suppressed a shiver. "But I am very grateful you didn't."

The walls I'd built crumbled into dust beneath his voice. "Thank you for coming for me, Alexander."

"I will always come for you," he whispered.

I felt him step away, but I remained. I heard him rifling through the jacket I'd removed from him and hung on the end of the bed. He stepped back up behind me, a soft clinking of metal barely audible.

"Lift your hair for me, please."

My body twitched, wanting to turn around and look at him, to question him, but I didn't want to shatter the moment we'd created. Instead, I did as he asked, and used my good arm to lift my hair from my neck, letting my eyes drift closed.

Cold metal met my skin, a heavy round presence landing on my chest. A familiar presence. My eyes shot open as the clasp snapped into place, and I looked down to see the red crystal necklace Henry had given me around my neck once again. Tears burned in my throat as I reached up to touch it. "You found it."

"I did. That first night, I went back to the river after you'd fallen asleep." He hesitated a moment. The prickle of his anxiety tingled on the back of my neck. "I was waiting until we could trust each other to give it back. And then... well, then we never had time."

"Thank you," I whispered, my heart swelling as my fingers rubbed over the smooth stone. Again, I ached to turn around and wrap my arms around Alexander's neck, but the peace was too fragile.

His hands found their way to my hips, resting on either side of me, and he squeezed just firmly enough to remind me exactly whose hands were on my body. I froze, warring with myself whether to lean into his embrace or step away. Leaning back may open the path for forgiveness, while stepping away might close the path for something more between us. So, I stood, still as a statue, as his fingers flexed against my skin.

Slowly, his small puffs of breath got more concentrated, and then his lips were on my neck. It was a soft kiss, but it sent a jolt through my body. My fire responded, racing through my veins and swirling in excitement.

One of Alexander's hands tugged at my waist, spinning me around to face him. The tenderness in his face knocked the breath from my lungs. He smiled, reaching up his hand to rub a thumb over my cheek and cup my face. "It seemed important to you. I'm sorry I haven't had a chance to give it to you with all that happened."

"It is important," I agreed, letting myself get lost in the ocean of swirling blues in his eyes. "It's the only gift I've ever been given."

Hurt and rage flashed in equal measures across his face. His other hand left my hip, joining the one holding my face, and he tipped my head back to meet his gaze more fully. "I will give you a gift every day for the rest of your life."

I huffed a laugh. "Don't be dramatic, that's hardly necessary."

He shook his head. "It's not dramatic. You deserve to know how valued you are."

"Thank you," I said, my voice quiet. My mouth opened, wanting to ask him to kiss me, but then I closed it with a click, biting down on the inside of my cheek. Warmth spread through my soul, pulling the oxygen from the room. My limbs tingled, remembering the last time he'd kissed me and what it had felt like.

Somehow, he moved impossibly closer, and his eyes darkened as he rubbed his thumb over my cheek, catching beneath my chin and raising my face to his. His voice was dark as he spoke. "What were you about to ask me, Katrina?"

My face burned, but this time, I could not tell if it was from desire or embarrassment. My eyes darted down to his lips, which curled into a smile.

"Can I kiss you, Katrina?" His voice was breathy, but I heard him as clearly as if he'd pressed his mouth directly to my ear, his words skating down my spine.

Instead of answering with words, I surged up to meet his lips with mine, consumed by the fire raging in my heart. The groan he let out in response vibrated against my face, and his hands tightened as he pulled me closer.

I wanted to touch him, but holding the dress and my injured arm had both hands occupied. For a split second, as our lips moved against each other, I considered my options, deciding to let the dress fall to the floor between us so I could wrap my hand around his neck and pull him back to me with more ferocity.

Our tongues met, our breath mingling as we kissed. But it wasn't enough. None of it was enough. One of his hands left my face and traveled down my neck, skimming the side of my breast before wrapping around my ribcage. He slid it down until it rested on my hip, burning a path down my body.

I groaned into his mouth, and he swallowed the sound, pulling back slightly to kiss at my neck and down my chest as we both panted for air. My hand moved down to fist the front of his shirt, and I pulled his face back up to mine, unwilling to let us part. Fire surged through my body, and I wanted nothing more than to be consumed by it. Consumed by *him*.

His hand curved around my hip, tracing over my skin, and wrapping his fingers around the back of my thigh, he pulled my leg up around his own hip. His other hand plunged into my hair, tilting my head to deepen the kiss. I could feel him *everywhere*. It was maddening, both too much and not enough all at once.

Finally, our franticness slowed, our movements becoming languid, but no less fiery. My fingers itched to untuck the shirt from his pants and run my hands over the skin of his stomach, and I almost did, but the twinge of pain in my shoulder pulled me back to reality.

Reluctantly, I pulled back, dropping my forehead to rest on his chest. He bent his head and pressed his lips to the top of my head, squeezing my thigh gently before letting my foot fall back to the floor while his fingers traced a path back up to my waist.

"We need to train." My voice was hoarse, but I didn't care. Raising my head, I traced my fingers over his face, catching the prickly hair along his jaw. "Thank you for returning my necklace."

He breathed out a laugh, rubbing his thumb over my lip. "If that is the thanks I get, you are profoundly welcome."

His words pulled a smile from my lips, but I rolled my eyes, anyway. "You said we had more important things to focus on, and that has not changed. We need to prepare."

He licked his lips, watching me intently for a moment before bowing his head. "As you wish."

"Lo! Death has reared himself a throne.
In a strange city lying alone."

-Edgar Allan Poe,
The City in the Sea

Thirty-Five

Summoning every ounce of my willpower, I stepped
back from Alexander and bent to pick up my dress
from the floor. Holding it in my hands, I wondered
how I would get it back on without his help. Wordlessly, he
tugged the fabric from my hands and helped me back into it,
easing it over my bound shoulder and pulling it over my
hips. Despite what we'd just done, his hands moved with
methodical efficiency, not lingering on my body. Not even
on the parts he'd just been gripping and squeezing.

Neither of us spoke as I followed him from the cottage
and into the clearing we'd practiced in before, still gingerly
holding my arm against my stomach. Alexander's shoulders
were heavy as he walked ahead of me, and I knew that
despite resting, he had not yet fully recovered from the hit of
his mother's magic.

He stopped in the middle of the clearing, turning
around to face me. "All right, are you ready?"

I scoffed. "We don't have time for me to not be ready.
Let's begin."

The weight of his stare made me want to fidget, but I

fought it back. He'd asked to kiss me, and that had given me a surge of confidence I hadn't known I needed. Perhaps I should have been looking for that confidence in myself, rather than in him, but for now, I would take it whenever I could. I bit the inside of my cheek and clenched my fists as I met his gaze, determination burning away the anxiety in my soul. I needed to do this. There was no other choice.

Finally, he nodded, waving his hand as the purple haze of his spirit realm descended over us and his head disappeared. The spirit magic was thick, and I reached up to rub at the ache in my ear from the pressure change.

Alexander stepped toward me, his voice louder than usual as he spoke. His words carried every bit of confidence I hoped to emulate one day. "Focus on visualizing your fire. Picture it building in your chest and moving through your arms down to your hands. Now, keep it there, don't let it go. Just keep it in your hands."

My heart squeezed, knowing his volume was for my benefit now that I couldn't read his lips. Taking several cautious steps away from him, I took a deep breath and closed my eyes. I straightened my injured arm and held my hands out to my sides. The fire that ran through my veins thrummed, and the heat pulsed as I called the flames into my palms. They swirled, agitation pressing against my skin from the inside, but they did not obey, deciding to spread through my body instead.

Gritting my teeth, I opened my eyes and ignored Alexander's looming presence as I focused on my hands, trying to follow his instructions. Slowly, finally, the heat in my body seemed to move, the flames licking through my veins as they gathered in my palms. I pushed my hope and excitement down, my brow furrowing as I tried to pull the flames from beneath my skin to rest in my hands.

With a slight pop, the flames emerged, dancing and flickering in my palms.

I couldn't help the smile that broke across my face, my eyes lifting to look at Alexander. My voice was slightly breathless, but the pride in it was clear to even my own ears. "I did it."

"Sustain it," his voice sounded, echoing slightly. "Don't let it go, Katrina. Keep it in your hands."

Looking back down at my hands, my fingers twitched, pulling at the flames. They grew, the flames licking up into the purple-tinged sky. I turned over one hand and pushed, directing the flames at the ground and concentrating as I visualized a small ball of flames leaving my fingers. I almost leapt with joy as the fire followed my instructions, landing on the ground and sputtering out against Alexander's magical shield.

The flames in my palm regenerated, both hands alight once more.

An unusually sharp gust of wind surged, picking up the heft of my curls and blowing them off to my side, whipping the ends of my dress. My fire extinguished as my focus shifted to keeping my balance in the strong wind.

The trees rustled, and it grew silent, the wind stopping at once. Unease pricked the back of my neck, clinging to the hairs and sending goosebumps down my arms. Stepping slowly closer to Alexander, I whispered, "Something's happening."

Before he could respond, a crow cawed. I flinched at the sharp noise and at the knowledge that the bird was back. The trees shook again, and then waves of black emerged as hundreds of crows joined the cawing, swarming in the sky.

The sky, already a dusty gray, darkened before my eyes as wisps of smoke rose from the trees. My eyes widened and fear thundered through my chest. My gaze stayed fixed on the swarming birds. "You said she can't pass the wards, right?"

"She shouldn't be able to." But his voice was wary, and even without being able to see his face, it was clear his answer was to calm himself as much as it was me.

"Should not is not the same as cannot, Alexander," I replied, fighting back the building panic. Sweat beaded and rolled down my spine. Wiping my clammy palms on my dress, I focused on the fire in my chest, trying to pull it back into my palms. "If she's coming, what do we do?"

A thick plume of black smoke rose from the trees, shooting up like a pillar and encompassing the birds above us. I could hear faint noises coming from them, like a high-pitched scream, and although I couldn't make out specific words, I knew we were in trouble.

"Katrina, get back to the house," Alexander ordered, his voice sharp. "She's summoned the sluagh here."

Icy fear washed over my body, and my eyes widened as I stared at the mass of swirling darkness above. "I'm not leaving you."

"Don't be foolish. You need to get inside. They cannot get to you there." He tugged on his gloves, his muscles bunching beneath his clothing as he adjusted his stance, preparing for the fight.

"My fire can hurt them," I protested, though I honestly wasn't certain why. I should be running as fast as I could for the house, but I couldn't stomach the thought of leaving him here to face this alone, after he'd already been so taxed by the previous night. I couldn't bring myself to leave. "Let me help."

The mass descended, spiraling toward us and drawing our attention upward.

"Fine, we don't have time to argue. Get ready," he said, extending his hand as the whip I'd seen last night appeared once more. Now that I could focus, I could tell I had been right. It was a human spine.

"Alexander, is that a *spine?*" I gulped out. "Whose spine is that?"

"Now is not the time," he snapped. "Get out your fire. Now."

The sluagh grew closer, and I focused on my hands, trying to will the fire out despite the panic clawing at my throat. My flames flickered, but quickly retreated into my palms as the heat curled around my heart.

"Katrina, NOW!" Alexander yelled as the mass of darkness surrounded us, blocking the dim light of the sun.

Nearly sobbing, I tried to push my flames out, but only tiny flickers appeared, lighting the darkness briefly and illuminating the birds surrounding us.

Screaming sounded, the high-pitched noise hurting my ears as the voices of the spirits inside the smoke keened their laments. Birds flurried around, their wings knocking against my back and tangling in my hair. My breath heaved as my vision blurred. A bird flew into my face, cawing loudly as its beak pecked at my hair. Crouching down, I raised my arms to cover my face, the pain in my shoulder not even registering against the fear that had its hold on my body.

And then, as quick as they'd descended, the day lightened; the silence leaving a ringing echo of screams in my head. Alexander's purple spirit realm was gone, and I looked at the clear green grass. Slowly, I uncovered my face and lifted my head to look around.

Alexander was gone.

I jumped up and whirled around, my eyes searching for any sign of him. The sluagh had taken him. My heart thundered as screams joined the sound of my blood echoing in my ears. I'd failed to push them back with my fire and now he was gone.

Out of the corner of my eye, I spotted movement at the edge of the tree line. I blinked rapidly to focus my vision on the emerging sight in front of me. Death, with her white hair and black eyes, stood there, draped in the blood-red cloak Ciara had worn.

Death had taken Alexander, and now here she stood, smiling with her gleaming teeth. Her smile only widened when she noticed me watching her and she stepped back, disappearing into the forest.

Rage took over my body, and before I realized what I was doing, I ran after her.

My feet crunched over the decaying leaves as I burst through the trees, searching the woods for any sign of the red cloak she'd stolen from Ciara's corpse.

"Bring him back!" I shouted as I moved deeper into the forest. "Why are you doing this?"

My words lingered on the wind, echoing into the emptiness. My heart shattered like the branches beneath my feet. I dropped to my knees, unable to bear the weight of what had just happened. Looking down at my hands, I growled. What good was having this power if I could not use it? The burden of my failure had once again struck, and this time Alexander was its victim.

Tipping my head back, I screamed into the trees. I screamed until my throat was raw and my body shook. Slumping to the ground, the echoes of my sorrow rang in my ears.

I rocked back on my heels, sitting up straight as my chest heaved.

Standing, I felt my fire roiling beneath my skin, spurred by my determination once again. My fear would smother my fire, but my persistence, it seemed, would let it out.

The forest quieted as I made for the clearing. The path

didn't take me to the house, though, but to the stable where Liath stood, grazing on hay.

She looked up as I approached, a sense of understanding reflecting in her dark eyes.

"I need you to take me to Sleepy Hollow," I told her, reaching out my good hand to brush against her nose. "Can you do that?"

She snorted and stomped her front leg as if she'd understood me.

I rubbed at her nose. "Good. Let's go save your master."

And with Liath's cooperation, I found myself hurtling toward Sleepy Hollow.

The bridge came into view, and my heart sped with anticipation. Would anyone believe me when I told them what happened? Would anyone care? Liath didn't slow as she carried me across the bridge, her flaming hooves thundering over the wood and onto the dirt of the path into town.

A town that would surely be waiting for me, given the noise of my arrival.

As we turned the last bend, I saw a large group already gathered. Fidgeting with the reins, I pulled Liath to a stop as we approached.

I could see the townspeople whispering to each other. Ichabod stood in the back with Brom, both of their eyes wide and fixed on me. Sliding from Liath, I kept my chin up and my shoulders back as I faced them.

"My parents are gone. And Death is coming for Sleepy Hollow."

"*Conquer such whims, and endeavour to strengthen your mind. No existence is more contemptible than that, which is embittered by fear.*"

-Ann Radcliffe,
The Mysteries of Udolpho

Thirty-Six

Waves of silence washed over the gathered crowd. And then, a flurry of shouting and outrage began.

"What do you mean gone?"

"Death?"

"What have you brought upon us, girl?"

Their words blended, fading into the background as my fire burst to the surface, encompassing my hands.

"Bring me the Ciallmhar." When no one moved, I snarled, "Now."

Someone in the back of the group scurried away, crossing the town square, and knocking frantically on the Ciallmhar's door. Their house overlooked the area, and I watched the door, waiting for the Elders of Sleepy Hollow to emerge while the crowd continued murmuring. I let my eyes sweep over their faces; some looked concerned, others angry. My eyes caught a familiar face. Henry. He was beside Priscilla, and the moment our eyes locked, his filled with tears, the sadness etched in his face. Before his tears could trigger my own, movement at the house pulled my focus back.

The Ciallmhar emerged, taking their time as they approached. Their slowness irked me, and I ground my teeth as they shuffled in front of me, expressions ranging from boredom to curiosity written across their faces.

"What is the meaning of this?" Tiernan, one of the council members, said. He was one of my mother's most trusted and one of the more vicious ones. He stepped up in front of me, peering down his nose as his lip curled. "You are supposed to be dead."

"According to whom?" I replied, letting the fire burning in my soul push back my anxiety. These people had never respected me. But they would now.

"Our sacrifices to the Dullahan serve a purpose, you impetuous child," he snarled, taking another step closer. My knees wavered slightly, but I held my ground. "You, of all people, should know that."

"My parents are dead." The shocked expression that passed over his face pleased me. I took a step closer to him, only a mere breath between us now. "They were killed when Ciara summoned Death to Sleepy Hollow to get revenge for the sacrifice of her brother."

"Preposterous," he spat. He waved a hand at the gathering crowd, which had grown since I first appeared. Even more whispers swept through them. "Your parents are dead because you are alive."

"Do you want this town to survive?" I asked, my flames licking up my hands. I turned to the gathered crowd and raised my voice. "Do you want to survive?"

No one replied.

"If you want to live, we need to act," I continued. "Death is coming. She's taken the Dullahan, and she won't stop until—"

Tiernan grabbed my injured arm, wrenching me back to face him.

Crying out, my fire surged, wrapping up my arm and burning away the sleeve of my dress. He yelped, pulling his hand away as I burned him. I panted through the pain, clenching my teeth as it dulled and my fire went out. Turning to him, I glared and gritted my teeth. "Never touch me without permission again."

He merely returned the glare, holding the wrist of his injured hand.

Ignoring him, I turned to the rest of the crowd and the other Ciallmhar. "As I was saying, the Dullahan cannot help us. Death has taken him, and we must get him back."

"Why?" someone asked. Turning to the voice, I saw it was Brom's father, Devlin. "Isn't that his purpose? To protect us?"

"You cannot truly be so stupid to believe that if Death kills the Dullahan, she will not come for us next," I spat back.

Before he could respond, a crow landed on the branches behind him, pulling my attention. Icy fingers wrapped around the back of my neck as it stared at us.

"What are you looking at?" he snapped, turning to see what had grabbed my focus.

The bird tipped its head back, opening its beak. But what came out was not a caw, but Death's melodic voice. "Hello, phoenix."

"What did you do with him?" I clenched my fists at my side and breathed through my nose. Alexander had mentioned the crows served as her eyes, but hearing her speak through one was something I'd not been expecting. I dug my nails into my palms to keep my hands from shaking.

The crow blinked rapidly, tilting its head from side to

side. "I think the more important question is, 'What will you do to get him back?'"

The words stuck in my throat.

"If you want your protector returned, you will hand over the phoenix. For every moon that rises, and she is not in my possession, I will unleash one of my creations upon this place. The price for your refusal is death, Katrina."

With that decree, the bird closed its beak and flew off, leaving the town silent.

My knees buckled. Tensing my muscles, I fought to keep upright, despite my vision swimming. This was wrong, all wrong. I whirled around to find Henry's eyes in the crowd.

A heartbeat passed.

And then chaos broke out.

Everyone was shouting and talking over one another. Accusing fingers pointed at me as people turned and ran, presumably back to their houses.

"Now, now, everyone calm down." Cyrus stepped forward. The frail-looking old man that I knew was anything but stopped in front of me, glancing back at the branch the crow had been on. "Phoenix, eh?"

I narrowed my eyes at him. "You're not surprised."

"Of course I'm not. The others may have been willfully ignorant of your power, but I see things as they are, girl, not as they appear to be." He tipped his head to the side. "Death is truly here? You saw her?"

"Yes," I replied, straining against the weight of the panic clawing at my mind and telling me to hide and run. "She's here, and she took Alexander."

His brows furrowed. "Alexander?"

My cheeks heated. I'd known Alexander had gone to meet with Cyrus, but I seriously doubted he'd told him the truth of his identity. "The Dullahan. His name is Alexander."

He eyed me carefully. "I see."

"Why are we talking?" Devlin asked as he pushed his way to the front of the crowd to face Cyrus. "You heard what she said. Give Death what she wants and keep the rest of us safe. This is her fault, anyway."

Murmurs of agreement stabbed through me like knives, and tears pricked my eyes. I shouldn't have been surprised. They'd already been ready to sacrifice me once. A second time would be nothing to them.

"How is it her fault?" Henry asked, pushing through the crowd and stopping in front of me. "Her only sin is wanting to survive, which is the same thing you are doing now. Who decides your life is worth more than hers?"

"We should work together to stop Death." A surprising voice came from the back of the crowd. Ichabod stood to be heard. His eyes met mine, shining with apology. "This town is filled with great power. Surely, if we worked together, we could stop her and rescue the Dullahan."

Silence met his words. Silence that gave me the town's answer. They would not be entertaining that option.

Finally, Tiernan gave voice to the sentiment. "We will not die for her crimes. This is on her shoulders."

The rage and hurt that had been building erupted, and fire consumed my arms and sent Cyrus skittering back. I turned to the town, my arms ablaze. I willed the fire to my eyes, to my heart, to my mouth, to make what I had to say resonate with them.

"The only ones at fault here are you all. For centuries, you sent an innocent person to their death, leaving behind those they cared about. Is it truly a surprise that one of those left behind struck back? This only happened because Ciara was grieving, and she shouldn't have been." Angry tears streamed down my face now, my chest heaving as I stepped forward. I raised a flaming finger to point at the townspeople. "*You* have brought this upon yourselves."

Once again, silence met my words.

I scoffed, pulling the flames back into my body. They did not deserve my anger or my power. They deserved nothing. My eyes landed on Henry and the ice around my heart melted slightly.

"Then what do you propose we do?" Brom's voice carried, but it was softer than I'd ever heard before. Snapping my gaze to his, I found that his face showed only remorse.

"I can stop her," I said with a nod. "I simply need time."

"We do not have time to give you, girl," Tiernan snapped, still holding his burnt hand. "It is nearly sunset, and whatever creatures Death sends will soon be upon us."

Cyrus cleared his throat, interrupting the retort I'd prepared. "I propose to the Ciallmhar—and anyone else who volunteers—to protect the town for two nights. We can certainly fend off a magical attack for that long. We owe Katrina time, at the very least."

"And if she cannot accomplish it in that timeframe?" Devlin asked, crossing his arms. "Will you ask us to defend the town another night?"

"Why are you so against defending your home?" I asked, irritation getting the better of me. "Are you truly *that* entitled you believe it beneath you to fight for your own life?"

His face reddened, and he opened his mouth to speak, but I turned my back to him, facing Cyrus.

"Thank you for the time," I said. I hesitated, weighing my options, knowing I truly only had one. "If I've not found a way to stop her by sundown the night after tomorrow, I will hand myself over to her."

He nodded, turning to the town. "Those of you who will join us, go and prepare to meet back here at sunset." He turned to me and then nodded at Henry. "You best get started, Katrina."

Cyrus left, moving to meet the other Ciallmhar, who waited for him off to the side. Henry took his place, looking at me for a moment before pulling me into the tightest hug I'd ever experienced. It hurt my shoulder, but I didn't care. I hugged him back, squeezing him as tightly as I could as tears rolled down my cheeks.

"You silly girl," he said before pulling back to look at me. He shook his head fondly. "Only you could try to escape the Hollow and end up with the Dullahan, after all."

My laugh was watery as I reached up to wipe at my face. "Priscilla told you?"

He nodded. "Everything, yes."

"I'm sorry you have to see me again, Henry." My lip trembled as the love in his eyes overwhelmed my senses. It was a poor joke, reminding him of the last words he'd said before he sent me on my way, but if I didn't say something, I would surely break down further.

"Don't be silly," he said as he pulled me into another hug. "I am glad to have you back. We will fix this, Katrina."

A faint cough broke us apart. Wiping at my eyes again, I glanced up to see Brom and Ichabod waiting for us. Ichabod bowed slightly. "Katrina. Henry."

My eyes remained fixed on Brom. "You tried to kill me."

Henry's head snapped toward Brom. "You did *what?*"

Brom ducked his head as his cheeks flushed. "I thought I was doing what was best for the town. I truly and deeply apologize, Katrina. What I did was wrong. I shouldn't have listened to your mother."

A humorless laugh escaped my lips. "You only say that now that I have power, Brom. You are not sorry. And you have only ever done what's best for you, not anyone else. Do not fool yourself into thinking you are a good person."

He reeled back as if I'd slapped him. Even Ichabod's mouth dropped open slightly. I'd never spoken to anyone like that in my life, but I was finished making myself smaller to enable others to feel bigger.

I turned back to Henry, presenting my back to both men who I'd once considered acquaintances. "We have work to do. Where shall we go?"

Henry reluctantly pulled his attention from Brom, but before he could reply, Priscilla stepped up next to him, smiling softly at me. "I have just the place for us, my dear."

Ignoring Ichabod and Brom, I slipped my uninjured arm through Henry's. He grinned at me and patted my hand as we walked away, following Priscilla. "So, a phoenix, girl? I knew you were destined for great things."

This time, my laugh was genuine.

Such is the general purport of this legendary superstition, which has furnished materials for many a wild story in that region of shadows; and the spectre is known at all the country firesides, by the name of the Headless Horseman of Sleepy Hollow.

-*Washington Irving,
The Legend of Sleepy Hollow*

Thirty-Seven

I growled, puffing my breath to move the strand of hair that had fallen in my face. "This isn't working, Henry."

"You'll get there. Just try again."

We'd been trying to tap into whatever powers my phoenix magic could offer for hours now, the afternoon sun dipping behind the horizon in the distance. In a small courtyard behind Priscilla's shop, they'd both taken turns trying to help me access my powers, but so far, I'd only achieved more of the same.

Gritting my teeth, I tried again, pushing the flames out from my chest and into my hands. Spheres of flame appeared, and while only days ago I would have been in awe, now I was frustrated. Flexing my jaw to ease the ache of a forming headache, I willed the flames out, lobbing the spheres at a wall of water Priscilla had conjured. Steam hissed as the two met, and I turned around to face the two older witches observing me.

"I can't do it without being afraid for my life. Which is very unhelpful because I can't remember what I was thinking or feeling at the time." I rubbed at the back of my neck roughly, trying to ease the twinge spreading across my shoulder. My body was wound tight, ready to snap like a bowstring. This frustration would get me nowhere.

Blowing out a breath, I rotated my head, clenching and unclenching my fists as I tried to relax and focus on my powers.

"You are putting too much pressure on yourself," Priscilla called, looking up from the books spread out in front of her on the table she'd had Henry bring outside.

Henry nodded. "You cannot be afraid of yourself. Fight it or accept it, fear it, or control it. You cannot do both, dear girl."

"Let it come naturally to you," Priscilla added.

"We don't have time to let it come naturally." I tried not to snap at the woman, but from the raise of her brow, I wasn't positive I succeeded. My cheeks flushed, but I didn't apologize. "We have to save him."

Sighing, she marked her place in the book and closed it, standing up. She walked over to me and took my hands. "Katrina, Alexander is a powerful man. He will not break so easily. We have some time."

"He's in danger because of me." My voice broke on the last word, the dam I'd put up around my emotions crumbling like sand as tears burned in my throat. "This is my fault, Priscilla."

Even with my vision blurred by tears, I could see her shaking her head. "Not in the slightest."

"Katrina," Henry muttered, stepping up and taking one of my hands from Priscilla. "You have led a hard life, my girl —one I wouldn't wish on anyone. But your vision is clouded by it. None of this is your fault. The fault lies with your parents, with the Ciallmhar, with Death. Even some of it with the Dullahan himself. But none of it is your fault."

"If I would have gone to Ciara sooner, made her listen..." I blew out a breath. "Her brother is alive, and I never got to tell her. Maybe it would have changed things."

"Ciara was grieving," he said, shaking his head. "You cannot fault yourself for that either."

"Alexander said he tried to tell the Ciallmhar that he wouldn't take the sacrifices." I rubbed the toe of my boot into the dirt to avoid meeting either of their gazes. I was struggling to keep the tears from spilling. "Why didn't they listen?"

Priscilla sighed. "Because tradition blinds those who live by its rules. It leaves no room for growth."

"I hate them," I whispered as a tear escaped, rolling a path down my cheek before dripping from my chin into the dirt. I covered it with my boot and sniffed, raising my head.

"No one blames you for that," Henry reaffirmed. "No one at all."

As much as I wanted to drop to my knees and cry, rage at the town that had doomed us to this fate, I knew I needed to get up and do something. Death wanted *me*. I would not be like my parents; I would not let the innocent suffer for my actions. Alexander was taken, and I needed to get him back.

Newfound resolved burned in my stomach, an ember flickering to life. Squeezing both Priscilla and Henry's hands, I lifted my chin high. "Let's try again."

"That's my girl." Henry gave a proud smile, patting the top of my hand. He and Priscilla stepped back as I moved to the other side of the courtyard.

"Focus on your confidence, Katrina," Priscilla called. "You can do this. But you must believe you can."

Nodding, I continued until I reached the back left corner of the courtyard, moving all the way to turn and face the water wall along the opposite corner. Rolling my shoulders back, I took a deep breath.

Focus, Katrina, I told myself, rolling my neck side to side. I closed my eyes, visualizing the flames crawling beneath my skin and remembering the feeling of the fire consuming me. My hands warmed as the flames built, and then the warmth spread, encircling my forearms. I didn't want to open my eyes to look, lest I ruin it, so I squeezed them closed even tighter, willing the flames up my arms before seeing them as coils of embers.

The heat spread up my arms, reaching the creases of my elbows.

And then it died. The cool breeze of the early evening washed over me, leaving goosebumps in its wake.

Opening my eyes, I deflated, shoulders slumping as I realized the fire had gone out, yet again. Faint gold light from the setting sun lit across my fingers.

"Maybe we should take a break," Priscilla offered. "Come sit with me and look through the books—see if we can find something about Death there. Maybe we can find some weaknesses we can exploit."

Shame coursed through me, acidic and bitter on my tongue as I swallowed it down. Looking at my hands, so pale and scarred, I wanted to vomit.

You are useless, Katrina. Truly, a waste of magic. My mother's words from our first and only magic lesson came back, swirling through my mind and scorching a path through my heart. *You disappoint me.*

My head hung low with the weight of her cutting words, but I pushed back, allowing Henry's support to surface. That it was *their* fault, not mine. They made me this way.

I made my way back to the table, flinging myself onto

the chair without a care of how it jostled my sore shoulder. I deserved the pain.

"I'll go make us some tea." Priscilla stood, patting Henry's hand. She threw a pointed look at him as she left.

Henry sighed. "What is it, my girl?"

"Perhaps I should just give myself to Death," I said, picking at my fingernails instead of looking at him. I could not bear to see the disappointment on the face of my mentor. My fingers crept up to the pendant nestled between my collarbones, rubbing my fingers over the stone.

One of Henry's age-ravaged fingers tucked under my chin, raising my eyes to his. His eyes were shiny with tears, and his lower lip trembled slightly. "Katrina Van Tassel, if you ever say that again, I will kill you myself. I wanted you to leave the Hollow so you would have a chance at a life. And while that didn't happen, this old man's sentiment remains. You have such a life ahead of you, such a life beyond these trees. The world is not reduced to Sleepy Hollow, my dear. And for all the pain it's wrought on you, you owe it nothing. Yet here you are. And that makes you better than most."

"If my sacrifice will save them—truly save them—is that not a worthy death?"

"No, it's not. Because your sacrifice to Death would not save them. Just like your sacrifice to the Dullahan would not save them. It is beyond time for Sleepy Hollow to step up and save itself for once."

"The town wants me dead." My voice cracked, the reality settling in that many of the townspeople hadn't thought twice about my being named Roghnaithe, nor had they questioned Death's proposal to hand me over. What kind of town was this—that so readily would give the life of one of their own? "They need me dead. In their minds, that's the natural order of things, the only way for Sleepy Hollow to survive."

"This town can burn for all I care," he bit out. He leaned back, his brown eyes shining with determination. "All I care about is you, Katrina. I need you to live."

His words rang through my mind, while indecision rivaled in my soul. I wanted to live, to see beyond the edges of the Hollow, to step out of the shadow my parents had cast. But then I'd met Alexander, and I couldn't leave him to die, just so I could live. I chewed on my lip, debating how to phrase my thoughts to Henry, but no words would do them justice.

But I didn't have to worry about that. The sky darkened in a heartbeat's time, gray clouds moving in as if heavy breath had blown them in. A chill came with it, bringing both a drop in temperature and an electrified feeling that clung to the hairs on my neck and arms. Standing, I looked up at the sky, turning my head in every direction, looking for what was coming.

Henry stood with me, tapping my arm until I brought my gaze down from the clouds. "We need to go inside, Katrina."

A scream pierced the air, every muscle of my body flinching as I squeezed my eyes shut. My body was frozen, paralyzed by the knowledge that, ultimately, I was the reason for that scream. Images of the creatures I'd seen in the book of Otherworld monsters flashed through my mind. I wondered which one had been summoned to Sleepy Hollow.

Henry pulled at my hand. His lips moved, but I could hear no words, nothing but the thundering of my heart.

I reached up, rubbing at my functioning ear until my body knew what I was trying to accomplish.

"—'side now," he finished, tugging me toward the door again.

Priscilla waited in the doorway, her eyes glued to the looming sky.

I let myself be led inside, despite the screams echoing deep into my bones. Henry sat me down on the lounge in Priscilla's office, kneeling in front of me. "You are not to blame for this."

"I need to go help," I whispered, though my common sense screamed at me to do anything but.

"No," he said firmly, turning around and sliding a book from the table. He pushed it into my lap. "You need to find a way to defeat Death. That's the only way to save Sleepy Hollow."

Reluctantly, I nodded, curling my fingers around the book numbly. He nodded, patting my knee as he stood. "Good girl. We will all research. We will find an answer. Let the Ciallmhar do their jobs tonight."

A bitter silence drew over the room, the three of us flipping through pages as the faint sounds of panic trickled in from outside. My fingers tightened around the book.

"Henry," I called. He met my gaze and tipped his head questioningly. I took a deep breath. "I will live. I will live, and I will save this town, whether they like it or not. I will be the villain in their story, so long as they live through it."

He smiled, the expression not quite reaching his eyes. "Katrina, the villain depends entirely on who is telling the story. And this is your story. Not theirs."

"Men are simpler than you imagine my sweet child. But what goes on in the twisted, torturous minds of women would baffle anyone."

-Daphne du Maurier, Rebecca

Thirty-Eight

P riscilla and I sat across from the table from each other the next morning, both silently waiting for Henry to return with news. At dawn, he'd left the bookstore, heading to the Ciallmhar house to gather information about the previous night's attacks. The teapot between Priscilla and me sat untouched. I was too nervous, too frightened of what Henry might tell us, to put anything in my stomach. From the way it swirled and twisted, I knew whatever I managed to drink would just come right back up.

I watched as a sliver of morning sun traveled across the wood in front of me, slowly inching closer and closer to the table's edge before sliding to the floor and continuing its journey. Priscilla reached out to me, catching my attention and pulling my gaze up to her.

"It'll be all right, Katrina." She smiled softly as she slid my teacup closer to me. "Whatever happened last night, it's not your fault."

Biting the inside of my cheek, I swallowed back everything I wanted to shout at her. Priscilla had done nothing to deserve my anger. Not when I was truly angry with myself.

Instead, I picked up the teacup and gulped it down, wincing as the scalding hot liquid moved down my throat. I relished the heat, focusing on the burning in my chest instead of the potentially awful information Henry would be bringing us.

Priscilla sighed, her eyes sad, but thankfully her attention darted to the door behind me, cutting off anything she'd been about to say. Turning in my chair, I watched as Henry entered the bookstore and hung his cloak by the door.

As he began toward us, my stomach dropped at his expression.

"What happened?" I demanded, standing, and meeting him halfway.

He released a heavy sigh, his eyes full of despair. "There were casualties last night. The Ciallmhar couldn't stop the creature before it killed five people."

The world fell out from beneath my feet, my knees buckling as my vision swam and ringing filled my ears, drowning out any words that Henry might have said as he caught me. People had *died* last night. While I slept.

My vision filled with Henry's face as he cupped my cheeks in his hands. The ringing faded, replaced by his concerned voice. "Are you with me?"

Unable to speak, I just nodded, reaching up to rub at the knot that had formed in my chest.

"What was it, Henry?" Priscilla asked, her voice calm.

"The three-headed vulture," he responded, his hands still holding my face as he looked over my head at Priscilla. "The Ellén Trechend."

Priscilla sucked in a sharp breath. "That beast was destroyed centuries ago."

"She is Death," I croaked out, images of the death bird carrying off townspeople flashing behind my eyes when I blinked. "She can raise whatever she wishes."

Neither of them said anything.

I pulled away from Henry, looking between them. "Who was it?"

Henry shook his head, standing and moving to sit in the chair across from me. "No, Katrina. I'm not telling you that. You will put their deaths on your shoulders, and I won't allow it. This was not your fault."

I exploded. Bursting to my feet, my hands lit up with flames, climbing up my wrists and forearms until I wore gauntlets of fire. I snapped, "Then whose fault is it?"

They both looked at me, though neither wore frightened expressions. Henry simply tipped his head toward my flames. "Perhaps you should take notes on how you feel right now."

That was the last thing I wanted to do, but as my flames sputtered out, flickering as they died back down to my hands, I knew he was right. If I wanted any hope of being able to take on Death and save Alexander, I needed to figure out my powers.

"We should go back outside," I murmured, too ashamed to meet their eyes after my outburst. "We're running out of time."

"There is still another day," Priscilla said.

I snapped my head up to look at them. "No. No, we figure this out today, or I turn myself over before sundown."

"You will not." Henry stood from his chair. "I won't allow you to sacrifice yourself, Katrina."

"The Ciallmhar clearly cannot be trusted to protect the town."

This town needed a protector. It needed the Dullahan. Alexander could protect Sleepy Hollow better than I ever could. If exchanging myself for Alexander meant that both he and the town would survive, it was a trade I would gladly make. "So we had better get started."

IT WAS MIDDAY, the sun high overhead, when Priscilla appeared at the back door, calling us back inside from our practice in the courtyard and back inside where she'd been researching. "I think I've found something. Come look."

Henry and I shared a glance as I shook my hands, extinguishing the flames I'd held for several minutes. From here, I just barely heard her words, but the look on her face told me how urgent her findings were.

As we approached and followed her inside, she didn't say anything else, only turned the book sitting on the table around to face us as she took her seat again. My eyes devoured the words, my heart speeding at the contents, both familiar and yet not.

A flame grows in the darkness,
Alone and blazing bright.
Screams bloom coldly in the wind,
On wings as black as night.

Death demands an offering,
Only those with sight can see.
Ash and dust surround the world,
No one to hear your plea.

Veils of smoke and shadow hide
The truest hearts of stone.
And with the dead to help her,
Death will build a throne of bones.

Run, little phoenix,

Run far, run fast.
For Death will always find you,
Your peace
It will not last.

Blood and embers fill the streets,
The world ready to become
An endless maze of bodies.
Oh, how quickly you'll succumb.

Ashes rain behind you,
Falling back to earth.
Begin your life again, again,
Bestowed your power upon birth.

Born of flame and bathed in blood,
Never shall you rest.
Lies and offerings freely given,
Will surely bring the best.

Blinding, brilliant power,
Fueled endlessly by ire.
Again, again, on restless wings
Will lie atop the pyre.

SLITHERING dread coiled in my stomach. The poem—the prophecy—I'd found in Alexander's journal, but this one... there was more to this version. And I didn't like what the additional lines seemed to imply.

"I've seen part of this before," I admitted, my eyes still fixed on the three new verses. The ones that spoke of offerings and ashes and beginning life again, and a pyre.

Priscilla looked up at me, her expression guarded. "Where?"

"In a book at Alexander's house." I lifted my eyes to hers. "What do you think it means?"

She didn't answer me, her eyes flicking to Henry. That was all the confirmation I needed.

This prophecy said I would have to die.

I would willingly give my life to Death.

I was numb. For once, no tears burned my throat, no anxiety wrapped around my throat, no fear squeezed my lungs. I was simply floating out of my body. I could hear Henry and Priscilla speaking, see them pointing at the book and turning the pages, and feel the cool wind through my curls. But none of it mattered.

"I need some air," I whispered, turning to head out the back door into the courtyard without waiting to see if they'd heard me.

Entering the courtyard, I stopped once I'd reached the middle, tipping my head back to gaze at the gray morning sky. I sucked down heavy breaths, the crisp air sharp against my nostrils and throat. Slowly, the looming claws of panic scratching at my mind receded, and I lowered my chin.

My feet carried me to the back wall of the courtyard, the echoes of the screams I'd heard last night wrapping around my shoulders like a shroud. Sighing, I turned my back to the brick and slid down, landing in the dirt with a thump that stung my tailbone and had me clenching my teeth at the jolt in my shoulder.

I deserved the pain. People had died because of me last night. People I could have saved had I just given myself over.

The numbness was a solace, an icy balm that frosted over my soul. I was nothing. I *felt* nothing. Nothing but emptiness. Opening my palm, I summoned a small ball of flames into my hand, watching it flicker across my skin.

Henry had promised I'd never be alone, but promises were the sweetest of lies. I was alone, alone in the hell my parents had forged. There was no escape for me.

Closing my palm around the dancing ball of fire, I snuffed it out, ignoring the sharp tug as my curls caught on the brick behind me.

I was uncertain how long I'd sat there, staring at the dirt, blank and empty. My legs had long ago lost feeling in them, heavy stumps I could see but not feel attached to my body. Though they were tucked beneath me, I couldn't be bothered to move.

Voices drifted in over the brick wall, the wind carrying their words to me.

"She went quickly, but I simply cannot bear..." the woman's voice faded into sobs.

"I know." The answering woman's voice had my head snapping up. Ciara's mother. The woman rarely left her home, so if she was out now, I needed to hear what she had to say. I turned my left ear up, and the gods must have decided to punish me, because every word she spoke was clear as day. "I've lost my son, and now my daughter. And Katrina Van Tassel is the cause of it all. She has brought death upon this town."

"She is a monster," the woman agreed, her words devolving into keening sobs.

"She is," Ciara's mother said, their voices beginning to fade as they passed the courtyard. "Whatever fate awaits her will be well deserved."

My heart fractured, the shards piercing the fabric of my soul, leaving behind gaping, jagged holes. Despair swept in, filling the holes like a raging current seeking gaps on the coast.

Standing, I ignored the needle-sharp pain racing through my legs, forcing them to move despite still not being able to feel them. I needed to get Alexander back. He could fix this. He could save these people and give them back hope and safety.

Adelaide and my mother had been right all along. And Sleepy Hollow needed their protector, not their destroyer.

Casting a last glance back at the bookstore, I reached up to rub at my necklace. Taking it off, I set it on the ground. Henry would find it, and hopefully, he would know what it meant. I loved him dearly, and now I would prove it. I would do whatever it took to ensure his safety.

Tears clogged my throat as I looked at the red crystal shining in the near midday sun. I squeezed my eyes shut, forcing the tears back as I turned and left the courtyard, turning my path toward the cemetery.

It was time to summon Death. It was time for a trade.

"But to die as lovers may -
to die together, so that they
may live together."

-J. Sheridan Le Fanu,
Carmilla

Thirty-Nine

T he streets were empty as I made my way to the wrought-iron gates outside the Sleepy Hollow cemetery. I felt oddly at peace as I stepped through the posts that stood guard, moving among the headstones until I reached the mausoleum in the center where Death had first appeared.

Pulling my cloak off, I laid it across the bench. Blood still stained the grass where my parents' bodies had lain, the color dried and brown, but thankfully, someone had collected their remains. I wasn't certain who, and I wasn't certain I even cared.

I blew out a harsh breath, spinning in a slow circle once as I scanned the cemetery. Holding my arms out wide, I tipped my head back and yelled into the sky. "Death! I am here."

My voice echoed across the headstones, clashing with the startled caws from the birds in nearby trees. The wind picked up, goosebumps skittering across the back of my neck.

"Finally come to your senses, then?" Death's voice came from behind me, sharp and clear.

I whirled to face her.

Death stood straight, her shoulders draped in a thick black velvet cloak that cascaded over her wine-red dress. The hem brushed along the grass and her bare feet. Atop her head, a crown of blackened branches twisted into the sky, and on her shoulder sat a crow that gawked with glassy eyes. Death's lips split into a smile and her eyes slowly tracked down to her side, bidding mine to follow.

On his knees before Death, hands bound behind his back and mouth gagged, was Alexander. His eyes widened at me, and he shook his head minutely. Dragging my eyes from him, I focused back on Death. If I looked at Alexander any longer, I might change my mind, and I could not do that. The town needed him to protect it, not me. No one needed me. Death could have me if it meant his freedom.

"You swear you will spare the town if I trade myself?" I asked, my shoulders back and chin high, a cold calmness in my voice that I didn't quite like. It reminded me of my mother, but I supposed, at least, it would serve me well.

I had to ensure Death wouldn't harm those I left behind, though. That she would take only me.

Death peered at me, pursing her lips. "Why do you care so much about them, little phoenix? My pet heard what they said to you after my ultimatum."

"Why do you care? You wanted me here, and here I am." Despite my intentions to not look at him, my eyes trailed down to Alexander, who looked upon me with suspicion and sadness. As if he'd known exactly what they'd said to me.

"Don't you want to punish those who wronged you?" Her head tilted to the side. "You could wipe them off the map with a mere thought."

Yes, I wanted to scream. Of course, I wanted to punish them, but more than that, I wanted Alexander freed, and Henry and Priscilla safe. And this was how I would achieve that. "You will release Alexander, and you will spare Sleepy Hollow. That was the agreement, yes?"

She sighed, trailing her hand through Alexander's hair. He stiffened, but didn't pull away. "You both are pathetic, truly. This silly little infatuation. *That* is what you will choose to die over?"

"Sleepy Hollow needs him."

Alexander's eyes narrowed, and I knew he'd seen through my words and what I truly meant. He struggled against his bindings, thrashing and tugging, but they held fast. Tears pricked my eyes, my lower lip trembling, but I held my head high. I'd made my decision.

Death looked between us before tipping her head back and laughing. "Oh, this is truly glorious. Dullahan, she *loves* you." She stopped laughing and tapped her chin with her long nails, putting her hand on Alexander's shoulder, her fingers curling and bunching against the fabric of his shirt. "Perhaps I will kill you both then, so you can be together in the Otherworld."

The bottom of my stomach dropped out. *No. NO, she was supposed to spare him.* Fire swirled in my stomach, fueled by the fear that mirrored in Alexander's eyes. "You said this was to be a trade."

"Darling, this is whatever I want it to be," she cooed, further digging her nails into Alexander's shoulder. He winced, trying to shift away, but she gripped him tightly. "Surely he told you that."

"Take your hands off him." My voice was cold fury, infused with the kind of fire that burned so hot its flames licked blue into the sky.

"Love is a weakness," she snarled. Even from a few steps

away, I could see darkness blooming against his shirts beneath the tips of her nails. "I do not tolerate weakness."

"I will say it once more," I said, not even needing to will my flames to obey as they swarmed to my fingertips, eager to feed on the flesh of the woman in front of us. "Remove your hand from him."

She eyed my flames, pulling her nails from his flesh. She bent down and whispered something in Alexander's ear, her eyes fixed on me. The red of her lips made it easy to see them move, but I still couldn't make out the words. Whatever it was, Alexander froze at first, looking up at her before thrashing harder than before, trying to get out of his bindings.

He got the gag out of his mouth, spitting the fabric out to fall around his neck. "Katrina, don't do this. Please."

Death smiled widely at me as shadows swirled up from the ground, twining around her arms. With the flick of her finger, a tendril of thick black smoke wrapped itself around Alexander's mouth, silencing him once more.

"Touch him again, and I promise you, I will be the one to kill you. No matter the consequences," I vowed, my flames mirroring her undulating shadows.

In some part of my mind, perhaps I'd known that it would not be so easy as simply trading my life for his, but the thought of him in her clutches... Sleepy Hollow was a distant memory. And I would do whatever it took to ensure Alexander survived.

She paused, her smile growing even wider. "I would be very careful with your words."

"If you want me, you will let him go free," I said, bordering on begging. And I would beg if that was what it took. "I won't fight you. Not once he's free and safe."

"This is not a negotiation, phoenix. Not anymore," she said, raising an eyebrow. The corner of her mouth ticked up, as if she'd thought of something amusing. "Perhaps I will go into town and collect that old earth witch and his water witch friend you seem so fond of."

Images of Henry, torn apart by whatever creature Death would send to do her bidding, flashed through my mind, and before I realized what I was doing, I'd sent balls of fire hurtling for her. It was impulsive and foolish, but I would not let her threaten the people I cared about. Those people who could not defend themselves against her.

If this was how I died, defending Henry and Priscilla, it would be an honorable death.

Alexander's eyes widened, and he ducked just in time to avoid being struck. Death dodged, too, but she was just slightly too slow, the flames impacting off her left shoulder, sending the crow skittering into the night with a loud caw. Unlike the night she'd appeared, my flames only sent her staggering a step back this time.

My vision swam red, and my entire body felt like it'd been dipped into the open flames of a candle, thrumming with burning energy.

Shaking her head, Death tutted at me, stepping back up behind Alexander. "That was a mistake, phoenix. And now, your beloved Dullahan will pay."

Time slowed as she pulled a silver knife from the depths of her cloak, the metal glinting in the sun. My body froze, and all I could do was watch with abject horror as she grabbed Alexander's hair and pulled his head back as she lifted the knife.

And then, with a smile that could only be described as evil, she drug the blade across his throat.

The world fell away.

My eyes met Alexander's, both wide with terror. Ringing filled my ears, my vision swimming. All I could see was blood pooling around the blade.

When she pulled away, a smile still stretched across her face as she watched the blood run down his neck.

Death stepped back, letting Alexander fall to the side, his hands still bound behind him as his blood soaked the earth. His mouth opened, but no sound came out as his head went limp. Still open, his eyes stared at me. But I couldn't see them. Couldn't see anything beyond the blurring tears.

My feet carried me to him, despite Death standing a mere arm's reach behind him. Throwing myself to the ground at his head, I pulled up the end of my dress, bundling and pressing the fabric against his throat in a panicked attempt to at least keep some of the blood inside his body.

"Do not waste your efforts." Death's teasing voice broke through the ringing and pounding in my ears. "Immortality does not protect against me. Not even for my children."

I ignored her, pulling Alexander's head into my lap as I bent around it, the tears burning my eyes now flowing freely. His hand twitched against my knee as his eyes fluttered shut, his body slumping.

I could hear myself crying, the gut-wrenching sobs clawing from my throat, though it didn't feel like the noises were coming from my body. Tears streamed down my face, dripping onto Alexander's face as I rocked back and forth, rubbing my hand over his forehead. Blood smeared from the touch, mixed with my tears as they landed on his skin and rolled down his face.

Death laughed.

I couldn't think—couldn't *breathe*—as I blocked out the sound of her mocking laughs, eyes searching Alexander's face, dotted with streaks of red and my tears, looking for any sign of life, any sign that this was a mistake, a trick, and that he was still alive.

But there were none. He was gone.

Once again, I was alone.

My sobs transformed into screams—gasping screams that stole my breath and wrapped around my throat, screams born equally of pain and anger. Alexander hadn't deserved this. I hadn't deserved this. Both of us had so much taken from us already.

Death's laughter broke through my agony again. My head snapped up at the mirthful chuckle, heat flooding through my body in a crashing wave of fury. Fire pulsed through my veins, flowing easily as it erupted, wrapping around my back like a shield, curling over my shoulders and hugging around my middle. I watched Death through the tendrils of red flame; the smile dropped from her face as she looked at me.

Carefully, before my fire could burn Alexander's body, I slid his head from my lap and stood. The flames swarmed and cocooned me.

Monsters weren't born. They were created.

And now, Death had created me.

Wings of fire sprouted from my back, tingling in my shoulders blades as the tips of them passed through my peripheral vision. My heartbeat pounded in my ears, deafening me to everything else.

Turning my attention to Death, my flames acted of their own accord, racing toward her. I didn't stop them. Instead, I encouraged them as they streamed from my body, endlessly bright and burning. My rage only fed them, the fire growing brighter, now an almost blinding white as it struck, again and again, like a viper. Tendrils of flame wrapped around Death, pulsing wildly as they spun like thread around her body, singing away at her cloak and lighting the ends of her crown of branches.

She swatted at the fire, pushing her shadows from her

hands in a futile attempt to ease the onslaught. My lips curled up as I watched them fail, the flames swarming her further.

Careful steps across the grass took me to stand in front of her, the soles of my feet scorching the grass. Her moonlight-pale skin turned pink with each strike of fire.

She bared her teeth at me, pushing more shadows from her hands. "I have killed hundreds of versions of you, phoenix. You will not succeed at killing me. You are too soft, too weak to go through with it."

I didn't recognize my own voice as I spoke. "Perhaps I will be the first. Perhaps the others were merely lacking in proper motivation."

"You don't know what you're doing," she snarled, her crown singed down to ashes and the flames licking at the ends of her hair now. "You kill me, and you risk upsetting the balance of the world."

"How unfortunate." I didn't care. I cared about nothing save seeing her charred body at my feet.

My flames overwhelmed her shadows once again, pushing with more vengeance this time. Visions flashed through my eyes. Visions of Brom's face as I tumbled down the riverbank. Visions of Adelaide's missing eyes. Visions of my mother's sneer. Visions of Ciara's lifeless body. And now, visions of Alexander's blood, running in rivers of red from his body and feeding the earth.

My rage was palpable, the aura of fire around me pulsing. I leaned into my power, feeding the beast with more memories, more visions of my mother's disappointment, my father's apathy, the glares I'd gotten from people in the street, Devlin's hand on my arm, the words Ciara's mother had spoken beyond the courtyard. All of it fed the monster in my soul. The fire grew higher, whipping out from my body violently with jerking movements.

Anger was freeing. Anger was better than guilt, than grief, than the tears I'd shed over Alexander's body. The anger was cleansing.

Death's black eyes widened slightly as I advanced on her, wings snapping out wide as they tugged on my back, on the very core of my soul beneath my skin. She took a step back, the hot air pushing from my wings, lifting her hair from her shoulders, now singed off up to her shoulders and still smoldering. "You'll never kill me, phoenix."

"Let's find out," I whispered, and unleashed all the rage that had been brewing. My vision blacked out as the roar of flames mixed with the thunder of my heartbeat. I let my eyes slide closed, relishing the sounds of Death's screams as the flames bubbled across her skin.

Was this power? Was this what I was meant to be?

The satisfaction that flooded through me at the sounds of Death's pain told me that this was what I was meant to be.

A destroyer. Not a savior.

Adelaide had been right all along.

The screams of the being who'd taken everything from me faded and I opened my eyes slowly. My heart thundered in my ears, pounded in my throat as my vision cleared. Death stood before me, her entire body consumed by flame, what used to be her face stretched open in a scream. With a beat of my flaming wings, the statue of cinders crumbled into ash, floating away on the wind.

Was she dead?

I couldn't imagine any being could survive being burned into ashes, but there was no way to be sure.

Only the taste of ash and smoke remained, the taste heavy on my tongue. I'd done it. My breath shuddered from my lungs in a cry. I'd done it. I'd saved Sleepy Hollow, saved *myself*.

Specks of black rose into the sky, catching my attention before disappearing into the distance. My gaze fell from the swirls of ash to Alexander's body, lying in the grass, his hands still bound and his blood pooling. Crimson was smeared across his face and neck from where I'd held him, trying to keep the life inside his body.

I fell to my knees, just out of reach of his body. Still wreathed in flames I didn't care to call back. I didn't want them to touch his body. I wanted him whole, to bury him properly.

Sleepy Hollow had taken everything from me and from him. I'd saved them, but lost one of the few people who mattered to me. One of the few people who cared about me. I was alone once more.

I'd saved Sleepy Hollow, but I'd failed Alexander.

The ground began to shake, a rumbling that vibrated my very bones. I squeezed my eyes closed, tears once again falling down my cheeks and dripping onto the earth. The rumbling faded slowly.

When I finally opened my eyes, nothing seemed different about the cemetery, about the forest beyond. Though the lingering pile of ashes from Death's body had disappeared entirely. Perhaps I should be worried about what would come next, about the consequences of killing Death.

But I felt nothing but an endless hole in my chest.

A sob ripped from my throat, which turned into a scream that had me throwing my head back and cursing at the sky until my throat ached and my ears rang.

Whatever retribution the Otherworld sought could find me. I'd had enough.

*He who wins a thousand
common hearts is therefore
entitled to some renown;
but he who keeps
undisputed sway over the
heart of a coquette is
indeed a hero.*

-Washington Irving,
The Legend of Sleepy Hollow

Forty

My flames wrapped around my naked body as I cried, tinting my vision with reds and oranges as they coiled around my head, shooting off around me in flickering movements. I needed to get up, to pull the fire back into my body and find a way back to Sleepy Hollow, to Henry and Priscilla. But I couldn't bring myself to move. I could barely bring myself to *breathe*.

"Katrina." The wind carried a whisper that barely reached my ear.

My sobs faltered at the sound of my name, and I squeezed my eyes shut, bowing my head as I felt the blaze grow around me. The voice sounded like it belonged to Alexander, but he was lying dead on the grass. I clenched my fists to keep from lifting my head to look. It was a trick, surely, and I would not fall for it.

Perhaps I'd not killed Death after all, and she was punishing me. Or this was my consequence from the Otherworld, to be haunted by Alexander's voice as punishment.

I took another shuddering breath and forced my eyes

open. If it was Death, if she was going to kill me, I would look her in the eye. Before I could stand and turn around, though, my ears popped, signaling a change in the air, and purple fog snaked through my spirals of flame.

Purple like Alexander's spirit magic.

I snapped my eyes closed, squeezing them tightly to fight off the burning tears. They quickly gave way back to my rage, and I stood, forcing down the nausea and dizziness that had come with the quick movement. Whatever this was would not trick me. Not anymore. The time for games and whispers was over. Taking a deep breath, I called my flames to my hands, intent on destroying whatever was playing this cruel trick.

"Katrina. Open your eyes," a soft voice said, directly in front of me now.

My eyes snapped open, and a breath punched from my lungs. *Alexander.* "How are you..."

He stood before me in his spirit form. Still missing his head, though his body was covered in blood, he reached out his hand for me, but I flinched back. It couldn't be real. This was just my imagination, my punishment from the Otherworld. Or maybe Death herself, taunting me.

Tears pricked at my eyes, and I turned around, putting the deception behind me. "You are not real."

Not-Alexander stepped around in front of me, blocking my steadfast stare at the cemetery gates. "No, Katrina. I'm real, I'm here. Don't do this. Don't push me away."

My heart skipped, wanting to believe he was real, if just for a moment. I shook my head. "No, you're dead. She slit your throat." I looked down at my body, but the dress that had been covered in his blood had burnt away. "Your blood was on me."

"You brought me back," Not-Alexander said, his voice softening.

I desperately wanted to believe him, to believe that for the first time in my life, I was *enough*. But that just brought my anger back anew, thinking of all those in Sleepy Hollow I'd not been enough for. That I'd failed simply by being alive. My fire flared.

He reached for me again, his ungloved hand wrapping around my wrist.

The touch sparked inside me. This was real. I gasped as my mind sifted through the possibilities. My heart raced and my stomach twisted in glee. He was alive. "How?"

His hand moved from my wrist to reach into my flames and wipe at a stray tear on my cheek that had somehow survived my flames. "Your tears, Katrina. Phoenix tears are healing."

I reeled back, the world swaying at the edges of my vision. I'd healed him? I had been so certain I'd brought about his death, and had been ready to burn the world for him, to fight Death and risk my own demise in his name. And all along, I had saved him. Was it possible to have this all? To have this victory so readily? It didn't feel like it.

I was waiting, my breath catching in my chest as I waited for reality to hit and the truth to be revealed.

But nothing happened.

Alexander simply rubbed his thumb over my cheek in gentle circles. His hand was engulfed by my flames up to the wrist, and he never flinched.

I should have been grateful. I should have flung my arms around him and embraced that he was alive. I should have been celebrating that the flaw my mother hated, my propensity for tears, could be valuable instead. But I was none of those things. I was hollow, filled with nothing but emptiness.

My throat tightened, and I pushed Alexander's hand away. "Let me go, Alexander. You're not real."

"Yes, I am, Katrina. This is real." He reached for my hand again, but I pulled back. "Katrina, don't let her win. You won. You defeated her. Sleepy Hollow is safe."

My wings of flame flared, stretching wide. My hazy mind fed the sparks that flickered off my skin. "Sleepy Hollow is filled with people who hate me, with the ones who made me this way. All I wanted was to be loved, to be accepted. And all I got for my troubles was pain. The Ciallmhar deserves to die. I will burn them to ashes. That will save the town."

"You are better than them, Katrina. Don't let them win." He reached for my hand, taking hold of it inside the flames surrounding me. "Don't let her win. Call your flames back."

The smell of burning flesh penetrated my senses, stinging my nose. My eyes snapped to the source, realizing I was the cause of it. I was burning Alexander, even in his spirit form. His other glove had singed away, leaving only his bare flesh, and yet he still held his hand out to me, holding mine. Crying out, I pulled away, staggering back. "I burned you."

He still reached his hands out to me, his face calm despite the angry blisters across his skin. "Yes, you did."

At his confirmation, my fire died with an unsettling *whoosh*, leaving me standing before him, cold, naked, and completely at his mercy. My chin wobbled as my vision blurred behind hot tears. "Why did you let me burn you? Why aren't you afraid?"

With a slight popping sensation in my ear, the purple haze around us faded, and Alexander appeared in front of me, human and whole. A puckered pink line stretched across his throat, but he was otherwise just the same as he was before. My eyes tracked down to his hands, both peeling, blistered, and red on the palms, the backs, the fingers.

His proximity to me had resulted in his shirt being scorched. I'd burned holes into the fabric, and the visible skin beneath was bright pink.

I had done that. To him.

He stepped up, pulling me into his arms and tucking my head into his chest. "How could I ever be afraid of you, Katrina? You saved me. You killed Death because of what she did to me. I could never fear that."

The reality of all I'd done—of all I'd wanted to do—rushed back at his words. My anger at the Ciallmhar hadn't faded, but my shame surfaced, quenching the anger slightly as I buried my face into his chest. His skin was soft and warm, and damp from my tears. "I can't go back there, Alexander. Not anymore."

He pressed his lips to my hair, lingering there and letting his words be muffled by my curls. "You never have to."

I wrapped my arms around his middle, squeezing, if only to prove to myself that he was real, that he was here. We were both here. "What will happen now?"

"Whatever you wish."

"Won't something come for me?" I asked, nodding toward the patch of scorched earth where Death had stood. "She said I couldn't upset the balance."

"We will deal with it together, Katrina." His head dipped and his lips brushed across my forehead, then dipped lower to the tops of my cheeks. Tucking one of his blistered fingers beneath my chin, he raised my face to look at him. He looked at me for a moment, his eyes searching my face. He pressed a gentle kiss to my lips. It was barely more than a brush, but it nearly made my knees buckle. He pressed another, firmer kiss to my cheek. "I never want you to sacrifice yourself for anyone, ever again. I am not worth that. Sleepy Hollow is not worth that. No one is worth that. You are worthy of living, and I will never forgive those who made you think otherwise."

There was nothing I could say to that. Nothing that would appease him, at least. He was worth that.

"We can leave, Katrina. I can take us away from here, and I can keep you safe."

Before I could respond, bustling movement behind us caused both of us to stiffen before pulling apart. The tension bled out of me when I saw Henry and Priscilla coming from town, rushing toward us with matching looks of alarm.

"We are safe." Alexander stepped in front of me to shield my nakedness. "We're both fine."

Priscilla unhooked her cloak, handing it to Alexander without a word as her eyes looked over us. "What happened?"

Securing the cloak around my body, I stepped out from behind Alexander.

Henry didn't give me a chance to answer, instead grabbing my arms and pulling me into his arms. He squeezed me tightly, tighter than I believed possible for him. After a long time, our breaths the only sound in the cemetery, he pulled back, looking at me with glassy eyes. "You are lucky that you're alive, or I would have killed you myself."

I let out a watery huff, unable to form any words to express that I was sorry for hurting him, but I would have done it again in an instant.

"I am so proud of you, Katrina," Henry said, his voice a hushed whisper. "You have always exceeded every expectation I've had of you."

"Did you succeed, Katrina?" Priscilla asked, interrupting our moment. Her face was still panicked, and for good reason.

I turned in Henry's arms, nodding. "Yes, I did. She's gone."

It was like the world had heard me because the clouds parted and the sky lightened, the afternoon sun warming us all.

"What will you do now?" Henry asked, still holding me. "Will you return to Sleepy Hollow?"

I tensed in his arms, shaking my head as I looked up at Alexander. His words had echoed in my mind, though I hadn't had a chance to respond to them yet. "No, I don't think I will."

Henry looked over my head to Alexander. "You will take care of her? Take her somewhere safe?"

"I do not think Katrina needs anyone to take care of her," Alexander said, his voice equal parts serious and amused. "But I will. It's time Sleepy Hollow learned to protect itself."

"I couldn't agree more, boy," Henry said. He pressed a kiss to the top of my head before stepping back and squeezing my hand, pressing a bundle of cool metal into my hand. My necklace. Tears stung my eyes, and I opened my mouth to thank him, but he guided me toward Alexander. "You two take care of each other, then. And I don't want to see you back here. I mean it this time."

"Will you be safe, Henry?" I asked, concerned for any repercussions from the Ciallmhar that had opposed my survival. My thumb ran over the stone of the necklace, the familiarity of tracing the contours calming my racing heart.

"Of course I will," he said, waving a hand. "I am far more concerned about you, Katrina Van Tassel."

"Where will you go?" Priscilla asked, her attention flitting between Alexander and me.

"There are a few places I have in mind," Alexander said, then looked at me with a smile.

I would go with him anywhere—anywhere, as long as it was not here. "There's an island off the coast of Ireland. It's a similar haven, but different enough to be a fresh start. We'll discuss and decide—together—if that would be the place for us."

Together sounded very nice. The firebird in my heart soared as Alexander pulled me to his side. We were safe, Alexander was alive, and I would never return to Sleepy Hollow again.

A flame grows in the darkness,
Alone and blazing bright.
Screams bloom coldly in the wind,
On wings as black as night.

Blinding, brilliant power,
Fueled endlessly by ire.
Again, again, on restless wings
Will lie atop the pyre.

A fter a long discussion, Alexander and I had decided against going to the island haven. At least, at first. There was something else I needed to accomplish before we crossed an ocean.

Thankfully, Alexander was supportive of my request. I suspected it would be a long time before I was ever not taken by surprise at how supportive and thoughtful he was.

As if sensing my thoughts had turned to him, Alexander's hand slid across the bench seat of the carriage we occupied. "You are thinking quite loudly," he murmured. "Are you all right?"

I chewed on my lip, trying to find the right words to explain how I was feeling about our intended task. "What if he doesn't want to see me? What if he turns me away and is angry at me, like his mother?"

"He would not have replied to our letter if he did not want to see you, Katrina." He ran his thumb over the back of my hand, chasing away the tension. Pulling our hands to his mouth, he pressed a kiss to each knuckle.

Blowing out a long breath, I still felt the nerves gnawing

at my spine. "We did not reveal the whole truth in the letters. He doesn't know why we're truly coming."

"No," Alexander agreed. "But it is a good sign that he replied, and that he's in the same place that I left him."

"But what if—"

Alexander cut me off by leaning down to press a kiss to my lips, moving his hand to rest on my cheek. "Stop." He pressed another kiss to my lips, then one to my forehead before returning to my lips for another kiss. This one lingered, a promise. "It will be all right, Katrina. I swear it."

Sighing, I leaned into his embrace as he wrapped his arms around me, using his warmth to chase away the troubles in my soul. "How much longer to Kentucky?"

"Several hours still, but we should arrive by sunset. Get some rest."

I doubted I'd be able to sleep, between my nerves and the bumping of the carriage wheels along the road, there was far too much to keep me awake. But Alexander tucked his fingers into my hair and began massaging my scalp, and I sighed again, letting myself relax further against him.

"KATRINA, WE'RE HERE," Alexander said, pulling me from the clutches of sleep.

The nerves that had eased with sleep were back in full force now as the muffled sounds of people bustling past our carriage registered to my ears. We were really here.

I couldn't do this. I had let Alexander convince me that Torin would welcome us, would be grateful for knowing the truth about his sister. But now, *here*, I wanted to run and hide. This had been a mistake. He would be angry, no doubt. Just like his mother, he would blame me for her death. I did not think I could handle that.

Turning to Alexander, I opened my mouth to ask if we were really about to do this, but my panic was interrupted by a loud knock on the carriage door.

"Breathe," Alexander reminded me as he reached across my body to push open the door. He inclined his head. "Now, get out of the carriage."

My limbs felt heavy, and I moved carefully to keep from making a fool of myself in front of our coachman as I clambered out of the carriage. Alexander stepped out behind me gracefully, bowing to the man who'd accompanied us all this way. He pulled me back into his embrace, tucking me into his side.

Alexander said something to the man, but I couldn't hear it over the pounding in my ears. Swallowing hard, I pressed my hand into my stomach and willed myself to calm as I slowed my breathing.

I could do this. I owed Ciara this much.

"My friend is nearly here," Alexander murmured, pressing himself into my side. "He will take us to Torin, but only once you're ready."

My eyes scanned the throngs of people moving through the streets, but quickly landed on the only one who was looking at us. A tall man, taller than Alexander, with shoulder length dark hair approached us, a smile spreading across his face with each step.

"Who is that?" I asked. Alexander had mentioned we'd be meeting one of his friends before we spoke with Torin, but he'd been lax with the details beyond that. And in my anxiety, I hadn't pushed.

"And who might you be? I know this fool, but how did he come across a companion as pretty as you?" The man smiled widely at my burning cheeks as he stepped up in front of us.

"Katrina, this is Lochlan. Lochlan, if you smile at her like that again I will make you swallow your own teeth."

"A bit testy, aren't we?" Lochlan slung his arm around Alexander's shoulders for a brief semblance of an embrace. He clapped his hand on Alexander's back. "Let's go somewhere a bit more private and chat."

My mind was still bouncing between anxiety and bewilderment, so I let Alexander pull me along behind them as Lochlan led us to a quiet pub. Once we were all seated at a table in the corner of the room, my nerves had also settled some. Alexander was at ease with this man, and if he could trust him, I could too. Or at least, I could try.

"So, shall we get down to business?" Lochlan said, clasping his hands together. "I've arranged for Torin to meet us here shortly. I guessed you would like to talk to me first."

"You guessed right," Alexander said. He tilted his head toward the dark-haired man. "Katrina, Lochlan is another Dullahan. He protects this area."

I almost swallowed my tongue.

Lochlan snorted. "I thought you said you told her about us?"

Tucking my hair behind my ears, I took a deep breath. "No, he did, I just wasn't expecting to meet one *here*, is all. He failed to mention your name or your...status."

"I like her." Lochlan leaned back in his chair with a grin. "You two will be good together."

Glancing at Alexander, I half expected him to be scowling, but instead his cheeks were flushed. We'd grown closer over the course of the journey from Sleepy Hollow but no amount of closeness prepared me for him leaning down to press a kiss to my temple in full view of everyone. "Yes, we will be."

Before I could collect my thoughts from where they swirled above my head and string them together to stutter out a reply, the doors of the pub swung open.

My heart sank to my boots, all joy gone as I recognized the man who entered. Torin.

He recognized me at the same time, smiling politely as he made his way over to our table. We all rose to greet him, Alexander stepping in front of me to extend his hand. "Torin, thank you for meeting us."

Torin's face was older, but he was still the spitting image of his mother. His eyes were exact replicas of Ciara's and I found myself dizzy with the realization. Closing my eyes, I forced back the sound of Ciara's neck snapping, the vision of her body on the ground.

"Let's have a seat," Alexander said, his hand on my lower back.

I almost fell into the chair.

"Katrina," Torin said slowly. "Why have you come all this way?"

Beneath the table, I dug my nails into my palms. I'd told Alexander I needed to be the one to give Torin the news; he couldn't take that from me, as much as he would have liked to spare me. Alexander's leg pressed against mine, a solid and silent reminder of his presence. Of his support.

"Your sister." I cleared my throat. "I'm here about Ciara."

I saw the instant Torin realized what I was not saying. His eyes widened, and then his jaw tightened as he looked to Alexander. "Was she named Roghnaithe?"

"No." I shook my head. "I was."

Torin's eyes settled back on me, his face falling as he realized the alternative. "Then what happened? She's dead, isn't she?"

Ash coated my tongue as I nodded. "Yes, she's dead."

"How?"

"Ciara was trying to avenge you. She found a spell, and she tried to summon Death. To force her to bring you back."

It was as if my words had punched the breath from Torin's lungs. "*What?*"

"Death killed her, after Ciara completed the summoning. She used my parents' deaths..." I shook my head. "That part isn't important."

"It's all important, Katrina." His voice was hard and his fists rested on the table. "Tell me all of it."

Alexander reached his hand to rest atop mine, stopping me from the story I'd been about to tell. "Let me." He turned his gaze to Torin, and I gladly let him, despite knowing it should be me. "Ciara used Katrina's parents to summon Death, to bargain for your soul. She didn't believe us when we told her you were not dead. Death snapped her neck."

Torin let out a sob, his fist pressed against his mouth. My vision blurred, eyes stinging with my own tears that built and spilled over my cheeks. Reaching out, Torin and I clasped hands, clinging to each other.

"Death is gone," Alexander continued. "Katrina destroyed her; she'll never come back. She'll never harm anyone else."

"That does Ciara little good," Torin snapped. I flinched at his words, drawing my hand back. He took a shuddering breath, pulling my hand into his before I could move away completely. "Wait."

I felt Lochlan's eyes on me. They were no longer friendly and casual, but assessing. Alexander had apparently not told him everything about me. "You killed Death?"

"Yes," I replied, not taking my eyes off Torin.

"My mother?" Torin asked, his eyes frantic.

"She's alive." I couldn't bring myself to admit that she now hated me, but she was alive. That much, I could attest to.

Torin whirled to Lochlan. "I need to get back home."

"You can take our carriage in the morning," Alexander said, his hand settling on my knee. "It will take you back to Sleepy Hollow."

"Is it safe for me to return?" He hesitated, looking at Alexander as he pulled his hands back from mine.

"My parents are dead," I reminded him. His attention settled back on me. "The Ciallmhar still exists, but they know the truth about the Roghnaithe now. You can return."

"Did you take over the town? Will you return with me?"

Alexander and I shared a look. "No," I replied, squeezing Torin's hand. "I doubt I'll ever set foot in Sleepy Hollow again. But I wanted to tell you this in person."

"Thank you," he said. He turned to Alexander, and then to Lochlan. "Thank you both, for your mercy and protection all these years."

"Do not thank us," Lochlan said, waving his hand. From the way Alexander pursed his lips, I knew he'd been about to say the same thing. "Go get your things ready, the carriage will be waiting for you at first light."

Without another word, Torin pulled me to my feet and into a tight hug before he left the pub in a flurry of movement.

The three of us settled back into the corner. I couldn't find the right words to say, so I let the silence take over.

"So, you killed Death." Lochlan repeated his earlier words, but this time, it was not a question.

"Phoenix."

"Ahh."

Silence took hold once more.

"Where will you go now? If you're not planning to return to Sleepy Hollow?" Lochlan picked up his untouched mug and took a large drink.

Alexander took my hand, resting them on the table. His eyes settled on me, and never left as he spoke. "Wherever she wants to go."

Not caring about the amused smirk on Lochlan's face, I cupped Alexander's cheek in my palm and leaned in to kiss him. "As long as I'm with you, I am home."

And I was. I'd never thought I would find a home outside of Henry's pottery shop, but now I had, and it was not in the arms of the Headless Horseman or the Dullahan. It was in the arms of Alexander.

"That's remarkably sweet and all, but that's not a destination."

"First, I think we'll go anywhere you are not," Alexander said, his eyes never leaving mine, even as the smirk grew on his face. He pressed one last kiss to my lips before leaning back to grin at his friend.

I couldn't help but smile along with him. Wherever we ended up, we would be just fine.

Leave a Review

I hope you enjoyed this book!

If you did, I would really appreciate if you could leave a review, even just a short one, on your preferred retailer sites.

Your ratings make a world of difference for authors, and help spread the word about books you've enjoyed!

Thank you!

Jessica

What's Next?

Did you enjoy Hollowed?

Enter the depths and dive into the Seas of Caladhan duology today!

This dark fantasy duology will take you into the depths and into the world of Brigid, our bloodthirsty syren, and Caelum, a pirate with a heart of gold.

Start with book 1: The Syren's Mutiny

Acknowledgments

Thank you to everyone who made this possible. This book was something different, but something I think I needed to write, and I appreciate beyond words all the support I've gotten for my spooky little baby!

A special thank you to my husband and my family, as always. And a shout out to Nebula, my cat, for keeping me company when I needed something to squish as I drafted.

If I had the space, I would list out every single person who's supported me with this writing thing, but that would take up it's own book, so a very special thank you to Leah, Leez, Gabbie, Aleera, Vanessa, and Whitney, among many, many others. Your support means the world to me, and I doubt I would be here without each of you.

Thank you to Fran, for a gorgeous cover and bringing my vision to life in a spectacular way.

Thank you to Christin, for the amazing illustrations you see on the title page, chapter headers, and scene dividers. They are awe-inspiring and I am so grateful!

Thank you to Ashley for the stellar feedback once again. You guys are the best and make me feel like maybe I actually do know how to do this whole writing thing!

And to my readers, thank you. Thank you for taking another chance on me. I love you beyond words!

Follow Jessica S. Taylor

Stay connected with Jessica at the following places:

SUBSCRIBE TO THE NEWSLETTER:
https://www.subscribepage.io/jessicastaylor

BOOKBUB:
make sure you enable New Release Alerts to get emails about sales and releases
https://www.bookbub.com/authors/jessica-s-taylor

WEBSITE:
https://authorjessicastaylor.com

INSTAGRAM:
https://instagram.com/authorjessicastaylor

FACEBOOK:
https://facebook.com/authorjessicastaylor

FACEBOOK GROUP:
https://facebook.com/groups/syrenscove

TIKTOK:
https://tiktok.com/@authorjessicastaylor

About the Author

Jessica (she/her) is a mythology enthusiast and author of her debut fantasy romance novel, The Syren's Mutiny.

As a child, Jessica all but lived at her local library, devouring whatever books she could get her hands on. When that wasn't enough, she began writing her own.

Jessica was born and raised in Kentucky, but is currently residing in southern Maine with her husband and cat, Nebula.

Visit her website to learn more:

www.authorjessicastaylor.com

Content Warning Locations

- Recurring parental neglect/emotional abuse (throughout)
- Non-explicit references to sacrificial practices (throughout)
- Explicit depictions of depression, anxiety and panic attacks (throughout)
- Ableist language used against the hard of hearing FMC (Chapters 3, 4, 6, 17, 22)
- Moderate, brief depictions of suicidal ideation (Chapters 32, 37)
- Explicit descriptions of death/murder (Chapters 24, 29, 30, 38, 39)
- Explicit injury descriptions, blood and gore (Chapters 24, 30, 31, 32, 40, 39)
- Brief mentions of non-consensual drug use (Chapter 28)
- Mild sexual content & situations (Chapters 21, 22, 34)

9 798985 492873